*& September 2001
London jg*

RIDING THE WHIRLWIND

An Ethiopian Story of Love and Revolution

Bereket Habte Selassie

The Red Sea Press, Inc.
Publishers & Distributors of Third World Books

11-D Princess Road
Lawrenceville, NJ 08648

P. O. Box 48
Asmara, ERITREA

The Red Sea Press, Inc.

Publishers & Distributors of Third World Books

11-D Princess Road		P. O. Box 48
Lawrenceville, NJ 08648		Asmara, ERITREA

*Although based on recent Ethiopian history, the characters
and events described in this novel are fictitious, and any
resemblance to real people or events is coincidental.*

*The name of the protagonist, Desta, was chosen by the
author to memorialize his deep gratitude to his friend
Desta Wolde Kidan. The latter risked much to save the
author's life in November 1974 by driving him out of
Addis Ababa, all the way to the North, putting him in
touch with Eritrean liberation fighters.*

Cover art and design by Carles Juzang

Book design and typesetting by Malcolm Litchfield
This book is composed in Berkeley Oldstyle and Lithos

Library of Congress Number 92-40942

ISBN: 1-56902-047-4 Paper

Printed in Canada

I dedicate this book to the memory of

AMAN MICHAEL ANDOM
YOHANNES MENKIR, AND
YOHANNES ADMASU

martyred friends who practiced what they
preached to the bitter end.

AUTHOR'S NOTE
TO THE PAPERBACK EDITION

Over the the last three years, following the publication of *Riding the Whirlwind,* many readers have urged me to come out with a paperback edition. The most insistent voice came from the faculty of African Studies departments in American Universities, where the book has become standard "Recommended Reading" despite the price of the clothbound edition. Obviously, for most readers in Africa, the book is even farther out of reach.

I have received many favorable comments from readers, including two published reviews and one forthcoming review by an African historian and man of letters. Their support and encouragement in this, my first work of fiction, is deeply appreciated.

The remarks of one prominent Ethiopian, however, were downright intriguing: "I always knew," he said, "that despite your Eritrean nationalist claims, you are still an Ethiopian at heart." My "nationalist claims," mind you, not my involvement or commitment or dedication! I think he must have sensed my uneasiness, for he hastened to add: "We miss you, you know." Well, it is nice to be missed, of course, but at what price?

Also, it seems that many readers believed, despite the written disclaimer, that Desta, the principal character of the novel, is Bereket in disguise. It shows the risk involved in writing a novel covering recent events, in the first person. The ending of the novel has also raised expectations of a sequel. I can only say that if that were to happen, it will not be written in the first person. I have learned my lesson. I am more keenly aware now of the technical limitations of writing in that form.

At any rate, I hope that this paperback edition will reach a much wider readership.

—Bereket Habte Selassie
Asmara, Eritrea, January 1997

Part I

UNDERGROUND

ONE

The Emperor paced back and forth behind the large mahogany desk, cracking his knuckles. He always did that when he was angry.

He fumbled with the lapels of his famous cape and cracked his knuckles again, then stopped pacing and threw a ferocious look at his ministers.

His foremost minister stood with bowed head, waiting for the storm to pass. Prime Minister Akalu was in his early sixties, of medium height with light brown complexion. He had broad shoulders, and his prominent forehead, beady eyes and aquiline nose dominated his face. His gray hair gave him an air of distinction, enhanced by his well-tailored light-gray suit.

As the Emperor resumed his nervous walk, like a restless lion in a cage, the Prime Minister approached the imperial desk slowly and surreptitiously, as though he were about to stroke a dangerous cat. Three ministerial colleagues followed behind Akalu, looking like frightened school children summoned by an irate headmaster.

"May it please Your Imperial Majesty," the Prime Minister ventured, obviously anxious to break the intolerable tension.

"Silence!" the Emperor roared back, stopping his movements. "Keep quiet, and speak when you are spoken to."

"Yes, Your Majesty," Akalu said meekly, bowing his head.

"We warned you," the Emperor said. "We warned you many times, and you told us you had everything under control." He used the imperial plural on all public occasions, and at times even in private talks.

"We told you again and again!" he fulminated, his voice rising to a high pitch. "We told you that they will stop at nothing and you said everything would be under control. But what do we get? More insolent demands. More riots. More demonstrations. What next, Prime Minister, what next?"

The Emperor spat out the words "Prime Minister" with sarcasm; they must have stung the hapless Akalu like arrows. But Akalu was used to such moods and knew that he had to answer or face severe sanction.

"All that Your Imperial Majesty has said is true," he said with diffidence. "Your wisdom is unquestionably higher than that of all your humble servants put together."

This language, which may seem farcical to the reader, was the stuff of which Imperial Court etiquette was made. Akalu called it the ego massage.

"But these are difficult times," Akalu continued.

"Don't tell us the obvious! Every child in Ethiopia knows that these are difficult times. The question is: what are you doing about it?"

As the Emperor spoke these last words, the clock on the wall behind him chimed, and he looked at his gold watch which was fastened on the palm side of his left wrist. He adjusted the wrist band with his delicate hands, then looked at the Prime Minister with renewed fury. It was as if the chime had forced the tension out into the open, symbolizing the break with the idyllic African past.

"Your Majesty—" the Prime Minister persisted. "I beg Your Imperial indulgence to speak."

The Emperor looked at him searchingly. "Well?"

"We have inside information that their movement is divided. The leadership is a squabbling band of demagogues, and I have given instructions to the minister of security to redouble efforts to exploit this division."

The Prime Minister turned for confirmation to Zerfu, who took his time in replying. Akalu looked anxious; he distrusted Zerfu, the minister of security, who was known for his ambition to become Prime Minister. The Emperor turned his gaze to Zerfu.

"It is true, Your Majesty," Zerfu said finally. "But we have not been able to find what the issues of division are. We think it is a struggle for power."

"What power?" the Emperor exploded.

"These students are talking about power to the people. But we know they mean power to themselves," Zerfu said.

"That is preposterous!" the Emperor said.

"Our agents inside their movement are very good, Your Majesty," said Akalu, visibly relieved that Zerfu had confirmed his claim. "Before long we will have an idea how to exploit the division. We will also find out more about their weak links and foreign connections. We can then strike to paralyze their movement."

At that point, the aging Emperor seemed to calm down. He sat back on his throne and assumed his familiar pose, joining his finger tips with his two thumbs meeting on top to make a heart shape. Akalu knew by this that the storm had blown over.

Akalu had a way of calming his imperial master, an art which he had perfected over his long tenure of office. It was an art which only a select few had the ability to master, and in which few could claim to equal this Sorbonne-educated son of a peasant. It was a matter of common knowledge—and a sign of esteem—that the Emperor never used insulting language on Akalu, whereas he regularly assaulted his other ministers with abusive words, comparing one to a monkey and another to a hyena.

The Emperor's hair glistened under the chandelier, seeming to stand on end like the bristly quills of a hunted porcupine. The Emperor's hair and high forehead made him look much taller than his five feet, four inches. His flashing eyes arrested everything around them and seemed to burn everyone caught in their fiery gaze. This day they were blood-shot with anger and fatigue.

Prime Minister Akalu lowered his head, pretending to bow, and also no doubt wishing to avoid those hypnotic eyes. As I watched, I was reminded of an Ethiopian war song in praise of kings whose fiery visages burned all around them. The faces of the ministers contorted with fear gave that song fresh import.

In the Imperial Court fear was a weapon of governance. Fear of the unknown, of what the Emperor might do to you at any moment. My father used to warn me against getting too close to the king, for he could burn; my father, of blessed memory, had added that staying too far in the outer fringes of power would not do either. But he did not tell me the way out, once you were ensnared by an imperial notice and appointment.

I had to puzzle that one out myself. In the meantime I was living a double life, having joined the underground movement, even as I was serving in a high position in the imperial government.

His Majesty cleared his throat and looked at his watch.

"Very well then," he said. "Make sure that there is no more trouble. And don't quote us the provision in the constitution about freedom of expression. We know it by heart. We granted it to our beloved subjects. But we will not allow it to be quoted back at us in support of riots and demonstrations. Is that clear?"

"Yes, Your Majesty," the Prime Minister said.

The Emperor gave a dismissive wave of his hand and the audience was over. Prime Minister Akalu and his colleagues scrambled out to the ante-chamber, where they were greeted by a pack of rumor-hungry lesser ministers and minor dignitaries, all anxious to know what the government was going to do about the worsening political situation.

The Prime Minister was not exaggerating when he said that Ethiopia was experiencing difficult times. It was the understatement of the season, and a remarkable one coming from a French-educated man.

The subject had begun to haunt him, as evidenced by the frequency of cabinet and sub-cabinet meetings devoted to the "student movement." That movement had begun to spread its influence; leaflets and pamphlets were appearing with increasing frequency. Although there were a few leaflets of a personal nature indulging in *ad hominem* attacks on individual dignitaries, much of the writing was concerned with far-reaching political and social issues.

Perhaps because of his French education, Prime Minister Akalu was given to drawing parallels between conditions and events of his day and those of France during the *ancien regime*. He was a very worried man in the Autumn of 1969, as I could see daily. As the chief cabinet secretary,

I heard all the woes of the Prime Minister and his colleagues as they sat over tea or coffee awaiting the convening of their cabinet meetings. I cultivated the habit of listening. Some ministers poured their hearts out when they found a sympathetic ear.

The Prime Minister walked through the ante-chamber and out to the steps leading to where his car was parked. A couple of his colleagues approached him, but he ignored them and soldiered on, making it clear that he was in no mood to be bothered.

But he stopped to greet a military officer who was standing alone, arms crossed, outside the ante-chamber.

"Brigadier Iman," the Prime Minister said, "what brings you here?"

"I don't know why I am here, your excellency. I was summoned by His Majesty's private secretary."

"Come to my office after your audience."

"Yes, your excellency. But I don't know how long I may have to wait for my audience. The traffic is heavy," Iman said, flashing a smile.

"Come as soon as you are able. Desta will admit you immediately to my office," the Prime Minister said, turning to me, and I nodded.

The Prime Minister continued his walk toward the stairs, where he was met by Getu, the minister of agriculture.

"When can we meet privately?" Iman whispered to me.

"I'll ring you up tonight, after eight at the usual place," I whispered and hurried to catch up with the Prime Minister, leaving Iman behind.

Getu, an old classmate and close friend of Akalu, followed him all the way down the stairs. I caught up with them, carrying some files. When we were at a safe distance from the rest of the crowd, Getu took Akalu by the arm. "How was he?" he asked.

"He was not amused," Akalu said in French.

Getu, who usually enjoyed Akalu's humor, did not laugh. It was no laughing matter. Getu was never on good terms with the Emperor, and he owed his job to his friendship with the Prime Minister, although he was an able man by all accounts. Ability, in and of itself, was never enough to qualify anyone for an elevated position in the Imperial Court; indeed, there were cases where it proved a liability.

It was also widely rumored that Getu's young wife was a secret mistress of the Prime Minister. I tended to discount such rumors as the work of jealous colleagues, or even of the Emperor's rumor machine, which was part of his arsenal of political weapons.

Getu, who was a former guerrilla fighter during the brief period of Italian occupation, often spoke using military metaphor: "Akalu, I think we have lost a sense of long-term strategy. We have been living on a daily menu of tactical maneuver, reacting to events instead of shaping them. We do the Emperor's bidding at all costs, and in the end it will cost us dear. We are—"

"*Ca suffit,*" Akalu interrupted. "I have had enough bashing to last me a month. Don't add to my pains, please. Enough."

"No, it is not enough!" Getu answered with unusual vehemence. Only Getu could speak so boldly to the Prime Minister, as a close friend. The two men looked at each other, and Akalu shrugged his shoulders which appeared unusually hunched. Getu patted his friend on the back as they walked toward the main gate, and I followed a short distance behind.

Getu broke the silence. "I hear they are now organizing the secondary school students."

"Yes, I know," Akalu said. "It will not stop. You are right, of course, about our lack of strategy. I am afraid we are in for a bad time, my friend." He lowered his voice, as if revealing a closely-guarded secret. "The old man is losing his grip. I have never seen him so jittery and angry. It is as if he has a foreboding of losing his throne."

"Frankly, *mon vieux,*" Getu rejoined, "I am more concerned with losing my life. It has come to that, and the sooner we realize it the better for everyone."

"What do you want me to do, tell the Emperor to abdicate, or organize a coup?" Akalu said in exasperation.

"Why not?"

"Come on, be serious."

"I am serious about organizing a coup," Getu said. "All you have to do is to convince the chief of staff of the armed forces, who likes you. The police chief is a commoner like you and me, and he would be delighted to join in. You don't need anybody else. The rest would fall in line, once you pull it off. As they say in America, nothing succeeds like success."

"You and your American sayings! Would your American friends help? I am sure the CIA would inform on us, and before we knew what hit us we would be hanging from a eucalyptus tree. And you know how I hate the smell of eucalyptus."

They both laughed and stopped the heady dialogue with the arrival of the Prime Minister's limousine. We all jumped in; I sat in front with the chauffeur.

As we drove past the main gate into the outer courtyard of the old palace, we saw a large crowd of petitioners and imperial favor-seekers milling around the gate, hoping desperately to catch the Emperor's eye on his way out.

The hour was approaching for the Emperor to leave his executive chores behind and assume his role as chief judge of the land. At twelve noon every weekday, he would arrive at the imperial bench and stand for a whole hour hearing cases. It was more a sophisticated form of exercizing social patronage than dispensing justice, although the appearance of the latter was cultivated with infinite care. The Emperor did not only reign, but must be seen to administer justice regally.

The crowd at the back surged forward, pushing those in front into the orderlies holding the gate. One of the orderlies cracked his long whip twice, and then landed it on the back of a peasant who happened to be near him. The peasant moaned and fell to the ground. Another orderly cracked his whip and approached the crowd, which surged back leaving an open space between it and the gate.

The Prime Minister shook his head in dismay. "Look at them," he said. "The students shout slogans like 'power to the people.' They mean people like these."

"Well, not only these, and perhaps not even these people," Getu said.

"What do you mean?"

"I mean most of these are probably small landowners who want more land, or are fighting over a tiny plot."

"You know what I am talking about," Akalu said with an impatient tone. "And you are being technical. In fact you have become too damned technical since I gave you the agriculture portfolio!"

"Not at all, *mon vieux*," Getu said. "I am talking the essence of politics."

They argued all the way to the Prime Minister's office in the Sidist Kilo region of Addis Ababa. Upon our arrival, I left them and entered my office, where a mountain of files awaited me.

TWO

The last days of the Emperor's reign, over which Prime Minister Akalu expressed such anguish and anxiety, saw the explosion of protest movements, principally led by university students and gradually spreading out to engulf the whole country. Those days also saw the obscene display of opulence in the midst of mass misery such as had never been witnessed in that unhappy land. Or so I though at the time, having traveled widely and being a close observer of the Imperial Court. I witnessed daily cruelties routinely inflicted by the powerful on the powerless, from the top down to the governors of the sub-districts to the local agents of the landlords. I saw the endless feasts and venal pursuits of pleasure of the rich, who seemed to be driven by an irrepressible will to flaunt their wealth.

The Emperor himself gave symbolic approval to all these indulgences and incongruities, by feeding dogs and cattle while his people starved. I personally witnessed him several times throwing huge chunks of choice meat to a pack of dogs while hungry peasants watched with watery eyes, and no doubt with watery mouths.

I never thought things could get worse. I did not know what the future had in store. To ordinary mortals like myself the future seems always bright, especially in youth.

That was how I saw things then, until the revolution exploded in our faces long before we were ready for it; long before the squabbling factions of our movement could heal their mutually inflicted wounds. And the revolution threw up from its womb unexpected forces and individuals that surprised us.

I was a part of a privileged generation, of a few hundred university graduates who were suspended between the old order—which still held sway, despite the growing shocks and challenges—and a new order waiting to be born, assisted by us of course.

Some among the educated thought that it was a misfortune to be born in such a period. I did not share such a pessimistic view. I belonged to what I proudly considered to be the *creme de la creme,* young people who believed that they were summoned by history to play a special role. I thought it was a rare privilege to belong to such a group. My companions and I condemned those who abdicated such a historic responsibility, for whatever reason. We also looked down with contempt on the new nobility and feudal aristocracy, whose privilege derived from birth or wealth, in contrast to our own which came with enlightenment and was acquired by hard work and learning.

It is a curious thing. I had known members of the elite class as students in England and France, and some of them did indeed have nobility of spirit. I also knew a good number of treacherous "commoners"; I myself was betrayed by one such commoner. Yet I drove from my heart any sentiment of solidarity with the elite. You might call that class bias; I called it class consciousness.

As a fraternity of the enlightened, we thought we could do no wrong. We planned a strategy of gradual infiltration of key positions in the government, and of cultivating key officers in the armed forces for the final day of reckoning. We were utterly convinced that we could bend events to our will; that we could organize important social forces like labor unions and students and harness their energies to implement our ideas and dreams of a better future. It took time and some painful experiences for us to recognize the arrogance and naiveté implicit in our belief.

Passion, ideas and dreams, move people to do incredible things. My father, an adventurous soul himself and a veteran partisan fighter in the war against foreign occupation, instilled the spirit of adventure in me. But I owe the pursuit of power and the urge to excell at school and in life not to my father, but to my mother. "You can do anything you want, if you exert yourself. You can reach the top!" my mother used to say. It was a constant theme that I imbibed with the milk with which she suckled me. "My son is second to nobody," was her well-known boast. It showed in the games I played and in my school record. My parents turned me into a fighter.

In retrospect, as I review my life, I suspect that behind the ideological passion and the "summons of history" which my companions and I embraced, there was another hidden passion driving me. There was an irresistible need to prove myself. And how could I prove myself except through the crucible of danger? I suspect that this was the golden knot binding me and my companions, including Brigadier Iman.

Despite the revulsion I felt toward the wild deeds of the oppressive regime, I was drawn to the centers of power. I was thrilled by imperial notice, by power and privilege, by being an insider and privy to important secrets. Why was I then drawn to the underground? Basically it must have been for the same reasons, and the mystique of the underground revolutionary may have added to the appeal.

Thus I ended up a minister, a trusted lieutenant of the second most powerful man in the regime, and at the same time a secret member of a revolutionary underground. There was adventure as well as danger in both roles.

Melaku, who was the leader of our revolutionary group, used to say that we were the midwives of history—which was waiting for us, pregnant with momentous happenings. He would add jestingly, "And without us, those moments will be stillborn."

I was very close to Melaku, the economist turned poet and revolutionary. Our association went back to our student days at the London School of Economics.

Midwives of history. That was a powerful metaphor. It held a seductive vision of our future role, and I never for one moment doubted that we were destined to be part of history in the making. That belief was further reinforced by what I had seen and experienced since my return from studies abroad.

Every sign of decay that I saw in the empire, every excess in the sprawling bureaucracy with its decrepit command structure and frustrating bottlenecks, seemed to validate Melaku's vision of our historic mission. My comrades and I organized our lives with that vision as our guiding light. It defined our attitudes toward practically everything, including our relations with people around us at home and in the workplace. It dominated our thoughts. It permeated our consciousness.

The impact of those exciting days remains an important part of my make-up today. I am an unrepentant revolutionary, unlike some who have "graduated" to a more "pragmatic" view of life, and others who shudder at the thought of their past which they try to forget. You will meet them all in this narrative, and perhaps wonder which route you might have chosen, placed in a similar position.

There were six of us making up the leadership. We called ourselves the Central Committee.

There was Melaku with his dreamy eyes and perpetual smile. Diminutive in build, he had a booming voice, an engaging personality, and a sense of humor that I always thought was one of the essential elements holding our group together. He was so generous and good-natured that nothing offended him. "Except," he said one day, "the outrage of oppression and exploitation."

Then there was Bekele, another diminutive figure with dreamy eyes, but without Melaku's sense of humor. What he lacked in wit and eloquence he made up with tenacity and organizational skill. An engineer by training, he set about his revolutionary duties with the precision and thoroughness of his profession.

Yohannes was the member to whom I felt closest. He was a tall, good-looking man in his mid-thirties, like me, and was married, like me. Our wives got on moderately well. Although they did not fall into the trap of competing, they tended to copy each other in the clothes and other things they bought. Yohannes and I thought this was funny.

A lawyer by profession, Yohannes was a well-established member of Addis Ababa society, frequenting the Rotary Club and rubbing shoulders with the business and professional elite. He felt periodic pangs of guilt for this, and it was I who chided him for feeling guilty and urged him to extend and deepen his professional and social contacts.

Aberra was the member about whom I knew the least, because we had moved in different circles before he joined the Central Committee in the early months of 1969. But more about Aberra later.

Berhane was the youngest member of the group. At twenty-eight he was well grounded in the theory and practice of revolution. His Eritrean origin and contacts with the important rebellion there would prove critical in my adventures.

The revolutionary upsurge of the late 1960s was spearheaded by the university students of Addis Ababa. We therefore paid special attention to students and teachers, including foreign teachers, notably the American Peace Corps volunteers.

Some members of our group regarded the Peace Corps as part of the problem, while others, including Melaku, saw their potential value. The question of how we should deal with them was one of the few issues on which we experienced serious differences of opinion.

We met at Melaku's apartment one Friday evening in early November 1969 to discuss the issue. Melaku lived in a two-room apartment in Building 82 in the modern sector of Addis Ababa, within sight of the Emperor's palace. Building 82 was one of the earliest high-rise structures began in the late 1950s in response to demands for modern housing. One of the earliest visible testimonies to the process of modernization, an architectural expression of the growing social cleavage, it stood at the center of the imperial capital with mud huts and shanties dotting the urban landscape around it.

Building 82 was convenient for meetings, not only because of its central position, but, more importantly for our purposes, because it facilitated anonymity. The spacious parking lot facing a large thoroughfare made it difficult for the ubiquitous imperial security agents to monitor people's movements in and out of the building.

We never traveled in groups when going to a meeting. We filed in one by one at decent intervals, so that no observer would think we were going to the same place. We made certain no one saw which room we entered, walking casually past the apartment first. Occasionally, we would carry bouquets or wrapped gifts to give the impression that we were heading to romantic assignations. The building had its fair share of young women residents, mostly airline hostesses, embassy secretaries and other professionals.

The meeting started when all the members were present. Melaku had urged full attendance due to the weighty nature of the item on the agenda.

It was 8:30 in the evening and Melaku served us his favorite dish, spaghetti, followed by a salad bowl and fruits. During the meal, we exchanged pleasantries and gossip of the city.

Then Melaku called the meeting to order. He cleared his throat, seemed to hesitate, and creased his faced with a broad smile. "Let us pray," he said.

Aberra who did not know Melaku's humor, was confused. The rest of us laughed.

Melaku then put on a serious face along with his reading glasses, and looked at the agenda.

"According to agreed policy," he began, "we don't carry copies of the agenda of any meeting or any other paper having to do with our movement, unless expressly authorized for a specific purpose. And even then, the paper must be burned and flushed down the lavatory.

"It was not possible to give an advance notice of the agenda of tonight's meeting. But I think we all know the reason for this special meeting."

"Why don't you read all the items and invite questions if there are any?" Yohannes counseled.

"Okay. The main item is about our relation with the Peace Corps teachers and other foreign nationals teaching in the university and at the secondary schools. It also raises the question which has been of some concern to a couple of our comrades. How do we deal with the Americans? Should we maintain relations with them?"

Melaku stopped and scanned our faces, as if expecting questions or comments. There were none.

"Let me frame the issues and then you can all jump in. First of all, you know my view that on a tactical basis there is nothing wrong with using the ready-made resource which the Peace Corps provides. I emphasize the *tactical* nature of such a use. The question then is: how do we use this resource to our advantage with minimal risk?"

"But that is the point," said Yohannes, who had been finishing an orange. "How can we be sure that there is no risk involved?"

"Just a minute," said Aberra, who had previously expressed an aversion to dealing with any foreign nationals for revolutionary purposes. Self-reliance in all things was like gospel to him. "Before we talk about tactics, we should first agree about principles. We are here, are we not, to consider both aspects?"

"That is correct," Melaku said.

"Very well, then," Aberra pressed. "Before we talk about tactics, should we not agree on the principle?"

"Right again," Melaku said. "I was not in any way trying to gloss over the point of principle. If it is the wish of the committee to argue that point, we can spend as much time as necessary on it. I was simply introducing the subject."

Melaku then asked Aberra to make the case against any involvement with foreigners.

I remember vividly the cogent arguments of Aberra, and the passionate intensity of his presentation. As secretary of the committee, I kept the minutes of all our meetings, and hid them together with other related documents in the most unlikely place—my filing cabinet at the office of the Prime Minister.

Aberra did not carry the day, despite his eloquence. None of the rest of us could see any problem of compromising principle in maintaining occasional and discreet contacts with sympathetic foreigners. On the question of caution, we spent more time, defining procedures for members to follow.

Melaku summed up the proceedings of the meeting clearly and concisely. At the end of his summary, he referred to the fact that he had spent a few months in America. He happened to be in Washington, he said, at the time of President Kennedy's inaugural speech, in which he appealed to the generous instincts of his fellow citizens.

"I did not realize until then that there are two sides to Americans, as to all human beings, I suppose," Melaku said. "There is the side which gives full play to the forces of greed and violence. And I never allow myself to forget that America was built with greed and violence. Then there is the other side which yearns for justice and puts compassion above politics. It is the side of the good Samaritan."

He stopped and peered at us over his glasses, which slid to the tip of his nose. He did this when he wanted to make a humorous point.

"I take it we all know who the good Samaritan was," he said. Even Aberra joined in the laughter.

"Yes," Berhane said. "Some of the Samaritan's best friends were Jews."

The tension was released. Aberra settled back to listen attentively as Melaku continued:

"Many, if not all, of these young Americans are drawn from the idealistic tradition. I took it upon myself to talk to some of them while they were in training. I think that with a bit of luck and with a good deal of caution, we can turn their presence to the advantage of the revolution."

He stopped and turned toward Aberra, as if to implore him to say, "Yes, let's give it a try." One of Melaku's best leadership qualities was his genuine love of consensus reached by persuasion. Aberra returned his gaze, but did not budge.

I felt uncomfortable and tried a diversion. "How about some coffee?" I said, getting up and moving towards the kitchen.

There was general agreement. After a few minutes I returned with the coffee pot and cups on a tray.

After drinking his coffee Aberra rose to go. "My wife is not feeling well," he said.

"Oh, I hope it is not serious," Melaku said.

I offered to drive Aberra, whose car was in the garage for repairs. Yohannes had brought him to the meeting, and he too offered to drive him home. There followed a brief argument as to who was the youngest member of the group—the one to do errands, according to tradition. I would have been disqualified as being six months older than Yohannes, but I defied tradition and begged to drive Aberra home. "Besides," I said, "I have always questioned my six months seniority over Yohannes.

In his village they did not keep registers of birth."

"And they did in your village, I suppose?" Yohannes countered.

"Yes, we are the custodians of the country's culture and civilization, and every household has a priest confessor who writes the names and birth dates on the back of the Good Book," I said.

I left amid laughter.

On the way out of the apartment, I noticed that Aberra looked glum. In the elevator I asked him if he was worried about his wife.

"Not really; but she is expecting a baby, you know."

"No, I did not. Congratulations!" I said. "You old son of a gun. Why didn't you tell us?"

"Well, I thought I'd wait until I was sure."

"Are you sure now?"

"Yes, the doctor has said she is three months into pregnancy," he said, smiling for the first time.

I was happy to see him smile. Aberra's mercurial moods and petulance in advocating some issues had worried me from time to time.

When we reached the ground level, I realized that we had unwittingly broken one of our rules. We should not have come down together. But it was too late. We agreed to separate and meet about one hundred meters up the road.

"I will stop just before the point where the road forks," I said. Aberra nodded and left.

Before I opened my car door, I turned to see if anyone was watching. Two men were standing in the shadows of the northern wing of the building. I didn't like it.

When I picked up Aberra a few minutes later, I told him about the two shadowy figures. He said he would phone to alert the others in Melaku's apartment.

"No, don't," I said. "Remember that the security ministry has listening devices. We have to assume that our phones are tapped."

"All our phones?" he inquired.

"Well, perhaps not all. But it is safer to work on that assumption."

Then I tried to lighten the subject by teasing him. "Why do you ask?

Have you been cheating on Hirut, now that she is pregnant?"

"Not a chance! She has become even more beautiful. I am crazy about her, Desta."

Of the six members of the Central Committee, Aberra was the man I knew the least. I knew that he had studied engineering at a university in California, and that he'd had a brush with the law there. He himself told me one day that he had been close to the Black Panthers, and that the Panthers had an impact on his life and thoughts.

In fact, I had volunteered to drive him home that night hoping to find out more about his vehement objections to our contacts with the Peace Corps volunteers. Was this anti-white sentiment fostered by his association with the Panthers? Or did it reflect deeper undercurrents of hostility? I wanted to probe a little deeper.

"How was life in Berkeley?" I asked. It was a shot in the dark.

"Those were exciting days," he answered without hesitation.

"Is it true that you knew Huey Newton?"

"Yes, a little."

"What sort of man was he?"

"A brilliant man. They were great men, the Panthers! They were the only people who understood America." He grew more animated as he spoke.

"In what way?" I asked.

"America was built by violence. It can only be reconstructed by violence."

"And you think the Panthers can do that?"

"Not by themselves. But they have shown the way."

"Were they anti-white? Did they exclude all whites from their party?"

"They were not anti-white, but they had a strict policy of not getting involved with white organizations of whatever political stripe."

"Was there any incident which caused this policy?" I asked.

"Yes, indeed. They were betrayed two or three times." His tone grew sad as he went on. "In fact it became their undoing in the end. They were infiltrated by FBI agents who played their leaders one against another."

He stopped for a moment and turned toward me. "Desta," he said, "I am worried about tonight's decision. I don't trust those Peace Corps people. They are a bunch of busybodies and curious do-gooders. They will stop at nothing to advance their own interests."

We had arrived at a narrow street leading to Aberra's house. Except for the dim lights of the main street, it was pitch dark.

Aberra asked me to come in. It was a customary gesture, and he knew I could not oblige, because I had to get back to the meeting and warn the others about the suspicious characters outside the building.

"So, I hope all goes well," I said. "Give my best wishes to Hirut, and I'll see you soon."

"Good night, Desta, and thanks for the ride."

"Good night," I said and left him in the dark

As I drove back, I tried to make sense out of the evening. An inner voice sounded the alarm that something was not right. But I couldn't put my finger on what it was.

I thought of Aberra's story about the Panthers and the infiltration and betrayal. The political trajectory of my life was very different from Aberra's. I saw the light, so to speak, in Paris and London, where revolutionary politics was a gentlemanly affair compared to America in the late 1960s. And I had left Europe long before 1968, the year that saw the overthrow of de Gaulle in France.

I decided to put my misgivings to rest following my brief exchange with Aberra. I felt that a revolutionary movement would be paralyzed into inaction if beset by doubts all the time. And should our worst fears be realized—should there be betrayal—only Melaku, as Chairman, knew the names of the leaders of the cells at the sub-central committee level. I, as secretary, knew them only by their assumed names. And we had all made solemn vows of silence, on pain of execution, not to reveal the identity of the leader.

With these comforting thoughts, I stuck to my decision to ignore my inner doubts. I stopped back by Building 82, and then proceeded to my next meeting—with the soldier I had encountered at the palace earlier in the day.

THREE

A short, dark-skinned man was standing outside Mama Zen's salon. For a moment I was startled when he turned his gaze toward me and smiled.

My immediate impression was of controlled vitality which could erupt at any moment, of a sincere dedication to a cause, and of a willingness to use violence in advancing that cause. Strange how impressions are formed so quickly, then resonate in the consciousness afterwards.

"Good evening, sir. Are you Dr. Desta?" the man asked.

"Good evening to you. Yes, I am."

"We have been expecting you. This way please."

He led me through a back entrance to the salon, where three men sat around a coffee table drinking beer: Brigadier Iman and two others. They were discussing strategy, as I could see from the papers and maps on the table which they quickly folded and put away. When I joined them I took off my raincoat, revealing the military uniform I wore.

"I always knew that you were one of us. Now the uniform has sealed your fate," Iman said with his inimitable laughter. He then introduced me:

"Gentlemen, this is Dr. Desta. The uniform is a disguise which I recommended over Desta's objection."

"Good evening, gentlemen," I said. "As you can see, I am uncomfortable in uniform."

"No, it becomes you," one of the men said, introducing himself as Colonel Haile. He was about Iman's age, slightly built but wiry in his movements. He had kindly eyes that blinked incessantly.

The others were younger, probably lieutenants. They did not introduce themselves, and as Iman did not tell me their names I assumed that their anonymity was important. Of the two, the darker one who had met me outside left the strongest impression. He exuded confidence, was deliberate in his movements and measured in his speech. They were all in civilian clothes, which made me feel even more uncomfortable in my uniform. Seeing Brigadier Iman in civilian clothes, I realized that his image in uniform, with his red-rimmed cap and rolled-up sleeves, was part of his powerful mystique. All officers worthy of their rank imitated his style: his straight posture and swaggering walk, his vigorous handshake, and his winning smile. In my school days, when his fame began to emerge as a full back on the army soccer team, we even spoke of a special Iman style of playing the game. Of such things are myths made and personality cults built.

That afternoon Iman was relaxed, wearing a navy blue blazer, gray flannels and open white shirt. The contrasting picture reminded me of his reputation in the armed forces as at once disciplined and relaxed, stern and scathing toward weakness and indecision, yet compassionate in administering military justice in the units he commanded. He was easy to talk to and frequently mixed with his soldiers. He ate what they ate, and slept on the ground in the field—which gave rise to the expression that the sands of the Ogaden were his mattress.

"Sorry I'm late," I said, sitting on Iman's right.

"Well, we are used to civilians not being on time. You are only ten minutes late which is not bad."

"I am usually punctual and very fussy about appointments."

"Never mind." Iman brushed aside my embarrassment and rang for a waitress. When she appeared, he ordered five beers. After she had brought them and left, he assumed a more serious countenance.

"Desta, I wanted you to meet three of my most trusted comrades."

At that point the officer who had met me outside stood up, snapped to attention and bowed—not to me but to Iman.

"I hope I will be deserving of your trust, sir," he said and sat down.

There was no expression on his face, but his eyes showed excitement by darting left and right.

Iman began introducing me. "As I have told you men, Desta is our civilian contact." With a barely perceptible smile, he added: "Desta, of course, would say that *I* am *his* military contact. But we have no quarrel on that score, as we are working for the same cause."

"Our group does not pretend to represent the whole of civil society," I commented. "No particular group, army or civilian, can make such a claim."

"I'll drink to that," Colonel Haile said, raising his glass.

The dark officer looked puzzled. "May I offer my opinion, sir?" he addressed Iman.

"Of course. Go ahead."

"Well, I have talked with some of the students and their teachers at the Haremaya College. They speak and act as though they represent the whole population."

"Desta can speak to that," Iman said.

"Well, students and teachers here are influenced by students and teachers elsewhere in the world," I said. "And in the present political climate and student mood, they think they are the vanguard of revolutionary forces. That does not mean that they can or even want to form a government of students and teachers."

"Some of them say they can," the dark officer said.

"Some army officers also say they can," I responded.

"What we need is a coalition of forces, out of which a proper government can come," Iman said.

"So, the question is—how do we build such a coalition?" the Colonel said.

"Yes, and that is our most urgent and delicate task," Iman said. "Would you drink to that, Haile?" He erupted into infectious laughter and everyone joined in.

"I am willing to risk going to jail to make that happen," Iman said, resuming a serious tone. The others seemed to swing with his moods, alternating between cheerfulness and seriousness. They sat, riveted, as he explained how such a coalition might be built. Of the three officers, the dark one was the more controlled, not exhibiting undue enthusiasm, but following every word uttered by Iman and occasionally taking notes.

"Where did you meet the Haremaya students and teachers?" I asked the young officer during a lull in the discussion.

"In places like this," he said. "Don't worry, we are very careful, although they tend to be adventurous."

"He is a skillful recruiter," Iman boasted.

"Perhaps we should compare notes," I said.

"We will, when it is appropriate," Iman said.

"We are singleminded about the cause," the Colonel put in. "But we take care not to expose ourselves, and above all our leader."

It became increasingly clear to me that the military wing of the revolutionary movement was better organized than we were. Brigadier Iman's vision of a better future, combined with his personal qualities, had inspired many young, idealistic officers to join his secret organization.

As we left Mama Zen's at the end of the meeting, I wanted to test the Colonel. "Do you have a family?" I asked casually.

"Yes. I have five children, all going to school."

"And are you sometimes afraid they may get hurt if you are betrayed?"

"I would not be telling the truth if I said that I am not sometimes worried. But I came from a poor background and have made it to the top by hard work. My children would find ways to take care of themselves and their mother. The revolution is a serious affair; I must give it my best. I have become single-minded about it. Iman is like a human dynamo that moves us all. He and the revolution he leads totally absorbs us."

It was an informative meeting, and a reassuring one. But the dark, unsmiling officer with the darting eyes and expressionless face troubled me. Call it intuition, an inner sensor that picks up seemingly insignificant facts: a certain hungry look, a certain demeanor, nothing that can be explained rationally. I was getting protective of Iman and of my own fate, perhaps. I was seeing yellow caution lights at the beginning of a long journey.

FOUR

There are times in the life of a community when a single passage in the admonition of an elder, or the sermon of a preacher, becomes a spark illuminating the darkness of ignorance, bringing to the surface seething social turmoil. Such an occasion was the annual service at the Church of the Holy Virgin, St. Mary of Zion, in the center of Addis Ababa. That fateful day is etched in my mind; I remember events as though they happened yesterday.

It was a sunny day with a clear sky: Sunday, November 30, 1969. I remember the texts of the sermon and I particularly remember the concluding remarks of the preacher, subsequently to be called prophetic. Toward the end of the morning mass, His Holiness Abuna Yonas, the bishop of Tigray, startled a fatigued congregation by injecting the political temper of the times into the soothing religious ceremony. His words hung in the air like menacing swords suspended between heaven and earth; at any rate, that was how people remembered them and talked about them for years.

Many people, including myself, who heard the sermon that morning wondered what inner force prompted the good bishop to say what he said. His "prophecy" did not take months, or even weeks to come true. In fact, the fulfillment began soon after the end of the church service, a fact which caused the *kerkedions* (members of the dark side of the imperial security machine) to insinuate that the bishop was part of the underground conspiracy. The security forces were always suspicious of prominent people who did not belong to the ruling group, as was the case of Abuna Yonas, who was of Tigre. He was an immensely popular cleric: learned, articulate and compassionate, in contrast to the patriarch who, though articulate, was not attuned to the needs and aspirations of the great mass of the faithful. The wily patriarch, who was from the Gojam region and a member of the ruling group, was forever complaining that Yonas and "his ilk" were undermining the fabric of authority. In the Ethiopian context "authority" could be interpreted to mean the authority of the established Church, or of the Emperor.

But that day, the faithful were solidly behind Abuna Yonas, and most seemed to be confirmed in their belief that he was indeed a holy man and thus privy to divine foreknowledge of things to come. The powers that he castigated in no uncertain terms at the mass were in no position to do him harm.

The texts selected for reading at the mass were themselves significant, it seemed to me upon reflection. The first text was from the Epistle of Peter, Chapter 2. It read:

Behold, I am laying in Zion a stone, a cornerstone, chosen and precious, and he who believes in him will be put to shame. To you therefore who believe, he is precious, but for those who do not believe, the very stone which builders reject has become the head of the corner, and a stone that will make them stumble, a rock that will make them fall, for they stumble because they disobey the words as they were destined to do.

The clarity and verve with which the bishop read that passage in his ringing tenor voice was itself remarkable. It was clear that he held the attention of his congregation, at least those in the front whom I could see—all the VIPs, dressed in their holiday best.

His reading was followed by a long silence, a pause full of suspense, as he cast a meaningful glance at the corner where His Imperial Majesty was seated on an improvised throne. The Emperor's inscrutable face did not move an inch. He sat like a statue, staring in front of him and holding his fingers in his usual pose. He was a believer in the axiom that in silence there is power, and the more stony the silence, the more power.

The bishop resumed his reading of Peter's Epistle:

But you are a chosen race, a royal priesthood, a holy nation, God's own people; that you may declare the wonderful deeds of him who called you out of darkness into his marvelous light . . .

Now in the history and mythology of the Ethiopians, it is written that the true Ark of the Covenant had been give to us, and that we had become the chosen people following the rejection of Christ's coming by the Jews. This belief was a powerful weapon in the development of the Ethiopian state. Moreover, the kings claimed direct descent from a union between King Solomon and Queen Sheba. Fact or fiction, that claim had a powerful hold on the Ethiopian mind. Remember also that such a descent would make Ethiopian kings kinsmen with Jesus Christ. You only have to read the gospel according to Matthew, which begins: "The book of the Genealogy of Jesus Christ, the son of David, the son of Abraham." Solomon was the son of David, and thus a progenitor of Jesus as well as of the Ethiopian kings.

Abuna Yonas read another text before he delivered his political bombshell. This time the text was from St. Matthew, Chapter 26, verses 42–46:

Again, for the first time, he (Jesus) went away and prayed, "My Father, if this cannot pass unless I drink it, Thy will be done." And again he came and found them sleeping, for their eyes were heavy. So, leaving them again, he went away and prayed for the third time, saying the same words. Then he came to the disciples and said to them, "Are you still sleeping and taking your rest? Behold, the hour is at hand, and the Son of Man is betrayed into the hand of sinners. Rise, let us be going; see, my betrayer is at hand."

The bishop of Tigray kissed the Bible and gave it to the deacon to take around for the faithful to kiss. As the deacon was going round among the congregation, Abuna Yonas moved away from the lectern holding the microphone in his hands, like a rock star. In his brief sermon, he mingled words from the morning's text with words from traditional Ethiopian religious writings. I remember one particular story he related. It was about the Holy Virgin, conducted on a tour of Hell by Jesus. In one corner of Hell she saw columns of fire to which people were bound. When she asked her Son who they were, He told her they were princes and noblemen and other men of authority who had disobeyed His Word on earth. The bishop left out kings from the list, but they were implicitly included in the words "other men of authority"; at least, that was how we in the congregation interpreted the words.

Instinctively I looked toward the corner where His Majesty was seated. It may have been my imagination, but it seemed to me that the statue-like figure of the Emperor shifted on the throne and his hands were fidgety.

Was he getting the message? I wondered.

Then the bishop continued: "Now let us turn toward our own sad condition," and he reviewed the contemporary state of the empire, in which the poor were like a flock of sheep abandoned by their shepherd. He dwelt on the utter lack of concern of men of power. Then he dropped his bombshell.

"I ask you all to join me in the Lord's Prayer. But, before we say the Lord's Prayer, let us pray for the embattled state of our nation. Let us pray for our young people, the innocent youth against whom the sword of injustice will be drawn."

The impact of that statement was heavy and immediate. The Emperor's mask fell, revealing anger that could consume like fire. But the bishop of Tigray stood firm, seemingly unconcerned about the Emperor's anger. He seemed more interested in the reaction of the rank and file in the congregation. The congregation first gasped in disbelief, and then there was ululation from the women's section. Ululation is the traditional expression of joy or jubilation uttered by women at weddings or during the triumphal entry of a hero.

The ululation was then drowned by the music of the choir, accompanied by the pounding of drums. The master of the choir took the microphone from the bishop, who was now seated, and led the choir in a Yared number. Yared is the finest classical Ethiopian musician, whose music is as soul-stirring and sublime as that of Bach or Handel. That day, in my state of excitement, the melodic chants of the choir and their ritual dance seemed a heavenly gift. Although I liked classical Ethiopian music, it tended to bore me. But I have always marveled at the power of the human voice in all its variety and richness—in opera, in oratorio. And that day Yared's oratorio on the Messiah acquired a new meaning for me.

Later that day, the spark illuminated in the Church of St. Mary of Zion seemed to spread far and wide, as if by magic. There was a sense of exuberance in the air that goes with the shattering of age-old taboos. The imposing facade of the monarchy was rudely shaken, challenged by an open and direct assault on the person and dignity of the Emperor, who had hitherto been regarded as sacred, his dignity inviolable and his power indisputable. That centuries-old rule of tradition was written in the constitution of the empire. Imagine then, the shock of delight mixed with bewilderment people felt on that bright day in November.

The Emperor had just come out of the church and his motorcade was heading to the Great Palace to receive members of the high clergy and other dignitaries in a reception. I was in the motorcade five cars behind him, sharing a car with Teferra, the Emperor's private secretary, and Debebe, the Prime Minister's private secretary. We three often rode together because we had similar jobs and our work brought us together on a regular basis. Detractors unkindly referred to us as the unholy trinity.

We were chatting about the bold and provocative words by Abuna Yonas. It was past midday, after the Emperor's motorcade turned toward Patriots Square, when we heard gunfire. Members of the imperial bodyguard jumped out of their vehicles and started running toward the Emperor's Rolls Royce, which had just turned onto Patriots Street. The cars in front of us stopped. A member of the bodyguard came out of nowhere and started giving orders in a loud voice: "Come on! Move! Move!"

Teferra, who was driving our car, accidentally killed the engine. His hands trembled. The officer came at us with a menacing look, barking, "Come on! Move!"

"Give me time to start the damned engine!" Teferra said angrily.

If eyes could kill, Teferra would have dropped dead then and there from the way the burly bodyguard looked at him.

"What is happening up there in front?" I asked the officer, trying to defuse the situation as Teferra struggled with the engine. I was concerned that the officer could take the law into his own hands and do what he pleased with us. Disobedience of a member of the imperial bodyguard was considered an insult to the Emperor; that was why everyone feared the guards and did their bidding.

"Nothing to worry about," the bodyguard told me. "Just get a move on!" And he left Teferra to struggle with his ignition key.

The engine started and we raced to catch up with the motorcade. We turned onto Patriots Street right behind a black Mercedes. I could see the rest of the motorcade snaking around the square, with the Emperor's Rolls Royce at the head of it.

Suddenly, more rapid gunfire was heard, and the crowd at the curb became agitated. The black Mercedes broke the line and raced ahead, careening through the contorted traffic. Teferra, who feared the worst, followed suit, and we found ourselves in the middle of a jostling crowd engaged in a mad fight with the police. Most of them looked like young people. What had been a leisurely ride, disciplined and dignified, had thus become a chaotic scene on that November day of the Holy Virgin.

I was suddenly seized with an impulse to get out of the car and mix with the crowd. I felt I belonged out there taking part in the fight, on the right side of the great issues of the day; besides, curiosity was consuming me. Again, the sound of gunfire came, this time from the direction of University College. By now, Teferra was all nerves. He was a kindly sort who couldn't hurt a fly, known for his distaste for violence of any kind. "I think we should break out of the motorcade and go home," Teferra said.

"That would be a dereliction of duty," Debebe said with a touch of contempt.

"I think you are right!" I said, supporting Debebe more out of a desire to find out what was happening than from any sense of duty.

The bodyguard who had given us the command to move was trying to maintain discipline in the motorcade. This time he was carrying an Uzi submachine gun and was accompanied by several police officers and constables. The police were pushing the crowd out of the street and onto the curb. Several hundred students were shouting slogans and hurling insults at the police and bodyguards. "Imperial running dogs!" one shouted.

"Oppressive pigs!" another said, and someone was struck on the head with a rock. More firing followed—into the air, because I saw no casualties. We moved faster and finally passed Patriots Square, entering the university area. There the traffic again slowed to a standstill, and I thought of a way to satisfy my curiosity.

"Stop! I think I see the Prime Minister's car surrounded by students," I said, getting out of the car. "He needs help. See you later!"

"Let me come with you," Debebe said.

"No, go with Teferra; I'll manage," I said. Before they could say another word, I disappeared into the crowd.

I was crossing the street, going northward to where the firing had come from, when I was stopped by a young police officer, who recognized me.

"Sir, you should not go that way. It is too dangerous," he said. He was a captain named Abate whom I had taught history at the police academy some eight years before.

"Why? What is the matter?" I asked.

"His Majesty's car was attacked by those ruffians," he said. "And there is going to be more trouble."

"Anybody hurt?"

"His Majesty is all right. But one member of his entourage got hit in the face and was taken to the hospital."

"Who were the culprits?" I wanted to hear what Abate would say.

"Students, and God knows who else. These communists are out to destroy us!"

"What Communists?" I asked in disbelief.

"Well, you know, the Russians, the Chinese. The students can't be acting alone, sir. They are too well-organized."

"You mean we Ethiopians are not capable of organizing?" I asked. By provoking him, I hoped to draw more out of him.

"Well, sir. You may not know the ruffians as well as some of us who have to deal with them daily."

"Are you in the criminal investigation division, then?" I asked.

"No, sir. I am a member of a special squad established to deal with the situation. The squad is made up of experienced officers from different sections of the police force and from the intelligence branch."

"Oh, I see. Well, that is quite a task, and I wish you all the best in your work."

I thought it wise to end the conversation there. The police are trained to be suspicious of everybody, even members of their own family.

"I thought I saw the Prime Minister's car surrounded by a crowd," I said. "That is why I came out of the motorcade, to help out."

"No sir, his excellency is all right. I have seen him; his car was next to His Majesty's car."

"Well, then I am relieved. But I am afraid the vehicle in which I was riding has left me. So I'll make my way home, and you should go about your duties. Please don't let me detain you."

"That is quite all right, sir. It will be a pleasure to escort you home myself. My car is parked nearby."

Suddenly a caravan of police trucks arrived. Eight trucks made their way toward the university gate, and one by one stopped at strategic positions along Patriots Street. Riot police jumped out of the trucks. They split into squads of twenty and took positions all around the university. A voice blared from a loudspeaker, ordering the crowd to disperse and go home.

As if expecting this, groups of students emerged from the university compound, jumping over the fence. There was firing into the air and the students started throwing stones and bottles. The police threw tear gas, and the students were driven back behind the walls of the compound.

The crowd outside on the streets picked up stones and broken bottles and started hurling them at the police, who charged at them wielding long sticks. As the police charged, a pregnant woman who must have been coming out of St. Mary's Church was caught in the melee and trampled.

By that time Captain Abate and I had come closer to the scene of action. No one seemed to be willing or able to help the unfortunate woman. I drew Abate's attention, and he and I carried her to safety on the curb. The captain brought his car and we took her to the nearest hospital. But by the time we reached Menelik Hospital, the woman had miscarried.

I was told later by Captain Abate that the woman herself had survived. The student movement was to use her case to demonstrate the police brutality under the Emperor's regime. Even some foreign newspapers told her story.

Captain Abate took me home in his car. On the way I asked him to tell me more about his own background. He hesitated, as all Ethiopians do. But after a little prodding, including a brief history of my own life and my peasant background, he told me his story. He was from the Gojam region, the third son of a family of four boys and three girls. He had worked as a servant in the household of Ras Belew, a nobleman, who helped him to go to night school and gain admission to the police academy. As a child he had been dazzled by the shining uniform, cap and pistol of the provincial police officer in his district. He regarded the day of his graduation as his second birth. It was obvious to me that he wore his uniform with immense pride.

He said some flattering things about my class at the police academy and about the way I treated the cadets. He was a man who appreciated respect both ways in the social ladder. I decided to probe him a little further.

"How do you think we should handle the student problem?" I asked.

"I don't know, sir. It is not my place to speak about high policy, which is the task of your excellencies."

"Come one," I teased. "You can't mean that. We are all responsible for our country. And as a member of the security forces who are in the front line of the battle, your views are of great value. You have a right and a duty to offer opinions."

"Thank you for your confidence, but I still think that these are not matters for me to decide," he said.

I had tried to break the wall, or at least to lower the fence, separating us. But Ethiopian culture is strong. It places a high value on hierarchy and maintaining a respectful distance between those on different levels. Of course, there was the flip side to that condition. If I were to fall out of grace (as I would later) the respect would dissipate like the morning dew; and the distance would be reduced to contemptuous familiarity.

The officer knew my house. He drove me there while I was engrossed in the conversation. The special squad, or the police in general, knew the residences of all the "excellencies" as the captain called us.

At my house, the officer got out of his car—a Peugeot 403—saluted and bade me farewell. I made the customary gesture, asking him to come in and have a drink, but he respectfully declined. I thanked him and wished him good luck in his work. "If there is anything that I can do to help you, please do not hesitate to call on me," I said.

That seemed to move him. "Thank you sir," he said saluting again, and left. He was a tall and handsome man in his late twenties. His overall conduct, including his compassion for the pregnant woman as well as his words, showed me a man who was deeply religious, patriotic, and a chip from the conservative granite of Ethiopian life.

But an altogether appealing figure, even to one who was dedicated to destroying the old order.

FIVE

When I entered my house I found my wife, Hanna, and my brother-in-law, Admasu, her oldest brother, glued to the radio. They were listening to a damning commentary charging that the students were biting the hand that feeds them, a disgrace to their families and society, and more in that vein. The voice belonged to Mergemu Wonaf, a newscaster with a unique voice and forceful delivery. He was selected for special occasions such as this, and was later to fulfill the same role for the military regime that overthrew the Emperor's government.

"The dastardly deeds of foreign powers and their mercenary hirelings from the student body—" Mergemu intoned, and Admasu turned the radio off with an expression of disgust. Admasu was a university professor.

"The media war is on," I said.

"How can you be so facetious," Hanna said. "Do you know that they actually struck the Emperor's car?"

"Yes, I heard," I said.

"You heard!" she screamed. "Where were you? I imagined all kinds of horrible things happening to you. I am scared to death. And all you have to say is, *I heard.*"

"Well, I am sorry. I was not actually near the Emperor's car. Is it your wish that I should have been there?"

"Of course not! Don't twist my words."

"Okay, you lovebirds, break it up," Admasu said with his usual directness, which was disarming.

Hanna looked at me with frustration for a moment, then said lunch was served and was getting cold.

"Why did you wait for me? I thought you had eaten," I said.

"You know better than that," Hanna scolded. We ate in silence for a few minutes, overwhelmed as we were by the events of the day. Then Admasu told some funny stories. There was the student at Haramaya College of Agriculture who was asked by the Emperor, during an agricultural exhibition: "Which of these fruits is better?"

"Whatever Your Majesty likes better is the better fruit," the student replied.

And then there was the story of a little boy in the first grade in "Bethlehem" where His Majesty was born. (The town was known by another name, but was renamed Bethlehem by provincial sycophants.) The Emperor was visiting the school and wanted to know if they were being taught their history properly.

"Who was born here?" the Emperor asked the little boy.

"I was," the little boy answered.

Admasu roared with laughter telling those stories. He obviously relished them. He was not the Emperor's favorite university professor, but that didn't bother him.

After lunch was over we were joined for coffee by Melaku and Woinishet, who was courting him. In those days a woman courting a man openly (or chasing him) was frowned upon by polite Ethiopian society. But our family had its unconventional ways, with which even Hanna went along.

I had not planned to meet with Melaku, but the events of the day had prompted him to sound out my views on a special meeting. It was clever of him to bring Woinishet to make it look like a friendly visit. Woinishet was the gossipy type whose interest in politics was minimal, which was why Melaku had resisted her advances and told her to put any thoughts of marriage out of her mind. But she was persistent. She also seemed to get on well with Hanna, which made things easier for us.

That afternoon's conversation drifted through gossip and platitudes before settling on the events of the day. A curious neighbor looked in to ask how we were—or rather, how I was—after he heard the radio. He did not stay long. He was a civil engineer by the name of Kebede whose two boys, ages five and six, were fond of Lemlem, our four year old daughter.

After Kebede left it was Woinishet, of all people, who brought up the incident of the day. Her question was unexpected. "How do you feel at times like this, when the Emperor's dignity is openly violated?" she asked me.

"How would you feel in my place? Outraged of course," I said.

"We are all outraged, or should be. But what I mean is, it is getting close isn't it? An attack on the Emperor is an attack on his ministers and all their aides."

She looked at Melaku as if searching for approval. He played it safe. "I suppose Woini is right," he said. "The Emperor is the keystone of the whole edifice. But Desta and his like are only technicians who run things, not policy makers. So if you are worried about his future, I'd say your worry is misplaced. Now, if we are talking about the Prime Minister, that is a different matter."

"I wouldn't be too sure about that," Hanna cut in. "I think Desta is in it every bit as deep as the ministers. And you know, the funny thing is that he has the responsibility without the corresponding wealth and privilege. We don't even own our home."

"It is paid for by the government," I pointed out.

"Yes, and it can be taken away any day that you are out of favor," she said, bringing up an old favorite subject. Her eyes rolled sideways, a sign that she was angry or worried.

"And Melaku—" Hanna continued. "Whose side are you on anyway? As a friend of Desta's, you should find him some teaching job in Europe or America, or even Africa, and get him out of this trap." We all kept quiet, a little surprised by Hanna's last outburst.

"At least Desta has been very helpful to people from his present position," Woinishet said.

"That is absolutely right," Melaku said, "and I think everyone appreciates his help. You see, Hanna, it is not wealth or privilege that matters, at the end of the day. It seems to me that you are worrying too

much. Your man is a gift to the nation, and we need people like him
in high places to take care of things for us."

Hanna seemed to be mollified. But I was not. Although I did not
want to admit it, the double life I was leading was taking its toll on me.
I felt guilty keeping secrets from Hanna, who was always honest and
straightforward with me, as with everyone she knew. But on the other
hand, if I disclosed the secrets of my underground life, I would not
only be breaking a vow of silence, I would be jeopardizing her and our
daughter. Also, she would always be worried, and she might even object
politically. So I maintained my silence. I knew she suspected something,
but she had no idea of the depth and extent of my involvement in the
underground movement.

Hanna's love and devotion was a precious thing, which I sometimes
took for granted. I treasure it even today, after losing her. The memory
of our life together, of our shared laughters and sorrows, has struck
deep roots in me. I look back to those days and see her beautiful face
with her high cheekbones and wide bright eyes, and that swing of her
hips when she walked. She had a sterling character: honest, forthright,
generous and kind. She suffered no fools, but she defended the underdog—which in her case often meant siding with the maids in their
disputes with the male servants of the household. She could be stubborn and rude on occasion, but she held no grudges. She could be
jealous, especially of women I had known in my student days. But at
heart she knew that, despite a flirtation and an occasional frolic, that I
was devoted to her.

That day her flashing eyes showed alarm. Her voice, though firm,
had the plaintive tone of a worried woman. She was obviously afraid
that I could be caught between the hammer and anvil of the revolutionary process that was unfolding with increasing speed.

Admasu left for work. Hanna took Woinishet to the bedroom to
show her the new clothes she had bought, leaving Melaku and me
alone. The two of us reviewed the events of the week quickly, before
the women came back from the bedroom. We agreed to hold an
emergency meeting the following evening at Melaku's apartment. We
divided the people we would inform about the meeting. Then Melaku

and Woinishet left; I saw them to the door.

Hanna was standing in the corridor when I returned. Suddenly, she ran to me and put her arms around me. I felt her body tremble with sobbing. I held her tight and caressed her; then I took her face in my hands and kissed her, tasting the salt of her tears. I looked into her eyes. They were vulnerable, like the eyes of a hunted deer.

"It is okay. Everything is going to be okay," I whispered. I felt dizzy as a mixture of emotion and desire stirred within me. We stood like that for a while, then walked toward the bedroom in a close embrace . . .

SIX

The Prime Minister stepped out of his black Cadillac before his chauffeur had time to get out and open the door for him. He always got out fast when he was agitated. I was waiting for him on the curb outside his Sidist Kilo office; we were late for the emergency meeting of the cabinet which he had ordered me to arrange. It was the day after what became known as the Holy Virgin Incident.

The Prime Minister walked a few steps toward the door, then stopped and turned to survey the emerging scene on the street.

"*Merde alors!*" he cursed between his teeth, sucking on his Gauloise cigarette. The scene was a menacing one, with students gathered in large numbers outside the government compound, and riot police in full gear positioned to deny them access. Akalu had told me the night before, when I went to see him at his heavily guarded residence, that he feared the end was near. He did not elaborate; nor did he tell me what had transpired at the palace when he was with the Emperor, following the incident. This reticence with me was unusual. Such was the bond between us that we were referred to as the "Sorbonne Mafia." That bond and his confidence in me often pricked my conscience as the implications of my underground activities deepened.

The scene at Sidist Kilo was not quite a replica of the previous day. But it was clear to me that the student movement had gained impetus and was moving to unexpected levels of agitation. The students had tasted blood. Whether their stones had struck the Emperor's Rolls Royce or not was immaterial. What mattered was that the first stone, and with it the die, was cast. To put it another way, the contending forces of revolution and reaction had locked horns.

The morning sun bathed the autumn air with its warmth. Eucalyptus trees covered most of the city from the Entoto hills to the north and northeast down to the flat land to the south. I could smell the faint fragrance of jasmine coming from the fence of the compound. The incongruity of the violence on the street and the beauty of the day reminded me of the artful public relations slogan about Ethiopia being the land of thirteen months of sunshine. Prime Minister Akalu was associated in some people's mind with that slogan, not because he invented it but because the thirteenth month of five days was a metaphor for something defective or transitional. In the pre-Gregorian Ethiopian Calendar, the five-day month, lying between the old year ending in August and the new year beginning in September, was an anomaly. Akalu was considered just such an anomaly in imperial politics.

Just as Akalu reached his office where the ministers were waiting anxiously, a loud cheer came from the direction of Sidist Kilo University campus. The cheer was echoed by the crowd outside the Prime Minister's office, and the police became fidgety. There were a few hundred students outside the main gate and around the little garden across the street. But the police had successfully contained most of the students inside the campus, where they demonstrated and shouted slogans.

Prime Minister Akalu called the meeting of the cabinet to order. His voice was grave and there was a somber look on his face. He looked haggard and much older than his years.

"My friends," he began, "we are facing an emergency unlike any we have faced before." He lit a Gauloise and inhaled deeply before continuing:

"You hear the sound of loud cheers outside," he said. "That is the enemy. The enemy is uttering war cries from the place in which we expected quiet and creative work. The enemy consists of our own children for whom we have tried to do our best. The place of learning

has been turned into a battleground, an arena of destructive warfare."
He stopped to crush his cigarette in a large ashtray. "The difficult part
of this warfare, gentlemen, is that the enemy is not clearly identifiable.
We cannot, without hesitation, pile upon it the sum total of our
collective rage as we would upon an alien invading army. These are our
sons and daughters, and the majority are gullible victims of a handful
of troublemakers."

Tesfa, the minister of information, an impetuous man in his forties,
interrupted.

"How long are we going to go on believing that only a handful of
troublemakers are to blame?" he said. "How do we know that? I saw the
crowd cheer when His Majesty's car was assaulted."

Akalu, normally a patient man and a good listener, cut Tesfa short.
"You were not the only one who saw it," he snapped. "I am sorry to
deprive you of such a rare privilege."

Everyone laughed except Tesfa, who folded his arms as he always
did when he was in a sulky mood. The laughter of the others was
nervous, and of short duration. The Prime Minister continued by first
half-granting Tesfa his point. Akalu was nothing if not a consummate
diplomat.

"I know that there is a sense in which what Tesfa is saying is true,"
he said. "We did witness the cheering following the outrageous act. The
question, however, is: do we shoot or incarcerate everybody who
cheers? Do we detain all our students and close the university?" He
looked at Zerfu, the minister of security, who was obviously itching to
speak.

"I say we close the university," Zerfu said.

"And detain the students?" Akalu probed.

"Yes, detain the damned bastards!" Zerfu said.

"And how many of them are there? Do we have enough space for
them in the detention stations?"

"There is enough room. That's not a problem," Zerfu said. "And
once we begin our interrogations, we will know who the real culprits
are. Then we can deal with them. We have been treating these bastards
with kid gloves. We have been preoccupied too much with due process

and adverse publicity in the world media."

"World media is not what concerns me right now," Akalu said. "What concerns me is the internal repercussions. If we begin to detain students then we will have the entire student body in the nation to reckon with, to say nothing of their immediate and extended families. There will be boycotts and riots by the secondary and even elementary school students everywhere. What would you do then? Do you have a contingency plan in the event of such student activities?"

"Yes, I do," Zerfu said. "But I am not sure this is the time or place to reveal it." There was a murmur and exchange of glances among the cabinet ministers.

"Stop writing! This will be off the record," the Prime Minister said, speaking in my direction. I put down my pen, not knowing what to expect next. Akalu's eyes flashed with anger.

"And when and where, pray, would it be opportune for you to tell us of your contingency plan. Or shouldn't I ask?" he said in an acerbic tone.

"That will depend on what we decide today," Zerfu said.

"Do you mean to say that if we decide to authorize you to make arrests today, you might share your plan with us?" Akalu pressed. The Prime Minister had scented a power play, for which he had the most sensitive nose in the empire, second only to that of the Emperor.

"I didn't mean that," Zerfu mumbled defensively.

"Do you mean, then, that we will be kept in the dark whatever we decide today. Is that it?"

"You are taking my words out of context."

"No, I am not. I am asking to make your words clear and comprehensible to us who are slow."

The other ministers watched and listened, apprehensively. It was clear to me from their faces that they sided with the Prime Minister in what appeared to be a bid for power by the minister of security, who had special access to the Emperor.

It was Getu, the agriculture minister, who spoke next, intervening to conciliate.

"If you will permit me, Prime Minister," he said. "We are all in this together, and we are in it up to our necks. I have always thought that we should be ahead of the students. We should take bold initiatives and not react to events provoked by others. We should steal the thunder of their demands and forge ahead with our own reforms."

"What kind of reforms?" Zerfu asked.

"Land reform, for instance. And administrative reform," Getu answered.

"But there is a land reform bill pending in Parliament," Tesfa said; the minister of information had apparently recovered from his earlier rebuff.

"And how long has it been there?" Getu said. "How long have we talked about reforming local administration?"

"And do you think the students, or whoever is behind them, will be satisfied with what we have proposed?" Tesfa countered, gesticulating profusely as he spoke. His use of his hands was attributed to his Italian education, although Heaven help those who would say so. Tesfa hated the Italians, and resented any association of his behavior with them.

"It is action, not talk, that the students demand," answered Getu. At that moment, as if to underline his remark, a loud chorus of cheers came from the direction of the university—followed by gun shots. The Prime Minister went to the window. We all rose and filed behind him to see what was happening. It was not possible to see the university from our vantage point, but we could see the effect of those cheers in the street below the office, where students and police were locked in battles. More shots were fired as the police tried to stem the tide of students trying to crash through the main gate.

In these circumstances, rational discussion did not seem possible. Akalu looked at me as if to ask what he should do next, and I felt sorry for him. "Your excellency," I said. "Do you think we should perhaps call the Chief of Police and seek more information?"

"That's exactly what I was thinking," Akalu said; and I had no reason to disbelieve him.

I went to the outer office to make the phone calls. I located Lieutenant-General Dima, the Chief of Police, who said he would be at the Prime Minister's office within ten minutes. I then called the office of

Lieutenant-General Gemechu, the head of the imperial bodyguard, though I suspected that it would not be so easy to persuade him to come. I knew he enjoyed a cordial relationship with the Prime Minister in an implicit tactical alliance against the chief of staff of the armed forces and the minister of security, who were potential leaders of a surprise *coup d'état.* I had once even overheard the Prime Minister and Gemechu speaking of the necessity of having bodyguard intelligence officers infiltrating the office of the general staff. I never knew what came of that.

I was not successful in reaching Gemechu himself, but I spoke with his special adjutant, an alert and amiable major who was politically sensible. His name was Asfaw and he frequently came to my office with delicate messages from Gemechu, and whenever we spoke he surprised me with his candor and keen interest in political matters.

Major Asfaw told me on the phone that the general was with His Imperial Majesty, who was having an audience with the American ambassador. Asfaw volunteered to deliver the message in person, since he had an office in the Emperor's palace. I reported all this to the Prime Minister, who had ordered a lunch recess of the meeting and was in his smaller office making phone calls on the "hot line" to the palace. I assumed that he was speaking with the Emperor himself, since he sprang from his seat when the line was answered, stood at attention while speaking, and even made periodic bows toward the phone. Such was the hold of the imperial will on those who were most closely associated with it

As I left the Prime Minister to finish his phone conversation with the Emperor, I saw fear and anxiety on his face. When I went to my office, I felt a pang of guilt nearly overcoming my revolutionary commitment. My world had become a battleground of competing demands: loyalty to the cause and to my underground comrades on the one hand; and on the other, personal loyalty to a man who had been kind and helpful to me over the years. This double life was not one to recommend to anybody.

Akalu was basically a decent human being who tried to use his office, his considerable political talents, and his personal charm to advance the cause of progress—"In an evolutionary manner," he repeatedly reminded me. The imperative of survival in office, which meant staying in the good graces of the Emperor, invariably dictated that he take cautious steps. Such steps, he knew, compromised his ideas of reform.

One thing was indisputable even among his detractors: Akalu was above the vulgar scramble for wealth in which most of his ministerial colleagues were engaged. He lived a modest life in a modest villa, and few accused him of stashing money in Swiss bank accounts, which he could have done easily since he had a Swiss wife. The only privilege he indulged was fishing and boating in one of the lakes south of Addis Ababa. And he enjoyed his cognac in the evenings in the company of his European friends, some of whom had unsavory reputations. That did indeed trigger occasional rumors that he was using European businessmen to siphon money abroad. Those rumors did not bear up under the close scrutiny that followed the revolutionary upheaval four years later.

Now, the impatient forces of history had pushed Prime Minister Akalu into a corner. Being part of these forces of change, I felt acutely the responsibility for the Prime Minister's plight. But I was able to justify my own role in larger, historical terms—in terms of revolutionary necessity. I also felt that in a sense he had brought his plight upon himself by compromising with the conservative imperial regime. He knew that the Emperor needed him as part of a calculated balance of forces.

Sitting in my office alone, I lit a cigarette and watched my smoke rings rise toward the high ceiling and disappear. I was surprised to find myself dogged by these persistent inner questions and doubts. Did my double life involve deception that could conceivably cost the life of this good man? Was it morally repugnant to work so closely with Akalu and use my position for the benefit of a higher calling whose outcome no one could predict? My answer came—a resounding No! No, it was not morally repugnant. I had resolved the whole question in my mind long ago when I had decided to enter the revolutionary compact, knowing that it would undoubtedly affect some innocent people. Besides, even as decent and basically progressive a man as Akalu was an actor in the game of power, not just a victim. He obviously enjoyed the power game; and now he was reaping the harvest of that hazardous exercise: a powerless spectator to the clash between irreconcilable forces which he had imagined he could tame. For him, there seemed no rational and reasonable way out of the emerging crisis.

As I sat and reflected, I remembered the incident that had pushed me to join the revolutionary underground. It was a fine November morning a few years earlier, and I decided, on the spur of the moment, to park my car near the Yugoslavian embassy and walk to work. I was single then.

I mixed with the pedestrians going about their daily business, most of them clad in khakis or traditional cotton clothes. Most were barefoot; a few had sandals, and fewer still wore shoes and socks. I let myself be carried by the wave of the crowd, tuning in to their conversations which ranged from the hopes they pinned on their children's education, to the rising prices, to the corruption of the judges and other public servants. What a contrast to the old days! I thought as I walked and listened. Casting my mind back to my childhood days, I remembered the muffled conversations between my father and our neighbors engaged in similar talk. But in those days there was an element of certainty about the modest bribe (or "gift" in kind) that a judge expected; and he in turn was expected to be merciful to those who could not afford to pay. For the most part, justice was rendered whether or not bribes were paid, and people were more or less satisfied with the result. There was an element of humanity and community spirit in the transaction. Even the "gift" was given openly.

These days the machinery of justice had become impersonal, and judges showed no mercy if you could not afford to pay. Money, the magic store of value and solvent of values, had become the arbiter of public affairs.

Absorbed in this reverie, I reached the area of the Jubilee Palace, where the crowd was stopped by police. Ahead, the Emperor's car was surrounded by a large crowd. I pushed forward and asked a policeman what was going on.

"It is none of your business. Now go away," he said nervously moving his hands toward his holstered pistol.

"I am a public servant just as you are," I told him, and challenged him to let me pass.

"If you are a public servant, all the more reason for you to obey the law!" he shouted back menacingly. He walked over to me and pushed me.

I pushed him back and we were soon engaged in a wrestling match. He blew his whistle and two other policemen rushed in and started kicking me and beating me with their batons. I fell to the ground and they handcuffed me.

By that time the Emperor's car had moved on, but a small crowd was left near the spot where it had stopped. I was forced to sit on the curb, handcuffed, to await a police car. What followed then became a turning point in my life. An ambulance arrived and picked up what seemed to be a wounded man from where the little crowd was gathered. I was taken to the ambulance and pushed inside, together with two other handcuffed men. The wounded man seemed to be in a coma.

"What happened to him?" I asked my fellow prisoners.

"He was shot down from a tree," one of them said.

"What was he doing in the tree?" I asked.

"He was a petitioner. He thought he could get the Emperor's attention that way. He must have climbed the tree before dawn."

"Shut up!" the police guard shouted.

We were taken to Menelik Hospital where I was treated, then released through the intervention of powerful friends. The unfortunate petitioner died on the way and was taken to the morgue. It is a mystery to me to this day whether or not the Emperor knew about the shooting. The fact of the matter was that a powerful branch of his security system had shot down an innocent man without even asking who he was or what he wanted. And no one cared. My attempts to raise a stink about the case became a laughing matter in the city.

SEVEN

As the Prime Minister emerged from his office to resume
the recessed cabinet meeting, General Dima, the chief
of police, arrived. He was ushered into the meeting
room by a uniformed guard, and he gave a military salute to the
assembled company. The ministers all rose to greet the general as
though they hoped he had answers to the burning questions of the day.
Seeing the ministers rise, the general was nonplussed; and abandoning
his stiff military posture, he took off his cap and bowed in the traditional manner to show his appreciation of the courtesy they were according
him by rising. They had never done that before, and their new courtesy
was not lost on Dima.

General Dima, a career officer, was a man in his mid-fifties with a
round face and somewhat bulging and kindly eyes. He was of medium
height, thick-set with broad shoulders. Comfort and lack of exercise had
added what he himself called "ministerial substance" to his belly, and
there was an element of a penguin wobble in his walk. He spoke slowly
and clearly and looked you straight in the eye as he spoke.

Dima shook hands with everyone present, and sat down next to the
minister of security, Zerfu, who was theoretically his superior. The noise
coming from the university and outside the Prime Minister's office had
subsided by the time Dima arrived. Everyone was eager to hear what he
had to say; whether he had solutions up his sleeve, and more particularly whether his analysis of the situation differed from that of his boss.

Relations between the two were strained, because Dima was not in favor of harsh measures if they could be avoided.

The Prime Minister called the meeting to order and came straight to the heart of the matter.

"General Dima," he began, "thank you for coming so promptly. I want to know, as do my colleagues here—is the situation ripe for drastic action such as mass arrests and closing the university? What are your thoughts?"

"I thank you, your excellency, for inviting me to the meeting," Dima said. "I hope that my thoughts are worthy of the office I hold and of your confidence."

He took a file from his briefcase and looked at a page with some figures.

"I have with me," Dima said, "the preliminary report of the special squad appointed to study the crisis."

Aha! I thought, Captain Abate's squad; and I felt a strange sense of satisfaction that I knew something even the Prime Minister did not know.

"What special squad? Who appointed it?" Prime Minister Akalu asked.

"It was appointed under a special order of His Majesty," Dima said. "I believe with the knowledge and, I might add, at the behest of his excellency the minister of security."

Anticipating another flare-up between the Prime Minister and the minister of security, Getu intervened. "May I ask you, General—was the special squad given any police powers in terms of arrest or detention?"

"No, sir," Dima said. "Its function is strictly investigative."

"I see; and how long has it been in operation?" Getu continued.

"About two weeks. This report is very much a preliminary one. The investigation is continuing."

Dima passed the file to the Prime Minister, who glanced at it for a few seconds, then asked: "Has His Majesty been brought up to date on this?"

"He has," Dima said. "As a matter of fact, he asked for it last night and I took him a copy of the report myself. I thought perhaps that the minister of security . . ."

Getu again intervened, with his main concern of the afternoon in mind. "I think, Prime Minister, it may be a good idea if you had a chance to study this report and then tackle the question of what measures should be recommended to His Majesty."

The Prime Minister surveyed the faces of the other ministers in his customary manner of soliciting questions or comments. There were none.

"If there are no questions, we will do just that," he said in a voice showing signs of fatigue. "I also think that Zerfu should come to our next meeting prepared with his contingency plan," he added, looking at Zerfu, who nodded gravely.

"Meanwhile," the Prime Minister said, "Zerfu and General Dima and I will meet in my office at the end of this meeting."

Then he smiled for the first time in the whole day. "As a cabinet we must either hang together or hang separately," he said, paraphrasing a British Prime Minister of bygone days. "But there are those whose necks are out in front!" And he laughed, enjoying the pained look on Zerfu's face.

At that point the usually voluble Demessa, the minister of finance, who had kept quiet throughout the meeting, answered the Prime Minister's witticism.

"Yes, but we must not forget that Louis XVI was executed for the sins of Louis XIV."

It was a jibe at imperial Ethiopian history. Demessa came from a conquered "minority" tribe which is not a minority in numerical terms. No one laughed, not because of a deficiency in Demessa's wit, but because the meeting had lost its sense of humor—a good reason for it to end. It was recessed until December 5, and everyone left except the minister of security, General Dima, and Prime Minister Akalu, who ushered them into his office.

"Desta, you may go home for lunch," he told me. "I'll give you a ring if need be!"

The prime minister called Debebe, his private secretary to give him some instructions, and I left. I made my way through the crowded streets, which the police now had under control. But instead of going home, I decided to go to Melaku's apartment. I could call home from there and tell Hanna not to expect me, and give her a number where I could be reached.

EIGHT

I arrived at Building 82 at about three o'clock. The area was unusually deserted for the time of day. There were a few cars in the parking lot in front of the building, Melaku's Fiat among them. No one saw me when I went up the elevator.

I rang the bell of Melaku's apartment and then knocked at the door—six knocks in beats of two which he would know was my signal. There was no answer. I rang again and repeated the knock before I used my key to open the door. Yohannes and I were the only ones with keys to Melaku's apartment, which we used when we needed privacy to work on movement papers. Not even Woinishet had a key.

I opened the door and shouted, "Anybody home?" I was heading toward the phone in the corner across the living room when I saw Melaku lying on the floor, face down. At first I thought he was sleeping. Then I froze there on the spot, terror-stricken. I knelt down and lifted his head, then let it drop abruptly as I saw the blood on the corner of his mouth. My heart pounding, I rushed to the bathroom where I vomited and stayed for what seemed an eternity.

I did not know what to do. I had always thought of myself as a cool and competent person, capable of handling any emergency. Now, face to face with the moment of truth, I failed the test. How could I not fail the test—when one of my best friends and comrades, one of the most remarkable human beings I had ever known, lay on the floor, lifeless? It was not the first time I had seen a dead body, but this one belonged

to a person with whom I had shared great moments, a person full of life
and dreams who was the guiding hand of a struggle for which I was
prepared to lay down my life if necessary.

My mind raced; I was not able to focus on anything; I could not
concentrate. I remember being seized by a sense of the absurd. I
thought of Albert Camus, of his view of life as absurd and how he had
met his death absurdly, in a car accident. Strange, how the mind works.
How could my mind travel from that room, from that situation, to
Camus! I am puzzled to this day.

After the initial shock was over, I collected myself and began to
examine the scene. There was no obvious sign of a struggle—no articles
knocked down, or out of place. There was no bullet or knife wound.
Could it have been an accident, or a heart attack? But Melaku was a
specimen of fitness and good health. He took karate twice a week at the
Y.M.C.A.

Karate! Could he have been surprised by an assailant who was a
professional? I approached the body again and raised the head with
trembling hands. I could have sworn that there was a faint smile on his
face, an ironic smile as if Melaku accepted his fate with the same
graceful humor that he had brought to everything.

Whoever did this must be a professional, I thought, and must have
caught Melaku by surprise. He must have gained entry somehow and
waited in ambush for Melaku to enter the apartment. I had no clue as
to who the actual killer was, but there could be only one possible
source of the order to kill. Melaku used to say that one measure of the
progress of the revolution is the desperate steps that the oppressors are
forced to take.

I cast my thoughts back a few weeks to the night of our Central
Committee meeting, and the shadowy figures I had noticed outside the
apartment building . . .

Looking back today, I think of the fact that Melaku did not live to
see the ultimate day of reckoning, when the Emperor was taken from
his palace in a Volkswagen to a detention camp. I often wonder how he

would have regarded that event which was observed—nay, celebrated—
by half a million residents of Addis Ababa. I like to think he would
have felt as I did—sad. Sad not because the old tyrant was overthrown;
after all, that was a revolutionary objective and we were revolutionaries.
No, sad to see an old man nearing his grave whose vanity and love of
power had blinded him beyond redemption. The sheer folly of it all was
saddening. At the same time, I think today amid the ruins of a revolution gone astray, amid the broken pieces of our dream turned to
nightmare, that Melaku is perhaps better off than those of us who
survived him . . .

My mind drifted as I sank into an armchair near Melaku's body. I
thought of the old Ethiopian saying: *Why is a dead body respected?*
Because it is silent. I felt a deep rage as I reenacted in my mind the scene
when the order was given, and then the invasion of Melaku's apartment
by the murderer. I made a pact with the silent one. I vowed vengeance.
"May my father's bones become arrows and pierce me if I do not avenge
your murder," I said addressing myself to my departed friend.

It suddenly dawned on me that I had been sitting there for over an
hour. I realized I had to do something. But what? First I had to inform
the others. I got up and went to the phone and dialed Yohannes'
number. Yohannes was perhaps Melaku's closest friend, his childhood
companion, and a sort of alter ego.

I looked at my watch as I waited for someone to answer. It was after
four in the afternoon. I knew Yohannes did not go to work that day.
The phone rang several times and I was about to hang up when a
sleepy female voice answered. It could only be Saba, Yohannes' wife,
one of my favorite objects of suspicion. In the business of revolution,
you tend to distrust everybody, rightly or wrongly, because you are
dealing with people's lives, including your own.

"Hello, is Yohannes there?"

"Just a minute," she said with irritation.

Bitch! I thought, almost cursing her aloud. She knew my voice, or
else she would have asked my identity.

"Yohannes, this is Desta," I said when he came to the phone. "You must come quickly. I am at Melaku's place."

"Why? What is the matter?"

"Please come immediately. I can't tell you on the phone."

"I'll be there in half an hour," he said and hung up.

I heaved a sigh of relief. The expectation of sharing the burden of my horrible discovery with a comrade and friend was enough to take a load off my mind. I thought of calling others but dismissed the idea. Yohannes was resourceful and more savvy in the ways of Addis Ababa than most of us. He would help in planning the next steps.

Yohannes was as good as his word; he arrived in less than half an hour. I got up to greet him, meeting him near the door.

"What is the matter," he began—and then saw. He glanced at me for an instant before rushing to Melaku's body. He felt the pulse by placing his hand on the chest. Yohannes had worked for several years as a medical officer before switching to law. Wearily shaking his head, he rose slowly to face me. His eyes glistened with tears, but his voice was steady.

"Well," he said, putting his hands on my shoulders, "the mantle now falls on your shoulders." Those words were so unexpected that it took a while before their meaning sunk in. Almost immediately, Yohannes insisted that I call an emergency meeting of the Central Committee. No sentimentalities, no expressions of sorrow—

I did not know whether to tell him to go to hell or to cry. I sank onto the sofa and buried my face in my hands.

"We have to keep cool," he said. "When you call the others, don't show any signs of distress. Remember, you are the acting leader now, and at a time like this others look up to the leader. Every word, every syllable, every inflection may make the difference between continuing the struggle and despondency."

Watching his face and listening to him, I was struck by the fact that although he was saying that I was now the leader, in fact he was behaving like the leader. That annoyed me, and I was irked by the fact that I was annoyed. At a time like this! Then the tension within me exploded suddenly and I heard myself saying:

"Yohannes, you should be the acting head of the committee."

"No, of course not," he said. "Revolutionary legality demands that you succeed Melaku."

"Revolutionary legality, my foot!"

"Yes, revolutionary legality," he said. "Even in a revolution we follow legality, or else the fabric of our organization would break up. Besides, you are the natural successor."

"What about him?" I said, pointing to the silent one. There was an accusatory edge to my voice, and Yohannes bowed his head in shame.

"I have not forgotten him," he said at last. "He is gone, and no amount of tears or mourning can bring him back. My soul is pained as much as anyone's, but we are revolutionaries with a noble cause. Melaku would want us to be steadfast, to keep our heads and get on with the job."

"What do we do about the body?"

"First we must tell the others," Yohannes said. "Then we must notify the police, for all the good that will do. If we don't notify them soon, they will use it against us."

"Do you think the police did it?" I asked.

"Not the police," he said, "At least not the ordinary police. You know that there are counter-insurgency agents in every branch of the security force, including the army and the imperial bodyguard."

"I know." I thought of the ministerial meeting and General Dima's "special squad."

Yohannes knelt to examine the body more closely. "The blood dried on his mouth is from internal bleeding," he concluded. "Probably karate blows. He was obviously surprised."

"They must have been watching us for some time," I said.

"Perhaps. Or maybe they were tipped off by someone."

"Who?"

"Who knows? We have to consider all possibilities," he said. "We are engaged in a dangerous enterprise. As Mao once said, 'the revolution is not a tea party.'" He sat down looking dejected.

At last, seeing a more human reaction, I forgave Yohannes his earlier clinical competence which I had resented. But for some reason, I did not share with him my solemn vow of vengeance.

We agreed on a plan of action. Yohannes would locate the other four members and convene them at Bekele's house near the old airport, and I would report the murder to the police. If, for any reason, the police detained me, the meeting would proceed with Yohannes as acting chairman. Yohannes would also inform Melaku's brother and uncle. They could take care of notifying his estranged Anglo-Indian wife who lived in London with their two daughters. The tumultuous life of a committed revolutionary was hardly the future she'd had in mind when she married him, although I remember her sitting at his feet with awed admiration when he chaired political study groups at the London School of Economics.

I decided to go home and tell Hanna the sad news before notifying the police. I dreaded the prospect of telling her, for I knew what would follow: loud cries and wailing. Hanna was fond of Melaku and she linked his fate with my own. I knew she suspected something, though she had no idea of the depth of our involvment in the movement.

NINE

Melaku's death became one of those events that mark a turning point in the course of a struggle. It marked a personal turning point for me as well. There could be no easy transition from my position as principal assistant to one of the most powerful men in the empire, to principal protagonist in the opposition camp. The boundary that I had so carefully built was about to be removed.

As we had planned it, the funeral was to be a simple affair. We wanted to avoid trouble that might be caused by unforeseen emotional outbursts. Accordingly, Yohannes, Bekele and I spoke to Melaku's brother and his uncle, and offered to take the body to his native area in Wollo for burial.

A funeral is a serious affair in Ethiopia, as in much of Africa. It is the occasion when the grieving family and other relatives of the departed are treated with the greatest of care and respect. It provides opportunities for social interaction, for the reconciliation of enemies and the mediation of old conflicts. For all these reasons, elaborate rituals attend African funerals, and the family of the deceased expect, and often demand, that the body of their member be brought to their village to join his ancestors.

Melaku's brother and uncle were grateful when we offered to take the body to Wollo, and to pay all costs and handle the arrangements. Dessie, the capitol of Wollo, lies some three hundred kilometers north

of Addis Ababa. We agreed to start the journey to Dessie the following
morning, before dawn.

But this was not to be. Our plans were shattered the next day when
we discovered that Melaku's body had disappeared during the night.

At first we did not know who the culprits were, though our suspicions naturally were directed toward the government. The hospital
authorities were shocked and embarrassed. The administrator had just
finished his interrogation of the policeman guarding the morgue when
Yohannes and I entered his office.

He received us with the deference that Ethiopians reserve for the
high and mighty, by bowing deeply and standing up while he talked to
us. I had difficulty getting him to sit down, and had barely succeeded
when the phone rang. He answered it and listened for a long while
before asking: "Where do they have the body now, sir?"

"They found it? Who? Where?" I demanded.

"It seems," he said as he put down the receiver carefully, "that the
university students have the body. That was the minister of health on
the phone and he said that the chief of police told him so."

I asked if I could use the phone, and he got up and walked around
the desk to sit on one of the chairs reserved for guests.

I thanked him and occupied his chair. I called General Dima's office.
"May I speak to the general, please. This is Desta Kidane-Wold."

"Yes sir. Just a moment, sir," the secretary said.

"Hello!" came Dima's inimitable voice.

"General Dima," I said. "What is this I hear about the university
students holding the body of my friend Melaku?"

"I am sorry, Desta," he said. "But it is true. Success is going to their
heads."

"Success? What has success got to do with snatching the body of an
innocent victim?" I said—and immediately regretted the phrasing of the
question.

"Perhaps you should ask them that question yourself," he said. I
detected an unusually tense note in his voice, and my heart sank with

growing apprehension.

"Who are they? Who would I ask?" I said, holding my ground.

"All we know so far is that they snatched the body a little after midnight, and that they are holding it at the main campus of the university. The entire student body has barricaded itself inside the campus, and our assumption is that it was not the work of an isolated group."

"Thank you, general. I will talk to you later," I said. I hung up, puzzled and more than a little frightened.

Later in the day we learned that ultra-radical elements in the student movement, hearing of Melaku's sudden death, had decided to use it to advance their own sectarian agenda. How they got past the police guard in the hospital morgue was not clear to anyone at the time. Apparently the police suspected that I had a hand in it, which explained Dima's cryptic remarks and the tone of his voice.

Melaku was known among the university students as a great poet, and not as a leader of a revolutionary movement. He had lectured on African literature in general and Ethiopian poetry in particular. He had also organized poetry reading and writing workshops. On one occasion his poetry reading had been reported by the security service as inflammatory, and the Prime Minister had sometimes teased me about my "wild poet" friend. But I did not believe anyone suspected Melaku to be a leader of a revolutionary movement. And I had no reason to believe that Melaku had kept secrets from me concerning contacts with anyone outside our party. He was too honest and disciplined to do that.

Yohannes and I went from the hospital to my house, where we were later joined by Bekele. I telephoned the Prime Minister to brief him on developments. The previous day I had asked him to give me leave for three days to attend to my friend's funeral, and he was very sympathetic. Hanna was in great distress. She, too, had told her supervisor at Alitalia airlines that she was not coming to work for two or three days. She wanted to go to Dessie with us.

Yohannes, Bekele and I reviewed the events of the day and discussed how to meet the challenge of the new situation. The question facing us was: do we expose ourselves by joining forces with the errant student faction, or do we side with the family and the forces of law demanding the surrender of Melaku's body. It was a cruel dilemma, filled with irony. In the middle of our discussion, Maaza, Melaku's brother, and his uncle came to my house unexpectedly. They carried an injunction from the high court ordering the students to surrender the body forthwith, on pain of criminal prosecution.

"I advised them to do that," Yohannes said. "They are within their right and it did not take long to obtain the order."

"The students are out of their minds!" Hanna said, bursting into tears. She was joined by Melaku's uncle, who stood up and began to walk up and down our living room with his hands on his head, wailing in the traditional manner:

"Oh my son, my son!" he cried. "Oh lion of Wollo, lion of London, what was our covenant? Is this how it will end! Oh lion of Wollo . . ."

Maaza joined him, and the rest of us sat sobbing, unable to control ourselves. My house was thus suddenly transformed into a funeral home without the body, which made the poor family's grief even more poignant.

A couple of neighbors heard the cries and came over. One of them was Almaz, the wife of an old friend whose house adjoined mine. The other was Colonel Gebreab, a retired army officer, who happened to be passing by. They came in puzzled, asking, "What happened?" Hanna recovered before the rest of us and invited them to sit and told them the story.

"Crying will not bring him back," the colonel said, pulling Melaku's uncle to sit down. "This is an outrageous thing the students did. What can they gain by this scandalous act?"

"How can they do this to us?" the uncle said, wiping his nose. "What an outrage! Have they no shame?"

He then turned toward me and said, "Sir, you must help us. Only you can help us. I don't think a court order can help us."

The poor man had no idea of the limits of my power. As a traditional Ethiopian, he persisted in his belief that the Emperor and his government were capable of anything and everything. For people like Melaku's uncle, the Emperor was all powerful and the imperial system was immutable. The quickening tempo of the revolutionary struggle which was evident everywhere was, for them, an aberration that would pass like the clouds.

"I will do everything I can, but I can't promise miracles," I told him.

"Meanwhile," Yohannes said, "you must take this court order to the police. They can issue an ultimatum on the loudspeaker, using the words of the injunction. It will be an open violation of law if the students refuse to comply, and the police will be under an obligation to taken forcible steps."

"With God's help," the colonel said.

"Of course," I said. "But God helps those who help themselves."

"All right, then," the uncle said. "We will take this order to the police." He and Maaza left. I saw them to the door with expressions of encouragement and hope.

"I will join you soon!" Yohannes told them.

The colonel also rose to leave. Hanna and Almaz left for the kitchen, leaving Bekele, Yohannes and myself alone again.

"So what now?" Bekele asked, looking at me.

"Yohannes may have more clues on this surprise action of the students," I said.

"Not really," Yohannes said. "There is only one thing that came my way that you may not know yet. A student leader who is in the law school called me to discuss a paper that he is writing on criminal procedure. I met him last night because he insisted that he had to submit it today."

"A paper? So what?" Bekele asked, puzzled.

"Well, it was not about a paper at all," Yohannes said. "He told me that the student leadership was divided on a number of issues. He said that he was told by a close friend, who is in the inner circle of the top five, that there had been an assassination—of an important underground leader."

"Did he say it was Melaku?" I inquired.

"He did not know the name, but his friend did. His friend also told him that the top leadership was going to take drastic steps related to the assassination. Now we know what the drastic steps are."

"How did the students know about Melaku's assassination so early yesterday?" I asked.

"I don't know," Yohannes said.

"Unless, of course," Bekele said, "they had a hand in it."

"Oh come on," I said. "Are you serious?"

"Anything is possible. The revolution devours its children and all that." When Bekele made a shocking statement, he usually had an impish smile and a twinkle in his eyes. Neither smile nor twinkle accompanied this devastating remark.

"That is a serious charge," I said. "Do you know anything we don't know?"

Bekele took his time before he answered. He was the Central Committee member in charge of student affairs, with Aberra as his deputy. Aberra also acted as liaison between labor and student affairs and was in charge of labor matters. The two of them seemed to get on well, despite their different personalities.

Bekele had cultivated, over the years, the appearance of a revolutionary with long unkempt hair and a beard, and he liked to quote revolutionary maxims from Voltaire, Marx and Mao. Although he had a brilliant mind, he was slow in speech and readily deferred to more articulate colleagues. He was educated as an electrical engineer and often used the language of his profession to illustrate points. He was technical manager of a branch of the state-owned telecommunications corporation and also a part-time lecturer in electrical engineering. He was the only member of the Central Committee who did not have success with women. But he was content to devote his spare time and energy to the cause.

Aberra, in contrast, always dressed smartly and was clean-shaven. He was brisk in manner, precise in language, and uncompromising in argument. Women found his brutal charm irresistible. A tall, handsome man, he was the object of intense competition among young women in his student days. To his credit, he never abused these assets; he was no philanderer and was evidently devoted to his wife.

Bekele took out a pack of Viceroy cigarettes and lighted one before he spoke. He looked at both of us intently.

"You probably think I have been holding out on you," he said. "But I have not." He inhaled deeply, then continued. "Have you heard of a student leader by the name of Gebre-Meskel?" he inquired.

We both nodded. "He is in charge of organization of the university student union," I said.

"He is that and something else besides," Bekele said. "He is a KGB agent."

Bekele watched our reaction with what I thought was devilish delight. Before we could ask him to explain, he continued: "He is the leader of the ultra-radical faction, and on Sunday night, following the assault on the Emperor's car, that faction rushed through a resolution to give the leadership authority to take any and every measure to maintain the momentum of the revolution."

"Including assassination?" I led him on.

"Exactly," Bekele said. "It was not stated so explicitly, of course."

"Are you saying that Gebre-Meskel and his group are responsible for Melaku's murder?" Yohannes asked, incredulous.

"I am saying that he is directly or indirectly involved in the body snatching, which means that he knew about the murder."

"What is your source for his KGB connection?" Yohannes pursued.

"A member of the opposing faction."

"That could be politically motivated," I said. "You know factional politics can lead to strange things."

"Right. In fact it is factional politics—his factional politics, and his inordinate ambition," Bekele said.

"Is your source trustworthy?" Yohannes asked.

"My source has an unimpeachable record for objectivity and fairness."

"So our assumption that the government ordered the assassination is wrong?" I asked.

"We cannot rule it out completely," Bekele said. "But the preponderance of evidence points to Gebre-Meskel's group as the real culprit."

"And the KGB," Yohannes added.

"Whether the KGB directly had a hand in it; whether they instigated it, or condoned it, I cannot say," Bekele said. "But I would say they are implicated. The knowledge of Melaku's movements, and the professional job done in killing him, as well as the efficiency with which the body snatching was carried out, supports such a conclusion."

By that time Yohannes was getting fidgety, looking at his watch. "I'd better go to police headquarters to help Melaku's brother and uncle. I'll see you tonight," he said and left.

Bekele did not have his car, so I offered to drive him to his office at the center of the city. On the way, he suggested that I use my ministerial connections to probe the question of KGB and other foreign involvement in student politics.

"If I were so much as to suggest that the KGB may have been involved in Melaku's murder, people would want to know how I got that idea. And that would be awkward," I said.

"Perhaps your friend Dima may have some lead," Bekele said.

"Perhaps. I am going to see him later, and I'll see what he can tell me. I will report tonight."

Bekele got off near the intersection of Mexico Square, and I drove off in the direction of the Prime Minister's office.

When I reached my office I found an urgent message from the British embassy asking me to return the call. The Prime Minister had been summoned to the palace and had left before I arrived. All seemed to be quiet in the campus. Too quiet, I thought, and wondered if it might be the calm before the storm.

I made a few phone calls to find out the latest on the case of Melaku's body. I could not concentrate. General Dima had also been summoned to the palace, together with the minister of security. I decided to call the British embassy as much out of curiosity as anything; I normally ignored such calls from embassies.

"Hello, this is Desta Kidane Wold from the Prime Minister's office," I said when I got a female voice on the line.

"Oh, yes, sir! We have been trying to reach you. Hang on please, sir. I'll put you through to his excellency," she said.

"Hello, Ato Desta," said a booming voice in what is usually known as the Queen's English. "My dear fellow, how very kind of you to ring up. We were wondering, my wife and I, if you could honor us with your company tonight at a small, quiet dinner."

"Well, it is . . ." I began, and he read my mind.

"It is an awfully short notice, I know. But I feel sure that you might find the company rather interesting. Sir Geoffrey Hicks, who is an old acquaintance of yours, I believe, is here, and he especially asked to meet you."

"Oh, how nice," I said. "I know Sir Geoffrey very well. How long is he staying?"

"I am afraid he is leaving tomorrow for Kenya."

"All right," I said. "I'll be there. But I may have to leave early."

"Agreed," he said and we both hung up.

Sir Geoffrey was an amiable, portly gentleman of middle age, with full white hair and a long moustache. I knew him from London and from Paris, which he visited for research on French colonial history. I never knew what he actually did; only that he was a gentleman of leisure who traveled to Africa and the Middle East a good deal. I had a suspicion that he was a member of British intelligence. That suspicion was enough to draw me to the embassy dinner that evening.

The dinner company was made up of three couples and the British consul, in addition to the Ambassador and his wife who was a gracious hostess. I have always thought gracious hospitality came naturally to the British, especially to their middle class. They make you feel at ease with everything they did and said; even when you make a *faux pas* they react as if it were their fault.

Sir Geoffrey took me to a corner and made some very interesting statements.

"I hear that the Prime Minister has asked the Emperor to relieve him of his duties," he said, lighting his pipe. "Is there any truth in that?"

I decided to play poker with him. "The Prime Minister is not a quitter, as the Americans put it," I said.

"I am sure he is not," Sir Geoffrey said, applying more matches to his pipe. "But the story is that he has asked the help of his old friend the French president to find him refuge in France."

"Interesting," I said. "And what is the source for that story?"

"Oh, I can't reveal my sources, can I? Let's just say it is an unimpeachable one."

I decided to be provocative; the events of the past two days had had a corrosive effect on my habits of polite conversation. "As unimpeachable as Her Britannic Majesty's Secret Service?" I shot back.

Bingo! Sir Geoffrey's face turned red all over as his hands fumbled in his pocket for more matches. But he recovered soon enough and managed a weak chuckle.

"My dear chap," he said. "What business is it of Her Majesty's Secret Service to meddle in such matters?"

"I did not suggest meddling, but an expression, shall we say, of legitimate interest."

"Quite so. Nevertheless that sort of thing is well above my mere mortal head." Sir Geoffrey withdrew behind his pipe, almost sulking. But I did not wish to let go.

"At any rate," I said, "the story is a wild guess. If your source is the press, then I'd say it may be based on information fed by enemies of the

Prime Minister."

"No, my sources are not the media. If you must know, I heard of it from a French colleague who is well connected with the president of France. I was in Paris a couple of days ago."

"Sir Geoffrey, I hope I did not offend you when I made reference jestingly to the secret service." I decided that a different tactic might mollify him.

"Not at all, my dear chap," he said. "But tell me, how are things going? The students are restless, I hear. Dash it all! They are getting restless all over the world."

"Well, we are trying our best," I said noncommittally.

"In my humble opinion," he said, "you should make a show of force."

"Oh?"

"With all due respect, you are being too gentle. You should chop off their leaders."

"Chop off?"

"Well, not literally. I think that an example should be made of the ringleaders. Thirty lashes on the backside, what! And if there are more protests, more arrests and then send the rest to dig ditches in the remote provinces under the tender care of the army. That would teach them a lesson. Eh, what!"

"Easier said than done," I vetured.

"Not at all, my dear chap," he said, just as our gracious hostess announced that dinner was served.

I was seated next to Sir Geoffrey with the Ambassador's wife on my left. The food was plain English cooking, and I did not have much appetite. But the wine was excellent, and the conversation sparkled like the champagne that the Ambassador himself opened and poured. After we finished eating, he dismissed the servants except for one southern Sudanese, who was dressed in the uniform of domestic servants with a red fez adorning his head, a relic of the colonial past. The sight of the servant would have been amusing, but for the fact that he himself seemed to be proud in that garb.

"A toast, a toast," the Ambassador said, rising. "To Sir Geoffrey!"

"To Sir Geoffrey!" we all said and sipped the champagne.

Sir Geoffrey seemed pleased with the gesture. As all eyes turned toward him, he rose and made a pretty little speech. I don't remember what he said, for my mind was busy mulling over the information he had given me.

Finally, I rose to leave, apologizing profusely. Sir Geoffrey walked with me and the host and hostess as far as the outer door. The Ambassador and his wife bade me good night and I thanked them for their hospitality, and they went back to the other guests.

"I am sure you know the French ambassador," Sir Geoffrey said.

"Yes, I do; rather well," I said.

"Forgive me for presuming, but might I suggest that you talk to him? He is *au courant* on things." And he winked with a broad smile. "Cheerio, old chap."

When I left the embassy it was little after nine, and I was late for my meeting at the "special place."

The "special place" was a small bungalow within a large compound of the Villa Bianca, a restaurant owned by an Italian named Enrico Vitarelli. The establishment of Enrico and his Ethiopian wife served fine food, and also catered to other, more intimate needs.

The Villa Bianca lay at the southern tip of Addis Ababa on the periphery of the red-light district. There, the most basic human commodity is packaged and offered for consumption, with its bare animal essence adorned by ritual courting, peacock fashion. Masculine arms stretch to grab feminine waists and to smack bottoms. But no kissing; it is taboo. You only kiss your wife. In the district, the oldest profession reigns supreme over the affairs of men, pushing all daily cares to the background, including business and family. Even politics.

When I arrived at the Villa Bianca, the restaurant was filled with clients, mostly Europeans, and soft Ethiopian music was playing—a contrast to the raucous rock music heard on the way throughout the red-light district. I greeted Lula, Enrico's wife, who was working at the cash register. She was a beautiful woman in her early forties with a constant smile.

Our "special place," which was procured courtesy of Lula, was one of the bungalows where VIPs were assured total privacy. In order to camouflage our meetings, we were often forced to commit sins, or appear to do so, for the sake of the cause.

As I made my way through a side corridor into the courtyard to go to the bungalow, Enrico saw me.

"*Bona sera, eccelenza,*" he said.

"*Bona sera, Enrico. Come sta?*"

"*A! Grazie, siamo bene, e lei!*" He whispered that the "commodity" he had procured for me that evening was special, very special indeed; then, winking, he left me.

I joined my comrades, who were playing cards while three girls looked on, bored. One of the three looked up at me and stood when I came in. She was such a stunning beauty that I could not help staring before I sat down to play.

We used the card playing gimmick to dismiss the girls when we needed privacy to talk. To look authentic, we even pretended to play for money. But when we told the three women to go and look for greener pasture in other bungalows, one of them was offended. It was the stunning beauty I had noticed coming in, who was quite articulate. She even made fun of our card game with a sophisticated double entendre:

"My lords," she said, "how can you mix hunting and gambling?"

"Shut your damned mouth," Aberra said, putting her in her place. I was embarrassed by his abusive language, which I though was not becoming to a revolutionary. I was even more embarrassed when she answered him.

"I am sorry. I thought I was in the company of respected gentlemen," she said. "Respected and respectful—the two go together." She began to walk away with her head held high.

"Wait," I said and went to her. "What is your name?"

"Zeleka. But they call me Mimi."

"Please excuse my friend," I said, quite taken by her beauty and spirit. "He has had a hard day and playing cards with small money is a way of relaxing for some of us."

She seemed to regret her own reaction and, smiling, said, "I am sorry."

"Perhaps I will see you sometime," I whispered, and stuffed a fifty dollar bill into her hand. She squeezed my hand as she returned the money.

"Your kindness has been reward enough, sir," she said, then added: "I'll be waiting."

I was dumbfounded by this unusual self-denial and dignity. Where did old Enrico find such a call girl? I wondered.

As the girls closed the door behind them, I immediately called the group to order. It was our first full meeting since Melaku's death.

"Our first order of business should be to confirm you as acting chairman until the Congress meets in the spring," Yohannes said.

"I second that," Aberra said.

"Are there any questions, or any discussion?" I asked. There was only silence.

"Do I take your silence as approval, then?" I asked testily.

"Yes," they all said.

"Bekele, do you have something to report before I go to the next item?" I said, and Bekele seemed to hesitate. "Shall I tell them what you told me and Yohannes this afternoon?"

He nodded, and I related the story about the alleged connection between Gebre-Meskel and the KGB.

"I am not surprised," Berhane said. "Gebre-Meskel is a psychopath. He would do anything to satisfy his crazy urges."

"Why do you say that?" Aberra asked.

"Because I know him."

"Well, explain to us. We don't know him," Aberra said aggressively.

"Is this an interrogation?" Berhane demanded.

"No, it is a simple question flowing from your assertion."

"Well, you can take it or leave it," Berhane replied.

"Is this the way scientific socialism works?" Aberra pursued.

"Who said anything about scientific socialism?" Berhane said. "I was talking about a psychopath. Do you want me to define a psychopath for you?"

The tension was rising, so I had to intervene. "Comrades!" I said. "We have enough problems on our hands without adding a new one. Let's separate the issues and address them rationally."

We were discussing Bekele's suspicions that the KGB had had a hand in Melaku's death, when there was a knock on the door. Mimi came in carrying a tray with five glasses and a bottle of Chivas Regal.

"Mr. Enrico sent this with his compliments," she said; then she secretly placed a folded note in my hands, which I put in my pocket.

"Tell him thanks," I said. She looked at me and at the others, all sitting awkwardly around the table, obviously not playing cards.

"See what you have done, Mimi?" I said in mock irritation. "After your devastating remark, we all felt guilty about playing cards."

"I didn't mean to . . ."

"No, its quite all right," I interrupted.

Yohannes helped me out. "Telling each other stories and laughing at our own lies is probably just as relaxing as playing cards!"

"I understand," she said cryptically and left with a flashing smile directed to me.

"I think she has taken a fancy to you," Bekele said to me.

"No, not me. Aberra perhaps. He is the lady-killer here," I said. And we all laughed for the first time that evening.

"Let us calm down," I said pouring scotch into the glasses. "Perhaps this will help."

"Our leader, our dear comrade, is dead," Aberra said. "And his body is possessed by power-hungry students, and there is nothing we can do."

"I know, I know," I said. "This thing pains me as much as it pains anyone. But we can't change the fact of his death. The best way to honor his memory is to carry on with calm and resolve."

"Desta is right," Yohannes said. "Everything has happened so suddenly that we have become disoriented. We must find a way at least of recovering the body and giving it a decent burial. That will clear our minds and our consciences."

"Any ideas?" Berhane asked.

"Yes. I was at the police headquarters this afternoon. The chief sent a company of armed police led by his deputy, a Major Abate, who spoke to the students with a bullhorn and told them that if they did not surrender the body, they would be prosecuted."

"Do you think they care?" Aberra asked.

"I think they do. They were holding a meeting to decide how to respond when I left."

"Were you there yourself?" Bekele asked.

"Yes. I even spoke through the bullhorn, challenging them in the name of decency to surrender the body to the family. I told them I was the family lawyer."

"Do you think they will give it up?" I asked.

"I think so. Anyway, we will know tomorrow morning. They can't go on forever with a rotting body on their hands."

"So what was the purpose of snatching it?" Aberra asked.

"Publicity and provocation," said Yohannes.

"Or madness," added Berhane.

"Now here is the hard question," I said. "What do we do if they refuse?"

"I say we denounce them," Aberra said.

"I agree," Bekele said. "I will work on our contacts to organize their rank and file to have the action condemned, and then use it to overthrow Gebre-Meskel and company from the leadership."

"Is that feasible?" I asked.

"You have my word on it," Bekele said with a determined look.

"This is probably premature and perhaps improper," I said. "But I will say it anyway so that we can all give it a thought. I think that Melaku would want us to use his death to the advantage of the revolution. Let us reflect on it."

I then suggested that we call it a day and relax a little. I poured more scotch and went to the toilet. There I opened the folded note Mimi had left in my hand. In fine handwriting it said, "Meet me at the small bungalow, outside and to your right as you enter the restaurant. I'll wait for you all night if need be."

"The cheeky bitch!" I thought. The strange thing was, I was excited. It was hardly two days since the death of my friend, his body was lying unburied, and this mysterious beauty was inviting me into her chamber. Another strange thing was that I did not feel any guilt.

When I returned to the table I found my comrades engaged in a philosophical discussion.

"Judge not, that you be not judged," Bekele said.

"Don't give me that biblical nonsense," Aberra replied.

"Who is judging whom?" I intervened.

"I was telling Aberra that we could also be accused of being power-hungry" Bekele said. "I was referring to his remark about the students being power hungry."

"There are some among them who are not only power hungry but who are dangerous psychopaths," Berhane said.

"Well, if there are psychopaths among us—" Bekele began and I interrupted.

"This is not the time and place for philosophical or psychological or even sociological debates," I said. "We will have time enough for that later."

They all bowed their heads. One thing I remember from that meeting was the deference they paid to me. I couldn't help but wonder whether it was deference to my position of acting chairman of the group, or to me as a man who walked in the corridors of ministerial power. I did not find the answer to that question.

"I think we should call it a day," I said. It was already past midnight, and we agreed to stay in touch. Yohannes, Bekele and I would call each other and meet in the morning.

"I will contact the chief of police" I said. "I will also find out what the Prime Minister is doing in all this."

ELEVEN

We left our "special place" one by one for security reasons. I was the last to leave. Instead of going to my car, I walked toward the bungalow to the right of the restaurant. It was a small brick house with two windows.

I knocked at the door and a voice answered softly.

"Who is it?"

"It is me."

"Who is me?"

"The card player," I said, laughing a little.

The door opened slowly and there she stood in a red dressing gown over cream-colored lingerie. Her long black hair was spread over her shoulders, with strands falling down the side of her face; she had worn her hair up earlier. She wore red lipstick but was otherwise without make-up. That was one thing that had caught my eye earlier: her simplicity in dress and make-up, in contrast to the two others.

"Did you expect another?" I asked, trying to be nonchalant, even though my heart was beating fast.

"No. But I wanted to be sure. I don't open the door for everyone." She stepped back to make way for me to enter and gracefully pointed to the sofa.

I sat down and smiled at her. There was an awkward silence.

"Are you hungry? I have cooked something special."

"I am not that hungry," I said. "But if you took the trouble to cook something special, I might be persuaded."

"I'll go and warm it up," she said. "Meanwhile, please help yourself to a drink."

There was a tray on the table near the sofa, and on it there was a fifth of scotch, a bottle of soda, and several bottles of beer.

"My God! Another Chivas Regal!"

"Don't you like it?"

"I like it. I was just thinking of the other bottle we finished tonight," I said. It was not hard to guess who the provider was. The question that intrigued me was: what was a bright and beautiful young women doing here? What was her relation to Enrico? Why did he go to such lengths to procure her for my pleasure? How strange, I thought, that so many surprises had met me in such a short time. There was Sir Geoffrey's intriguing story about the Prime Minister, then this. To say nothing of the blood-curdling incident of Melaku's death and the body snatching.

It was all absurd. And I was attacked once again by that mordant guilt that was eating away at my entrails; the scotch only numbed it. Then I found myself getting excited by this mysterious, beautiful woman. It was as if my mind had become the battleground between two demons: the demon of free will, saying: "to hell with all scruples!" emboldened by the seductive presence of Mimi; and the demon of over-caution and self-censorship. I even thought: what if this is a trap? What if she is an imperial agent? But by the time she returned with the food, I had already decided to let the demon of free will win the battle.

"Do you have a telephone?" I asked as she placed the basket of food on the table.

"Yes. It is in the bedroom." She led me to her bedroom and closed the door behind me.

I called home and told Hanna I was going to be very late, perhaps even spend the night out. She was groggy with sleep and complained that I had not called her earlier.

With that settled I went back to the salon, where Mimi had removed the red-embroidered cloth which covered the basket. I sat on the sofa and she sat at my feet.

"Come and sit by my side," I said.

"No. I will sit at your feet."

"No! I insist," I said, half rising.

"And I refuse," she said, smiling. "You can whip me if you wish. But I refuse. You can also whip me if my food is bad," she said without a smile, placing a handful of steaming *fitfit* in my mouth. She held the *fitfit* with her right hand and placed her left fingers around my cheeks squeezing them gently, and I opened my mouth. It was heavenly.

She fed me a few times, and each time she ate what remained in her hand, licking her fingers before she put more in my mouth. Her eyes, which were large and black, burned into my soul.

"Do you like my *fitfit?*" she said.

"I have eaten better," I teased.

"Are you going to whip me?"

"No, not tonight."

It was part of the game. It was part of the culture. "Anyhow," I said, "I don't see a whip in the house."

"I can get one."

"Not tonight."

"One more," she said, standing and pushing my chin up and stuffing the biggest lump of the *fitfit* into my mouth. Then she licked her fingers making kissing sounds, and caressed my lips and cheeks with the same fingers.

In Ethiopian culture, you only kiss your wife; and the "fallen woman" cannot presume to take your wife's place without your permission. Her fingers feed you and make do for kissing. It has to be the fingers of her right hand, because the left hand is associated with unmentionable functions.

The feeding was over. I resisted her entreaties for more, finally getting up and going to the toilet to wash my hands and face. On my way back I noticed a large framed picture hanging from the wall near the door leading to the bedroom. It was a picture of a bearded man.

"Your father?"

"No. My uncle."

"He looks distinguished."

"He was. He is dead now. He brought me up. Father and mother died when I was very young. I hardly remember them."

"What did he do?" I asked, pointing to the picture.

"He was a judge of the high court."

"Where?"

"In Wollo."

"Oh! Your are from Wollo?" I said, surprised. "So you must know Melaku Mekonen."

"I do. I mean I did." She began to weep softly.

I waited for her weeping to subside. "Who are you, really?" I asked, sitting beside her.

"It is a long story."

"Why are you in this place? I mean, any man would give his right hand to find a woman like you."

"I might ask you the same question," she said, recovering her poise and her quietly defiant spirit.

"Quite so. But we are not talking about the same thing," I said.

"Aren't we?"

"Are we?"

Suddenly, she took my hands and kissed them. "I have known about you for some time" she said.

"Many people know about me. That is one of the hazards of being a public figure."

"Do you remember Saba Lemma?" she asked.

"Let me see. Wasn't she a university student a few years back?".

"Yes. She took a course in history with you when you taught as a part-time lecturer."

"I remember. What about her?"

"She had a crush on you. She used to tell me about you."

"Is she a friend?"

"A cousin. She is married now and lives in America. Her father also knows you."

"I am still puzzled," I said.

Mimi poured me more scotch and poured one for herself for the first time. Then she continued her story.

"We lived together in a rented house here while she studied. I was married then. I ran away from Wollo to come to live with her."

"Why did you run away?"

"Because I was forced to marry a local big man. He was one of the top men of His Royal Highness, the Governor."

"Who forced you?"

"My uncle was not in favor of it. But he had no choice. The Prince's minions ordered him. I was only fifteen years old and doing well in my studies."

"Why didn't you run away before the wedding?"

"It was not an ordinary wedding. After I showed resistance, I was abducted when I was going from my home to school in Wollo."

"And how long did you stay married?"

"Three years."

"How was it?"

"It was horrible. But I accepted my fate and did not even think of running away."

"So how did you run away?"

"That is where Enrico comes in," she said, smiling and studying my face. Her tone had changed from sadness to one of pride in a narration of adventure.

"You mean Enrico helped you escape?"

"Not exactly. Can I trust you?"

"Of course."

"I want you to swear on your word of honor," she said.

"I swear on my word of honor as a gentlemen."

"I must trust you. For if they knew, the Prince's minions would harm her and her relatives."

"Her?"

"Lula. It was Lula, Enrico's wife, who planned and organized my escape. You see, she was a friend of my mother. One day she saw me at a funeral and kept looking at me. Finally, she approached and asked if I was the daughter of Asselefetch. I said yes, and she began to weep. After she told me who she was, I invited her home for coffee and told her my story. The result, you see before you."

"I see. And your husband has given up?"

"Fortunately, he is dead now. He was killed in a car accident last year. But I changed my name."

"Is that why they call you Mimi?"

"Yes. When I introduced myself tonight I slipped up and told you my real name first."

"Don't worry. My friends didn't even notice." I told her I was still puzzled over the nature of her work with Enrico, and asked why he had arranged for her to meet me.

"I asked him to," she said.

"How did you know I was coming here tonight?"

"Lula told me. One of your friends phoned to reserve the bungalow for your card game."

"Do you do this sort of thing with other public figures?"

"I won't lie to you. I have done it a couple of times. But I have been dreaming of this for a long time."

"You mean Saba Lemma's infatuation with me was transferred to you?"

"You might say that. But I have also heard good things about you from other people that you helped. Also, Melaku often talked about you. And I have seen you here a few times."

"I don't remember seeing you here before."

"Lula keeps me protected. I help her with the accounts and other odd jobs. She has become like my mother."

"So she also planned our meeting."

"Yes. But Enrico knows too. She trusts him and he does not mind if I create a relationship with a VIP." She laughed at her own statement.

"Why are you laughing?"

"Because Enrico has a son by a former wife who wants to marry me," she said.

"And you are through with marriage?"

"I didn't say that. But not now, and not to Enrico's son."

"Do you know that I am married?"

"I know, and her name is Hanna."

"Wait a minute!" I said. "Do you know everything about me?"

"She works for Alitalia. She is beautiful. Enrico knows her too. He is a friend of Alitalia's manager."

"So the circle is closing," I jested. "And when can I expect my capture?"

She looked serious for a moment. The dimly lit room did not do justice to her beauty. But even in that light I could see the changing expression of her face corresponding to her moods. I was reminded of a famous Swedish actress, and I remember telling Mimi that she could become a great actress.

"You are mocking me," she shot back.

"No, I am not. I am paying tribute to your physical and mental qualities."

"Let me tell you a couple of things more, and then you judge me," she said with an arresting finality.

By then the Chivas Regal was dulling my faculties somewhat. But I was alert. "Tell me. I am all ears," I said.

"First," she said, "you are right: this place is not for me. But I love these people. They have been good to me."

"Believe me, Mimi," I told her, holding her hands, "I am not passing any judgment against them. From what you told me, they are admirable people."

"The second thing," she continued, "is that Saba encouraged me and helped me to continue my education. I finished twelfth grade attending night classes."

"Terrific," I said.

"I also took courses in bookkeeping and typing, and Lula paid all the costs."

"How nice," I said, kissing her fingers. She pulled my hands to her and enfolded them against her chest.

"So it is not their pressure that has kept me here," she said. "Lula wants me to make it out in the world."

"But the world is a sea full of sharks," I said.

"I can look after myself. Meanwhile I feel an obligation to them. So I have played in this game."

"Is that the end of the story?" I asked.

"Not quite." She lowered her head bashfully.

"Mimi, is there anything else?"

"Yes!" she said, looking me straight in the eye. "I want to be your lover. I want to be with you all the time, if I can. But I know I can't. I want to cook for you and fuss over you."

Her eyes became misty, and she turned her face away.

"Is it possible? Oh, God, is it possible?" she said turning her face back toward me. "My beloved lord!"

"Don't call me your lord," I said.

"My dearest love," she said. "I have sighed for you for so long!"

She rose from her kneeling position and slowly took off her dressing gown. Through the transparent lingerie I could see her shapely brown body. Her large firm breasts with dark nipples pointed at me like the muzzle of a double-barreled gun. I touched her breasts and caressed them gently. Her eyes closed and her mouth opened and she fell on top of me. Her hot breath became short gasps—sighs of pleasure accompanied by rhythmic moans.

I could not resist any longer. I put my mouth over hers, enfolding her completely and holding her tight. It was a prolonged and passionate kiss. When we broke off to catch our breaths she looked at me adoringly.

"You kissed me," she said. "Oh my darling . . ."

"Shshsh," I admonished her. Her face was flushed.

She unbuckled my belt. I kicked off my shoes and took off my socks. She pulled my trousers down and pulled off my underwear, running her hands gently over my private parts, closing her eyes and uttering a low moan. I pulled off her lingerie, and we stood up naked. I lifted her up and she wrapped her arms around my neck.

In no time we were on her bed, our bodies melted into one. In the pitch of night our love burned like a coal fire crackling until the smoldering embers consumed us.

Part II

ON RAZOR'S
EDGE

TWELVE

I woke up early in the morning. It was dark in the room and Mimi was sleeping. Soft purring sounds accompanied the slow movements of her bosom, which touched my chest as she exhaled. I lay awake for a while watching her and listening to her breathing. I felt a surging desire to make love to her; but it would be cruel, I thought, to wake her up from such a peaceful sleep. She must need it, after last night. God, what a night!

Quietly and very slowly, I got out of bed. I tiptoed to the bath and took a cold shower, which woke me up and drained my desire away. As I dressed, I was surprised to find that I felt neither guilt nor shame. These are facts of life, I told myself. Joy. Sorrow. Love. Death. Life is too short for regrets or crippling pangs of guilt. Take life as it comes, I thought to myself. Why question a magnificent gift of life such as Mimi! Besides, this gift did not diminish my commitment to the cause or my resolve to avenge my friend's death.

I opened the window and greeted the day. The morning air was bracing, with the faint smell of cow dung coming from a nearby shed, mixed with the fragrance of freshly cut grass, accompanied by a chirping chorus of sparrows perched on a nearby lemon tree. As the sun's rays appeared on the eastern hills, I saw a lonely crow flying and squawking, perhaps in search of its lost mate. Smoke came from several isolated houses in the foothills beyond.

I scribbled a note and left it on the couch on top of Mimi's nightgown. It simply said, "If all goes well, I'll go to Wollo with Melaku's body. Wish me well or pray for me, whatever comes easier. No need for a whip in this house. It was wonderful!" And I left Mimi's ready to face the day.

By the time I arrived at my office, people were gathering near the university. It was a little before seven and I started making phone calls. I tried Bekele first. He was out. I tried Yohannes next; he was out, but Saba was in. She told me he was on his way to meet me. "Did he say where?" I asked.

"No, but I thought he was going to your house," she said.

I had a slight attack of nerves as I faced the prospect of talking to Hanna. When I called home, I found that Yohannes had come and gone.

"What is happening?" Hanna asked in a subdued tone which surprised me.

"I see some people converging on the university campus," I said.

"Are they students"? she asked.

"Actually, there are all kinds of people, including students," I said.

"I wish to God these students would give us the body," she said.

"I wish so too. Don't worry, we'll find a way," I said. "Did Yohannes say where he was going?"

"He said he was coming to your office," she told me. She asked me to let her know what was happening. I promised I would, and hung up.

As I tried other numbers, I watched the scene around the campus from my office window. More people arrived, swelling the ranks of the crowd. I tried General Dima's home, and found him just preparing to leave.

"General Dima," I said, "I am in my office. Do you know what is happening here?"

"Yes, I do," he said. "I just received a radio message from the city police. It seems that the whole city is demanding the surrender of the body."

"Good for the citizens of the city!" I said.

"Let's hope they succeed where we failed," he said.

Presently I saw Yohannes' car arriving in the compound of the Prime Minister's office. I went down to meet him.

"Thank God you are alive," he said. "I've been calling all morning. You were not in your office. You were not at the Prime Minister's residence. You did not spend the night at home. God! I thought you had joined Melaku."

"Did you tell that to Hanna?"

"No, of course not," he said. "The poor girl is distressed enough."

"Thanks," I said gratefully.

"I will not ask where you were," he said, assuming the countenance of a headmaster. "But in the future, you have to tell us where you are."

"I will. Thanks again. What is happening?"

"Well, Bekele has worked all night and wrought miraculous deeds."

"How? What?"

"He sent his student minions, the best and brightest, to wake up every home in their neighborhoods and persuade them to join in the crusade."

"Crusade?" I was puzzled.

"They appealed to parents as well as to churchmen in the name of Christian decency to help them recover the body."

"Brilliant!" I said.

"Wait. That's not all," Yohannes said. "He organized a girls' contingent and a secondary school contingent to help out. The girls part has a touch of genius to it. Something about the *unmanliness* of snatching a body."

"Do you think it will work?"

"We shall see what we shall see," Yohannes said, imitating his favorite character in Dickens.

We drove closer to the university campus and parked where we could observe. Loud cheers followed a short speech given by a young student. We could not hear his words, but he was interrupted by cheers as he spoke. Then he launched a slogan which was repeated all within earshot.

"Surrender the body! Surrender the body!" the crowd thundered.

Yohannes and I got out of the car to mix with the crowd. We saw placards with slogans written in large letters. I recognized Bekele's handwriting in several of them.

A human body is not a carcass!

You are turning into cadaver peddlers!

In the name of decency, surrender the body!

The slogans were shouted again and again and reverberated throughout the area as curious onlookers joined in. By now there were several thousands. The students will not dare resist this public outcry, I thought. We saw girls running toward the gate of the university compound; they flung their skirts at the students inside, who cowered under this traditional insult.

They had no choice but to surrender. Eventually a small delegation came out bearing a white flag. One of them gave a note to a police officer, who ran to give it to his superior who sat in a Land Rover surrounded by armed guards. The officer emerged from the Land Rover and announced the news on a bullhorn.

"Citizens, ladies and gentlemen. The students have agreed to surrender the body," he said, and was greeted by a loud cheer.

People embraced one another. Then I saw Bekele emerging from within a closely guarded part of the crowd. He beamed with joy and smiled broadly when he saw Yohannes and me. But he did not come to us. He was too busy giving instructions to the young people around him, who listened attentively, bowed slightly, and disappeared in the crowd.

The gate opened and several students carried Melaku's body out and surrendered it to the police officer. I went up to the police officer, but before I could introduce myself he saluted me.

"I understand that he was your friend, sir," he said.

"Yes he was. His brother and uncle must also be in the crowd," I said. I asked the officer to call their names.

"Will Maaza and the other relatives of the deceased come forward to receive the body!" he shouted.

Maaza came forward, accompanied by his uncle and a few other close relatives. Meanwhile, Aberra had had a coffin made, which he carried to the Land Rover. We placed the body in the coffin. The police offered to take the body to a waiting hearse. Aberra had also arranged all of that.

And so ended one of the strangest incidents of that strange time.

We set out, a cortege of ten vehicles, at about ten that day. It was a bright, warm day with a cloudless sky. The road to Dessie was paved, save for a few strips where the Imperial Highway Authority had torn up the asphalt for repair, creating dusty conditions.

I sat next to Maaza and his uncle's wife, who wept most of the way, joined by Maaza from time to time. I looked at the countryside. The fields had turned brown and there were few trees until we began to wind down the escarpment. In the lowlands, the acacia trees and other thorn bushes presented a dramatic change in the scenery.

The road was eroded in several places in the lowlands, and highway workmen were replacing stones from piles of crushed gravel. The men stopped work as we passed, took off their hats and made a sign of the cross or bowed their heads. So did the peasants; some of them climbed off their mules and made motions of scratching their faces as a sign of commiseration.

The journey in the lowlands took longer because we had to cross several streams and negotiate winding, narrow passes. We reached the outskirts of Dessie a little after three o'clock, after five hours of non-stop driving. A crowd waited for us near the marketplace. The cortege stopped and I got out to consult with my friends. Maaza also got out, because he recognized a cousin in the crowd.

There followed a general wailing and utter confusion. Women bared their chests and started pounding them in the age-old tradition which church authorities have tried but failed to discourage. Melaku's relatives surrounded the hearse and threw themselves at it. It was total pandemonium, with clouds of dust adding to the confusion.

Finally, the ever-alert Yohannes took out a bullhorn and addressed the crowd. "Dear friends," he said. "We will not do proper honor to our beloved Melaku if we spend the rest of the day in this condition. Good people of Wollo, friends, and relatives. Please listen to me. We have to go to the burial place and inter the body before sunset. Some of us may have to go back to Addis Ababa."

At that point a young priest, a bearded man with a white robe and white headpiece, came forward and took the bullhorn from Yohannes. "In the name of the Father, the Son, and the Holy Spirit—" he began. And the wailing gradually subsided to a few isolated cries.

"The gentleman who spoke is right," The priest said. "But he omitted one essential thing. We have to go to the church where Melaku was christened and offer prayers for the salvation of his soul."

There was a murmur of approval. The priest thanked Yohannes and returned the bullhorn. The cortege began to move slowly, and I decided to walk with Yohannes. The town was surprisingly empty, except for a few country folk driving their donkeys and a handful of military men walking in small groups. There were few vehicles, and some two-wheeled horse-drawn carts.

We passed the main town square, where more people converged, walking slowly or standing on corners. The Church of the Savior was about half a kilometer north of the town square. The cortege stopped outside the compound of the conical church with its red-tinned roof. They carried the coffin to the inner gate. The service was mercifully brief and the young priest was to the point. He admonished the women to spare us all the pain of watching them beat their breasts and fall ill. Melaku, he said, would not approve.

"Daughters of Wollo," he said finally (quoting Christ in Geez, the ancient language), "Don't cry for me. Cry for yourselves."

The burial rite was also a brief affair. A few people spoke about Melaku's childhood in Dessie, mentioning that he was the wonder boy of the town with his phenomenal memory and respectful manner. Others spoke of the kind help they received from him when they were in Addis Ababa, where they knew nobody. I spoke briefly on behalf of his friends.

They lowered the coffin into the grave. The priest took some of the earth from the edge of the grave and sprinkled it on the coffin. His words, "Dust thou art, and unto dust thou must return," were drowned with the deafening cries of wailing. Then they filled the grave with earth.

Ah dust! Glorious dust, I thought. We are all dust in the end. Fugitive dust. Dust, that ubiquitous, inescapable substance of nature is also a symbol of our destiny. Our advent and collective destiny. How often I have contemplated on, human destiny, picking up a handful of dust and letting it slip through my fingers!

Almost immediately after the grave was covered and a cross made from splintered wood was placed on it, there was a thunderstorm. It rained hard.

"He is a righteous one!" said an older woman.

"The Virgin Mary is weeping for him!" said another.

Their sentiments fit the traditional view of people in the area. If it rains on the occasion of your burial, the Good Lord shall receive you on his right side and count you among his fold. I said "Amen," and Yohannes looked at me curiously.

We were led to the home of Melaku's oldest sister, who acted as the convener of the family on such occasions. A large tent had been pitched outside her modest house. People brought food from every corner of the neighborhood for the mourners. We were all seated and served.

For the first time since we had started the journey, I saw Hanna. She was sitting beside Melaku's oldest sister and weeping with her. The women were seated on one side of the tent, the men on another.

The rain had stopped, but the sun was going down over the mountain range west of Dessie. Soon the lights which had been fixed on all the corners of the tent were turned on. Our party, consisting of

Yohannes, Bekele, Aberra, and myself, was seated on sofas to the left and right of Melaku's brothers and uncles. There were two other brothers in addition to Maaza, both in their early twenties.

Just when dinner was about to be served, we heard cries of men outside, getting louder as they approached the tent. It was a cavalry contingent from the village of Melaku's origin. Their arrival created a commotion. When they arrived outside the tent and dismounted, the young people got up and went out to meet them. Some of the young people led the horses away, and the others joined in the cavalry's cries. The uncles also left their seats to join in. The wailing began as disorganized cries and then took on order and discipline, almost like an orchestrated musical number, with a chorus leader repeating Melaku's name and the names of his illustrious ancestors. It was very moving. The women remained seated in the tent, but resumed their cries.

My comrades and I were left behind, torn between joining the melee in the wailing ritual, and remaining behind the tent quietly weeping. No one present could remain unaffected by that moving scene. The people were bereft of one from whom they had expected great things, for much was expected from the lucky few, such as Melaku, who were educated. The cries we heard were no mere ritual. The people felt Melaku's loss acutely, as the loss of a son and of an asset for their region.

After a while the elders rose to intervene. They coaxed and cajoled the cavalry contingent and the uncles and other relatives to halt their cries and be seated. It took a great deal of coaxing before the mourners could be persuaded. "Crying is one way, but not the only way," said one elder. "Remember also that some of the relatives have been crying for two days. Think of them."

Finally the mourners filed in one by one to take their places in the tent. A few of the women continued their weeping; the elders admonished them from time to time, but to no avail. They were led by a professional mourner, an *areho*. For her, wailing was not only a matter of her daily bread; there was also an element of artistic satisfaction in her ability to organize and channel disorderly wailing into something that had rhyme and rhythm.

"The cardinal is here," the Areho intoned.

"Wai wai!" the chorus chimed.

"The rases are here."

"Wai wai!"

"All the world is here."

"Wai wai!"

"Your friend Desta is here."

"Wai wai!"

"Yohannes is here."

"Wai wai!"

"They have come to mourn you."

"Wai wai!"

"Even the birds cry."

"Wai wai!"

"The sparrows cry."

"Wai wai!"

"The swallows cry."

"Wai wai!"

"The doves and the crows."

"Wai wai!"

"They all cry like me! Because you are lost to them as to me."

"We all cry. Because you are lost to us!"

And so on and on until all names that counted were mentioned. The *areho*'s mourning songs are a sort of liturgical communication, which binds people together in a common stance toward life and death. In between the "wai wai" choruses, the *areho* improvises, spicing up things to break the monotony. Everyone listens to capture a gem of a word or phrase to comment upon for weeks, months, or years afterward. I was surprised to hear our names mentioned; but then, the *areho* is not only an artist, she is also a good researcher who collects information in advance.

Dinner was served. That is the time when people greet one another and quietly exchange news and general information about their lives—harvest, market prices, local gossip, and so forth. It is also the time when ambitious types come forward to make acquaintances among the big wheels and seek favors. Mercifully, I was not approached by anyone, but I was amused to see Yohannes surrounded by local lawyers. He kept looking at me and Bekele, but there was no way we could rescue him. When he finally extricated himself and came back to his seat, embarrassment was written on his face.

"Mr. Attorney-General!" Bekele said.

"Damn you!" Yohannes said. "I looked at you two, hoping you would rescue me."

"We thought you were enjoying it," Bekele joked.

At that point, two officers were brought and seated to the left of us. One of them smiled and gave me a special military salute before he sat. I recognized his face but could not remember where we had met. He must have noticed my puzzled look, for he scribbled a note and passed it through the line of mourners to me.

"Greetings, sir. We met at Mama Zen's with Brigadier Iman, some time ago," the note said. It was not signed.

I then remembered. How could I have forgotten the expressionless face of the man who met me outside Mama Zen's salon? He was thinner then, and wearing civilian clothes. What was he doing at Melaku's funeral anyway? I knew that Melaku had been invited a few times to read poems at the military academy outside Addis Ababa. Perhaps he knew him from there. But where did he come from to attend his funeral?

As if he sensed the question going through my mind, the young officer stood up to speak.

"My elders, brothers and sisters. Please forgive me if I am interrupting your quiet conversation," he began. "On occasions such as this, it is the privilege of the elders to speak. Forgive me for usurping that privileged role."

He stopped, I felt sure, for effect. That quiet officer had an aura of authority about him, in spite of his seeming diffidence. And as he went on to explain why he had risen to speak, that initial diffidence disappeared. It was as if a house cat had been transformed into a roaring lion. The word that came to my mind was charismatic.

As the young officer heaped praise on Melaku, the sobbing which had subsided resumed with renewed fury. Some of the women rose to strut on the floor, wailing loudly. The officer calmed them down by switching his oratory to a more soothing tone. He controlled the occasion completely.

Finally he said:

"Melaku is gone, but his spirit lives. His work must go on. I am here on behalf of myself and many others, not only to pay homage to a hero, but to vow on my honor as an officer and a gentleman that his work will continue."

Then he stepped out into the night as suddenly as he had come. Nobody knew his name, where he came from, or where he went. He left us all in the dark. In my mind I began to make an association between the power of his speech and the power of darkness.

All eyes turned toward me, including the eyes of my friends Yohannes and Bekele.

"Perhaps he is from the local brigade. Perhaps Melaku did him a favor," I equivocated.

Yohannes was not satisfied with my remark. "Do you know the man?" he asked in a whisper.

"Not really. I met him once, through our military contact. But I don't know his name."

"Well, he certainly knows how to speak. He could be a successful lawyer," he said, not in jest.

"He could also be a successful stage actor," Bekele said.

"Do you mean his presence and his pretty speech could be a cover for something else?" Yohannes inquired.

"Something like that," Bekele answered. "After all, the military does have an intelligence branch which does dirty work for the regime."

They both looked at me.

"Don't look at me," I said.

"But you are our expert on the military," Yohannes said, rubbing it in.

"We can't eliminate the possibility of foul play from any quarter, of course," I said. "But I am inclined to believe in the sincerity of the man's speech and sentiment. He is obviously an admirer of Melaku."

"We'll see," Bekele said. He was obviously not convinced by my theory. Nor was I. The old doubts and alarm signals came back to me. But I could not express them. As the leader I felt I could not say or do things that might have a demobilizing effect.

THIRTEEN

W hen we got back to Addis Ababa the following day, we found that the police had put a road-block outside the city. Hanna and I rode with Yohannes and Bekele. Hanna had calmed down after the funeral. She was almost her usual self-controlled self. And when a policeman walked up to see who we were, Hanna was in charge.

"What is the matter, officer?" she asked him calmly, with a slight edge of condescension in her voice.

"We have our orders, madam," he said. "Where are you coming from?"

"Dessie," she said.

"What do you have in the trunk of the car?"

"Nothing. You can see for yourself." She looked in my direction, and I got out to open the trunk.

"You see? There is nothing," I said. "What were you expecting, guns?"

"We have our orders," the policeman said, letting us by. We were stopped a second time near the Kebenna bridge, this time by army soldiers. A young second lieutenant saluted and came closer to examine our faces.

"Are you the group from Dessie?" he asked.

"Yes," I said.

"Okay, let them pass," he said, and the soldiers made way for us.

"I wonder what is going on?" Hanna said.

"Probably just routine checks," I said.

"We should have asked the lieutenant. He seemed like a nice officer," Hanna said. "But how did he know we came from Dessie?"

"The police at the first roadblock must have radioed him," Bekele said. "I saw one of them inside the hut with a walkie-talkie."

"Things have not been the same since you electrical engineers invented those things," Hanna said in a light mood.

"I suppose not," Bekele said. "But we have also lightened the burden of household chores."

"The burden of the household chores is still on the backs of women," she shot back.

"But it is lighter than when our mothers were your age," Bekele said.

"I wonder sometimes," she replied. "It is easier for men, that is for sure."

We reached Bekele's house. He asked us to come in for coffee, but we declined; we were all tired and it was already past seven in the evening. When we got to Yohannes' house, he insisted on our taking a few minutes rest. We agreed. Saba had prepared some food in expectation of our arrival.

Yohannes took her aside and came back. Hanna went to the kitchen to talk to Saba. Yohannes looked worried.

"What is it?" I asked.

"They have been looking for me," he said.

"Who?"

"The security people."

"Probably to find out about the funeral."

"Why would they want to know about the funeral?"

"Did Saba say if Aberra has called?" I asked, remembering that Aberra had returned ahead of us.

"She didn't say. But I'll ask her."

"Something may have happened in these last two days in our absence. We should look for him," I said.

Saba and Hanna came back with a tray of food and bottles of beer. Saba opened the bottles of Melotti and placed them on the table in front of us. "How was the funeral?" she asked.

"It was moving," I said.

"I can't believe that he is gone," she said.

"How have you been? How has the city been in our absence?" I asked.

"I have been busy answering the security people. They have been here twice," she said.

"What did they want?"

"They wanted to talk to Yohannes. They did not say why."

"Saba said Aberra called this afternoon," Yohannes said.

"So he is okay," I said.

"Is there any reason why he should not be okay?" asked Hanna.

"Of course not," I said.

"Then why did you say, so he is okay?"

"Because he was involved in the funeral arrangements. And if the police want to ask Yohannes questions, it must have something to do with Melaku's death. They always ask friends and acquaintances." It was flawed reasoning and I could see from Hanna's face that she was not satisfied with my answer.

Saba intervened. "Actually, Aberra said that the police investigation on Melaku's death has started and they have made some arrests. He did not know who was arrested."

At that point the phone rang. Yohannes answered it. He listened for a minute or so, then hung up.

"That was Bekele, saying that a student leader has been found murdered just outside the campus."

"Does he know who it is?" I asked.

"Yes. He is the leader of the Chinese faction," Yohannes said.

"Chinese, Russian, Cuban. Is there no one for good old Ethiopia?" Hanna said.

"What about us?" Yohannes said.

It was time to leave. As we reached the gate where our car was parked, Yohannes whispered to me: "Bekele said it was our man who was murdered." And he added quickly, "He is looking into it and will report tomorrow."

We said good night and left.

I found a note when we got home. It was from Captain Abate.

"I heard from reliable sources that they suspect you of leaking government secrets, and that you have association with subversive forces. I am giving you this advance warning so that you can be ready for any eventualities. If it turns out to be false, I will come to apologize personally. But, after a lot of soul-searching, I decided to inform you rather than regret it later. Yours faithfully, Abate."

My heart leapt to my mouth. My first thought was to go to my office and retrieve all the documents. But then again, if what Abate said was true, might they not be waiting there to catch me red-handed?

I tried to connect things: The security looking for Yohannes; Abate's note; the murder of the student leader. Was this a dragnet? If so, did the Prime Minister know about it?

There was only one way to find out. I sprang to my feet and put my coat on, telling Hanna: "I promised the Prime Minister to report back as soon as we returned."

"Won't this be too late? It is after nine. Can't it wait till tomorrow morning?"

"No. The way things are developing, he will want to talk to me," I said.

"And is this going to be another night out?"

"No. I'll be late, but I'll be back."

I was surprised at Hanna's calm. The funeral and the journey back seemed to have helped. I went to the small bedroom and kissed Lemlem, our four year old daughter, and left. The sight of her sleeping peacefully, clutching her brown teddy bear, and the thought of her and Hanna facing adversity without me began to haunt me. As I drove to the Prime Minister's house, thoughts of their future dominated my mind. It is strange, but it had never occurred to me before that I might be discovered; hence, the thought of my family facing privation and suffering had never crossed my mind. Abate's note changed all that.

The guard at the Prime Minister's home told me that his excellency was out, but that his wife was entertaining some foreign guests. I decided to wait. The guard opened the gate; I parked my car and was ushered into the waiting room. The servant took my raincoat, then went to inform Madame Akalu, who came out beaming. She was a fulsome woman in her late fifties with raven black hair (dyed of course). She wore a black satin dress with pearls on her bosom.

"Ah! Monsieur Desta."

"*Je vous derange?*" I queried.

"*Mais no, mais no. Pas du tout. Entrez, je vous en prie!*" She led me to the dining room, where two European couples and Mr. Lavine, a local import-export businessman, were seated.

"Ah, Ato Desta," said Lavine, getting up. Madame Akalu did the rest of the introductions.

"Monsieur Desta, I present to you Mr. and Mrs. Legrand from France and Mr. and Mrs. Duclos from my home town, Lausanne." And turning to them, she said, "Ladies and gentlemen, this is Monsieur Desta, the Prime Minister's *chef de cabinet.* How you say in English?"

"Principal cabinet secretary," I said.

"Desta is also a historian," Lavine said ingratiatingly. "He was at the Sorbonne, like the Prime Minister."

"It is a pleasure, Monsieur Desta," said the Frenchman. "I have heard a lot about you from many people."

"Thank you, Monsieur Legrand. I hope you heard good things."

"Oh yes. Nothing but good."

"You must be busy these days," the Swiss guest said.

"We are always busy."

"Yes, but especially nowadays."

"You might say that. Not a dull moment," I said and changed the subject. "Are you here on business or pleasure?"

"They brought us here with promises of vacation," said the French woman, who was in her early forties. "But it has been business, business, so far."

"I am sure that will change soon. Have you been to our lake district? It is beautiful," I said.

"I hoped to go there today. But it has been postponed for some reason. It is annoying," said Madame Duclos, the Swiss woman. She was also in her early forties. In fact, there was a striking resemblance between the two women, who were both tall and slender. Their husbands were older, probably in their late fifties. Legrand had a bald head and drooping moustache. The Swiss, Duclos, was distinguished looking with silver hair. He was tall and slim.

"Did you hear about the death of a student leader?" Lavine asked me.

"Yes," I said and kept silent.

"What happened to him?" asked Madame Legrand.

"I don't know. I just got back from Dessie. That is up north."

"Ah yes, for the funeral of the—what was his name?" That was Lavine again, poking the fire of controversy.

"Melaku," I said, and changed the subject again, asking the European guests, "Are you in government or business?"

"Monsieur Legrand is from the Quai d'Orsay, in charge of African affairs," said Madame Akalu.

"It is a recent appointment. Before that I was in overseas service," said Legrand.

"And Monsieur Duclos is a banker," Madam Akalu filled in.

My antenna of curiosity went up again, and my mind was busy speculating on the motives behind these people's visit. I remembered Sir Geoffrey's remarks. I should not jump to conclusions, I thought. But the fact was, I did jump to conclusions. There was also Lavine about whom it was persistently rumored that he laundered money for some ministers into Swiss bank accounts. He and his Ethiopian-born Armenian wife were close friends of the Prime Minister and his family.

"And Madame Duclos is a lawyer," said Lavine.

"Oh. How nice. What branch of law do you practice, Madame Duclos?" I asked.

"Public law. Both international law and criminal law."

"Then you must know Professor Plevin," I said.

"Yes, indeed. He taught me," she said. "Do you know him?"

"A little. I once asked him to prepare a brief for us on Swiss law concerning the right of heirs to money deposited by foreign nationals in Swiss banks—especially money left by dead dictators."

All eyes trained on me as if I had defiled something sacred. Lavine, especially, glowered at me. That seemed to me at least circumstantial proof that there was something to the rumors.

"More wine, Monsieur Legrand?" said Madame Akalu, and poured some Beaujolais into his empty glass. She also filled the other glasses except mine, which was full. The Swiss banker placed a cigarette in a long cigarette holder and lit it with a gilded lighter. He then rested his elbows on the table and leaned forward.

"I can tell you, Monsieur Desta, what Swiss law is on that subject," he said. "No one has a right to such assets unless the depositor executes a legal instrument instructing the bank to that effect. And no one has the right of access to information on such deposits." He turned to his wife who nodded.

"Not even the Swiss government?" I asked.

"Not even the Swiss government. Why do you think people entrust their money to Swiss banks?" he said with evident pride.

"No offense meant. But that also encourages the flight of capital from poor Third World countries."

"Well now, that is interesting," Duclos said. "We believe in the free flow of money and trade. And capital also flows from the developed countries to the backward countries."

"*Developing* countries," I corrected him. He neither accepted nor acknowledged the correction. I decided I didn't like him.

The Frenchman came to his rescue in a conciliatory manner. "In a sense, what Monsieur Duclos is saying is true, of course. But I grant Monsieur Desta's point. We in the West encourage or tempt Third World governments and individuals to invest in our banks their much-needed capital."

"But they have the freedom of choice," persisted Duclos.

"It is the choice of a lamb tied to a tiger," I said.

"Oh, that is an exaggeration!" Duclos said.

"Perhaps. But when you talk about choice, you are more than exaggerating yourself, with all due respect."

The conversation was becoming acrimonious and our hostess was embarrassed. The curious thing was that I didn't even care what she thought. Perhaps because of Captain Abate's warning, I accepted it as a fact in my mind that the suppressed demon of revolution was taking over. I even felt some relief.

I liked Legrand. And the women had listened with interest when the morality of the Swiss banking system was debated. But as for Lavine, he couldn't take it anymore and went to the salon to sulk.

We all followed him into the salon for coffee. The conversation drifted to platitudes like the weather and sports cars. Lavine dominated, speaking volubly about the latest cars he had in his auto shop in Addis Ababa. He also spoke about the fishing and hunting trips he and his friend, the Prime Minister, took. "His excellency hates hunting. He is a good fisherman though," Lavine said.

I left them at that point. Madame Akalu saw me to the door and said she would tell the Prime Minister I had come. "Good night, Monsieur Desta."

"Good night, Madame. And thank you for your hospitality."

"You are always welcome here," she said.

Even then, I suspected that couldn't remain true much longer.

I was tempted to go to Mimi. I couldn't sleep if I went back home, and I couldn't get hold of Bekele or Aberra. But my mind was filled with so many unanswered questions that I knew I would make disastrous company. The memory of the previous night with Mimi was so sweet that I didn't want to spoil it. I would make bad company, and a terrible lover.

I drove toward the center of the city, past the Shebelli Hotel and the commercial school. Everything seemed to be normal: the streets filled with people and cars; no signs of groups of armed police, only the usual patrolmen at strategic corners. I decided to go to the Hotel Ethiopia, where disgruntled intellectuals and other members of the urban elite gathered for drink and gossip.

I parked my car in front of the Rasta Pharmacy, which was open. The owner of the pharmacy, Dejene, an older man from Wollo, was known to most younger generation Ethiopians. His education did not go beyond the eighth grade, but he was a well-read, self-made man who had been trained in pharmacy by French doctors. He liked to talk about French literature and philosophy, and was well-versed in recent Ethiopian history, with which he engaged and entertained his friends and customers.

Dejene was standing at the door of the pharmacy when I got out of my car. He saw me and came forward to greet me.

"*Excellence. Quel plaisir,*" he said smiling. He always called me *excellence;* once you cross the ministerial threshold, you become transformed into a minor star in the Ethiopian mind.

"Greetings, Monsieur Pasteur," I answered. He like to be called after the man he most admired.

"What brings you to my humble shop at this time of night?"

"Well, I was on my way to the Hotel Ethiopia," I said. "But now that I am here, I must say we expected to see you in Dessie for Melaku's funeral," I said. I knew that the two of them had often talked about their native province and the city of romance, as they called Dessie.

"That was a bad business, what the students did. But I was glad to hear that reason prevailed in the end," he said.

"Well, it was not exactly reason," I said.

"Whatever it was, I am glad it ended peacefully."

Then, almost apologetically, he tried to explain why he had not gone to Dessie. "I had nobody to take over the pharmacy," he said. "Besides, I was not born in Wollo, really, although my roots are there. Do you know that I have not been there since the enemy occupation? That was thirty years ago, and I was twenty or so."

"It does not matter. I was only teasing you."

"How was the funeral?"

"It was moving." There was no other way of expressing it. And I did not want to talk about it.

Dejene stepped out of the door, looked left and right, and whispered: "If you ask me, Melaku's death is just the beginning. Did you hear about the murder of a student leader?"

"I just heard. Do you know if they have any clues about the culprits?" I knew Dejene had connections with army intelligence and the police. Some suspicious types even hinted that he himself was an undercover intelligence operative. I discounted that as merely the Ethiopian penchant for rumor-mongering, which the imperial regime fostered with great skill.

"I do not know if they have any clues," he said. "But maybe this will interest you. It is widely believed among reliable sources that your friend Melaku was killed by the KGB."

"Why would the KGB want to kill Melaku?"

"I am only reporting what I heard. Apparently Melaku was suspected of being in the pay of the Chinese and spreading the gospel according to Saint Mao."

"And the Soviets didn't like that?"

"Exactly."

"But Melaku was his own man. He was nobody's agent!" I said.

"I don't wish to speak ill of the departed, and he was your friend. But it is worth checking. I don't want this to harm your career. Yours is a promising career and one which . . ."

I interrupted him, although in normal circumstances I enjoyed his talk and was flattered by his tributes. But I was not in the mood. "I am grateful Dejene, believe me. But this is a wild rumor."

"Then who killed him? Have you any idea?"

"No. I have none. I have left that to the proper authorities. If what you heard turns out to be true, I will deal with it when it comes. But thanks, anyway."

We changed the subject to the usual inquiries about the health of family and wished each other good night. But after I had walked a few steps, Dejene ran after me and caught my arm.

"What I just told you is strictly *entre nous,* and I trust you implicitly," he said.

"Strictly *entre nous,*" I said and left.

The hotel was filled with people. I recognized a few faces at the bar and waved at them on my way toward the couches inside, where I saw some old friends. Many of them stood up to greet me and invited me to join them.

"This is indeed a surprise," said Asfaw, an old classmate at the Mekonnen Secondary School. He was slightly tipsy, and smelled of alcohol when he embraced me and kissed me on both cheeks, as close friends and family members do.

"Nice to see you, old boy," I said. He liked that appellation, which he had picked up at Cambridge University where he had studied mathematics.

"Same here, old chap," he said.

There were five others sitting and drinking whiskey. I knew two of them. One was called Fikre and worked in the ministry of defense as a procurement adviser. The other was called Mulatu and was a city engineer specializing in water resources. I didn't remember the names of the other three.

"We were talking about the Select Two Hundred and their recent meeting," Fikre said.

"In fact, they are having a meeting at the Ghion Hotel tonight,"

Mulatu said.

"I would have thought that you would be there too," Fikre said. "Are you coming from there?"

"No."

"Well, I have been told that the Prime Minister gave an opening speech," Mulatu said.

"No, he did not give an opening speech," Fikre corrected. "He sent Debebe, his private secretary, to open it."

I pretended that I knew about the meeting but had been out of town. Their story was of interest for what it said about the Prime Minister's predicament. The Select Two Hundred had been formed by the Prime Minister three years earlier in an attempt to build a base among young professionals in his struggle to advance reforms. The idea had been shelved when the aristocratic class complained to the Emperor that Akalu was trying to subvert the Emperor's authority. But if this report was true, I thought, then the Prime Minister was reviving the idea. That could mean he was facing a new threat. That especially would explain his absence from home.

Fikre and Mulatu were artists of gossip in Addis Ababa. In the absence of a free press, they and others like them spent a good deal of their time and energy in the collection, sifting and artful dissemination of information—and disinformation. Some of them were connected with the security services, while others pretended to be. Fikre encouraged the rumors that he was. To be the object of fear enhances status, and status was what the game in town was all about.

I note the subtle manner in which Fikre had broached the subject of the meeting of the Select Two Hundred. When he said, "I would have thought that you would be there too," knowing full well that I was in Dessie (he would know that), he was hinting at some secret game to which he was privy.

Fikre studied my face closely as the conversation rolled on. "Have another whiskey on me," he said, and before I could protest he snapped his fingers to summon a waiter who was standing not far from us.

"Another round for me and his excellency," he said. After the waiter left, Fikre leaned toward me. "Did you notice how the waiter was moving closer to us and listening while his back was turned?"

"No. Why was that?"

"Don't you know that all the waiters here are *ears*?" he said.

"That means they are members of the security," Mulatu explained.

"This one is a lieutenant!" Fikre said.

"How do you know?" I asked.

"I just know," he said, smiling wickedly. The unknown three at the table were impressed, as they were meant to be.

"Is it true that Melaku was a friend of yours?" Mulatu asked.

I nodded. They all trained their eyes on me, maintaining a customary silence as a sign of homage to the dead. Soon the waiter came with the drinks and placed them on the table. Everyone kept quiet until he left.

"*Pour la cause!*" Fikre raised his glass and swallowed half of its contents.

"*Pour la cause. Quelle qu'elle soit,*" I said as the unknown three looked on, puzzled.

"Justice and progress," Mulatu elaborated, raising his glass. We all drank to that with no questions asked. Who could be against justice and progress?

But Fikre would not let go.

"No. Mine is better," he said. "The cause embraces justice and progress. It is better as a toast because it is all-embracing. *N'est ce pas, excellence?*"

Asfaw, who stammered when he was anxious, answered him. "Don't try to in-in-involve my friend in poli-poli-politics," he told Fikre. "He is a ci-ci-civil servant."

"Asfaw," Fikre answered brutally, "politics is not comprehensible to you. There is no mathematical precision in politics. Politics is the art of the possible."

"Have you heard of mathe-mathematical prob-probability?" Asfaw answered.

"Yes. That is a far cry from the art of the possible," Fikre said. "And by the way, in Ethiopia there is no distinction between politicians and civil servants. They are all servants of the Emperor."

"What about engineers?" Mulatu asked.

"Everyone is a servant of the Emperor," Fikre answered, and repeated it loudly when the waiter moved closer again.

I decided it was time to leave. I was itching to get out of the stifling atmosphere of idle gossip and petty intrigue. I had to find some answers to the questions pressing on my mind.

"Thank you for the drinks," I said, rising. "Next time it will be my treat."

"You always say next time, but you don't frequent your old haunts as you used to," Mulatu said.

"That's tr-true," Asfaw stuttered. "Come more often! We like you. Don't we, friends?" They all nodded.

I left them, weaving my way through the crowd of standing customers.

I drove to the Ghion Hotel, where the Prime Minister kept a special suite. I suspected that it was where the Select Two Hundred meeting was being held. It was short distance from the Hotel Ethiopia. The parking lot was packed with cars of various sizes and makes, and since I didn't hear any dance music, I assumed the cars belonged to people at a meeting.

So the story was true, after all. At least there was a reasonable presumption that it might be true.

I then decided, on the spur of the moment, to go to my office. Curious, how the mind works when you are faced with danger.

It was already past midnight. Should anyone question why I was going to my office at this hour, I decided to say I wanted to clear up some paperwork accumulated during my two-day absence. The guards would not question me unless specifically instructed to do so. And if they refused me entry, I would draw the necessary conclusions and be better prepared for what might come the next day.

The whole building was dark except for the lamps at the main gate and around the outer wall. I was greeted by the guard, who opened the gate after peering through the open windows of my car. He was half asleep, but he recognized me instantly.

"Was the Prime Minister here this evening?" I asked.

"No, sir," he said.

"Thank you."

I parked in front of the office and went in. I made certain that there was nobody around, either inside the building or outside. It would be a disaster to be surprised and caught with the incriminating papers. I turned the lights on in the corridor and in my office.

I opened the drawers of my desk, took out some ministerial files, and pretended to read for ten minutes. I then thought of a ruse. I took the files with me and went downstairs slowly, watchful for any movements. I opened the door and walked to my car, and looked around. There was nobody. Having made certain that there was no ambush, I then drove my car toward the outer gate, then stopped. I pretended that I had forgotten my house keys, left the car at the gate, and walked back to the office with the three files.

In my office, I deposited the three files in my desk drawers, then retrieved all the papers about the underground from a locked filing cabinet. I put these inside three folders with the letterheads of the Prime Minister's office and again left the office, trembling a little.

"I am becoming forgetful," I said as I picked up my car at the gate.

"We all are, your excellency. But you have so many important things on your mind," the guard said—bless his heart!

"Good night."

"Good night, sir."

So ended one major anxiety. With the documents out of my office, they could not confront me with any direct documentary evidence. But where could I hide the documents? I could not take them home. That would be jumping from the frying pan into the fire. I thought of a number of relatives and a few old friends—But could I trust anyone these days? If I was arrested, they might come forward out of fear that I might incriminate them under torture. Everyone knew that the security tortured their prisoners, especially political prisoners. What to do, then?

Mimi.

Mimi, I thought, was the only one who would not betray me. I felt instinctively that she would not. That assumed, of course, that I would not break down under torture and give her away—or any one else, for that matter.

Which reminded me: I would have to carry some cyanide. Then and there, I decided to go to Mimi and, on my way, pick up some cyanide from the Rasta Pharmacy. I would tell Dejene that I need it for mice in my house.

Was I being overcautious? How could I know that what Captain Abate wrote in his note was true? Could he be exaggerating, perhaps to curry favor with me? Or even setting me up, to observe my reactions and movements? But if that were the case, it meant that someone suspected me.

No. I was not jumping ahead. I had a horrendous responsibility as the secretary, and now acting head, of the movement. I was the custodian of all the names, including code names, of our membership. I had a responsibility to exercize the utmost precaution, both in my own personal interest and my family's, as well as in the long-term interest of the cause.

There was no problem obtaining the cyanide. Dejene was obliging. "You know, you need a doctor's prescription for this stuff," he said.

"I know. But I am so busy these days. No time for anything. Couldn't you stretch a point for a friend?"

"Yes, of course." He brought tablets of concentrated cyanide with *poison* written on the wrapping paper in red ink.

"Many thanks. But I don't think the mice will be thankful," I said, bidding him good night.

I parked at the Villa Bianca and walked to Mimi's bungalow carrying the files. I knocked softly. There was no answer. I knocked again louder a couple of times and waited. Again there was no answer. I looked at my watch. It was one o'clock in the morning. She must be asleep.

I went around the house and knocked softly at her bedroom window. I was about to leave when the light was turned on in the bedroom. I then went around the house again and knocked at the door.

"Who is it?" a voice answered.

"Desta," I said.

She opened the door. I entered the room and she threw her arms around my neck before I even had time to say "hello" or put the files on the table. She was dressed the same as the previous night. It was as if she had been expecting me.

"I hoped you would come," she said. "But then I thought you might stay until the third day of the funeral."

"How are you?"

"I am all right now. Oh, how I wanted to see you. You left before I woke up."

"I had to go. And you were sleeping so peacefully."

"I know. I stayed in bed most of the day, re-living the delight of the previous night. Can I make you something?"

"No. Thanks. I have eaten."

She must have read that all was not well from the tone of my voice.

"Is something wrong?" she asked, taking my raincoat and putting it on a chair.

"No. Well . . . yes."

"Can I help?"

"I don't know. I hope so. I hesitate to ask you."

"I will do anything for you," she said, running her fingers through my hair in a way that had a calming effect on my racked nerves. We sat on the sofa and kissed passionately. She started taking off my tie.

"No. Not tonight," I said.

"I just want you to relax, my darling," she said. "In any case, I was visited by the Red Cross this afternoon."

"The Red Cross? What were they . . ."

"My period. Silly!" she laughed.

"So, I was lucky I got here before them, the night before last," I said, matching her laughter.

She brought out the bottle of Chivas Regal and poured me a drink. "Now. Perhaps you can tell me in what way I can help."

I hesitated, then began telling her in a rambling fashion. "I know I can trust you. But I don't want you to be hurt on my account." I pointed to the files. "I will do everything possible to avoid any harm to you because of these."

"What are these files?"

"They are important documents that no one must find."

"And you want to leave them with me. Is that all?"

She shook her head in surprise and laughed, mocking me. "I thought maybe you had killed someone. This is nothing. I will hide them with my jewelry, where no one can find them."

"No one?"

"You don't trust me?"

"I trust you. But I fear someone may find the papers."

"If they can find my jewelry, they can find the papers."

"Do you bury them?"

"Yes. And no one but Lula knows where."

"In that case, I must find some plastic bags to put them in."

"Don't worry. I have plenty of plastic bags from the restaurant."

"Aren't you curious to know what the papers are all about?"

"Curious, yes. But I will not ask questions. You can tell me anything you want at any time and place you choose."

"I am relieved already," I said, and I took her in my arms and kissed her.

"When I woke up the other morning and found you were gone, my heart jumped out and followed you," she said.

"Did you know that we got the body and left the same day?"

"Yes. Later in the day I drove to town and visited a cousin who works in the bank. He told me that the students finally gave up."

"How are Lula and Enrico?"

"They are all right. They asked me about the previous night."

"What did you tell them?"

"Nothing."

"Why? Were you protecting my reputation?"

"Not really. I didn't know how to explain it. This is not like anything that has happened to me before. It is as if it was written in the stars that we meet. I have never felt anything like this before." She stopped for a moment and then said: "Desta, I am in love with you."

"Mimi. Don't put all your eggs in one basket. I am going to be trouble for you."

"What trouble? I don't care. I fear nothing and nobody. Not even death itself. Can't you understand?"

"I think I do. In a way, I have not felt like this before. I mean, I loved my wife from the time we met. But this is different. It is risky. It is dangerous. And I love it."

We kissed again passionately. I felt as if I had known her for many years. There was a simplicity and totality in her surrender. I had heard about the romantic nature of people of Wollo; but tasting it in the flesh, so to speak, was different. The thrill and sheer abandon with which I embraced this romance in the midst of a political crisis is hard to express. Maybe there was a connection. The odd thing was that, although I did not discuss politics with her, I felt as if she understood and supported the things for which I was working.

"You don't even want to know why a government minister is hiding papers?" I quizzed her again, after we recovered our breath and lay on the couch.

"Government minister or church man, everyone has something to hide," she said philosophically.

"Is this homespun folk wisdom from Wollo?"

"Wollo is a melting pot of different peoples and beliefs," she said.

"And that makes us tolerant, I think."

"And romantic."

"That's what they say," she said teasingly. "I know I am romantic."

"How romantic?" I whispered, grabbing her by the waist.

"Enough to risk everything for the man I love." She looked me in the eyes and added: "Even my life."

"Don't promise too much, Mimi," I cautioned.

"Try me," she said, looking at me with deep seriousness.

I began to feel that sense of divided loyalty. I thought of Hanna and her fears and anxieties. And I thought of Lemlem sleeping peacefully with her teddy bear.

"Would you risk your life if you had a four-year-old daughter?" I asked.

"I don't have a four-year-old daughter," she said.

"You did not answer my question."

"Is that what is worrying you? What would happen to your family if something happened to you?"

"It is always on my mind. Except when I am with you. You banish all those cares from my mind. That is the mystery of it all."

"Oh my love," she said, and sat at my feet looking up at me, leaning on my knees. "I feel you are in some kind of serious trouble."

"Don't worry," I said.

"I will do whatever you wish. I don't have means. But . . ."

"Don't worry," I repeated. "But I think I will take your phone number, just in case."

I wrote down her phone number and gave her a number to call in case of need.

"This is the number of my niece. Her name is Almaz. You can call and arrange to meet her in case you don't hear from me after two or three days."

"Are you expecting to . . ."

"This is just a precautionary measure. Tell her you want to learn about the travel business and give her your name. That will be your communication code."

"I understand," Mimi said. I saw a shade of fear pass across her expression. And she bit her lips without saying anything.

"Did I frighten you? I didn't mean to."

"I am afraid for you. And I don't even know where the danger lies. I don't want to sound like a wife." She interrupted herself and flung herself on me. I had risen to leave by that time. She kissed me hard, until it hurt. I kissed her back passionately, stroking her head and weaving her hair into strands. The incredible energy that flowed from her to me gave me so much courage that I felt I could face any adversity.

I left her standing at the door, her silhouette visible from the distance as I drove away.

FOURTEEN

The following day turned out to be uneventful. After leaving Mimi's I spent a sleepless night, or what was left of it, at home, and was awakened by Hanna rather late. I must have jumped up because I frightened her.

"It's after eight. You will be late for the office," she said.

I took a cold shower and got dressed quickly. I could not eat what she put on the table. "Just coffee, thanks," I said.

"You can't go on an empty stomach. You must eat something."

"I will eat something later."

"You didn't have a proper dinner last night," she said.

"Yes, I did."

"Where?"

I thought I noticed a cloud of suspicion. But it may have been my imagination, or guilt. I did not even answer her, and she sauntered out to the dining room.

There I was, expecting a knock at the door from policemen, and she was fussing over breakfast. Woman, whether she is mother, wife, or mistress, will never be happy unless those for whom she bears responsibility are properly fed and clothed. We men are never thankful enough for that gift.

I picked up my briefcase and left for the office. On my way, I bought some foreign weeklies and a couple of local newspapers and a pack of Rothman cigarettes. Nothing seemed out of the ordinary: the morning traffic was as horrid as ever. Cars were blowing their horns and pedestrians were running in and around the stalled traffic.

The drive to the office, five kilometers from my house, could be a pleasant experience in the morning before eight. After that the traffic begins to thicken, asserting its own peculiar sovereign flow, frustrating to the motorist who has to contend not only with other autos but also with country folks driving their pack animals into the city.

That morning I was late and the city seemed to be overflowing with people, cars and animals. A long line of pedestrians walking on and off the main road were moving faster than the cars. I sat in the traffic listening to the bleating of sheep. A police traffic officer hurled abuse on the country folk, telling them to keep themselves and their animals off the road.

The trouble was, there was no way for them to do that. The city had not been planned, but was instead the result of random development. The roads connected a warren of villages with the city center acting as the nodal point. The problems of Addis Ababa, including its maddening traffic, could be traced to its origin. Menelik, its founder, was an imperial conqueror. His palace stood at the center, with his feudal lords occupying the surrounding hills, all connected originally by narrow mule tracks. Building a modern city on such a foundation created a municipal nightmare.

It was a sunny day with a high cloudless sky, and the gentle breeze carried the faint aroma of eucalyptus mixed with the smell of exhaust fumes. I looked at my watch and saw that it was nearly nine, the time when I should be at the office. Anxiety took hold of me; I imagined the Prime Minister arriving and asking for me. I hoped he would be detained somehow. Every time I was stopped by the traffic, I felt as though the whole world was watching. The people on the sidewalks seemed like intelligence agents spying on me: the idlers, the shoeshine boys, the vendors carrying their wares on their chests, the women hurrying to the market, even the motorists at my side and behind me.

Checking to make sure my cyanide was on the inside of my breast pocket, I moved on. I was late to the office, but fortunately the Prime Minister had not yet arrived. He usually would go to the palace first thing in the morning to make his obeisance to the Emperor and report on urgent business.

The streets around the office were free of the congestion and noise of the previous days. The university campus was quiet at last.

It was all too quiet for my liking.

From the privacy of my office, I made a few phone calls. I gave my secretaries instructions that I was not to be disturbed by anyone except the Prime Minister. They were to hold all incoming calls and note the names and numbers of all callers.

The first person I called was Yohannes. He was not at home, which he used as his office. His wife, Saba, was not in either. I then tried Bekele, with the same result. Then I called Aberra's number. His younger brother, a university student who lived with him, answered the phone.

"Aberra has been arrested," the brother said.

"When? Who arrested him?"

"Some policemen came late last night and took him to the police station for questioning."

"Do you know which police station?"

"Yes. I followed them and saw them taking him to Prince Mesfin Street."

"How is his wife?"

"She is taking it very badly. She went to the station early this morning."

"Anyone with her?"

"Yes, her elder brother and other relatives. Sir, you must do something to help. I am especially worried about her. She is expecting a baby, you know."

"Yes, I know. I will do what I can," I said and hung up.

I called the police station and asked to speak to the chief. "This is Desta Kidane Wold," I said.

"Yes, your excellency. How can I help you?"

"I have just been informed that someone I know is in your station for questioning. It is Dr. Aberra."

"Yes, sir. He is in the criminal investigation division."

"Can you tell me what this is all about?"

"No sir. The criminal investigation division, or the C.I.D., in not under my jurisdiction."

"Can you tell me who is in charge of this investigation?"

"Yes, sir. It is Colonel Muluneh. He should be in his office now." He then gave me the number, adding: "This is strictly off the record, sir. I am not to be quoted. But I heard that Dr. Aberra is under suspicion for the murder of Mr. Melaku."

That news hit me like lightening. The funny thing is, at first I felt a mixture of relief and worry. Relief because it indicated that the police questions and their visit to Yohannes' house were probably related to the death of Melaku; and worry that their suspicion of Aberra might be well-founded. The implications of that would be far-reaching and disastrous. My earlier sense of unease about Aberra was revived, even though his behavior—particularly in helping with the funeral arrangements—had been exemplary. But then, that behavior could be a cover-up, I thought.

It is amazing how worries shift in the scale of importance. Earlier that morning I had expected to be arrested at any time. I had expected the Prime Minister to call me to his office to relieve me of my position, or at the very least, pose some tough questions about my involvement in the underground. I had prepared myself mentally for those eventualities, even purchasing cyanide to avoid torture. Now, faced with a different kind of problem, those worries withdrew into the background.

I tried the number of Colonel Muluneh a few times before he came on the line.

"Your excellency," he said. "What can your humble servant do to help?" I could visualize him making funny faces for his colleagues. He was a cynical police officer known for cruelty and corruption.

"Colonel Muluneh," I said. "I understand you are holding Dr.

Aberra. May I know the reasons?"

"I am not at liberty to divulge anything that is under investigation,"
he said, obviously angling for a price. It was common knowledge that
he took bribes in return for the "easy handling" of prisoners.

"I realize that, Colonel Muluneh," I said. "But surely it would not be
divulging police information to tell me, as his friend, what he is under
suspicion for?"

"With all due respect, sir, I don't want to sound stubborn or
uncooperative; but revealing that kind of information, even to you,
would be against the rules."

"Does that mean then that he is being held incommunicado?"

"Yes, sir, for the time being."

"I see. Well, far be it from me to interfere in police matters. I would
never presume to use my position to suggest that officers of the law
should break the rules. But I would be grateful if you at least inform the
family members how long you intend to hold him, so they can hire a
lawyer for his defense, if it comes to that."

Here I was playing a high-stakes game. I knew that under the law
no one could be held without trial beyond forty-eight hours. Although
this constitutional rule was honored more in the breach than in the
observance, when a well-known or well-connected person was involved
it could be used to browbeat the police.

"We have already obtained a court order to hold him under investigation for as long as necessary," Colonel Muluneh said.

"It must be a serious offense, then."

"You could say it is the most serious in the penal code," he said;
then amended himself: "Well, one of the most serious, at any rate."

"One final point," I said. "Dr. Aberra has a wife who is expecting her
first baby. I understand that she is under great distress and is in a
delicate state of health. Could you at least meet her and give her some
assurance that there will be no harm to him?"

"What kind of harm are you talking about?" Muluneh asked defensively.

"Don't misunderstand me, Colonel. What takes place within the four walls of an interrogation room may be different from what an anxious wife may imagine," I said.

"I see what you mean."

"Purely on humanitarian grounds, could you not talk to her? I don't see how that could be a breach of the rules."

"All right," he said. "On humanitarian grounds I am willing to speak to her. But I cannot give her any assurance that he will be released soon."

"Do whatever the law requires. But on humanitarian grounds, and on legal grounds I might add, you can surely tell her that no harm will come to him, beyond what the law prescribes."

"Okay. Send her to me. I will see her," he said.

"She is not with me, you understand. She may be at the police station outside your office. Her name is Hirut."

I then phoned Aberra's house and informed his brother that Colonel Muluneh would speak to Hirut.

"Thank you, sir," the brother said gratefully. That was a welcome piece of news to Hirut's brother, as it was to Hirut, as I later found out. In times of distress simple favors assume great significance. I was to learn this very well in the trials and tribulations that lay ahead.

FIFTEEN

Days passed. The Prime Minister took his foreign guests to the lake resort over the weekend. The students were quiet, stricken by internal squabbles. The security forces had the upper hand in the city, which was astir with wild talk about an impeding *coup d'état*. Our fears of our own arrests were momentarily allayed, but Aberra's case puzzled and intrigued us. We were outraged that the police could detain our comrade without evidence; at the same time, doubts and suspicions began to grow as we met as a group to discuss the matter. These doubts were beginning to have a corrosive effect on our relationships as comrades committed to the cause and to each other.

I even considered the possibility that the security forces had detained Aberra precisely to produce this corrosive effect on our group. This theory assumed that they knew about us. That assumption in turn proceeded on the basis of another assumption—that there was an informer among us. Or at least a weak link that leaked information.

Yohannes took charge of Aberra's case, frequently visiting his house and comforting Hirut. Bekele became more and more quiet, brooding at meetings. Only Berhane maintained an equanimity of spirit and a brave cheerfulness, even though he was the youngest member of the group.

During those days, while we awaited the result of Aberra's investigation, I carried the cyanide tablets and made certain that Mimi had concealed the documents. She told me that the papers were sealed in a plastic bag together with her jewelry and buried in a secret place which even Enrico did not know. She said she told Lula that they were her late uncle's papers about land disputes in Wollo. The girl was not only beautiful but also resourceful.

I spent more time at home with Hanna and Lemlem, taking them out for drives and buying them ice cream. But Hanna's worries did not diminish. Aberra's arrest did not help; her nagging was increasing almost every day. The result was that even when I made love to her, my thoughts were with Mimi.

One Sunday evening a couple of weeks after Aberra's arrest, Hanna dropped her bombshell. I was reading a book when Hanna came and sat down on the sofa. She looked at me for a while, and I sensed immediately that something was wrong.

"You think I don't know about you?" she said.

"Know what?"

"You can't go on pretending any more, deceiving me."

"What are you talking about?"

"Everything. Everything you do. What you do behind my back!" She started crying in uncontrollable fits that shook her entire body. I knelt in front of her, pleading with her to tell me what was wrong.

"Hanna. Will you stop it! You are driving me crazy!"

She suddenly stopped. "I am driving you crazy! Ha. Ha. That's funny."

"It's not funny. You go on nagging and sulking, and now you burst out crying. I don't know what is the matter with you."

"I'll tell you exactly what's the matter with me. I am the stupid trusting wife. I trust you. I don't ask questions. And you? You go when you please, where you please and meet anybody you please."

"It is my work. I have to . . ."

"Don't give me that. Do you do your work at *Casa Bianca*?"

I got up from my kneeling position and stood half paralyzed. How did she know? I should have told her myself, I thought. But how could I without giving the whole game away?

"I sometimes have to meet people in such places. But very infrequently," I said.

"Desta. I know. Don't pretend. I know."

"What do you know?"

"I told you. Everything. I don't know her name, but does that matter?"

"I don't know what you are talking about."

"Oh yes, you do, you do, and you should be ashamed of yourself, spending nights out pretending to be doing office work and sleeping in a whorehouse!"

"Hanna, please. It is not what you think."

"Really! What is it, then?"

"I can't tell you. It concerns other people."

"Well, thanks a lot. It is nice to be trusted!" she said with a short, sarcastic laugh.

"You are not being reasonable."

"Reasonable! Reasonable! Listen to him!" She flew into a fit of sobbing. She was a perfect picture of the wronged wife and she had every reason to be angry. But her incessant sobbing got on my nerves and I stormed out of the room.

"That's right. Run out. Run away. Go to your harlot and don't come back," she cried as I banged the door behind me. She followed me to the porch and repeated, "Go to your harlot!"

"She is not a harlot!" I shouted back—and instantly regretted it.

"What is she, then? Go on. Go to her. Get out of my sight. And don't bother to come back. I won't be here!"

A couple of neighbors looked out of their windows to see what was going on. Hanna and I had never made a public exhibition of our private squabbles. This time she didn't seem to care. I felt a strange sense of release.

The gatekeeper let me out, and I drove away not knowing where I was heading. At that moment I thought of Melaku, and of the times I had gone out for a drink with him after quarrels with Hanna. I missed him. He had a way of getting people back together, of putting things in a different light, invariably adding a comic element to the human condition. Hanna knew this about him and liked him. If he were alive I would have gone straight to him, and he would have joked and laughed and probably ridden back home with me.

But Melaku was gone. I drove aimlessly around the city for a couple of hours and then went to Mimi.

My face must have said it all. "Trouble at home?" she asked. I nodded.

"Never mind. Are you okay?"

"Hanna knows about us."

"What!"

"Funny thing is," I said, "I am sad and relieved at the same time."

Once more we became two lovers in sweet embrace, without a care in the world. Politics, family, and work lay prostrate at our feet, forgetful of us as we were forgetful of them all.

The drama unfolded with painful slowness. Aberra was still in detention, after more than two weeks. Berhane was in charge of communications between me and the rest of the Central Committee. We decided to keep meetings to a minimum. Yohannes reported that Colonel Muluneh was suitably provisioned with a fifth of Johnny Walker, Black Label, every night; and word came back from Aberra that he was being treated very well. His wife, Hirut, was over her shock and coping with the help of family members and friends.

Though I was assailed with doubts and suspicions, the comic spirit also intervened at times. I imagined a scenario in which Aberra was the real killer of Melaku, in league with the security. If that were the case, I thought, laughing, then Yohannes and the rest of us were compounding the irony by providing scotch for Colonel Muluneh's nightly consumption. There we were, young revolutionaries who thought of ourselves as the hand-maidens of history, scurrying around pathetically in reaction to the invisible actions of mysterious forces.

The Prime Minister was spending more and more of his time with foreign guests. The Emperor was in the eastern province at an annual pilgrimage for the feast of Saint Gabriel's. And when the cat is away, the mice will play, as the saying goes. Most of the other ministers were visiting their ill-gotten estates in the provinces, or bathing in the hot springs of Sodere, or swimming in the lakes in the south. At such times the invisible government ran the show, with the Minister of Security at the top, scheming and conniving. That did not suppress the widespread rumors of an impending coup. And in the north the Eritrean Liberation Front (ELF) was drawing international attention with a couple of spectacular hijackings of commercial airlines, as well as the ambush of an Ethiopian military convoy.

Berhane had spent some time as a guerrilla fighter in Eritrea before he was driven out of the field, disappointed by the brutality of the ELF leadership. He told me one day that a new and better organized splinter group, the Eritrean People's Liberation Front (EPLF), had established contacts among university students and others in Addis Ababa. He urged that we help them and send a contingent to Eritrea to be trained with them.

I wanted to wait until we had resolved the question of Aberra's detention along with Melaku's murder.

"Why should that be a factor for delay?" he asked me. "Sending a contingent would be a kind of insurance. If the worst happens here, at least we will have some people carrying on the struggle and preparing for the final onslaught."

"Perhaps you are right. But give me a couple of weeks," I said and we ended the conversation.

Meanwhile, I thought of using the breathing spell in the urban revolutionary upsurge to visit my ailing mother in Gonder, and gather some information discretely. So I telephoned the Prime Minister and asked his permission.

"Two days. And that is all," he said, warning me not to stray out of the city.

"I will stick to the city, your excellency. You know I am a city-slicker."

"No, I don't. I know you like mountain climbing," he said, and hung up bidding me a pleasant journey.

SIXTEEN

I t was around eleven o'clock one morning in late December when the DC–6 airplane landed at the airport in the city of Gonder. An elegantly dressed man in his late twenties met me at the airport with a black Mercedes. Everybody bowed or saluted. It was wonderful to come home as a noted figure. If they only knew my trepidations!

It was a beautiful day. As my host, who was the private secretary of the governor of Gonder, drove me toward the Grand Hotel, I noticed how small the buildings looked. In my youth those buildings, relics of foreign influence, had appeared gigantic. That was before I went to Addis Ababa and later to Paris and London.

Gonder looked deserted in comparison to Addis Ababa. "So how is life here?" I asked my host.

"Life is great here. I am from Addis Ababa, and I have been here a couple of years. Life is easier here. Food is cheaper and the people are good."

"Are you saying that to flatter me?"

"No sir, not at all. The people of Gonder are perhaps the most civilized in the empire. They are proud and sometimes suspicious of outsiders. But once you know them, there are no better people."

"I think you are right. But then I am biased."

"The people here are deeply religious and go to church all the time, not just on Sundays."

"I don't know whether that is good for development or not," I said. "What about work? Agriculture and development?"

"Well, there are some exciting developments in the lowlands in the Northwest. I own land there and I hope to start working it next year, if all goes well." He added excitedly: "Oil seed is the new gold of our times. I know people who had nothing five years ago, who are now millionaires."

"How are the students in Gonder?"

"Well, now that you mention it, they have become our principal worry. They are against everything. They want to destroy our traditions, our religion, and they are against development."

"Are they boycotting classes?"

"All the time. They wait for word from the university students in Addis Ababa, and then they go on the rampage."

We arrived at the Grand Hotel, which was one of the charming relics of the past, situated near the seventeenth century castle. The castle was a symbol of old Gonder, a monument to its past glory. The people of Gonder believe they are favored by history and look down on Ethiopians from two hundred kilometers to the south as uncouth barbarians.

I did not have to register at the hotel. There were rules for the many, and rules for the privileged few. The hotel personnel must have been told of my imminent arrival, for they all lined up and bowed and scraped. It was most embarrassing. My bags were taken to my suite, which I was told was the best room in the hotel, with the best view of the city and the castle.

"Thank you" I said.

My young host then drove me to the governor's office, a short distance from the hotel. I wanted to walk and recall the days of my youth. But my host would not have it.

"The people of Gonder would be outraged," he said, shaking his head. "It is not becoming for a Big Man to walk."

The Big Man obeyed.

The governor, a slightly built, kindly man in his early fifties, met me at the door with a beaming smile. We bowed to each other with a slow and dignified inclination of the head as befits Big Men of equivalent rank.

"What a pleasure to see you," he said, shaking my hand, then kissing me on both cheeks. The latter gesture was designed to convey to onlookers that we were close friends, if not relatives; in fact we were not friends but acquaintances.

"Your pleasure is no greater than mine," I replied, as he motioned me to enter his office.

"I thought we could chat for an hour or so here, and then go to my residence for lunch," he said.

"Oh, I don't want to impose. I hope your good wife has not gone to any lengths to prepare . . ."

"Not at all!" he cut me short. "This is an unexpected pleasure. And the house is full of servants. She does not have to lift a finger."

"But if my information is correct, she does more than lift a finger," I said.

That pleased him. His wife was the daughter of a popular nobleman, a liberal aristocrat whose children were brought up to like and enjoy work, including manual work.

"The ladies of Gonder are sometimes puzzled by her example. But they are getting used to her," he said with evident pride.

We settled on leather armchairs facing each other. I took out my Rothmans and offered him one.

"No. Thank you. I have never smoked," he said. He had a habit of twirling a small gold chain on his pointing finger, back and forth. I had seen him do it before, and he started doing it this time. Who knows, I thought as I lit my cigarette, maybe that chain saved him from becoming a smoker? I started to say that, but changed my mind for fear of offending him.

"Did you have a pleasant flight?"

"Yes. Very smooth. I like these DC 6s."

"Well, now. How many days will you stay? I hope for a week, at least."

"Oh no. I am afraid two days was all I was given."

"That is too short. I have thought of a hunting trip and picnics. You must relax a little, you know."

"I have never been a hunter," I said. "Never liked it. And really, the

Prime Minister was explicit. Two days, and no more. His words still ring in my ears."

"How is his excellency? How are things at the center of the storm?" the governor asked, frowning a little.

"Never a dull moment," I said cryptically.

"I'll say! We hear of wild deeds. Students smashing cars and snatching dead bodies. What is this country coming to?"

"It is the accumulated grievances of decades and maybe centuries," I said boldly, partly in order to hear his views on the revolutionary upsurge.

I knew him to be a decent man who did his best in his assigned jobs. I remembered him showing courage in the early 1960s when he was an acting minister of justice for a short while. He had shown mercy to a number of officers of the imperial guard who had joined in an attempted coup. Although he was married to a nobleman's daughter, his sympathies lay with the underdog. For that reason he was considered to be on the Prime Minister's side and was not trusted by the conservative forces.

"But two wrongs do not make a right" he said. "I fear the students will destroy many good things without achieving their objectives. Much of what they demand is right. If we could only have enough courage to say so and meet them half way, I think they would stop."

"I doubt it. I think it is too late."

"Is that the official view?" he asked with pained curiosity.

"I am not saying it is the official view. It is my reading of the situation as a close observer."

"You may be right. More is the pity. But I think there is still time. What are the ministers doing with the land reform bill? Why is everybody slamming the brakes on reform?"

"Because not everybody is like your illustrious father-in-law, Ras Amare, who showed the way many years ago by giving land to his tenants."

"That was regarded by some of his noble kinsmen as the act of a mad man," the governor said. "I remember some of them literally commiserating with us for what they saw as his madness."

"He must be having the last laugh," I said.

"On the contrary. He is sad, and still urges the Emperor to proclaim land reform."

"The bill under discussion may be too late and to little," I told him; then I changed the subject, asking, "How is the family?"

"They are all well, thank God. And yours?"

I felt a brief pang of conscience, thinking of Hanna and Lemlem. "Very well. But I have come to see my mother, who is not well."

"That is what I heard. If there is anything I can do to help, please let me know. I have seen her a few times in church."

"I was thinking of going to her now."

"No. I insist that you join us for lunch, and then my chauffeur can take you to her."

We were driven to his residence where we were met by his gracious wife and well-behaved children, who were legion. I remembered that one of them used to recite short poems of Melaku when she was six years old, in the days after our return from studies abroad when we used to frequent the home of the governor's father-in-law. The children often stayed with their grandparents, whose home was open to all educated young Ethiopians, Melaku and I among them. I always thought of Ras Amare's home as a model for Africa, combining traditional respect for the elders with progressive, open debate between the generations and across social stations. I will never forget the kindness of the old man and his wife.

The governor's wife resembled her mother both in looks and manner. She was attentive to her guests; her sensitive hospitality was the talk of all Gonder, where she was revered.

One of the governor's social functions was to preside over innumerable banquets, a function which was an exact replica of the imperial banquet in smaller scale. Social scientists have made endless comments about the banquet as a cementing factor in the imperial social order, as a periodic ritual bridge erected between social classes. The radicals among them, including myself, attacked the practice as archaic and reactionary. In the local vernacular the word for banquet is the same word for taxes. One Ethiopian novelist describes a scene in which a throng of invited commoners, trying to enter the palace gates, are struck with long rods.

"Why do people submit to such humiliation for one meal?" the novelist's narrator asks, then answers his own question: "They are paying special dues to humiliation." Material dues in the form of taxes are not enough. The Emperor's subjects have to pay psychological dues as well, he concludes.

No such humiliation was extracted in the home of Gonder's enlightened governor. All guests were treated with respect. As we ate, the conversation flowed freely at the table, without the restraint experienced in the home of other, even lesser, members of the nobility. In this atmosphere I wondered whether the revolutionary method, the *tabula rasa,* was the answer to the problems facing our country. Might not an evolutionary method of the Fabian variety be more appropriate?

Well, it was too late for all that. The beast was unleashed and there was no telling what lay ahead.

After the usual entreaties addressed to me, as an honored guest, to eat and drink, the small banquet was over and we retired to the salon for coffee. Then the governor rang a bell and when a servant came in, he whispered something in his ear.

A few minutes later, the door opened and the governor rose to greet my mother, who was helped into the room by my young niece and an elderly priest, Aleka Lemma, my boyhood teacher. What a surprise!

"I hope you will forgive me for springing this surprise on you. We wanted your mother to join us for lunch but she was delayed in church. Besides I know your time would be short, and I wanted to take maximum advantage." With these words the governor left us.

My mother rushed toward me, ululating in a cracked fashion, almost sounding like a hen that has just hatched its eggs. She stumbled as she rushed and would have fallen but for the alert Aleka Lemma, who caught her by the arm in the nick of time, and admonished her as he always did.

"Don't rush, old lady," he said. "Do you think he will run away from you? Come to her, my son, and spare us the pain of seeing her fall!"

I did as he bid. No one could resist Aleka Lemma's orders. Not even the governor whose home he frequented, as I was informed, teaching his children classical literature and religious studies. 'Aleka' is a title equivalent to professor.

"My son. My son. The light of my eye," said my mother as I bent to kiss her. "Let me look at you. You have gotten thinner. Doesn't that wife of yours feed you properly? These modern women, all they know is how to dress in short skirts and paint their lips."

"Mother, I have never felt better. In fact I have gained weight."

"Nonsense," she said, squinting. Her eyes were getting weaker but her mind, at eighty, was alert.

I was her last child and she had always tried to spoil me, provoking the wrath of my father of blessed memory. Aleka Lemma, who was a good friend of my father, took his place when he died as the only man who could tell my mother anything. Since his wife was also dead, they kept each other company, which pleased me immensely. At least her last years were not lonely. She spent her days praying and chatting with him.

"How are they treating you, those barbarians?" she asked me after we sat.

"Lady! Is that the way to talk about our rulers?" the Aleka said. "Remember what our king Theodor said? He said that where the king lives even the stones are gold. Barbarians indeed!"

"Well, they are still barbarians. They talk like barbarians and eat like barbarians, and don't try to talk me out of that one, Aleka. I know your old tricks!"

"What about our governor?" the Aleka said to provoke her. "Is he a barbarian?"

"There you go, trying to make me say bad things about that nice young man!"

Aleka Lemma laughed a hearty laugh, and they went on quite a while bantering, with my mother constantly looking at me and examining me closely. I wanted to go to our house and smell the earth and listen to the sounds of the voices of the neighbors, and chat with my mother into the small hours of the morning.

Later, we were taken by the governor's chauffeur to our old house.

Most of the neighbors I knew from childhood were gone. A few old women and a couple of old men and several childhood friends came to see me. The women ululated, and the children laughed when my mother gave them some of the sweets and biscuits I had brought.

My chat with the people was a rambling, sentimental journey back to my childhood. Most talked about the good things I did. Only one old woman remembered and dared to mention a bad incident. She said that one day she was carrying water in an earthen pot when I used the pot for target practice with my sling. They all burst into laughter when she finished and I bowed my head in mock shame, offering to pay for the pot with interest.

"You have paid us all in more ways, my son," she said, blessing me. There was a proud murmur of agreement. And my mother invited all and sundry to eat and drink and be happy. The governor had sent cases of beer and other stuff without my knowledge.

Aleka Lemma told us a few of his jokes and some vignettes from his own adventures. It seemed that he was once accused by jealous rivals of being a crypto-Catholic. He was brought before the governor of the area, who was at that time none other than the good Ras Amare, then a young nobleman. One of the accusers said, in summing up his case, that Lemma deserved to die not one but ten deaths. Whereupon Aleka Lemma said, "You want to gloat over my death ten times, eh? Well, I will die only once, just to deny you the pleasure!" He had the whole court, including the governor, in fits of laughter. Noticed for his presence of mind and wit, he became the teacher of the governor's children and a life-time friend of the family.

My young nephews and nieces, the children of my two brothers and a sister, all deceased, sat at my feet never taking their eyes off me. To them the evening must have seemed like a miracle. It was to me. You don't get that kind of warmth and community of spirit in the big cities. With all its material backwardness, the life of these simple folks was better at the spiritual level. Will it be there for long? I wondered. Will it be swept aside in the march toward material progress; and if so, can it be replaced by something remotely resembling it?

I didn't know then and I still don't know today. But one thing seems certain: by deciding to become active agents of history, we disturbed those ancient ways without offering any better replacements. My mother was the last to doze off at the end of that fortuitous gathering and celebration. Aleka Lemma left early. Finally the fire was turned to embers, which gradually gave out. That became the signal for all to leave. The governor's chauffeur, who had joined the carousing and fallen asleep, was awakened by my niece. I bade all a goodnight and left for my suite at the Grand Hotel.

The following morning, I was awakened by the bells of the Holy Trinity Church, known as the Mount of Light. What a change from the jarring sounds of the alarm clock that heralds every workday in Addis Ababa, I thought. The alarm jars you into the day where your life is defined by tight schedules and deadlines. Here the pace of life flowed slowly in tune with the church bells or the call of the muezzin to prayers.

Eventually I got out of bed, washed in the deep and spacious tub, shaved and dressed. I had eggs, toast and tea in the hotel restaurant. There were a few foreign tourists and hotel residents, and the head-waiter's attention to my breakfast service aroused their interest. One of them approached my table. He spoke the local language fluently, with an American accent.

"Greetings, my lord. You are Mr. Desta from the cabinet office, I think."

"Yes I am. News travels fast."

"Well, I confess I did check with one of the waiters. But I have seen your picture in a magazine. I am a Peace Corps volunteer, a medical doctor. I teach at the local college and also help in a local clinic."

"How nice. Please sit down," I said in English.

He shifted to English too. "Thank you. I won't take much of your time. I just wanted to make your acquaintance. My name is Dr. John Reed."

"Glad to meet you, Dr. Reed. Have you been here long?"

"Three years."

I was tempted to ask him questions touching on policy and politics, but that morning I was not in the mood. The previous night's session in the charmed circle of my people had transported me to the past, into the depth of the soul of northern Ethiopia, the historic Ethiopia that was the center of the country's culture. I was still committed to the cause, but the events of the previous few weeks had raised some questions in my mind.

Some of Dr. Reed's friends came over and introduced themselves, and before long my table became a hub of the restaurant.

"It is not every day that we get to meet a celebrity like yourself," said a young woman of about twenty eight who was also a Peace Corps volunteer.

"I hear you are originally from Gonder," said a young man with a red beard. He was British, judging by his accent. "It is a real honor to meet you, sir."

"Thank you. It is a pleasure to meet you all." I was somewhat embarrassed, and invited them to have tea.

"No, we've had our breakfast," one of them said.

There was a moment of silence.

"Are you all teachers?" I asked.

"Yes," they all said.

"And how are the students?"

"They are good. But there have been problems lately. Boycotts," the young Peace Corps woman said. "I believe the majority want to attend classes. But they are afraid of an organized minority which has control over them."

"So what are the prospects, do you think?"

A tall, thin man spoke up. "Addis Ababa is where the action is," he said. "It is like the French Revolution. When Paris sneezed, the rest of the country caught cold."

The rest of the company laughed. I was inexplicably annoyed. "A slight correction," I said. "The actual quotation is, 'When Louis the Sixteenth sneezed, Europe caught cold.'"

Another silence followed, with the thin man blushing. It must have been the effect of the previous night's journey into the past, but I was not in the mood to listen to a bunch of foreign teachers making fun of our predicament.

Then I was contrite and tried to make amends. "You people are doing a marvelous job," I said. "And we are grateful, although we may not show it all the time."

"We love this country," said the young woman. "We want to make a positive contribution. Our intentions are good, but we may make mistakes. There is so much we don't know. Oh, so much!" She was flushed.

"Well, it takes time and patience. Just do your best. And now, if you'll excuse me, I have to see the governor." I shook hands with all of them and went to the desk to leave my key.

"Your excellency, there are a couple of messages," the desk clerk said, giving me two slips.

One was from the governor, who said he would wait for my call. The other was from Addis Ababa. It was from Yohannes. It simply said: "Call as soon as possible. Urgent."

The governor rose to receive me. He moved from his desk to sit in the armchair. His expression was grave and his manner circumspect. "I have some bad news," he said, looking at me with those gentle and sad eyes.

"What is it?"

"I got a phone call late last night from the minister of security." He paused. "I don't understand what the hell is going on. But the minister's order was that you should be arrested and sent back in police custody, first thing in the morning."

"What! He can't do that," I protested.

"That is exactly how I reacted. But he said that the order came from higher authorities."

"That can only mean the Prime Minister, or His Majesty," I said.

"When was the last time you spoke with the Prime Minister?"

"The day before yesterday. I came here with his permission."

"Then there can only be one other authority . . ." The governor did not complete his sentence. He sighed and continued: "I did not want to spoil your good time. I heard you had a good reunion with family and old friends last night. And I wanted you to have a good rest this morning."

"I appreciate this."

"Don't mention it. It is the least I could do. There is some kind of intrigue going on in the center of the empire. I am afraid you may have been a victim of someone's game of power."

Not knowing what I had been doing behind the Prime Minister's back, and indeed in betrayal of his trust for the sake of what I considered a higher call, this man was sticking his neck out for me. And why? Not because he sought some favor, but simply because he was decent to the core. When everything seemed to be falling apart, men like him could keep a cool head and a kind heart and do what seemed just and proper.

"What do you propose I do?" I asked him.

"Well. The security minister's order was that you be arrested here. I have arranged a special flight. No uniformed men will accompany you. Instead two plain-clothes men will travel with you back to Addis Ababa. And don't worry about your mother. I will take care of her."

"I will not forget this," I said. "One favor. Can I call my wife?"

"Yes, of course, go ahead."

I called home. The housekeeper told me that Hanna was not home. Hanna had stayed with her sister since the night of our quarrel, and I had not seen or talked to her. I had hoped that she might return as she had a couple times before, following a similar quarrel, but she obviously had not.

I then called Yohannes.

"Desta. Did you get my message?" Yohannes asked.

"I did. I am at the governor's office in Gonder," I said to alert him to be careful.

"How are things?"

"I am coming this afternoon by a special flight," I said. "A special flight accompanied by special people."

He got the message. "Where will you go with these special people?"

"To the security ministry."

"Okay. I will be waiting there."

"How is Hanna?"

"She does not know yet."

"Take care of her and Lemlem."

"It'll be okay. Everything is going to be okay. Keep cool."

"I'll see you," I said.

SEVENTEEN

The "special flight" did not arrive, so I was taken back to the capital by Land Rover. We started from Gonder at two o'clock that afternoon, driving at breakneck speed. I was given the place of honor in the front seat beside the driver, a quiet young police officer with a lean and hungry look. The provincial security chief, a colonel, and two other officers sat at the back.

I was not in any mood for small talk, though the colonel tried several times to engage me in conversation. For the first fifty kilometers I withdrew into myself, reviewing the events of the past weeks and preparing my mind for the hard times ahead. I imagined sessions with hardened interrogators in secret chambers. I also imagined a showdown with the Prime Minister and the Emperor. I even thought of the possible questions and prepared my answers.

When we reached the lakeside town of Bahrdar, I emerged from my mental cocoon and decided to enjoy the countryside, one of the most pleasant in Ethiopia. I did not know when, or if, I would ever see it again, so I savored every bit of the scenery: every hill and tree and homestead. As the man said on the eve of his execution, nothing else concentrates the mind so wonderfully.

Surveying the countryside, it was easy to see why Gonder was once the imperial capital. At the end of the plains north of Bahrdar, a chain of mountains guards Gonder like a sentinel. Further to the north and east, the mountains are even more forbidding. To the north-west and west lie the impenetrable jungle wilds of Kuara and Armacho, where wild beasts and malaria stand guard. Thus protected, Gonder developed and nurtured a sophisticated culture for over three centuries, before decay from within and the rise of rival claimants to the south reduced it to a province of the empire. The center had become the periphery.

As I reflected on these matters, I regretted not spending an afternoon revisiting the interior of the old Gonder palace, with its fourteen gates, the six imposing castles inside the palace, and the large open-air bath built by one of the kings. Ah well! I should count my blessings, I thought, for the mere fact of the visit—for seeing my mother and Aleka Lemma again, and for passing an unforgettable evening with my people.

We arrived at Bahrdar a little after four o'clock. The colonel suggested a little coffee break. Would I mind! No, not if they didn't. We stopped for half an hour and the driver filled the tank with petrol. The hotel where we had coffee was filled with well-dressed young people who were probably employed in the town's textile industry. There were also a few students from the local technical college, volubly complaining about their Russian teachers and their bad English.

"Nobody seems to like the Russians," said the colonel, who was desperately trying to break the silence that hung like a dark cloud over our group.

I remember saying, "They can't help it if their English is bad. It is not their native tongue."

The colonel seized the initiative and launched into a long discourse about his experience in Israel, where he had spent a year in intelligence training.

"The children ran after us, calling us *cushi! cushi!*" he said.

"What is that?" asked one of his subordinates.

"It means black or negro," the colonel said.

"Negro! You?"

"Of course. We are all negro to them. Or slaves."

"I thought they were like us. I mean, I thought we were the same as them; you know, Semitic," said the puzzled junior officer.

"Captain, wake up," said the colonel. "To them you are a negro. I learned my lesson in Israel. We used to look down on Africans, but Israel taught me different. Mind you, these were the children. The older people were very nice and polite."

"Yes, but you know what they say about children," said the third officer. "They are the mirror of their families."

"I thought about that," the colonel said. "But I never experienced open prejudice from adults."

"Where did you live in Israel?" I asked.

"Jerusalem. West Jerusalem, as it then was. This was before the Six Day War. They are an impressive people, the Israelis," he continued, after a short silence. "There is so much we can learn from them. Even their Arab neighbors can learn a lot if they could only overlook the differences."

He launched into a long discussion on the origin and development of the Histadrut and on the Kibbutzim and Moshavim and so forth. He was obviously impressed by Israel, and who could blame him? But I was not inclined to continue the conversation.

It was getting dark, and we resumed our journey. The sun was nearing the horizon. Eventually, with the sunset, the woods turned dark and the moon appeared, outlining the shapes of the trees on the hilltops. From his tone of voice and the way he talked to his subordinates, I decided that the colonel was a good person. That gave me reason to hope that he might let me contact Hanna when we reached Addis Ababa. I also suspected, however, that one of the three, probably the quiet officer, might be an informer with a direct line of access to the minister of security or even the Emperor. That was the way things were organized. I would have to watch my step.

We reached Debre-Markos, the provincial capital of Gojam, at a little after eight in the evening and had dinner in one of the local hotels. I had no appetite and gave my dish to the driver, who consumed it with gusto. It was the only time I saw him smile. Perhaps he is the Emperor's man, I thought, noting the fact that he ate at the same table as the others—an unusual arrangement even for an enlightened colonel of the security.

The woman serving us was very attractive and all our eyes were focused on her. She knew this and showed it with a smile, revealing beautiful teeth lined by blue tattooed gums, a mark of beauty in local custom. She walked to and from the table with exaggerated swings of her hips.

"This one is new," said the captain.

"No, she is not" said the driver. "She used to work at the other hotel, and the owner made a higher bid for her and brought her here. The clientele of the other hotel moved with her. It is a tough business," the driver concluded, wiping his mouth with the back of his hand.

He is the special informer, I thought, and decided to engage him in conversation. "You seem to know everybody and everything," I said.

"Not everybody and certainly not everything," he said without a smile.

"He knows these parts, sir," the colonel said. "He is from Gojam and knows everybody who is somebody in Gojam!"

"And that woman is some body!" the captain said, following her movements with undisguised admiration. We all laughed.

I ordered beers for everyone. The colonel protested. I insisted, and we all drank two bottles each of Melotti. The beer relaxed the atmosphere.

"Nice place" I said. "Who is the owner?"

"The woman at the cash register," the driver said. "Her husband is a local district governor."

"And an astute businessman," the colonel added.

"Well, the country needs astute businessmen," I said.

"What the country needs is justice," the quiet officer said, and all eyes turned to him.

The beer must be having an effect, I thought. The colonel looked ill at ease and tried to divert the conversation.

"Gojam is one of the richest provinces in the empire," he said. "If only people would invest their time and money on productive enterprises like farming."

"And who controls the best land, colonel, with all due respect?" said the quiet officer—who had decided not to be so quiet any longer. "And who has the money?"

"Lieutenant," the colonel said, in a gentle but firm tone, "I am not saying we live in paradise. But if we persist and approach the right people with the right language, anything is possible."

"And at the right time, and in the right circumstances?" the lieutenant retorted, to the visible annoyance of the colonel.

"Yes. Anything wrong with that?" the colonel answered, raising his voice a little. The lieutenant relented and bowed his head in deference.

It was obvious to me that the men liked and respected the colonel; but whatever liberty he might give them for free discussion, there was a limit. After all, they were officers in a system where rank determined everything. At that point I thought I would intervene to guide the conversation to a safe landing.

"I don't want to sound equivocal," I began, "but you are both right. I think it is axiomatic that there could not be development without justice; people must feel that they have an equal opportunity and an equal access to resources before they can decide to spend their time, money, and energy."

"That is what I am saying," said the lieutenant.

"But people must also take initiative and risks," I continued. "Even with the best land in the world, there can be no development where people do not take initiative."

The two seemed to agree to that standard rhetoric. Only the driver seemed unconvinced as far as I could judge from his skeptical look.

"Wouldn't you agree?" I challenged him.

"Well, I don't know about other parts of the country" he said, "But here in Gojam people are suspicious of any laws that come from Addis Ababa, especially where their land is concerned. They have revolted before, and they would revolt again if land reforms were extended to this area."

"Are we talking about land reform?" asked the lieutenant.

"What are you talking about then?"

"Equal rights and opportunities for everyone."

"Well equal rights can mean equal land. And those who have any land are not willing to share it."

"Well that is too bad. They will have to live by the laws of the country," the lieutenant said.

The captain stepped in. "I would not grant equal access to everything," he said, smiling in the direction of the pretty woman, and we all laughed.

"Well, gentlemen. It is time to go," the colonel said, signalling for the bill.

"This is my treat," I said.

"No, sir. We have a *per diem* for this."

"I insist," I said. "You can use your *per diem* to buy presents for your wife and children."

He protested, but I prevailed and paid the bill, leaving a substantial tip for the pretty girl, who flashed a smile and bowed in gratitude. We left without knowing how her voice sounded; she had not said a word. Her face and movements spoke for her.

It is amazing what beer and conversation can do for a relationship. The tension was gone, replaced by the human bond that develops even between the prisoner and his jailer. By the time we reached the spectacular gorge of the Abbai Valley, which the moon-lit night made even more awesome, we had become almost like old friends.

We crossed the Abbai bridge and began to ascend to the plateau of Selale, winding our way up, changing gears all the while. The captain teased the driver with jokes about the way people of Gojam spoke. The driver answered with jokes the Gojam people tell about those from the other side of the Abbai Valley. Even the lieutenant told some interesting stories about his experiences in Gonder where people made fun of his southern words and accents. The colonel listened and egged them all on.

We did everything but sing. But then, as we got nearer to our destination, reality began to impose itself again. The talk became less natural and the tension returned.

It was about two in the morning when we approached the northern range of the Entoto Mountains, half an hour from Addis Ababa. I wondered where I would spend the night. Ordinarily a detainee would be taken to a police or security station. Finally the colonel broached the subject delicately.

"The agreement reached with the governor was that we would all spend the night, or what is left of it, at a guest house owned by him," the colonel said. "He has telephoned instructions to his agent who guards the guest house."

No one raised any objections. Even if an unknown agent of the Emperor were present in the group, it would be improper for him to countermand the "agreement." Decorum is an important concept in Ethiopian social life. The colonel's delicate phrasing regarding the "agreement" left room for speculation that higher authorities might have been parties to it.

The guest house turned out to be heaven-sent, and the governor's agent a kind of gift of providence. He gave me his private office to make phone calls out of reach of the security people, who were content to wait in the salon eating a hearty breakfast.

I called home. Hanna had not returned. I called Yohannes and Saba answered. "Desta, are you alright?" she asked. "Where are you?"

"In Addis Ababa, somewhere at a guest house."

She interpreted guest house as a euphemism for prison and started weeping. All my previous dislike for her disappeared.

"I am all right, I assure you. Now be a good girl and get Yohannes," I said and she did. Yohannes knew the place and said he would be there in a few minutes.

"No, don't come here," I told him. "Wait for me at the security ministry. Meanwhile try to console Saba. Any news about Hanna?"

"Yes, I told her last night as delicately as I could. She is all right now. Doctor Kassa gave her some tranquilizers."

"Dr. Kassa! Did she fall ill?"

"She became a bit hysterical. Apparently the police had been to your house. They left a message that you were wanted for questioning. When she called and asked them why, one of them said that you were a suspect of a capital offense."

"The bloodthirsty hounds! How is Lemlem?"

"She is staying with her aunt and is fine."

"Alright, Johnny. Thanks"

"I'll see you soon."

Yohannes was standing at the entrance to the ministry, reading a newspaper when we drove up at a few minutes before nine o'clock. When he saw us getting out of the Land Rover he rushed to meet me. The colonel walked a few steps away and signalled for his subordinates to do the same.

"Desta, are you okay?" Yohannes asked.

"Yes, I am fine. I am dying to know what they are up to. And I confess, I am a little scared."

"Don't admit to anything! They are saying at the police station that Aberra has confessed to the murder, and that you were part of the conspiracy. I am sure it is a trick to get you to talk about the movement in order to get off the hook on the murder rap."

"If this is true, if Aberra has confessed, then it is his word against mine, right?"

"Right. It may also be that Aberra was a plant from the start, that he has been an agent of the security pretending to be a revolutionary."

"We can't rule that out. After all, I am a revolutionary pretending to be an imperial loyalist," I said with a bitter laugh that left Yohannes unamused.

"That is a false analogy. There is no moral equivalence," he said.

I decided not to waste time in attempts at humor. "Anything else?"

"Just keep steadfast. Deny everything. If they persist, insist on being brought to open court and demand to have a lawyer present. Ask for me."

He spoke hurriedly and excitedly. The door opened and I left Yohannes to join the colonel, who led the way to the Minister of Security's office. The minister's private secretary greeted us, bowing deeply. I could tell he was ignorant of my changing status and fortune; if he knew, he would not bow at all.

"Thank you for everything, colonel," I said after the secretary went in to announce our arrival. "You did not treat me like a prisoner at all, and I am grateful."

"I don't consider you or anyone else a prisoner until a court declares you guilty," the colonel said.

"Now I know why a person of your education and background is in the provinces and not here at the center."

"I don't mind the provinces. The people there have rights, too. Besides, I like it there. It is more peaceful."

At that point the minister's secretary reappeared. He did not look as cheerful as when he had first met us. Without even looking at us, he took a piece of paper from a folder on his desk and went back to the minister.

"As you were saying, it is more peaceful in the provinces," I said. "And people are more courteous." The colonel saw my point and laughed. The secretary came back after some ten minutes and motioned for us to enter, holding the door for us.

I had never been to Zerfu's office before. He was not a favorite of mine, and I knew the feeling was mutual. I had always felt that he was a henchman eager to please his master—anyone who happened to be his master at any given moment—and that he would go to any lengths in that endeavor. I was apprehensive as we entered his office, which was more spacious and more exquisitely furnished than the office of the Prime Minister.

There was a large Persian carpet on top of a wall-to-wall carpet. A benignly smiling picture of His Majesty was hanging on the wall behind the desk, a picture that contrasted with the minister's scowling face. The desk was a semicircle of a dark gleaming wood. Tall, well-proportioned windows overlooked the garden outside, and there were several leather chairs arranged in groups around salon tables.

Zerfu was signing papers and did not look up to acknowledge our presence. I was familiar with this bureaucratic game, which is designed to build tension and put the bureaucrat on top of the situation. As if his power were not enough.

We stood there for a few minutes before Zerfu looked up briefly, only to shake his head in grave disapproval and continue signing his papers. The colonel and I exchanged furtive glances and I saw a knowing smile on the colonel's face.

"We are here, sir," he said.

"I am not blind," the minister answered curtly.

More silence.

"I was expecting you yesterday," the minister said continuing his signing. He seemed to sign the papers without reading them. My apprehension subsided, replaced by an academic curiosity: either he read the papers before, which is unlikely, or he puts much trust in his secretary, I thought. I knew the hidden power of secretaries and the vanity of ministers. The former enjoyed invisible power; the latter enjoyed the glory that went with status.

"Why were my orders not obeyed?" the minister asked, finally putting down his pen and folding his arms.

"I am not aware of any orders that have been disobeyed, sir," the colonel said.

At this, Zerfu flew into a temper tantrum, getting up from his chair and pounding his desk. "The order was that the prisoner was to be brought here immediately, which meant yesterday!"

"The airplane did not come as expected, sir, and we drove all night."

"My order was given two days ago. Even by car you could have brought the prisoner yesterday afternoon, at the latest."

The repeated reference to the prisoner implied a presumption of guilt, and I was about to protest when the good colonel beat me to it.

"Your excellency, I was not aware that Mr. Desta was a prisoner. I did not receive a court order to that effect."

"Is that so? And the order of your political superior does not count, I suppose."

"I didn't say that. But we officers of the law must treat everyone as a free person until his freedom is curtailed by a court decree."

"Colonel, spare me your Sunday sermon and your police academy lectures. Obviously you have forgotten that I am minister of security and your superior."

"No, sir. I have not forgotten that. I am only . . ."

"Never mind. I know who is behind this, and I will deal with that. You may go now; I will deal with you in due course." The minister dismissed the colonel with a flick of his left hand like a ping pong player hitting a backhand.

The colonel's eyes flashed with controlled anger. He gave a dignified bow and left. I never saw him again, but I later heard he was transferred to the central prison as a deputy warden. I will never forget him.

The minister sat down and rang for his secretary. "Get me General Dima on the phone," he ordered. Then for the first time he appeared to notice me, and motioned for me to sit down.

"I prefer to stand, since you say I am a prisoner," I said after the secretary left.

"There will be time enough for standing and worse," he said.

"What have I done to deserve this humiliation?" I challenged him, summoning all the force within me to sound aggrieved.

The minister emitted a shrill, staccato laughter. "You have two choices," he said. "Either you confess your reprehensible crimes and beg His Majesty for forgiveness. Or you continue to pretend innocence."

He lit a cigarette and blew a cloud of smoke straight at me, then continued: "The first choice, which I strongly recommend, might—I repeat, just *might*—elicit mercy from Our Gracious Sovereign. That may, and I repeat, *may,* help reduce the punishment. The second choice . . ."

"I have committed no crime," I interrupted. "I cannot confess to anything I did not commit."

"Young man" he said, although I was in my thirties, "we have all the evidence. Don't try to make matters worse for yourself, and think of your family. How old is your daughter?"

The last question was like a knife piercing my entrails, and I knew it was meant to soften me. I ignored it. "I have committed no crime," I repeated. "You tell me what crime I have committed. This is the twentieth century, and not the Spanish Inquisition."

That last remark threw him off balance. He was generally referred to by the literate public as the Spanish Inquisitioner, and he knew it. I knew that I would obtain neither justice nor mercy at the hands of Zerfu, so I deliberately acted defiantly with a hint of unspecified personal repercussions for him.

Fear is the first principle, I reminded myself.

"Very well, then," he said. "Have it your way. This protestation of innocence borders on stupidity."

"Thank you very much," I said sarcastically.

I knew that he was trying to trick me into signing a confession in the vague expectation of imperial amnesty. But I remembered the warning that Yohannes had given me, and his strategy of steadfastness and denial was the only course I would follow. I prepared myself for the worst. I still had the cyanide tablets tucked away in my underwear.

"Arrogance and sarcasm won't help you, Desta. You are being foolish and you know it. Before I hand you over to the interrogators," he said, dwelling on the last word with relish, "I want to give you another chance, as a favor to the Prime Minister who has pleaded for mercy on your behalf."

"Preposterous," I said. "The Prime Minister would not plead for mercy for a crime I did not commit. How could he, before even talking to me?"

"Well, he will talk to you. He wants to. In fact, General Dima will escort you to him."

At that point the secretary came in to say that General Dima was on his way.

"Desta. For God's sake be realistic," the minister pleaded, changing his tone to a soft, paternal one. "I am not your enemy, although I know you never liked me. I am trying to be reasonable. You will save yourself and your family much grief if you follow my advice." He crushed his cigarette in a large ashtray. "Believe me, once you are out of our hands and in the hands of the interrogators, it will not be pleasant. Besides, the evidence in incontrovertible."

"What evidence? And what crime? You say you are being reasonable, and yet you have not said one word about the offense I am supposed to have committed."

"It is a capital offense. And the evidence is overwhelming."

"Then bring me to open court and have me charged according to the law!"

"I knew you would say that. But you know very well that there are political considerations that sometimes justify handling matters quietly. You are an officer of the Emperor's government with ministerial rank. It would reflect badly on the cabinet as a whole if you were tried in open court."

He stopped to examine my reaction, and lit another cigarette. "Please sit down, don't be an ass," he said in a more genial manner. "Come on, sit down."

I sat.

"That is why we have special courts for security matters," he said. "If you insist on your day in court, it will be granted. But not before a thorough interrogation."

He ordered two coffees without asking me if I wanted one, and we waited for Dima's arrival. Zerfu resumed his signing, and I withdrew into a silent contemplation of my fate.

The Prime Minister, we were told, was on the special line when Dima and I were ushered into his waiting room. As we entered the vestibule, the police guard, an old sergeant of whom I was very fond, shook my hand and left a folded piece of paper in my palm. I waited for Dima's attention to be distracted and then took one of the magazines from the waiting room table. I opened the note and read it behind the magazine.

It read: "We are behind you. God be with you. Mimi has heard and wants to know what she can do to help. I am a first cousin of her late mother. It was I who first told her about you."

It was not signed, but I knew the handwriting from several applications which the sergeant had written asking for my comments and help.

"So that was what she meant when she said she had heard about my good deeds from others," I thought. That note was like a shaft of light in the darkened room of my life at that moment. It gave me an inner warmth and calm, and I felt gratitude to the guard.

I tore a piece from a page of the magazine and wrote: "Thanks. Don't say anything about her to anyone. Tell her I am okay." I folded the piece of paper and told Dima I was going to the toilet.

"I have to go with you," he said. "No offense. Just standard police procedure."

"Oh, don't be ridiculous. Call the guard outside and tell him to show me the way. He can wait outside the toilet if you wish. I am not going to hang myself." Dima agreed reluctantly and called the sergeant. I placed the note in his hand when Dima looked away, then followed him to the toilet. Actually, I did need to go. I remember I was thinking about a character in Arthur Koestler's *Darkness at Noon*. Before he was taken for interrogation that led to his execution he was advised to empty his bladder. He was thankful for that simple, prosaic act.

The red light on the Prime Minister's door went off and we were told to go in by a secretary.

I prepared to enter that room with which I had been familiar for so many years, like a stranger being introduced to a new place. I hesitated, conscious of the moral dilemma I had faced.

"After you," I said to Dima.

"No, after you."

"No, after you. Don't forget this is where I work," I said, adopting an air of nonchalance as if to warm up for the trial ahead. I followed him in and we were face to face with Prime Minister Akalu, who rose to meet us.

What a refreshing contrast to the stuffy and arrogant Zerfu! The Prime Minister came around the desk and sat on the armchair. We all sat, and Akalu took out his packet of Gauloise and lit a cigarette. He offered me one, but I declined.

"Now," the Prime Minister said, "I want first of all for you, General Dima, to repeat to Desta what you told me the other day."

Dima took out a black book from his small briefcase, and opened it at a place marked by a red ribbon. He cleared his throat and began speaking.

"First of all, your excellency, let me say that this is the finding of an investigation team. We think the finding and the concluding recommendations are supported by evidence. But a police finding is not the same as the verdict of a court of law."

"I know, I know. Go on," the Prime Minister said wearily. His face was the sad face I had seen the day after he was given a dressing-down by the Emperor following the motorcade incident a few weeks before.

"All right, sir. First of all, our agent who has penetrated the movement over a long time, has confirmed our suspicions about the extent of the underground, and some of its top leaders. I cannot reveal his identity, but your excellency has been informed about this and other related matters."

"General, please summarize, leaving the details for later, and come to the point concerning Desta."

"Yes, sir. Well, the essence of the case against Mr. Desta is that he has been, for some time, a leading member of the underground revolutionary movement dedicated to the overthrow of the government of the imperial system."

"Tell us, and tell him, what the evidence is."

"Well, there is no documentary evidence. That is something which we believe can be produced when Mr. Desta is interrogated. Your excellency's intervention has postponed that process. But we have the evidence of a witness, backed up by tapes of telephone conversations between Mr. Desta and other members of the underground."

"Is it lawful to tap people's telephones?" I interjected.

"Wait. You will have ample opportunity to raise questions," the Prime Minister said in a weary but calm voice. Thank God for this man, I thought—and felt more guilt at the same time.

"I can answer Desta's question," Dima said with pride. "The answer is definitely yes. This is not the United States or England. Even there, they use wire taps to track down criminal activities. It is up to the courts to accept or reject the evidence." He then continued his report.

The essence of the report was that for a least two years the security service had worked with the aid of Israeli intelligence gathering experts and surveillance devices, and established beyond reasonable doubt that I was a member of the underground. The Prime Minister did not indicate whether or not the security minister had alerted him to the suspicion, or if he had, how he had responded. That would remain a mystery for some time. But the Prime Minister did help in clarifying some questions, including the unspecified allegation that I was an accessory to Melaku's murder.

"That is still under investigation," Dima said when Akalu asked about it.

"What would be my motive for killing my friend, and if what you say is true, my revolutionary comrade?" I asked. The Prime Minister showed his concurrence with a nod.

"Perhaps you can answer that question yourself," Dima said to me, then turned to the Prime Minister to watch his reaction.

"That is one of the questions I have been waiting to ask Desta," the Prime Minister said. "If that can be proved, it would be indeed an unmitigated tragedy, and I could wash my hands of his case in good conscience."

"It is not true, your excellency. Why would I kill one of my best friends?"

"Let me say again what I told Zerfu and General Dima. My chief concern and interest is in the allegations that you have been a leader in the underground movement. When that question is answered we can turn to the other questions."

He then asked General Dima to leave us for a few minutes. The Prime Minister looked at me the way a concerned father looks at a son whom he knows to be guilty.

"Desta. Tell me, have I ever wronged you, or been unfair to you?"

"No, sir. On the contrary, you have been good to me."

"You have heard Dima's report. I want you to look me straight in the eye and tell me the truth. I can take it however much it may hurt."

"Yes, your excellency."

"Is it true, what they have said?"

"Not all of it, sir."

"How much of it is true? Which of it is true? Talk to me, man!"

I bowed my head in shame and kept quiet.

"Why, Desta? In heavens name, why?"

Tears started flowing down his cheeks. The sight of this good man crying, who had trusted me and defended me over the years, tore me apart. I cried too, not out of regret concerning my commitment to change the empire, but out of a sense of personal betrayal. It was a bittersweet feeling. There was an element of relief, that the moral questions which had tormented me were partially resolved. At the same time I felt sorry for this man, who had trusted me with many secrets and treated me like his son.

The Prime Minister took out his white handkerchief, wiped his face and blew his nose. He lit another cigarette and inhaled deeply.

"Don't you think I too want change? You should know me. You also know this country, at least I thought you did. It seems that I did not know you after all. I never thought that you, of all people, could be entrapped by the infantile rhetoric of radical students."

"I was a student radical, your excellency, before I returned from France."

"We are all radicals when we are college students. It is a stage in our lives. It is a rite of passage. But we grow out of it. 'When I was a child, I did childish things. But when I grew up into a man . . .'" he quoted Saint Paul, which surprised me. I never thought I would live to see the day when Akalu would abandon Voltaire for Saint Paul.

"What these students are demanding, and you with them it now turns out, will lead to nothing but disaster. They don't know the country. Evolution is the only way. Or, if it has to be a revolution, it has to be a controlled one."

He must have suddenly realized that he was overstepping the bounds of propriety. Why should he be confiding in me this way, after the way I treated him? After all, I had already betrayed his trust.

Akalu looked me in the eye and said: "I want to know from you two things. First, how much of the information to which you were privy as my principal cabinet aide has been divulged? Second, are you ready to confess and ask forgiveness?"

"The answer to the first question is that I have given very little information that would be of a security risk to the country or to you personally. What I provided were analyses of government policies and some facts and figures, none of them of a sensitive nature. And none of the information has been divulged beyond a narrow circle."

"Okay. What about the second question?" And he added: "Let me warn you that there are sharks out there. They have tasted blood."

I still needed his protection from the "sharks" who would only be too glad to get me. At the same time, I reminded myself that I should not relax my vigilance. I decided to answer his question with another question.

"Before I can consider confession, I need to know all the particulars of the alleged crime. Some of what I heard is not true. For instance, I did not kill Melaku."

"I know you did not. That was just to soften you up." Then he gave me more valuable information, wittingly or unwittingly, when he said: "Some of your fellow revolutionaries have been acting out a bizarre drama. Betrayal from within, not the vaunted surveillance, undid your unfortunate adventure."

I knew then that Aberra was the traitor, and a flash of anger must have been visible in my eyes. The Prime Minister gazed at me with curiosity. I thought of Melaku with vengeance in my heart.

"There is another thing," I said. "I know I am in no position for plea bargaining, but what guarantee do I have that a confession and petition for forgiveness would lighten my punishment."

"You have my word on that," he said firmly. "I cannot promise that you will be given red carpet treatment, but it is possible that you will be exiled in a province, under house arrest. The alternative, should you be obdurate, will not be pleasant, I assure you."

He then rang the bell and ordered that General Dima be brought back in.

"General Dima," he said, "Desta is contrite. He has confessed to his association with the movement. He was caught up in it and could not extract himself from it without endangering his life and family."

I was dumbfounded. This man I had betrayed not only forgave me, but was already trying to lighten my punishment.

The Prime Minister went on: "He assured me, and I have no reason to disbelieve him, that he gave away no government secrets of any consequence."

I was suddenly apprehensive that in order to be helpful he might even say that I was acting as double agent, informing on the underground. That I couldn't allow. I braced myself to deny it, even if it meant the "sharks." But fortunately, Akalu stopped short of that.

"I want you to prepare a confession, based on your report. Check it with Desta, have him sign it, and come back here tomorrow morning. Then we will go to the Emperor."

"Where will he stay meanwhile?" asked Dima.

"He can spend the night as your personal guest," the Prime Minister said. Turning to me he said, "I cannot authorize your return to your house. Some people are wild with anger already over your stay at a private guest house last night."

I bowed with deep gratitude in my heart, and left him. He followed my exit with the same sad eyes that had greeted me earlier.

EIGHTEEN

The memory of December 28 in the Imperial Palace is so vivid that when I think of it, it is as if it is happening now. I am sitting on a couch in the ante-chamber, waiting alone, observing the ebb and flow of the movers and shakers of the empire, as if for the last time before the curtain of life descends on me . . .

To enter the domain of the Imperial Palace is to pass through the looking-glass into a wonderland where appearance and reality are hopelessly mixed, where everything is topsy-turvy, and good and evil change places. In this imperial center, there are the few earthy types who do good within the limits of their power, whose heads have not been turned. And there are the many—far too many—who have forgotten their origins and shed their humanity, assuming the manner of petty gods . . .

Their behavior seems to me this morning particularly reptilian. Power has corrupted them absolutely. To curry imperial favor, they lie and cheat and sponge and spy and inform on people, including their friends and families . . .

I call them the *kerkedions,* because in Ethiopian mythology the *kerkedion* is a mythical rhinoceros-shaped minion of Lucifer. Most of these *kerkedions* are shabbily dressed, and their level of social awareness does not go beyond the point at which *homo sapiens* emerged. They are erratic and arbitrary. One minute they are smiling (or grinning, to be exact); the next minute they are heaping abuse or obscenities on some poor wretch who has strayed into their path . . .

No one speaks to me as I wait. I am not surprised. Last week I was somebody, a rising star in the empire. Today, I am a fallen star—ashes to be trodden under and spat upon. I am ignored or ridiculed in whispers. All this should amuse me, but I am also afraid . . .

It wasn't until much later in the day, when the traffic in the ante-chamber had thinned out, that I realized I had been waiting for eight hours. A stray minister who had just returned from a visit abroad saw me and rushed to greet me with open arms. Poor wretch, he was behind the news! The *kerkedions* looked at him with alarm, but he sat and kept me company, chatting about the latest fashions in shoes and ties! He laughed volubly, and created massive anxiety among the *kerkedions*. In doing that, he helped me more than he knew.

"Desta Kidane Wold!" cried the palace chamberlain. His voice echoed across the hallways, and my name was repeated by one of the *kerkedions* in the ante-chamber.

"Go on, don't just sit there! Move!" said the *kerkedion*. He came closer to push me (that is what they do to fallen stars) and I shoved him away, to the disbelief of those remaining in the ante-chamber. Before he had time to recover and strike me, I moved out of his jurisdiction and into the hallway leading to the Emperor's office.

I was stopped by one of the earthy types, who gently reminded me that running or fast walking was not allowed. He was a short, bald man (someone later remarked that most of the earthy types are bald, and joked that power did not go to their heads even thought their hair was making room for it).

My heart was beating hard and fast. I waited at the entrance; I could hear the Emperor's soft voice and other voices. Then the Emperor's *aide de camp* appeared from within and motioned for me to come forward. He was wearing a smile (a smile is a mask and a potent weapon in the palace). I moved forward through the red curtains and stood face to face with the Emperor, some ten meters away. The Emperor was sitting behind his desk, and the Prime Minister and the minister of security, Zerfu, were standing to his right.

The Emperor fixed me with a mildly amused stare. I had expected the burning glare of anger. What I saw encouraged me, and I switched my mind-set from the defiance I had silently rehearsed to one of deference and humility. (I must have been out of my mind even to consider defiance!)

The Emperor's gaze panned from my face to my feet like a movie camera. Then he turned toward the Prime Minister and prompted, "Yes?"

Prime Minister Akalu summarized the essence of the "confession" which General Dima and I prepared. Then, before Zerfu could spoil the game, he cleared his throat and made a final plea.

"Your Majesty," said Akalu, who loved Shakespeare as well as Moliere, "justice is best rendered when it is mixed with a quality of mercy. It has been said, and truly said by many foreign commentators, that Your Majesty's reign is distinguished from those of all your Illustrious Predecessors by the quality of mercy."

The Emperor nodded vigorously in approval, and Akalu continued:

"This young man has served his Emperor and country with distinction. But certain human weaknesses have caused a lapse. He lapsed into carelessness which I find to be not characteristic of this man. Once ensnared by evil company, he did not dare to cut loose and reclaim his honor and denounce the evil company. He stands before Your Imperial Majesty humbled, and begs for mercy."

The Emperor thanked the Prime Minister and cleared his throat to speak. I was relieved, because according to imperial etiquette, no one speaks after the Emperor. Zerfu cannot spoil the game after all, I thought.

I was mistaken. The Emperor asked Zerfu to speak next. My heart leapt to my mouth. I am finished, I thought.

"Your Imperial Majesty," Zerfu began, "The learned Prime Minister has summarized the case of Desta Kidane Wold fairly and competently."

What? Praised be the Lord! Was he agreeing with the summary?

"I have also reviewed the case with the help of General Dima and some members of my department. It is a very unfortunate case of a fine and promising young man led astray by doubtful loyalties to friends who did not wish him well."

"Hurry up," the Emperor commanded.

"I do not wish to repeat what has already been ably said by my brother Akalu. However, I think we need to emphasize, for the record, two important considerations in recommending mercy to Your Majesty. The first is that we should not be perceived as countenancing treachery in the ranks of our inner circle. That would be encouraging more treachery. The second consideration is the converse of the first; that is to say, we should not, by filing charges of treason in open court, reveal our weaknesses to the world. The most appropriate penalty therefore seems to be banishment to a distant province, where the offender will have no contact with other would-be offenders and where at the same time he can do penance."

As Zerfu finished his speech, I was wondering what had happened since yesterday morning, when he was after my blood. Why had he changed his mind? I was, of course, glad to learn he had moderated his views, especially since I would be under his ministry's jurisdiction if exiled. Much of my welfare (or its lack) would depend on his good will.

I felt sure, knowing his hostility to the Prime Minister—and to me— that no one except the Emperor could have persuaded him to come to his present views. And why, you may wonder, did the Emperor favor banishment instead of severe punishment for such treasonable acts as I had confessed to have committed? The Emperor was a consummate politician who knew how to use errant subjects to his advantage. Many were the men who had collaborated with his enemies and then been forgiven, or at least shown mercy. Their past sins make them more obedient servants. It was part of the imperial *modus operandi*.

However, the Emperor's motive did not matter to me at the time. Only the content of his verdict did. And the verdict was, as recommended, banishment to a province.

"Very well, then," the Emperor said finally, after exchanging a few words in whispers. "So be it."

He then turned to me and assumed a scolding frown.

"As for you," he said, "you have been a disgrace. You have disgraced yourself, and nearly brought disgrace on a man who had trust in you. You betrayed trust and peddled in the cheap marketplace of subversive politics. You were entrusted with unique responsibilities and given rare privileges flowing from the only legitimate source sanctioned by Almighty God. You were graced with our favor, basking in the sunshine of our glory and the warm comfort of your home. Why you chose to debase all those blessings is beyond our comprehension. Why did you stoop so low?"

It was a rhetorical question, and as the Emperor paused for theatrical effect, all present gave varying sounds of appreciation of his majestic eloquence. Neither he nor they expected me to answer the question. I simply bowed my head and stood meekly.

"The devil has many ways of tempting good people and leading them astray. He filled your heart with pride and arrogance and promised you the world. Well, the world he promised you is a denial of the good things that lie in loyalty and trust and truthfulness."

He paused as the clock chimed, and then gave the finale.

"You must exorcise the devil! In former times traitors and offenders like you were burnt at the stake. But we are a civilized and modern nation. Nevertheless, you must do penance and exorcise the pride and arrogance that twisted your heart. We forgive you and we hope that God will forgive you. Now go. Get out of Our sight!"

His last command hit me like the blast of a percussion instrument. I turned to go, and the *aide de campe* rushed to push me down by the shoulders, whispering: "Bow!" I slipped and fell flat on my face, and the Emperor's chihuahua came barking and stood on me, until the damned thing was taken away by the *aide de campe*. The Emperor could hardly repress a chuckle and his ministers broke into broad smiles. There was a popular belief that that the Emperor's dog could spot his enemies in any crowd. He carried it with him, until a bigger canine inhabitant of the palace killed it in a fit of jealousy. (An Imperial veterinarian later told me that he saw ministers weeping at its burial.)

So ended my last audience with His Imperial Majesty. I was led out of the office through the ante-chamber, and out into a security van which was waiting to take me away to an unknown destination on the periphery of the empire I had simultaneously helped rule, and sought to help transform.

Part III

BANISHMENT

NINETEEN

I was kept ignorant about my place of banishment until the last minute—until I got there. That was part of the punishment. They kept me in the dark and did not allow me to say good-bye to my family. That was also part of the punishment.

There was nothing remarkable about the journey except the severe discomfort. My body ached all over after traveling all night in a closed van. You see, once the security service took over the control of my life, all the niceties and courtesies to which I had become accustomed were thrown overboard. I had become a non-person. I was not exactly a nobody to be thrown about like a sack of potatoes. But I was not somebody of consequence either. There was no Akalu or Yohannes to cite the Geneva conventions on my behalf. Nor could I.

Speaking of Yohannes, I learned later that all my fellow Central Committee members, except Aberra, were arrested after my case was disposed of. Aberra was smuggled out of the country to a post-doctoral program in an unspecified university abroad. Melaku's girlfriend disappeared from the scene. Opinion was divided on her fate. Some speculated that she joined the student underground under a new name; others said that she was a government agent and was also smuggled out of the country.

When I was taken out of the van in the morning, after a sleepless night's journey, it was good to breathe the fresh air and stretch my limbs. Although my cramped condition in the van was painful, I did not forget that the alternative could have been the torture chamber. I was still suspicious and kept the cyanide tablets. Those tablets gave me a feeling of security, a sense of control over my fate. This sense of control is very important when one is in detention.

We stopped outside the gate of a large compound in what looked like a nice little town. The town was dominated by a mountain range to the east. Another mountain range lay some distance to the south; and beyond a wide green valley to the west, I could see yet another chain of mountains.

We entered the compound through a narrow gate and I saw a row of simple buildings no larger than sheds. On one side, standing by itself, was a larger guardhouse. The leader of my escort team, whom I had not seen all the way in the journey, led me to a rough-hewn bench and told me to wait while he went into the guardhouse. He was courteous but firm and did not engage in small talk. I sat on the bench, while my two other escorts stood nearby.

A uniformed policeman emerged from the guardhouse with three glasses of tea on a brass tray. That was the biggest surprise of the whole journey. He gave us the tea and went back in. I had a couple of sips and looked around.

"Where are we?" I asked.

One of my escorts, who had sat beside me crooning popular songs most of the journey, laughed and addressed his colleague. "These people don't know their own country." he said. "Yet they act high and mighty and lecture us on everything."

His colleague did not laugh; instead he gazed at me with curiosity and drank his tea with noisy gulps.

"Do you know Gonder?" I asked the crooner.

"No. Why do you ask?"

"Would you know where you were in Gonder the morning after you were taken there in a closed van?"

The other man laughed and said, "He got you there." The crooner moved a few steps away and started looking at the mountains, as if to find an answer from them.

"You are from Gonder, aren't you?" the quiet man asked.

"Yes."

"I know it. It is beautiful. I am from Tigray."

"Is that so?" I said with interest, knowing from experience that people from that northern region generally tended to be well-disposed towards Gonder. I felt a warmth inside me. It is interesting how loyalties shift to regional origins, when the bonds that hold the center are loosened and things fall apart.

"Yes. This place is on the outskirts of Assela, the capital of Arsi," he said.

"Thank you," I said and finished my tea in silence.

"You'll get used to it. It is not so bad. It is no Gonder, but the people are nice."

"The people?"

"The country folks."

"Am I going to be in their custody, then?"

The man smiled, revealing a gold tooth. "You never know," he said withdrawing into caution.

"Yes. I never know. And that is exactly the point of it, isn't it?"

He did not answer me. But there was a barely perceptible smile, which I read to say: "Well, at least, you are aware of an important fact about crime and punishment in Ethiopia."

The chief escort emerged from the guardhouse and gave a sign for me to go inside.

Meet Major Gashaw!

I was now, I discovered, in the custody of the provincial security, sitting face to face with an affable major.

"Your name?" Major Gashaw asked, writing in a file.

"Didn't they tell you?" I said, forgetting my dramatically altered status.

The major gave a soft chuckle while continuing to write. "It is my job to record everything. Standard security procedure," he said, laughing again.

Where does all this laughter come from? I wondered, studying his impassive face. And why is he laughing?

Gashaw was the chief of the provincial security. He was trained in Israel. He was acting this morning as the chief recording officer of the security archives. He seemed to enjoy knowing every detail about people, including their intimate personal lives and habits.

"You are a historian, I know," he said. "I love history. Perhaps you can organize history classes for us. Some of my colleagues are dreadfully ignorant about history." And he laughed.

"There is no worse fate than teaching history," I said laughing in my turn. But mine was a hollow laughter.

"Ah! Witty too. I like witty people. Me, I am not witty. But I enjoy wit." More laughter.

"Educational background?" he inquired in his best bureaucratic voice. "You were a student in . . . er . . . the Sorbonne, wasn't it?"

"Yes, the Sorbonne. Do you want me to start from there and work backward to my first grade schooling?"

"Yes, please. I love working backwards. And be as detailed as you can. You see, we in the police are trained to observe and note details that others may think are irrelevant or immaterial."

I told him about my education in France, and at the University College of Addis Ababa before going abroad, and before that in the secondary and elementary schools in Gonder. He intervened several times to ask questions to clarify obscure points . . .

Meet Major Gashaw. I mean really meet him.

There is more than meets the eye. The affable manner and incessant chuckling mask one of the keenest minds in the government.

His volunteering to go through the bureaucratic "standard procedure," doing the work of a junior archivist, reflects a devotion to duty rare in this kind of work; a diligence that borders on obsession. If he were an evil man (an imperial *kerkedion*) I would tremble.

But Major Gashaw is not an evil man. At the same time, he is not soft-hearted. He is a complex man who enjoys his work and does not allow himself to make mistakes, even while staying alert for the personal advantages that may present themselves in the course of his work.

After a hard day's work at the office, consisting of interviews (read *interrogations*) and reviewing of files, Gashaw drives home in his prized possession, a Toyota Corona. After dinner at home, he habitually goes to the Rosa Hotel, where the local grandees and businessmen congregate for gossip and card games, over beer or scotch.

He practices karate three times a week at the police club, and plays tennis every Saturday. He also runs a farm through a local agent just outside Assela, where he was born.

He is a fascinating mixture of modern enterprise and feudal charm— of which he has plenty. He is always perfectly groomed, from the point of his vaselined hair to the tip of his polished shoes. He is of medium height, fairly good-looking with a full head of hair and a bushy moustache. He leads an organized life evenly divided between work and pleasure. He rarely complains, and does not blame people or apologize. He is always smiling.

At the age of thirty-eight he seems to be a perfectly contented officer and gentleman. Is he for real? I am still wondering today.

How did I know all these things about the man and why am I spending so much time describing him, you may wonder. Well, to start with, Gashaw, like the *kerkedions,* leaves a vivid impression on the mind (though not for the same reason). Also he was an important link in the chain of command that ruled my life in exile. He, the governor-general of Arsi, and the judge of the high court of Arsi met once a month to review security cases. His reports and recommendations were rarely, if ever, contested by the other two.

And now for the other two . . .

Meet Governor Damtew and Judge Mengesha. They are both middle-aged men in their late forties. The governor, a slow-moving, slow-talking man of little education, represents the imperial dignity. He presides over all state ceremonies and sits on a replica of a throne. That throne, and the imposing little palace where he resides, are sources of immense pride for him. His conversation invariably leads to them; it is his way of reminding others that he is the little emperor in the province. Gashaw, who has a keen insight into the governor's character, plays on those symbols of authority and flatters him shamelessly.

Judge Mengesha is of a different breed. A church-educated, devout and literate man, his kingdom is not of worldly things. He likes to argue about legal and theological doctrines, demonstrating a firm grasp of both. He has a felicitous style of marshalling his arguments, courteously but tenaciously. I like him. (I liked him. Alas! He is no more.)

At the time when I was brought in to meet these three most important people in my life (or, at least, in my exile), I had already been in Assela six months. The meeting was, on the face of it, "standard procedure," a six-month review of a case. But the subject does not have to be present in ordinary circumstances. Apparently, someone had decided that my case was not "standard" and perhaps curiosity prevailed.

At any rate, when I was taken to the governor's office, it was a welcome change from the boredom and isolation that had descended on me. For six months, time had seemed to stand still. The events that regulated my day consisted of waking up at daybreak, aroused by the singing of the birds. Then there was breakfast, which consisted of tasteless porridge and bitter tea. I couldn't complain, and I didn't. I could come out of my room and sit, and walk within the confines of high walls. Lunch was served erratically, sometimes at about one o'clock, sometimes much later. Then came dinner after dark. The same tasteless, rubbery food was served for lunch and dinner. On Sundays, I was given one banana and sometimes an orange.

And I ate alone. All the time. No letters or messages were allowed in or out. I had nothing to read: no books, no newspapers, and no papers or pencils for writing. And . . . Ah, well! Six months is mercifully short, I was to be told by the governor-general, who said he had witnessed far worse fates in banishment procedures.

Six months of solitary confinement affects your consciousness. My confinement was mitigated by the presence of nature around me. I could hear the song of the cuckoo at all hours of the day. At dawn the hush of night was broken by the first sweet sound of a single bird, followed by a chorus of birds announcing their presence in their domain of the trees and the skies, their enchanting celebration of life.

The birds cheered me, almost making up for my lack of human company. At times I thought their chorus mocked me for feeling depressed. A film I had once seen, "The Bird Man of Alcatraz," came to mind, and I reminded myself that my predicament paled in comparison to the fate of the man serving life at America's most brutal prison.

During my waking hours I was sometimes transported to my youth in Gonder. At other times, I thought of Paris in the spring and the Bois de Boulogne. It was at night, when I lay awake in the dark, that I thought of Addis Ababa—of Hanna and Lemlem, of my friends, and above all of Mimi. And very often, I thought of revenge—of sweet revenge for Melaku's murder and for my own plight.

During the day I walked in the compound and exercized regularly. Or I sat in the sun, dozing. I once broke out into a cheery song, much to the surprise of the guard who must have thought I had gone mad. But he did not return my embarrassed smile or ask what the song was for. He had his orders. I was not to be spoken to.

My residence was a small room, three meters by four, with no window. My bedding consisted of an iron army bed, a stinking mattress, two rough sheets and a blanket.

I washed the sheets, my only shirt and underwear once every two weeks. The soap was given to me by a young police guard, along with a pail of water and a metal barrel cut in half which served as a basin. The guard took away the bar of soap with the basin; I had to chip off and save small pieces for washing my hands and face every morning.

I did not know where the food was cooked. It was brought from outside. My guard never spoke to me except to knock at my door to say "it is late" in the morning, or to grunt when I told him "toilet time" twice a day. I was led to the open air outside the compound.

I did not have any shaving things, no razor blade, no soap. When I appeared before the governor-general, therefore, I had a six month old beard.

"My goodness!" Gashaw exclaimed. "Professor, you have been transformed into a veritable monk."

"You mean the beard? Well, I am doing penance," I said. "If not ashes and sack cloth, at least a beard must do to show that I am repentant."

I smiled as amiably as I could, for I suspected that "good behavior" was a factor in determining the outcome of a review.

The governor-general and Judge Mengesha examined my appearance, momentarily interrupting their reading of what I assumed were copies of Gashaw's report on my situation.

"He looks fine to me," Judge Mengesha said. "It is becoming to wear a beard. And very time saving."

"Yes, very becoming," said the governor-general, who must have had in mind the Emperor's world-famous beard. The governor-general then returned to his reading. He was a very slow reader. It was at least another quarter of an hour before he finished.

"Please sit down, your excellency, I mean professor . . ." The governor-general lost his grasp, then regained it and said: "Please have a seat."

Gashaw's reference to me as "professor" had confused the governor-general. And his slip of the tongue calling me "your excellency" was by force of habit, for the governor-general had been to my office a few times pleading to see the Prime Minister, and I had helped him when I could.

I took my seat in front of the three provincial authorities. Gashaw had a file opened on the table in front of him and a small black book beside it. The governor-general had a notebook and an array of pens on his table. Only Judge Mengesha sat there without papers. The judge studied me. He had a pair of eyes that seemed to penetrate like X-rays. He wore a small goatee which he stroked constantly when he was not speaking.

"Is your beard grown by choice or because you have no shaving things?" the judge asked.

"Not by choice," I said.

"Do I take it then that if you had the necessary things, you would like to shave it?"

"Yes, your honor."

The judge turned to the governor-general and asked, "Are we ready?" The governor-general turned to Gashaw and asked, "Are we ready?" Gashaw said, "Yes, sir, I am ready to begin my report."

"Mr. Desta," the governor began. "We have brought you here to review your case. According to standing instructions issued in a ministerial circular, such review is made every six months. Ordinarily, only the file is brought before this special committee for review. But in your case, it has been suggested that you should appear in person to answer a few questions. You will do that I hope after the report is read."

He looked at the other two for any additional remarks. There were none, and Gashaw began reading a long report which summarized the reasons for my exile, his interview, the weekly reports on my "activities," and his own opinion. I realized at that point that it was Gashaw who had recommended my personal appearance, because it was his "considered opinion" (he said) that I had shown model behavior and that further incarceration was not justified. Indeed, his report stated, a man such as I could benefit the local community by mixing with them and helping in local affairs—under supervision, of course.

When he finished, he smiled broadly and handed a carbon copy of the report to the governor-general.

"Any questions from the panel?" the governor asked.

"Yes, just a couple of points of clarification," the judge said. "Mr. Desta, would you say that the report is fair and accurate?"

"Yes, your honor, I think it is fair and accurate."

"Would you also say that an involvement on your part in some local activities would be a good thing? If so, what kind of activities can you see yourself being engaged in?"

"I would welcome an opportunity to serve the local community in any way that is within my capabilities and where there is a need for my services. Beyond that, I cannot presume to say what I can or should do."

"Very well said," the judge concluded and resumed stroking his goatee. He had an ascetic face, almost emaciated, which enhanced the effect of his sharp eyes.

"Major Gashaw, do you have any questions or remarks to address to Mr. Desta?" the governor asked.

"With your excellency's permission," Gashaw began, "I would like to suggest to Professor Desta that he might consider teaching some of the provincial personnel who are able and willing to learn. I made the suggestion to him when we first met six months ago, and I think it would be a pity if such learning and experience possessed by Professor Desta were to lie unutilized."

Major Gashaw laughed and turned to the judge, who seemed to be intensely interested.

"You see, your excellency . . . your honor," Gashaw continued, "I hate waste. There is much that some of us can learn from the likes of Professor Desta. I mean, it is not often that we have such people in our midst." And he laughed again.

"Mr. Desta, what do you say?" the governor asked.

"I would be delighted. But perhaps we need to discuss the details of the curriculum and related matters."

"Of course. As long as you are favorable to the idea," Gashaw said.

I was surprised and elated. But I did not want to show it.

"May I suggest that his honor, the judge, join us in preparing the curriculum?" I said. The judge looked surprised and he demurred, but only out of the traditional need to show humility.

"I think that is an excellent idea. The judge loves talking about ideas," Gashaw said.

It was agreed. Then came the real surprise.

"And now you are all invited to lunch in my humble house," the governor said, with breathtaking modesty.

The governor's wife stepped out of one of the several doors of the house to greet us in the large reception room. She looked like a movie star come to make a film in a distant African location. She sounded like a movie star, and she had the clothes and the carriage of one. She was young and beautiful with a marvelous walk that told you she knew she was beautiful. With her copper skin and black hair, she looked like a perfect mannequin for the Christian Dior or Marcel Rochas gowns and jewels she wore. She might have been described as looking like Lena Horne in her youth.

Was it my beauty-starved senses? No, she was there, she was real. I heard her voice and shook her soft hand. It was obvious to me that her husband, who was almost twice her age, was proud of her and spent a great deal of money on her clothes and jewelry. Well, he had to pay some price to keep such beauty in distant Arsi. He asked her to show his guests their little palace, and we were conducted on a tour. The others had probably seen it all before, but they joined in.

The governor's residence was a two-story rectangular building inside a large compound with a big garden. The garden was full of flowers including roses, carnations and hibiscus. The walls were covered with bougainvillaea. There was a large dining hall for ceremonial occasions, a smaller dining room and waiting room, and a larger reception room and office. We did not visit the kitchen which lay outside the main house, adjoining the row of low-ceilinged servants' quarters.

It was said that when the governor's wife gave parties, there was always a good mix of people and good food. On this, my first occasion, there were only five of us, but the food was good. Before lunch, we were served cocktails on the outside terrace with a magnificent view of the town, the green valley, and the blue mountains beyond.

During the conversation over lunch, she was a good listener and spoke very little, urging others to do the talking while she presided over the service. Curiosity was consuming me. I wanted to know who she was, where she came from, what grade she had reached (that wretched habit of educated classes again!). I hoped that she or her husband would say something to enlighten me on these matters. But the only fragment of information that came up during lunch was that she had been in Paris last spring, following a pilgrimage to the Holy Land. That gave me the cue to ask her how she liked Paris.

"Oh, I loved it!" she said.

"She spoke about that trip for a whole month," her husband said.

"I still talk about it. But alas! It was too short."

"It was too long for me," the governor said in the only possible way he could publicly confess his love. Being a traditional man, he did not openly avow such sentiments which were considered unmanly.

"The professor stayed many years in Paris," Gashaw said.

"Really? How lucky you are. What were you doing?"

"Studying."

"I envy you," she said.

Her husband ordered more wine, and the servants brought chianti. As I sipped the wine I thought of the abrupt transition of my status from a prisoner in a dismal little hut to a sumptuous dinner with the Emperor's representative. The beautiful woman sitting as hostess was the equivalent of the Empress, and I was eating at her bountiful table. Where was this going to end?

My thoughts were interrupted when we moved to the salon to have coffee. The governor's wife was away supervising the servants. Judge Mengesha thanked her and her husband profusely for a wonderful lunch. Gashaw did the same.

"No one can be more thankful than me, your excellency," I said to the satisfied governor.

"Not at all, professor," he said, adopting Gashaw's favorite word. "And now there is this matter of your lodging. Major Gashaw had made some arrangements."

"Yes, professor," Gashaw said. "We have secured approval for you to move to a better residential quarters in the city. You can move tonight if you wish."

Coffee was over by three o'clock. Time for going to the office.

"Thank you again, your excellency and madame," I said to the smiling couple as I took my leave with Gashaw.

"We will see you again," she said.

"There is one question that has puzzled me, Major," I said to Gashaw as he drove me to the prison compound. "I know you are the architect of the change in my status. Why have you done this?"

"Wait a minute. I ask the questions," he replied laughing. "Remember, I am the policeman."

"No, seriously, I am grateful and I will not forget this. It is just curiosity, the curiosity of a historian."

"Well, I have had a helping hand. In fact, many helping hands. You are a popular man and have more friends than you know."

"You have evaded my question. But I am not complaining. On the contrary, I am grateful. I also realize that in your kind of work, caution is the first principle."

He just smiled and drove on. We reached our destination. He waited for me outside while I went in to pick up the few things I had in my prison cell, most notably my reversible London Fog raincoat.

TWENTY

The next morning Major Gashaw placed a medium-sized plastic sack on my dining table. He had settled me in a modest but comfortable house with a man-servant to act as my cook, housekeeper, and (I presumed) "guardian angel." That was the term we used to describe security agents working undercover.

"I kept all this for you until proper authorization could be given for you to read it," Gashaw said.

I opened the sack and books, magazines, newspapers and letters fell out. I sorted it all, putting the books and magazines on one side, the newspapers on another. I then shuffled the letters like a pack of cards and arranged them in their order of priority. I searched in vain for one with Hanna's handwriting. I was waiting for Gashaw to leave before reading them.

"Well, I'll see you later at the office," he said, finally. "We have much to discuss. And now I leave you to read your letters."

He stopped at the door and turned to face me again. "In case you are wondering. None of the letters have been opened. Word of honor. That is one thing I have never done or permitted, believe it or not."

"I believe you," I said. He left closing the door behind him.

I opened all the letters before I read any of them. There was nothing from Hanna. There were five from Mimi, one from my niece, and several unsigned letters from well wishers, including two in French and one in English.

Six months of altered consciousness had left its mark. Strange as it may seem, I was neither disappointed nor sad to find that Hanna didn't write. Of course, I was dying to know how she was coping and how Lemlem was feeling. But I knew that the extended family, one of Africa's unsung blessings, would provide a safety net for both of them. In times of distress—death, divorce or any separation—the uncles and aunts, brothers and sisters, cousins and nieces, immediately step in to help the affected family, fulfilling the material and emotional needs.

I glanced at Mimi's letters, beginning with the first and then the last. I wanted to read them later in the evening and savor every word; for now I read only the opening and closing paragraphs. She was discretion itself. No one but the most sensitive reader could guess that they were love letters.

Among the other letters, I was particularly intrigued by one in English, signed "an admirer from Gonder." It was written in a humorous vein, but there was a certain tension beneath the humor. I soon guessed that the author was the young Peace Corps woman I had met at the hotel over breakfast. She wrote:

"Dear Mr. Desta:

"During the Ethiopian Christmas break, I decided to spend some time in Addis Ababa and called at your office. I was told that you had gone away to a distant land. When I mentioned this to an American friend who knows your language better, she said 'going away to a distant land' can mean that you had passed away, gone to meet your Maker! I was saddened beyond belief. But I was not satisfied with her version, so I made further inquiries and was told by someone who was well informed that you were one of His Majesty's guests in a remote prison . . .

"Further research revealed the place of exile and I have taken the liberty to write you, hoping that this letter would reach you and find you in good health and spirits.

"Our brief encounter in Gonder and what I heard and read about you impressed me so much that you have become one of my heroes. There is no getting away from it. You are stuck with this admiring fan. And I am going to do everything that I can, which may not seem much to you, to see that justice prevails in the near future. I have adopted your cause. I have written to Amnesty International in London and to the International Commission of Jurists in Geneva, and to other human rights organizations . . .

"My first and most important demand is that you are not physically harmed. The second is that you must be allowed visits from friends and family. The third and long-term objective is to secure your release."

She went on to give details, but she kept her identity secret to avoid expulsion from the country. Even among her American friends, only a trusted few knew what she was doing, because if the American Embassy found out about it she could be sent back.

What surprised me most in her letter was the extent of her knowledge of the student movement and other revolutionary activities. I learned from her that during my six-month absence there had been more student demonstrations and riots. One of them was particularly grave. The students had demonstrated to protest the secret assassination of a student leader, and the police had opened fired, killing and wounding many. The university was closed and high school students boycotted classes in sympathy strikes. The momentum was increasing and the government had become more repressive. The Emperor had lost his legendary calm and in his nationwide address had used unseemly language. "He was almost without clothes" (the letter said), referring to the story of another king in another era, real or mythical.

I was excited and infinitely grateful to this wonderful, crazy (wonderfully crazy) American woman.

I then had a quick look at some of the press clippings and magazines. One headline read, "Amnesty International Takes up Mr. Desta's Case as a Prisoner of Conscience." Another one read, "Exiled Minister Said to be Secret Revolutionary Leader." This latter article was fantastically wrong, suggesting that I was China's agent in Ethiopia and that I had secretly visited Peking and met Chairman Mao.

That is the press for you. A mixed blessing.

The letters in French, which I read last, were from two different sources. Both were signed, but I did not know the names. One was very personal and emotional and promised to mobilize support in French government circles to help secure my release. It indicated that the Prime

Minister was *au courant,* discreetly informed by the French Embassy. The other was equally intriguing. It placed my predicament in a historical perspective and urged me to be consoled by the knowledge that I was part of momentous historical events, making reference to the French situation on the eve of the Revolution. It urged me to turn my exile to advantage, to study the peasants in the countryside, and so forth . . .

One of the books was a short history of the French Revolution, which I assumed was sent by the author of the second letter. Another book, on Catherine of Russia, was also in French, presumably from the same source. The books in English were works of literature, designed to help me pass my lonely days. I launched into these immediately and reserved the histories for later.

I was deeply grateful to the thoughtful people who sent all the books. But I wanted to know more about developments in Addis Ababa. I wanted to know how my comrades were and where they were detained. I felt it unfair that I would be the object of so much attention and concern, much as I welcomed and appreciated it. Perhaps Gashaw can help fill in the gaps, I thought, as I left my residence to go to the police club to meet him. I also hoped he would tell me something about my wife and daughter.

What a wonderful thing it is to have been a teacher! Wherever you go you find people who had been your students, some of them holding key positions, or the keys to important access. So it was at the police club at Assela. I was greeted by two smiling officers who had been my students at the police academy. When they saluted me the entire company of officers and men rose to follow suit. To be so treated the morning after walking out of a prison camp where you have spent six months as a non-person, is an experience barely short of a miracle. And a welcome one, I must say.

I did not bother to ask myself how they might have behaved the day before—before my return to personhood. It did not matter to me.

"Greetings, everybody. Well, well. Look who is here!" I said, shaking their hands.

"Nice to see you, sir. You have changed," one of them said.

"It has been quite a while. And now I have a beard," I said. I had decided to keep my beard as a memento of my days in isolation; and I had grown fond of it.

"Major Gashaw said he will see you at lunch time," said one of the officers. "He was called away by the governor-general on an urgent matter."

"So we can have a nice chat about old times," I said sitting on a chair in the officers quarters of the club.

"Can I get you tea or coffee?" asked the other officer.

"Coffee would be nice," I said.

During two hours of talk with the officers I learned that there had been several peasant uprisings in the Arsi area, following evictions by government-supported agribusiness development projects.

"So business is booming—I mean the police business," I joked.

"Yes, we are being kept busy," said one officer.

"I sometimes wonder why I ever chose to be a policeman," said the other.

"Nothing is easy, whatever your profession," I philosophized.

"Not like our profession," said the first officer, a captain. "Our choice is between the fire and the frying pan."

"I remember your lectures on the French Revolution," another said. "You said that progress is often accompanied by violence of one sort or another. You can see for yourself what has been happening and draw your own conclusions."

"But isn't agribusiness development part of the process of progress?" I asked.

"Well, if it is, then there is no justice in progress," said the captain.

"Surely, in the end, the increased income coming from these development projects will benefit everybody in one way or another," I said.

"How can it benefit the poor farmers after they have starved to death?" asked the captain.

"You have a good point. I'll have to see to be able to make a judgment. When can you take me there?"

"Anytime you are ready. Gashaw will have to give clearance, of course."

As if on cue, Major Gashaw rushed in, panting.

"I am sorry, professor. Urgent business kept me longer than I had planned."

"That is okay. I have been having an interesting chat with these former students."

"Oh, yes. They always talk about you. There are others too. You see, I knew about you long before we met six months ago." Gashaw joined us and asked for coffee.

"I am afraid that our discussion on the education project has to be postponed," he said.

"Trouble?" I asked.

"I have been summoned to Addis Ababa. I don't know the reasons. I will be away for a few days."

The captain told Gashaw that they had offered to take me for a picnic to show me the beauty of Arsi. Gashaw said it was a good idea. "But don't go too far," he warned. "There is talk about a peasant uprising spreading in the whole area. Take with you a company of policeman with enough arms. Perhaps you can do some hunting."

"I don't like hunting," I said.

"We'll teach you," said the other officer. "Before you know it, you will be a good shot."

I hated hunting as a sport, and I still do. But I did not want to spoil the chance of going on a small research expedition to observe the local scene. So I agreed.

"When are you leaving for Addis Ababa?" I asked Gashaw.

"This afternoon." He then asked to talk to me in private. The two officers moved to another table.

"I am not supposed to do this, but I'll make an exception in your case. If you wish to write a letter to your wife, I can see to it that she gets it; I can also bring one from her. Don't tell this to anyone."

"Thank you. That is very kind. I'll write a letter immediately."

"Please be quick. I have to leave before three. You can use my office to write the letter."

He led me to a private office in the officers section of the club. I wrote a long letter to Hanna. I expressed my surprise and disappointment that she did not write, and my hope that she was well. I did not dwell on the problems between us or ask her to forgive me. I begged her to write a few lines, if only to say that she was well and tell me about Lemlem. I told her of the change in my status and that I was being treated well. I sealed the letter and wrote the address of Alitalia on it.

"She works at the airline," I explained, as I handed the letter to Gashaw.

"I know," he said.

"Is there anything you don't know?"

"Many things. But this kind of information is part of the routine business of our work. Don't worry, I will take it to the office myself."

Then he left. It occurred to me that there was something about him that was missing. It was as if someone who had a moustache had shaved it: you realize something is gone, even as you wonder what it is. In his case it was not his moustache. I later realized that what was missing was his laughter. Major Gashaw had not smiled or laughed that day, for the first time since I had met him. Something was wrong, I thought.

TWENTY-ONE

I had never handled a rifle before. I owned a Colt .45 but had used it only once, for target practice. I had never killed a living thing. I tolerated the slaughter of sheep at Easter and other ceremonial occasions as something unavoidable, so long as I was not there to see the poor animal killed.

So imagine my horror when I was taken by the two officers on a hunting trip, properly attired for safari, including hat and camouflage chaps (as a defense against thorns and poisonous snakes). We set out in the morning, the weekend after our meeting at the police club. They were repaying me, they said, for the pleasure of my class. (I have always thought students exaggerate their teacher's performance; but you have to accept such compliments with grace.)

Our entire company of about twelve men seemed excited. I couldn't tell whether the excitement was in anticipation of seeing a city slicker shooting and missing, or whether they all loved hunting. I suspect they did love hunting; at least the two officers who had invited me did.

We set out in three Land Rovers, loaded with shotguns, ammunition, and cases of beer and food. The senior officer of the group, the captain who had been one of my students, sat with me in front and asked me how I felt.

"A little worried," I said. "I have never done any hunting. I always thought of it as barbaric and cruel. And here I am, going out to hunt."

"Don't you worry," he said. "You will like it. There are few things in life as exciting as the moment when the quarry you have been pursuing bolts out of hiding, and you fire away. You have to be very alert, ready to shoot again, because the animal may be only wounded, and there is nothing more dangerous than a wounded animal. That is the thrill of it. It is like an orgasm."

His face was flushed as he spoke, and the others approved, telling me: "You'll like it!" One of them, an older man, elaborated with a story of how he was once charged by a wounded boar, before he had time to reload his rifle.

"What happened?" one of the company asked eagerly.

"Well, the Good Lord was on my side that day. That's all I can say. There was another man beside me but he was unarmed; he was my boss. I tried to reload, and I couldn't. And all the time the bloody boar came charging, screaming like the devil—"

The officers all strained their necks to listen. The older man, a masterful storyteller, paused for effect.

"Don't keep us in suspense, sergeant. What happened?" said one of the men.

"Patience, my boy, patience. I thought it was curtains for me. I made the sign of the cross, ready to meet my Maker."

"And then? And then?"

"And then we were saved by a companion who saw the charging boar and shot it down. The good news is that he saved my life. The bad news is that he also saved my boss."

The men all roared with laughter.

We were on the road for hours. The road got steeper and steeper as we climbed a forested mountain. After crossing two small streams, we stopped at a clearing which gave us a lovely view of the eastern and southern area of the district. We had breakfast consisting of *fitfit* carried in an *agelgil,* a round basket made of hard straw and leather.

As we sat eating and drinking, the captain explained to me that the area where we were heading was not a wildlife reserve and the animals were not in their mating seasons, when they were protected. "So we can hunt with a clear conscience," he concluded.

"A clear conscience?" I queried. "You are saying that conscience is only a matter of regulations. To me it is not. I will not spoil your fun, but I'd rather you counted me out."

"Try just one shot, and see how it feels," he insisted. "There are wild beasts that are a menace to the local inhabitants, like hyenas and foxes."

"Well, maybe I'll have a crack at a hyena," I said. "I never liked hyenas anyway." They all laughed with relief. They seemed to be determined to initiate me into their hunting company.

"And on our way back we will see some development farms," he said, winking at me.

After breakfast we traveled another fifteen kilometers and entered a valley where we saw a wild herd of elephants.

"They are not for hunting," the captain said. "Although poachers are decimating them."

The company was ecstatic at the sight of the elephants. I could see from the look of some of the men that they would have gone on a killing spree, had they been by themselves. I was reminded of the saying that men like to destroy the things they love. This irony, it seemed to me, defines man's progressive despoliation of earthly paradise.

The beautiful sight of the elephants settled in my mind any question about hunting. Because I knew hyenas were nocturnal, I felt safe. Bring me a hyena, I said, and I'll shoot. But I will kill nothing else.

The company killed a couple of pheasants and one antelope. Satisfied with that modest harvest, they called it a day. We turned back and made a detour toward the agricultural development areas.

It was about four in the afternoon. The sun was dropping toward the western horizon. We saw a long trail of dust, partially covering an even longer line of people moving toward the south. The captain ordered the driver to stop and jumped out with his gun at the ready. He told the two drivers to move the Land Rovers behind a small hill

He left me with a loaded pistol and ran crouching toward a large stone nearby. He gave orders to a policeman who ran to the top of the hill. The policeman took out field glasses and surveyed the scene. He ran back to the captain and reported what he saw.

The captain stood up and walked back toward me, smiling. "Okay. At ease," he said to the relief of the company.

"What is it?" I asked.

"False alarm. We thought it was a rebel movement. They are people going on a pilgrimage to Sheikh Hussein, a famous shrine in the south. We are getting jumpy these days, because of the uprisings and rebel movements," he said apologetically as we climbed back into the Land Rovers.

We traveled for another ten minutes toward the pilgrims, who were crossing the land of one of the agricultural projects. There seemed to be no end to them. They walked in a single file which stretched as far as the eye could see in both directions. Most of them were elderly, both men and women. They carried their belongings in bundles on their shoulders or on their heads.

The captain ordered the driver to stop. He got out of the car and I followed him. I had heard of the shrine, but I had no idea that so many people went there. The captain addressed one of the pilgrims in the local language, which I did not speak. A group of the pilgrims stopped to listen to the conversation. Their faces were haggard and looked vacant.

"What did the old man say?" I asked the captain at the end of the conversation.

"I asked him where he came from. He said he came from Gefersa, a village not far from Addis Ababa."

"That is far," I said.

"He has traveled six days so far. And he said he was stopped on the way by the authorities who were looking for rebels."

The captain paused and was pensive. "I think some trouble is brewing. He said that the markets everywhere were empty. That is a sign of trouble."

"I understand," I said.

We scrambled back to the Land Rover and began our journey back to Assela. Some ten kilometers back north of where we saw the pilgrims, the hills opened up to a wide green valley bordered by a stream. I could see acres of cultivated land. I asked the senior officer the name of the place.

"The district is called Chilalo," he said.

"So this is Chilalo. I know about it from project documents at the cabinet office. It is beautiful."

"It is also controversial," the captain said. "This is what we were talking about the other day."

"You mean the eviction of poor farmers."

"Yes, farmers and herdsmen."

"But surely they have other areas they can use for farming and grazing."

"The other areas are less fertile. They are being driven from their fertile land."

"Did they own the land now being developed?"

"They had rights which nobody disputed. Of course, there are a handful of landlords who claim the entire province belongs to them," he said with mounting anger.

I could see that he felt strongly about the issue. I made up my mind to risk trusting him and find out more about the situation. This could be a model area for organizing the peasants to rise up in arms against the government. But I was going to take my time.

"In any case," I said, "title to land in these southern areas is a tricky thing, isn't it? I mean, the landlords have been there only a few decades at most, whereas the local population can claim ancient rights. Am I correct?"

"Absolutely. And no one even talks about that," the captain said.

"Are you from this area originally?"

"I am from another part. But my region of origin fares even worse than Arsi. At least here people from outside can come and report on what goes on. And the government . . ."

He stopped, realizing that the others were listening. "We can talk more about this in Assela," he said quietly.

"What is your exact position in the province?" I asked.

"I am district chief of police."

"Then I have come to the right place," I said. "It is better to be a guest in a district where the police chief is one's former student."

The captain laughed. "We will do everything we can to make your stay, shall we way, less unpleasant."

We reached the outskirts of Assela. The sun was on the horizon, and the ochre sky above the sunset tinged with crimson merged with the darkening mountains beyond the fertile valley. Shepherds drove their herds back to the villages outside the town. It was a peaceful evening typical of the African countryside. Here and there, groups of cattle grazed on the meadows watched by herdsmen standing in their midst, their silhouettes visible against the sunset. Dogs followed some of the cattle heading home, and parents called out the names of their children. I felt at peace with everything around me and with myself.

TWENTY-TWO

Two weeks passed, and there was no sign of Gashaw. I began to worry. Strange, isn't it? There I was worrying about a man who controlled my movements. I knew that this was a result of my new freedom and improved living conditions. Relativity assumed greater significance. It was in marked contrast to my attitude while I lived in isolation with the bare necessities of life. Those stark conditions had introduced a new dimension into my consciousness, a withdrawal and a dependence on spiritual resources. I had drawn on those inner resources as the body draws on fat to survive, becoming lean in the process.

During my imprisonment, I had gained a new insight into the process by which prophets and mystics acquire a higher (or at least a different) consciousness linking them to forces greater than themselves. Every person I have known who has spent any length of time in solitary confinement has conveyed a sense of serenity. I have spoken to South Africans who spent many years at Robben Island with Nelson Mandela. They all impressed me with this serenity, and with a capacity to be forgiving even of their monstrous captors and tormentors. My captivity was a picnic compared to theirs, but I learned to know and appreciate the inner spirit that guided their attitude.

A surprise visitor! And a most welcome one at that—Brigadier Iman, whom I found in the police club, surrounded by a band of admirers including the captain who had taken me hunting.

The officers must have known that the brigadier was a close friend of their boss, General Dima; this, in addition to their undisguised admiration, explained the unusual attention they were paying to him.

When he saw me he feigned surprise and exclaimed, "What on earth are you doing here?"

I knew he was playing to the gallery—to the ears of those whose job required them to report such meetings.

"Where did you think I was?" I rejoined.

"Paris, London, or some such place," he said.

"And what are you doing here, Brigadier Iman, hunting?" I asked.

"As a matter of fact, yes," he said. "Hunting and fishing in between official duties."

The captain whispered to another officer, at which point all but he left our table. He ordered beer for us and we settled back to hear Iman talk about hunting and fishing. Then he turned serious and told me that my friend the senior police officer was "one of us."

"That is how you have been spared the worse part of imprisonment," Iman added.

"I am very grateful," I said turning, to the district chief.

"I wish we could have gotten you out of the hole earlier," he said.

The captain left us alone for a while, and I asked Iman to bring me up to date on the political situation. He outlined the position of his followers in the army. They included the senior army officers and some majors, but excluding those who were tainted or hopelessly compromised. His followers were concentrated in the Third Division, which he had commanded. There were also some staff officers at the headquarters of the Chief of Staff and some ground forces in Addis Ababa.

"It is tricky, you understand," he explained. "One false move, one treacherous element admitted to the secret, and the whole plan would be in jeopardy. That would mean our necks. I am shadowed by the security people all the time. Even here I suspect that someone is following my movements."

"What about support from foreign powers?"

"My friends in various embassies and their contacts at the foreign office are aware of our plans."

"Does that include the British?"

"Yes. Especially the British. In my view the British are aware of the deteriorating situation here and are trying to disperse their eggs in different baskets. And my basket seems to be given the top priority. I am flattered, of course, and I will see what use can be made of this connection. But I am being cautious. So far they have been very helpful and encouraging."

"What kind of support can you expect? Let's say the student riots spread, joined by labor strikes and general public disaffection. And this is followed by paralysis at the center and rebellion in the periphery. What then?" I pressed.

"That is the most obvious scenario, and one which suggests a military coup," he said. "But the foreign powers are not convinced that an imperial government which is deeply embedded in the regional popular consciousness can be overthrown without a popular rebellion. The countryside would be opposed to the new military government."

"Do you agree with that?"

"Yes and no. If we prepare the ground properly, if the students and labor unions could be won over, the opposition could be crushed in a matter of days. The students have tasted power and they are becoming increasingly bold. I suspect your group was allied with them. You hinted as much to us last year."

"You are right," I said. "But there is no coherence in the student movement. Our group, which could have provided coherence and unity, has been decapitated. That is one problem I want desperately to discuss with you."

"You are wrong when you say there is no coherence in the student movement. There are factions within it, but sooner or later one faction will be dominant. The function which your group wanted to provide will be taken over by the student leadership."

"But a student movement is not a party," I said. "There is no disciplined leadership that can issue commands."

"I agree. That is where the armed forces come in. Even your group, with all due respect, left much to be desired, as we found out. The difference between the armed forces and your type of political move- ment can be summed up in one phrase: chain of command. Then, there is the critical matter of force. The army has the guns and is trained in the use of them. In a revolutionary situation, nothing can be achieved without the armed forces."

"But then it would be just another *coup d'état* and another military government," I answered. "We would have no guarantee of the fulfillment of revolutionary objectives, and no guarantee against a counter coup. Isn't that the problem facing much of Africa and the rest of the Third World?"

"That is true. I personally think the ideal solution in our case would be a joint effort between the armed forces and the civilian revolutionary movement," the brigadier said. "That movement should have a unified command comprising the students, labor unions, intellectuals and professional groups, and even some of the enlightened businessmen."

"Easier said than done," I said.

Our talk became a dialogue in which we considered different strategic options. We finally agreed that he would redouble his efforts (carefully!) in organizing officers in the armed forces, and that I would urge my group to intensify work among the student movement and exile groups abroad.

"But I want so much to get out of here," I said. "I want to go back *incognito* and revitalize our group."

"Have you thought of ways to get out of here?" Iman said, "One possibility is to escape to the north, to the Eritrean front."

"I thought of that. We have links with that movement."

"Good. We'll try to get you out," said Brigadier Iman.

It sounded easy. We were excited by the prospect of success.

After our talk, I wrote a long letter to Mimi and a short note to Hanna. I asked Iman to deliver the letter to Mimi by hand. I asked him to mail the note to Hanna, not knowing how she would react to him. I did not want to risk endangering his position or even his life, should Hanna report the communication. It may have been uncharitable on my part to imagine that she would do this, but recent events had taught me to exercise caution on all fronts.

Our parting words were short and to the point. "Remember, my friend," Iman said, "don't underestimate the enemy. This is a cardinal lesson in military science and in our case it extends to politics. A Chinese sage has put it this way: Despise the enemy strategically. Respect him tactically. Be bold and imaginative. But be vigilant."

I thanked him and said that his advice should apply to him more than to me, since he was in the front line of the struggle.

"We shall meet in victory," he said, ending our meeting abruptly.

He was a magnificent specimen of a man both physically and mentally. A man for all seasons, I thought, watching him go. My fervent good wishes went with him. As events would reveal later, much was to depend on him.

TWENTY-THREE

The teaching project was shelved until Gashaw's return. But the social gatherings at the police club, in which I was the center of attention, were becoming informal political seminars. Officers eager to learn more about world affairs asked me pointed questions about issues ranging from American elections to world peace to African politics. No one dared ask questions about current events concerning Ethiopia. I was grateful for this reluctance because it saved me the embarrassment of declining to answer on the grounds that it might incriminate me!

The captain Iman had called "our man" became my life-line with the world outside Arsi. As second-in-command of the district, he held the fort during Gashaw's absence. He had been slightly reserved before Iman's introduction, but he now surprised me with a gesture that amounted to comradeship. He asked if I would be his guest for dinner at the Rosa Hotel, which so far had been out of bounds for me. "There is good Italian cuisine," he said. "I think you need the change from the local food."

He also bought me a shirt. My only shirt had been worn out by weekly washing and the officer had observed that minor item. I was grateful and accepted both the shirt and the invitation.

Since the hotel was out of bounds for me, I wondered if the captain was taking a risk by inviting me; but I did not bother to ask him, for I welcomed the change. Being a product of Gonder, the first urban center in the history of Ethiopia since the decline and fall of the ancient empire, and having known Paris, London and Addis Ababa, I am essentially an urbanite. And hotels fascinate me as social centers.

The Rosa Hotel was owned by a northern businessman who employed a German manager to run it. I found out later that the German was a former Nazi officer who lived under a changed identity, and that the Israelis were researching his past. He later disappeared from the scene, probably tipped off by an insider in the local security.

That evening the German paid special attention to our table. He greeted the captain with exaggerated bows accompanied by grotesque compliments in the local language. When he spoke in the vernacular, the German made people laugh. The locals called him "doctor" because he procured all kinds of medicine which he claimed was supplied to him by doctor friends. I suspected he was acting as an unofficial agent for foreign pharmaceutical companies that were pushing their drugs on the African market.

The captain told me that the German was a bit of a Don Juan who had fallen victim to the beauty and charm of the governor's wife. He bought her perfumes and jewelry, which her husband did not mind. But when he began calling on her during office hours, on the pretext of showing her pictures in fashion magazines, he was told to stop. And he did.

Our waiter brought us the first course of spaghetti *bolognese* and the German followed carrying a flask of chianti, which he opened himself.

"With my compliments," he said.

"No. I insist on paying. This is my special treat for a special guest," the captain protested.

"Mr. Captain. This is nothing. Just a flask of chianti. Please accept. The house will be offended if you don't."

"Okay. We accept and thank you," I said in mitigation of the captain's embarrassment. The German beamed with a childlike joy and poured the wine, then went to attend to his other guests.

The restaurant was not full. There were some fifteen tables, occupied mostly by members of the local elite, with a few foreigners. Some of them were young Americans; I could distinguish their accents. They spoke loudly. At one point, the German bent over a young woman who pointed at us. He nodded vigorously as she whispered to him. By that time our second course had arrived. I chose *filetto alla griglia* with mashed potatoes and string beans. It was delicious, the more so because it had been months since I had eaten such delicacies.

The manager came to our table and handed me a note.

"There is a young lady who wants to talk to you," he said smiling and winking. "You are here one half hour and already you have made a conquest. Some people are born lucky. *Ja?*" His chest and shoulders shook when he laughed.

I read the note. What a surprise! It was my young Peace Corps guardian angel from Gonder. After I finished reading the note, I looked across the room and there she was, waving and smiling.

"An old friend?" the captain asked.

"An acquaintance," I said.

"Let's invite her to come over. Doctor, would you please be good enough to ask the young lady to join us," he told the German.

"*Ja, Ja.* I will do dat."

The German walked over and whispered in the young woman's ear. She got up, said something to her friends, and started toward us. She wore blue jeans and a white shirt that hung loose over her hips. I suddenly realized that I had forgotten her name. Names, Names! Remembering names was becoming a problem for me at the ripe old age of thirty-six. I hoped she would introduce herself to the captain and save me the embarrassment, particularly since she had taken up my case as a crusade.

"Mr. Desta! How wonderful to see you," she said shaking my hand. "I didn't recognize you at first. The beard has changed you. Oh my! It is great, I mean the beard."

"Thank you. Meet my friend, captain . . ."

"Captain Teferra. Pleased to meet you."

"Hi! Nice meeting you, captain. I am Gloria Sullivan."

Saved!

"Will you join us?" the captain asked.

"I'd be honored." She took a seat.

"This is good Italian wine," the captain said. "Would you like to try it?"

"Thank you, I will."

The captain ordered another glass. He then made the excuse that he had to attend to some business with the German, and left us. How accomodating the police were becoming! After he left, Gloria Sullivan said in a low voice: "It is so good to see you! I could not imagine how you would look after what they did to you."

"What did they do to me?"

"I imagined all kind of horrible things. I have been reading reports by Amnesty International. What people are capable of doing to their prisoners is incredible."

"It has been nothing like that, I assure you."

"Well, thank God! But of course there was no way I could find out."

"Tell me," I said, gazing into her hazel green eyes, "what have I done to deserve such kindness and attention?"

"You have become a cause for me. And there is no higher cause than justice. Did you get my letters?"

"Yes, I got all of them at the same time about two weeks ago."

"That's terrible. Don't they respect their own constitution?"

"We should be grateful when they do. How did you manage to come, and when did you come?"

"I came this afternoon. I have some friends who teach at a school in Assela. But wait till I tell you about my project."

"Project?"

"Yes, it is a ruse, but I am beginning to enjoy it."

"Tell me about it before the captain returns."

"Is he your guard?"

"More or less. But he is okay. They are all okay. So what is your project about?"

"There is a project within a project. I wanted so much to come and see how you were doing, and find ways of helping you. So before the end of the teaching season I applied to US-AID for some funds to do research in the Assela district. I chose Assela after I found out that it was your place of exile. I wrote a proposal on the role of women in rural development using Assela as a case study. In my application I told them my research will be in fulfillment of a requirement towards a

Masters degree in Rural Sociology. I wrote to my university in Pennsylvania and the dean, who knows me, accepted my application. It is nice to have friends everywhere."

"You're telling me!" I said.

"Anyway, to cut a long story short, US-AID in Addis Ababa accepted my project and agreed to give me a modest grant to do field research. This is my preliminary survey trip."

"You don't waste time, do you?"

"That is the outer project," she continued, ignoring my remark. "Now comes the inner project, the real thing. And that is you."

"Me?"

"Yes. I want to use the research project to be near you and consult with you and discuss ways of securing your release."

"You are not only energetic and determined, but resourceful."

"So what do you think?"

"I think it is extraordinary. I am flattered and grateful that you are taking all this trouble on my behalf. I don't know how I can repay this kindness."

"You can repay me by simply approving the project."

"You don't need my approval."

"Oh, yes, I do. I do. Are you going to approve?" she said with the eagerness of a child seeking a pat on the back.

"Of course I approve. Are you kidding? I not only approve, but I am thankful that this world has people like you in it."

It is difficult to describe the expression on her face when I said those words. Rapture comes nearest.

"You are imaginative in addition to everything else," I said.

"Yes, imagination is part of my armor, I have been told by my teachers. With an Irish father and an Italian mother, that comes easy."

"What a delightful combination. I like the Irish and the Italians."

"Delightful, yes. It can also be, at times, an explosive combination."

She then told me that she had funds for travel, accommodation, field assistants, materials collection, and an extra sum for "unforseen items." She asked if I knew of anyone who would be a good research assistant and interpreter. Finally, she asked if I was prepared to consider escape, if worst came to worst.

"Escape to where?" I asked her.

"Anywhere. To a neighboring country, to start with. Then we can go to the United States, if you wish."

"How? On what travel papers? Aren't you going too far?"

"I said, if worst comes to the worst. If there is any risk to your life, papers can be forged. I have friends who know how to deal with these things."

"Wait a second," I said. "Let's take things step by step. What you wrote in your letters about influencing international opinion is good. Let's work on that and see how things develop."

I did not want to appear ungrateful, but I had to bridle her fantastic imagination by concentrating on things that seemed feasible. Her breathtaking schemes and wild energy set off alarm bells in my mind. I even considered the possibility that she might be slightly mad.

Captain Taferra came back about an hour later and joined us. He told me if I wanted to stay on and chat with Miss Sullivan, I could do so. He would send a car to pick me up about midnight. I agreed and he left.

"You have really won them over, haven't you?" she said.

"Behind every policeman's badge, there lurks a human heart," I said, and she laughed.

"But some have stony hearts, I'll bet," she said. She grew serious and her voice dropped to a whisper. "If you want, we can continue our talk quietly in my room. I am staying in this hotel."

The alarm bell inside me rang again. "What about your friends?"

"Oh, I'll see them tomorrow. I am not married to them."

Perhaps she was slightly drunk. But there was an element of rashness in her, I thought. In the course of one hour she had told me her intricate schemes about my life, including a hazardous plan of escape. And now, to top it all, she was making what I considered to be sexual advances. Or was I jumping to conclusions—a typical male chauvinist, misinterpreting an innocent suggestion? Then again, what if she was making a seductive move? Why shouldn't she? Why should I mind, particularly since I had led a celibate life for over six months? Where was it written in the criminal code, I reflected with amusement, that exiled people could not have a fling if and when it became available?

"All right," I said, after such inner reflection. "I am ready whenever you are."

She was elated. "Let me say good night to my friends and make arrangements for seeing them tomorrow."

She got up and went to her old table. Her friends looked toward me with curiosity; one of them, a bearded man, even waved. I waved back. Gloria Sullivan put on her brown leather jacket and came toward me, smiling broadly.

Gloria's room was conveniently located in a cottage outside the main hotel. It was a conical thatched structure which had been added to the main building.

It had all the amenities of a modern hotel room, minus television. The age of TV had not reached Arsi yet. But there was a radio, and she herself had brought tape recording equipment for her research project.

The first thing she did, after asking me to make myself at home, was to select a tape and put it on the recorder. The sound of jazz filled the room, and Gloria Sullivan broke into dancing.

"Can I get you a beer, or a scotch. That is all I have," she said.

"I'll have a scotch, thank you."

She then excused herself and went to the bedroom. She came back wearing a long, loose African dress. She sat on an armchair.

"You probably think I am a crazy woman," she said.

"Did I give that impression?"

"Some people think I am slightly crazy. I guess I have to be crazy to do what I am doing."

"Is that a declaration or a confession?"

"You sound like a damned customs inspector," she said testily. "Let us be ourselves, for God's sake. Don't you trust me?"

"Let's say I trust you. Forgive me for sounding pedantic or even ungrateful. But what do you get out of all this? I mean, you hardly know me."

"Well, if you don't understand me after reading my letters, and after hearing me tonight, I doubt that anything else I say will help. Perhaps what I do will convince you."

She got up and walked about the room, then continued in a quieter tone. "I found you fascinating the moment we met in Gonder. I can't explain why. It is a fact."

"Well, I am flattered and most grateful," I said, changing my inquisitorial tone.

There was a momentary silence. She changed the music to Brubeck.

"I love Dave Brubeck," I said.

"Oh, so do I. You see, that is a good sign. At least we have something in common."

She sounded a little hurt, and sat in silence.

"So, where do we go from here?" I probed.

"Well, it is up to you, really." She gazed at me through her glass of scotch, then asked: "Has it been rough?"

"At first it was. The loneliness and not knowing what was going on outside. And no one talking to you."

"You poor man! I think I would go nuts in a week in solitary."

"I thought so too, at first. But after a while you adjust. And hope springs eternal, as they say."

"Yes. Yes. Oh, yes, you sweet, sweet man," she purred, coming over and sitting beside me on the sofa.

As I spoke about my experience, I felt the warmth of her body as she moved closer and closer. When I stopped speaking she put her arms around my neck and brushed my lips with hers. I yielded and kissed her hard until she moaned.

We released each other and I looked at her. "Did I hurt you?" I asked.

"No, it was delicious. Do it again."

"Do you believe in mixing business with pleasure?"

"Business? What business?"

"I am thinking of your project."

"Well, I am a liberated woman," she said with an air of defiance.

"And right now I have an intense desire to sleep with you. That is, if you want to."

Her defiance was emphasized by her snub nose, and her full lips tightened. Gloria Sullivan was no beauty. But she was an attractive woman in her late twenties with hazel green eyes, auburn hair and an engaging personality. The warm, seductive person that had emerged disappeared again, and her energetic half took over. I wondered whether the Irish or the Italian in her was in control of her mood.

"Are you a believer in women's liberation?" I asked.

"I have no old hang-ups, if that's what you mean. I don't believe in being coy and coquettish."

"Here in our culture," I said, "there is a certain decorum that goes with love-making."

"Am I pushing myself on you?"

"No. I didn't mean that. But I don't want to hurt you."

"What!"

"No, I don't mean physically. I am in love with someone, and I don't want you to feel . . ."

"I am a big girl. I can take care of myself. I was in love once. The bastard left me. But that was a long time ago."

"And have there been others since?"

"A couple. But not as serious as the first. Anyway, it is sweet of you to be concerned."

She got up and started walking slowly toward the bathroom door. "Don't go away," she said. "I'll be back in a jiffy."

That remark, accompanied by a modest attempt at coyness, was probably, I thought, the concession that she and other modern women in the United States made to decorum. And lo and behold! she came back naked carrying an orange towel over her left shoulder, covering one breast.

"God! Is this a new fashion. The hemline has disappeared," I said.

"I want you to see me in the nude," she said, walking over to me. She was tall and shapely, if a little on the plump side. She led me to the bedroom.

Afterward, I took a shower and then lay listening to jazz on the sofa with Gloria cuddled in my lap. A woman's presence can do wonders to release a man from tension. Already, the bitterness of isolation was behind me.

Yet, there was not that magic quality in it. When it was over my heart traveled somewhere else and Gloria sensed it as we lay on the sofa together.

I looked at my watch. "It is time to go. The captain said midnight," I said.

"I'll walk with you to the lobby," she said, putting her jeans and leather jacket on.

At the corner, before the entrance to the hotel lobby, she kissed me passionately under the cover of darkness. "I'll see you tomorrow?" she asked.

"Of course. We have much to talk about. I'll come to the hotel after nine."

"Okay. Good night."

"Good night, Gloria."

TWENTY-FOUR

Two more weeks passed. Major Gashaw did not return, but he sent me a note to tell me that he had personally delivered my letter to Hanna, and that she was all right. I was relieved.

But I had expected that hearing from me, she would write or even come to see me. I was beginning to get angry. In fact, I was beginning to hate her, although I was not willing to admit it.

Meanwhile the student movement had paralyzed the educational system. Class boycotts spread far and wide, reaching junior high and even elementary schools. Parents were confused, torn between two considerations. Most had sacrificed for the education of their children. The first generation of educated Ethiopians in modern times, that of the Prime Minister, and the second generation, my own, had achieved positions of prominence. People saw clearly that the key to such advancement was education.

On the other hand, many parents and community leaders were aware of the problem afflicting their society: rampant poverty, gaping inequality, corruption and injustice compounded by bureaucratic arrogance and incompetence. Now their children were not only speaking about these problems, they were proposing solutions. But the solutions they proposed were so radical that they worried most parents. So they begged the students to return to school

The students would bow their heads in deference to their elders and listen in silence in their homes. But when they met on the street corners or at other gathering places, their rebelliousness would be reinforced.

The problem facing the government was not one that the usual sanctions could resolve. What do you do with students who refuse to go to classes? You can't detain hundreds of thousands of young people. Not only would that present a logistical nightmare, it would leave the parents aggrieved. Far from being a solution, it would compound the problem. It would light the fire of sympathy in the breasts of hitherto dormant social forces, such as the armed forces, labor unions, taxi and bus drivers, and even the peasants who were a special, if belated, target of the underground movement.

The irony of it all! I was exiled to a province which had become one of the pilot projects for agricultural development. The same area was also to become one of the pilot projects of student agitation among the peasants, and a scene of great battles.

One Saturday afternoon, I was sitting on the front terrace of the Rosa Hotel chatting with Gloria over coffee. During the previous week we had worked on her research project. I had criticized some of the assumptions of her questionnaire and made suggestions for change. She had deferred to my judgment but was not quite convinced.

The questionnaire concerned the role of women in the cash economy sector of the rural areas, and the use of the disposable income by the head of the household, which was the husband. The assumption which I questioned, and which Gloria had revised, was that the cash should all be given to the wife; that the wife as the manager of the home should be the banker. My suggestion was that this should be the case only in respect to the income brought in by the wife, and that the remainder of the income should be left in the husband's hand, provided he did not squander it on drink or gambling.

Gloria was critical of my view as old-fashioned and male supremacist. We clashed and left the matter unresolved. We had just agreed to postpone the discussion and talk about rumors of the arrival of a delegation of student organizers in Assela, when I saw Hanna coming out of a hotel accompanied by her younger brother.

When she saw me she froze. I could not believe my eyes. I was not at all sure I was happy to see her. When I analyze my feelings in retrospect, there was more anger than anything else.

"Hanna!" I cried and got up to meet her.

"Hello, Desta," she said coldly—so coldly that instead of running to embrace her and kiss her, I stood there frozen. Then I introduced her to Gloria.

"Gloria, meet my wife, Hanna," I said.

I then went slowly to meet her. I bent to kiss her. She received my kiss on her cheeks and she went through the motion of kissing me on both cheeks. Gloria rose from her chair and came smiling to meet Hanna.

"I am so glad to meet you, Hanna. Desta has told me so much about you. I feel that I know you."

"Well, you have the advantage over me there, don't you? Because I don't know who you are, and I don't care to know. Now if you'll excuse me . . ." Hanna turned away.

I was flabbergasted. I felt an almost irresistible impulse to slap her. "Where are you going?" I shouted. "Why are you acting like this? Why are you so bitchy? Where is Lemlem, anyway?"

"Lemlem is in Addis Ababa with my mother. And don't raise your voice at me. I am not a person to be shouted at."

"I will raise my voice anytime I want to, anywhere I want to," I shouted back.

She seemed frightened. I noticed the furtive withdrawal of her eyes. I must have looked horrible in my anger. Her brother, a quiet and even-handed young man, came and stood between the two of us.

"Hanna, be reasonable. He has had a rough time. What do you know of what he has been through?" He then turned toward me. "Desta, please stay calm and try to deal with this matter reasonably. You are both my elders; it shames me even to presume to give advice to you. But things have come to this. I have to insist that you two sit down like responsible adults and talk things over."

"Why didn't you bring Lemlem?" I asked more calmly.

"I did not know in what kind of situation I would find you. I did not want her to be traumatized. It seems that I was not mistaken," she said, looking at Gloria with contempt.

"You are mad!" I said. "Don't you know that? You are stark raving mad."

"Am I the one who is yelling?"

"Thanks a lot! This is what I have been dreaming of for seven months?"

"So now you are blaming me for your banishment! You brought it on yourself. I have nothing to do with what you did, what you were scheming. I don't even know whether you had a hand in Melaku's death."

"What! You can't mean that, Hanna! You can't mean what you just said!"

"How do I know? Everybody is talking about it. Who am I to question the words of people who say they have evidence?"

"You are my wife, that's who. But never mind. That is the straw that broke the camel's back. Do you know what, Hanna? You can go on believing the lies they have concocted against me, for all I care. May you choke on them, along with all of those flaming bastards!"

I had lost all sense of balance. At that moment, I did not care what happened to me. Her brother came between us again, looking extremely concerned.

"Desta. Don't say that please. She only said it out of anger. You know how women can be sometimes. They say the most stupid things, the most hurtful things, to the people they love most. And they regret it immediately. Hanna has been under great stress. Please don't take to heart everything she has said."

"Look, I appreciate what you are saying," I said. "I know she has had a rough time. But this is beyond my wildest imaginings—what she just said. As far as I am concerned, she can go to hell."

His eyes, which looked like his sister's, withdrew with sadness, and he stood there looking downcast. Hanna had left for the hotel and he followed reluctantly.

Gloria stood there looking lost. She looked at me with apprehension, fearful that I might explode at her too, yet hoping I might say something to relieve her own fears. Quite frankly, I didn't care how Gloria felt, or how anyone else felt at that moment.

I walked away with quick strides toward the governor-general's residence. A crazy idea had seized my agitated mind. The more I thought about it, the more my crazy idea took hold of me.

At the gate of the governor's residence I was told "his excellency" was having a siesta and was not to be disturbed.

"What about her excellency?" I asked sarcastically.

The guard, who was an armed policeman, said he did not know. I insisted on being let in. The chamberlain, an old man with gray hair, came out squinting in the sun. When he recognized me he smiled and told the guard to let me in.

"His excellency is resting, but madame is awake upstairs," he said. "I'll tell her you're here." He led me to the small waiting room.

"Good afternoon, Professor Desta," said the governor's wife coming into the waiting room. She wore a white, ankle deep traditional robe with a green hemline.

"Good afternoon, madame," I said.

"Please don't get up," she said, bowing gracefully. She sat down on a sofa facing mine, then clapped her hands and a maid appeared to take a whispered order.

The governor's wife must have read from my agitated state that something was wrong. "Professor," she said, "if there is something wrong, I can wake up his excellency."

"Oh, no. Please don't disturb his sleep."

Call it feminine intuition: she hit on what ailed me immediately. "Is it a woman problem?" she asked, smiling amiably.

"Yes," I said without hesitation. Her easy manner was a welcome change from what I had just experienced. In fact, something about her reminded me of Mimi.

"How did you guess?" I asked her.

"I heard my husband mention something about a white woman being seen with you frequently. I also know that you have a family in Addis Ababa."

"My wife is here," I said. I then told her what happened, leaving out the details of my relations with Gloria.

"Can I talk to your wife?" she asked.

"By all means. But she is a stubborn woman. I doubt if a talk will change anything."

"Leave that to me. You men don't know much about us women. She is just frustrated. Some women don't know how to cope with pressures like this. I can't blame her, mind you. She must have had a bad time, worrying about you."

"Well, she has a strange way of showing it!"

"Don't worry. She will understand."

She then called her chauffeur and ordered him to go to the hotel and ask for Hanna and bring her to the governor's residence. "If she asks why, tell her the governor's wife requests the pleasure of her company for coffee."

I had gone to the governor's residence to confront him. I was going to tell him to send me back to Addis Ababa, where I would demand an open trial if I was suspected of the murder of my friend. Hanna's remark had struck a raw nerve. I imagined the cunning imperial rumor machine spinning tales linking me to Melaku's murder, and making sure that the stories reached my wife's gullible ears. Poor simpleton! She believed the rumors, and they had scored perhaps their cleverest victory by destroying my family. "Even his wife left him," they would now say.

"Professor," said the governor's wife, "don't worry. Things will get better. Your coffee is getting cold."

There was something singularly persuasive and reassuring about the governor's wife. I felt renewed confidence in my future, and decided to relax and chat about things that she liked, such as Paris. We must have talked for at least an hour. Finally, the chauffeur returned.

"Madame they are gone," he said.

"They?"

"Yes, she was with her brother" I explained.

"I drove about thirty kilometers hoping to catch up with them," the chauffeur said. "But they were nowhere in sight."

When the governor-general joined us it was past five in the afternoon. His wife briefed him on the events of the afternoon.

"Why didn't you wake me up? I could have called the police in Adama," he said.

"That would have made matters worse, my lord," she said. "Remember the poor woman's state of mind. The police stopping her would not have helped. No, we need another strategy."

"What?" her husband asked.

"We must arrange for Professor Desta to got to Addis Ababa."

"Are you out of your mind? We can't arrange that. We need the minister's permission."

"Not if the professor is gravely ill," said the indomitable woman. I was beginning to see that there was more to her than met the eye.

"But he is not gravely ill," the governor mumbled.

"He would be if the doctor certified that he was. It has happened before. Or have you forgotten?"

"I don't know. I have to think about this," said the hapless governor defensively.

Whatever she was referring to seemed to jog his memory. Her decisiveness and cool head aroused my curiosity about her past; I wondered how she had become the wife of such an important man. For Governor Damtew was a relative of the Prime Minister and one of his staunchest supporters. He was also related by marriage to the security minister, who was known to have made attempts to draw him closer to his orbit.

"My lord," the wife persisted, "a simple telephone call to Dr. Zairis can do it. Leave that to me. They can't dispute the word of a doctor."

She spoke as if the whole matter were settled. And it was. The poor governor could not resist her. There is more to the power of women in life—and in history—than our feminist sisters are prepared to admit, I thought, watching the governor's wife coming back to take her seat in front of me.

"Now, professor, what about it?"

"What about what?"

"Come on, be reasonable. That woman needs you and you know it. She must have been devastated to find you with that white woman, when she thought you were miserable all by yourself. And what does she find?"

"But I have done nothing with . . ."

"I know!" She interrupted me with a wave of her hand. "But she may have heard rumors."

"Rumors again! I have no control over rumors. If a wife believes every rumor spread against her husband there will be an end to the institution of marriage."

"I agree with you. But not everybody has the strength or the wisdom to stand up to that kind of warfare."

"She is right, you know," said the governor. "I mean, if Nura believed all they told her about me . . ."

"Yes my lord, I know," she interrupted him.

So that was her name: Nura. It suited her beauty. It also gave me a clue to her origin—a Muslim minority of traders in the center of Ethiopia. But she must have converted to Christianity. No Ethiopian could climb to or hold a prominent position unless he and his spouse were Christian. That was an unwritten law. What a fascinating story this woman could tell, I thought.

"So, are you in agreement with us?" she asked, coming very close to me.

"Let's reflect a little on this whole matter," I quibbled. "Suppose Hanna had heard rumors about me and the American woman before she came here. She comes here, and finds me on the hotel terrace with a white woman to whom I introduced her and flies off the handle. What does that suggest to you?"

"Nothing. That she is obviously in love, and also a jealous woman who can't bear the thought of her husband with another woman. That is why you must go to her and patiently explain everything. Show her your love."

"She is right, you know," the governor put in.

"Have you considered another possibility?" I challenged them both.

"What?"

"That she herself may be involved with another man, and that she came here to find an excuse."

"Would she have behaved the way a jealous wife behaves if that were the case? You yourself told me that she flew off the handle when she saw you with the white woman."

"She is right, you know." The governor had been reduced to a chorus echoing his wife's reasoning. Meanwhile, the conversation went back and forth between her and me.

"That could have been an act," I said. Why not, I thought. After all Hanna is a very attractive woman. Although she had never been the flirtatious type, the pressures of my detention and all the poisonous rumors could have had an impact on her.

A part of me almost believed these suppositions. Was I preparing the ground for what I really wanted, deep down? Was it not I who wanted an excuse to break with Hanna? Because there was Mimi, sweet beautiful Mimi. Was it not Mimi I thought about most? If I went to Addis Ababa, it would be to be with Mimi, just for one night.

I was rudely awakened from my reveries.

"So, professor? What do you say?" persisted Nura.

"Well, if it can be arranged."

"Good. Consider it done. I'll get to it right away," she said, and left us to make phone calls.

It was late when I reached my residence. My servant handed me a sealed envelope. It contained a note from Gloria.

"Dear Desta," the note said. "I am so sorry about this afternoon. I looked everywhere for you. You must hate me for what happened. Your wife obviously concluded from our being together at the hotel terrace that we are lovers. I wanted to tell her that we are not. But by the time I came back to the hotel she was gone. I became so desperate. Please Desta, don't hate me. I truly wanted to help. If you want me to go, I will. But please, please talk to me."

Poor Gloria! She was caught in a web of people and issues she did not properly understand. I felt sorry for her. I was sorry that I walked away from her; that was childish, I thought in retrospect. I decided to go to her hotel first thing in the morning, before reporting to Nura.

What a miserable revolutionary I am! I thought. I missed Melaku. I wondered how he would have handled the situation had he been alive and in my place. Well, he was not. I had to carry the cross of my own misfortunes on my meager shoulders. The warm consolation of belonging to a group lasts only as long as the group is intact. When misfortune strikes it is singular. Are the others feeling the same way? I wondered. Are they subject to the same doubts and remorse? Where are they, and how are they?

The more I thought about it, the more I welcomed the idea of going to Addis Ababa. I blessed Nura before I went to bed and turned the light off.

Gloria was up and in her jogging outfit when I knocked on her door.

"Desta! Boy, am I glad to see you!" she said, holding my hands.

I noticed she did not kiss me. The experience of the previous day had taken its toll. I kissed her on the cheek and apologized for my abrupt departure.

"That is quite all right. How are you?"

"I am okay now."

She invited me to sit down and went into the bedroom to change into her blue jeans.

"Listen Desta," she said through the open door. "I have an idea. Tell me if it is crazy, and I'll still do it!"

"What are you up to this time?"

"I want to go to Addis Ababa and talk to your wife."

"No. Definitely not."

"Why not? I want to try to convince her that it is not what she thought. I want to see your daughter and take pictures of her and bring them to you. If I can, I want also to persuade Hanna to come with me and bring your daughter. What's her name?"

"Lemlem. But Hanna will not do it. She is stubborn," I said. Then, since Gloria was bound to find out sooner or later, I added, "I may be going myself anyway."

"Oh, really! How? I mean, would they let you?"

"I will try to find a way. If it works, fine. If not, then we can talk about your plan. Okay?"

She did not look convinced. "Are you saying this to offset my idea of going?"

"Oh, no. I am serious. In fact, I am going to the governor's residence to talk to him about it," I said.

She looked puzzled. "Will you keep me posted?"

"I will, I promise."

"Cross your heart?"

"Cross my heart," I said, touching my heart.

I turned and saw her smiling with her arms crossed, leaning against the door.

"You know," I said in a parting shot. "At times like this I wish we had polygamy."

"Why?"

"Because all this aggravation and waste of time and energy would become totally unnecessary. We could all live happily as one family."

"We? Would I be included?"

"Why not? You are almost a member of the family now. In fact, you have been like one as far as I am concerned." I left her frowning and looking perplexed.

TWENTY-FIVE

I t was all arranged. Dr. Zairis had dutifully obliged Nura, for whom he harbored a secret love (who wouldn't?), and written a note attesting to the seriousness of my condition, which could only be properly treated in Addis Ababa. His excellency had written to the security minister explaining why he could not, in good conscience, as a Christian, accept the possibility of my untimely death for lack of proper medical attention. Besides, the enemies of the regime would undoubtedly claim that the government had poisoned me, and the governor was not prepared to shoulder the blame. He hoped that the minister would understand and approve my immediate transfer. Due to the gravity of the illness (as certified by the faithful Dr. Zairis) time was of the essence. Hence, the unusual step of acting on his own discretion and sending me before clearing the matter with the minister.

The entire operation was a masterpiece of political duplicity. "Thank you, madame, and your excellency," I said, overwhelmed.

"Don't you want to know what your illness is?" Nura said laughing.

"Yes, of course," I said. "What is it?"

"Kidney failure," the governor said. "I thought of that one, because I have kidney stones, which is one of the worst illnesses. I had to go to Israel to remove a stone."

"Several stones," Nura corrected him. "There were so many we could have built a house with them. Of course, you have to go to a hospital in Addis Ababa for the examination. But that is no problem. Dr. Zairis has friends and trusted colleagues there."

"I am most grateful for all that you have done for me. Can I go tomorrow?"

"I'll make the necessary arrangements," the governor said. "You will travel in my special Toyota cruiser, which has a comfortable bed in the back."

"What a difference from the van that brought me here!"

"Well, times change. *Al Hamd lilahi*," Nura said, turning to the governor with an air of defiance.

"She means God be praised," he said defensively.

Neither the driver nor the plainclothes policeman who were my companions on the journey knew of the charade. So I had to ride stretched out in the back of the Toyota, moaning and groaning in pretense of pain. When this became too tiresome, I would pretend to fall asleep and I could hear their muffled conversation.

I was surprised to find that both men knew about me and were sympathetic to my fate. My wife's visit and sudden departure, my "affair with a white woman," had become public knowledge in the small town, as I could gather from their conversation.

"The poor man didn't even have a chance to explain to the wife," the driver said. "I tried to catch up with her, but she had driven off like the devil."

"Perhaps he was too kind to her," said the policeman. "Women have to be kept in their place. These educated types treat them as equals, and the next thing you know, the woman wants to be the boss."

We stopped for lunch just outside Adama. I didn't eat much, though I was famished, because I wanted to seem sick. But an idea came to me as they enjoyed their lunch.

"I know an Italian on the outskirts of Addis Ababa who has doctor friends," I said. "He may be able to get me some medicine for pain."

"Our order is to take you to the Menelik hospital," the driver said.

"I know. But I will wait the whole night in pain, and then they will take me to X-ray tomorrow before I find any relief."

"Are you sure your friend can help?" the policeman asked.

"I am positive. One simple phone call and the doctor will be there. You know how these *ferenji's* are."

"Okay then," the driver said.

For the rest of the four-hour journey from Adama to the Villa Bianca, I lay awake thinking of Mimi. How surprised she will be to see me! How ecstatic. I would tell the two men to wait in the restaurant, while I sneaked into her residence on the pretext of seeing my Italian friend. They would not insist on coming with me, once I settled them with two bottles of Melotti each, served by seductive women, I thought.

My excitement was mixed with anxiety, though. What if Mimi was not there anymore? What if she had left the Villa Bianca? Well, there was no point getting worked up about it. Besides, where would she go?

It was seven in the evening when we arrived at the Villa Bianca. I led the two men into the restaurant which had a few customers. I had wrapped my head in a white shawl. Nobody recognized me with the nearly eight-month-old beard and the shawl.

We sat at a corner table and I invited the two men to be my dinner guests. I ordered spaghetti for both to start, and recommended the scallopini. I also ordered two Melottis for each of them. Since I was "sick" I did not order anything. I told them I would go to find my Italian friend.

"That lady at the cash register is his wife," I told them and walked toward Lula. I took off the shawl and smiled at her. It took several moments to register and then she nearly had a fit.

She sprang up and came around and kissed me on both cheeks. "Desta? Is it really you? Look at that beard! How are you?"

"I am very well, Lula. How are you? How is everybody?"

"We are all well. And 'everybody' will die with fright to see you," Lula said, referring to Mimi.

She called a young man to take over the cash register and took me into her office. "Desta. Is it really true? You are here? We have all been so worried."

"Well, here I am."

"There had been all kinds of rumors. Some said that you have been killed. Others said that you escaped and went to France."

"Rumors, rumors. How is Mimi? Is she here?"

"She is well. She should be here soon. Can I get you something?"

"Well, yes. I would love a beer and mountains of spaghetti. But I am supposed to be ill."

"What!"

"No, I am okay. I will explain later. But bring me something on the sly. Those two men who came in with me think I am very ill. That is why I have been brought here—for special medical treatment. It was the only way I could come."

She went out to order the food and came back with a bottle of Melotti. "Mimi won't believe her eyes when she sees you. Oh, what a blessed day! And you won't believe your eyes when you see her."

"Where is she?" I said impatiently.

Lula giggled like a teenager. "Let me go and see if she is back," she said and went out through a back door.

After a while Lula returned. "She is in her house, resting. I just told her that there is some guest who came from far away to see her."

She led the way through the back door. Before she knocked on Mimi's door, she whispered to me: "Don't be shocked. You will see a different Mimi."

"Come in," said Mimi's sweet voice.

There she stood in the middle of the room—transformed! She made an attempt to run toward me, or rather to wobble, and I stood dumbfounded on the spot.

"Mimi!" I managed to say finally.

"Dessie!" she cried and wrapped her arms around my neck; her protruding belly pushed into mine.

"What happened to you?"

"You mean, what did you do to her," Lula said, giggling again.

"You mean . . . Is this . . . Are you pregnant?"

"Of course. What else?" Mimi said wiping tears of joy from her eyes and cheeks.

She looked radiant, ravishing even, despite her pregnancy. Even in that state she caused a surging desire to run through me. I embraced her again and pulled her to sit by me on the same sofa where we first kissed on that magic-filled night months before.

"The silly girl did not want to complicate matters for you," Lula said, "so she considered abortion, and almost did it, twice. I intervened in the nick of time."

"Our baby!" I said. "Aborted! Are you out of your mind?" I scolded Mimi who flushed with shame.

"But I was so afraid of what it might do to your family. You have enough problems as it is. I also thought a baby might come between us. I was not willing to risk that."

"Nothing can come between us. And now, this baby has sealed our love." I felt her belly with my hands.

"It is going to be a boy. I had a dream," she said.

"You and your dreams!" I said.

They both laughed.

"How much longer to go?" I asked.

"So you don't mind?" Lula said.

"Mind? I am thrilled. I feel like shouting the news from the roof tops!"

"What about Hanna?" Lula asked.

Lula and Mimi kept very few secrets from each other. I could tell from that question that Mimi had confided in her about the quarrel between Hanna and I.

"What about her?" I shrugged off the question.

Lula did not want to pursue it. "Well, I will leave you two to talk. You have a lot to talk about," she said, getting up to go.

"When you go back, please tell the two men who came with me that I am resting and waiting for my friend."

"I will. Don't worry, I will look after them," Lula said and left.

Mimi's eyes glistened with tears of joy. My eyes, too, joined in the celebration. I kissed her and rubbed her belly gently. "Did you really think of abortion?" I asked.

"I was desperate. I missed you. I was worried. The rumors about your fate nearly drove me out of my mind. If it had not been for Lula, I think I would have done it."

"I am glad you didn't. This is a gift," I said.

"Part of you is within me."

There and then I made up my mind. Whatever Hanna had done or was going to do, I could no longer sit on the fence. It would be unfair to everybody to leave things dangling. I decided to escape. To escape from the tension. To escape from the country and take Mimi with me and lie low and, for the first time, devote my life to a person I loved.

But how? When? That was the question. It would be madness to attempt to escape with Mimi in her present state. I had to wait until the baby was born, then make arrangements for them both to leave. Then I would join them.

I remembered Gloria's promise to help me escape. Now, far from sounding crazy, it became the focal point of my salvation. A new situation—a new life and love—had altered my condition. I could only hope that Gloria would not back out.

But how would I wriggle out of the "medical" snare that had brought me to Addis Ababa in the first place? And how would I get in touch with Gloria?

"I like your beard," Mimi said stroking it playfully.

"It is a memento," I said absent-mindedly.

We gazed into each other's eyes and I was filled with a warmth of feeling I had never experienced before. It was as if all my travails, all my struggles, had led to this supreme moment. I knew the true meaning of love as never before. I forgot everyone and everything else.

"Well, you must rest now," I said. "I have a few loose ends to tie up before I come back. And when I come back it will be for good."

"Where are you going now?"

"I must register in a hospital and spend a few days undergoing tests."

I then told her everything that had happened in Assela over the past few days. I told her that I was finished with Hanna. I told her about Gloria and her idea of escape—everything.

Far from feeling guilty about Hanna, I felt a sense of release and a new avenue for the struggle.

"Are you sure you will not blame yourself later?" Mimi asked.

"I am absolutely sure. It is best for everybody. Besides, I can serve the revolution better from abroad at this stage."

"I will accept anything you decide. I will go wherever you go. Your life will be my life. Your friends will be my friends."

Mimi brought to mind the story of Ruth when she uttered those simple but reassuring words. I kissed her and left as quietly as I had come.

Money, the solvent of all obstacles, becomes the critical factor in moments of difficulty. Money had never held any fascination for me before. But now its importance was as clear as that of the pliers that cut through the barbed wire standing between freedom and bondage. And Lula provided enough of it to make our scheme succeed. I gave the equivalent of two months salary to each of the two men, plus an extra fifty to the driver, asking him to take a letter to Gloria. In the letter I asked Gloria to come immediately and ask for me at the Villa Bianca.

The medical side had already been taken care of by Dr. Zairis, Nura's secret admirer. He had written to his friends at the Menelik Hospital. Dr. Dimitrov, a jovial, stocky man in his early fifties, paid special attention to my needs. After X-rays and routine tests of blood and urine, he told the nurses he would handle my case personally.

"Your kidneys are both functioning normally," Dr. Dimitrov told me.

I must have looked worried.

"But don't worry, we will make more tests. Meanwhile, you need to rest. I am aware of your recent history and of your past history, and I like it," he said with a wink.

"What is the prognosis?" I asked vaguely.

"Politically, the prognosis is not good. There will be an explosion soon. Medically, in your case, there is nothing to worry about. Now all you need is rest, my friend. *Au revoir.*"

A few days later Gloria came to my hospital room, wearing a face furrowed with worry. "Are you okay?" she asked, rushing to my bedside.

"I'm all right. It is all a charade. I'm sorry I did not have time to explain to you before I left."

I then told her how and why I had come to Addis Ababa, and told her for the first time about Mimi and about my decision to escape.

She did not show the same enthusiasm for the idea of escape. But she agreed to help, adding a dash of humor. "Perhaps now I can look forward to becoming the second favorite," she said, laughing.

"Favorite of what?"

"I see you have forgotten your parting remark about how you sometimes wished polygamy was allowed."

"Oh, that," I said, somewhat embarrassed.

"Do you remember our first talk in my hotel room? You warned me about getting hurt. It was Mimi who was on your mind, wasn't it? Not Hanna."

"Yes," I said.

"Well, please don't think I am passing judgment, but don't you think talking to your wife is still worth a try? After all, that is why the governor and his wife helped you to come here."

Her statement hit me hard. She had become my conscience, and my fondness for her grew into respect. But I demurred.

"No, you are not passing judgment. But Hanna is not the helpless, abandoned wife that you may think. She can take care of herself. My mind is made up. My heart belongs somewhere else, and I know that in the end we will all be the better for it. You see, I just learned within the last couple of days that Hanna has been seen with a certain minister a great deal. She knows I am here, and has chosen not to visit me."

"Oh. That does change the whole matter, doesn't it," Gloria said. We kept silent for a while.

"In a sense, I am relieved," she said. "We can now attend to the matter of escape with single-mindedness."

"I want you to find out discreetly which is the safest and quickest escape route," I said. "I have my own ideas, but two hands are better than one. Besides, you are free to move about and ask questions; I am not."

"I'll get to it right away. It means goodbye to my Assela research project for the moment. What a pity! You know, I was beginning to enjoy it," she said.

Gloria was a miracle worker. She brought a chauffeur's uniform into

the hospital the next day, took a picture of me, and the following day
I had a passport with the picture of a uniformed, bearded man—me.
"You are now my driver," she said. "And I am the cultural attache
of the U.S. Embassy."
"And how are you going to prove—"
She interrupted me: "That I am a diplomat? Simple. I had that
forged too."
"Are you sure you are not a member of the CIA?" I asked.
"Let's just say that I have friends in the right circles" she said.
The next hurdle was to choose the escape route.
"I think the safest and quickest way is through the east to Djibouti,"
Gloria said. "I will not need a visa, and I can get yours easily for a
hundred bucks."
I took my hat off to this remarkable woman. It did occur to me that
she might be an undercover agent for the CIA. I shrugged off the
thought. "So what if she is, as long as she can get me out," I reasoned.
It was also possible that she was simply an adventurous woman
genuinely interested in helping me.
"What will you do after I am safely across the border?" I asked her.
"After a couple of weeks, I'll come back, hide the false passport, and
resume my real identity," she said calmly.
"What if you are discovered?"
"Then that would be the end of it. Deportation. Possible prosecu-
tion. What do I know?"
"But you are prepared to risk all that? Why?"
"Desta, we've been through this before, unless you are fishing for
compliments," she replied with mild irritation.
"I am not complaining, believe me," I said. And I let the matter
drop.

Dr. Dimitrov settled himself on the chair beside my bed and took
my pulse.
"The result of our tests shows a young man in perfect health," he
said with a cheerful smile. "You have been here now for twelve days,
and questions are being asked."

"What kind of questions? By whom?"

"Never mind, my friend. The prognosis, politically speaking, is not very good. I have done my best to keep things quiet. But the minister of health has been instructed to have your case reviewed by the medical board."

"When will that happen?"

"Two or three days from now; they may subpoena all our documents. The most I can do is delay things another two days. I can go to the lake district with my family and the Prime Minister's wife, and after that, God alone knows."

He looked at me with a paternal concern that was so moving that I got up and hugged him. "Thanks, Dr. Dimitrov. That will be all I'll need."

"What then?" he asked. "Back to Assela, to the sharks?"

"Maybe. God alone knows, as you yourself said. Don't worry."

He looked relieved. He then told me about His Majesty's deteriorating state of health. He was a member of the committee of doctors who examined the Emperor.

"I don't know how long he will hold out under the pressure of events. He is a tough man, but age and the students are wearing him down," he said.

"Only the students?"

"Well, they are the most visible force. But I am sure there are hidden forces behind them, including some members of the armed forces. But you should know more about these things than I do. I am an amateur."

"Cut out that false modesty," I said.

"No, really. I have lived here for ten years. I love this country. But I am still ignorant. You people are inscrutable. We Bulgarians are simple peasants compared to you."

"Will you go back to Bulgaria one day?"

"No. If I have to go anywhere, it will be to the United States. I have friends there. It is a doctor's paradise."

The good Dr. Dimitrov wished me all the best and left my room. I was never to see him again.

TWENTY-SIX

I t was so smooth and uneventful that it was almost disappointing, in the end. But I was grateful to Gloria Sullivan for the way she pulled it off. So faultlessly and smoothly did she handle my departure that the CIA theory gained ascendancy in my mind once more. And I dismissed it again. Who was I to complain, even if that were the case?

She had rented a Mercedes from a German businessman she had been involved with; he still cared for her but she despised him, she told me. She fitted the car with diplomatic tags—"a touch of genius," she said, giggling in understandable self-congratulation. Everybody in customs and immigration was suitably impressed when the car was loaded onto the freight section of the train to Djibouti.

All the questions and checks were perfunctory, followed by smart salutes by officers wishing us *bon voyage*. The sheer audacity of it all!

At dusk in Djibouti we walked side-by-side, dressed in light summer outfits. We moved in slow motion through the heat, staring at the tourists and townspeople who seemed to wander chaotically.

It was the first time in years that I had felt carefree. The sea breeze was bracing, though warm even in the evening. I breathed easier at sea level, a relief from the rarified air of the highlands. We did not talk much. We just walked, occasionally holding hands as we were jostled by the crowd.

After months of stifling banishment and, lately, weeks of unrelieved tension, it was dream-like to walk in the leisurely mood and manner of a holiday maker. It was also dream-like because I was holding hands with a woman I hardly knew. The short time that I had known Gloria Sullivan was so intense that, in a sense, I knew her as well as many lifelong friends. But we were still total strangers in many ways.

Thanks to Lula's munificence, we had registered at a first-class hotel, as befits a diplomat and her chauffeur. I thought Gloria deserved the best and overruled her objections.

The French clerk at the front desk, a sleek, sly-looking man of about thirty, winked with a knowing smile when he handed me the keys, as if to say: "I know the chauffeur business is a cover for romance." Besides, my French probably gave the game away. Ah well, *c'est la vie!*

The company of a woman—any woman, I think—sheds a wondrous light on the landscape of a place, on people and things. As I walked with Gloria through the streets of Djibouti, I found myself paying attention to details that would have otherwise escaped me.

But after forty-eight hours it was a dead end. Two days of the place was quite enough. The euphoria of freedom was dissipating, giving way to a restlessness which we tried to control through an orgy of eating and drinking. I was beginning to detest the place: its dizzying heat, its sweaty crowds milling in the streets or pushing their wares in my face, the pungent smell of cooking oil mixed with exhaust fumes, the chaotic traffic.

The hotel terrace was a welcome relief after a day of wandering. We ordered two iced teas for a change.

"So. What is the next step?" Gloria asked, sipping her tea.

"Mine or yours?" I asked.

"Mine is obvious. I have to go back to Addis Ababa. I mean yours, of course."

"I have a choice of two countries for asylum, France and Britain."

"And not America?"

"No."

"Why not?"

"For one thing, I don't know anyone in America, or next to no one. For another, America is too far away from home. I want to stay in touch with developments."

"So will it be France, or Britain?"

"Either would do, but my preference is Britain. Don't ask me why. It is too complicated to explain."

"I won't ask you. Do you want me to stay here while your application for asylum is processed?"

"No. That can take weeks. I would like for you to go soon and look after things, especially Mimi. Would you do that for me?"

"Of course. We are in this together."

"Three for one. One for three!" I mimicked the Three Musketeers.

"Be serious. I give you my word that I will take care of Mimi and eventually help deliver her to you, wherever you are. That means we have to work out communications."

"I agree," I said, and we decided on names and channels.

That evening, our last, I invited Gloria to a sumptuous dinner—"a dinner you will never forget," as I told her. As the meal progressed through the third course consisting of a huge chocolate-vanilla ice cream, she turned morose.

"Is this the last supper?" she asked.

"I certainly hope not."

"You really don't trust me, do you? I mean, there are still some doubts in your mind regarding my motives."

"Well, motives be damned," I said, touching her hand. "You have delivered on your promise. You probably saved my life."

"Can there be a small room in your heart for me?" she asked, squeezing my hand.

"I have a big heart, with rooms for honored guests. But I won't lie to you. The inner sanctum will not be shared."

"*Touché!* And I deserve it."

"Gloria. I want you to know that your help and friendship means a lot to me. Can't we leave it there?"

"Yes, dear man. Yes."

She wiped her eyes, looking away. Then she assumed a serious, business-like look.

"I will leave tomorrow. And don't worry about Mimi," she said.

Part IV

EXILE AND
REVOLUTION

TWENTY-SEVEN

It took about a month to process my application for political asylum in the United Kingdom. Sir Geoffrey, whose name I gave as reference, went out of his way to help expedite matters.

Out of diplomatic courtesy I also called on the French governor and informed him of my presence. He was probably relieved that I did not ask him to help find asylum in France; if I had done that the French government would have asked Akalu's views, and that would have put my erstwhile mentor and chief in a cruel dilemma. I wanted to spare the poor man that predicament. That was the main reason I chose England.

The British consul, an affable man with red cheeks, handled my case with the ease and charm that I have long associated with British officialdom. You never know whether they will help, but they put you at ease even when the answer is to be a negative one.

"Yes, my dear fellow," the consul said to me, when he got word from London, "your case has been approved. You can go anytime you want, and you will be the guest of Her Majesty's government. There are certain rules that have to be observed, of course."

The conditions were that I would not engage in politics that might jeopardize the diplomatic relations of his country with mine. But that did not mean that I could not travel or engage in research and "similar worthy activities." I took that to mean that I could travel to organize and communicate with my comrades, as long as I did so discreetly. I was ready to go to London.

A few months later, I was comfortably settled in a flat on Camden Street in north London. The British authorities honored my request to live under a assumed name: Mr. Hab Selous. My two-room apartment had a lounge which I used as a study.

The stipend was modest but sufficient to enable me to live a comfortable life. The British were aware that I was expecting to be joined by a young lady with a baby. Their sensitivity and discretion was such that they did not ask if she was my wife; they surmised that I would have said so, had she been.

The woman who took me to the flat was a model of British propriety. "When your fiancé—" she began, then modulated her subtle intonation. "I take it she is your fiance. When she and the baby arrive, there will be a revision of the accounts. An upward revision of course."

The British view of life, even at its harshest, is peculiarly uplifting. It is heroic without giving that impression. The French and others charge that the British are artificial and cold. I beg to differ. They appear to be cold, actually masking a sentimental nature. And the so-called artificiality is a reflection of a culture: a civilized conduct in which the views and sentiments of others are accommodated. One may experience condescension at times, but that is a function of a complex class society and it operates across national boundaries. I did not experience it, probably because of my educational background and previous station in life. I mixed and moved easily in the highest circles.

By the end of September 1970, Sir Geoffrey had introduced me to a number of people in educational and research institutions who helped find me funds for travel and research. I was given an office at the Institute for Commonwealth Studies and became friendly with the staff including the director, the librarian and some research fellows.

I got into the habit of walking in the parks of London, which helped in clearing the mind and soothing the soul. Gradually my evening walks turned to solitary dawn patrols under London's baleful oaks. These morning walks helped me to establish a rhythm for the day's activities, fortifying me, as it were, with a spiritual communion which nature can best provide. I felt a mystic chord of memory stretching across the centuries to my ancestors.

Once I got to my office at the institute, I would read and write and make phone calls, in tune with the reality of life as lived by ordinary people. This rhythmic interplay between natural and social reality defined my work habits.

When the end of October came, and there was still no word from Addis Ababa, I began to fret. Mimi would be delivered of the baby soon if all went well. I received no word from Gloria Sullivan.

I consulted with Sir Geoffrey, who promised that he would try to find out through the embassy in Addis Ababa; to that end I gave him Gloria's name and address. Meanwhile he insisted that I should meet some influential people around Whitehall and in his own club.

"The club is the best place, old boy," he said. "People are relaxed and you do business in that atmosphere better. Besides, you must be inducted into British social life. The very best of it."

"I would be delighted to visit your club, Sir Geoffrey," I said.

"Good show. It is all arranged then."

Sir Geoffrey's club was the Athenaeum near Saint James Palace. I met him in the late afternoon in Green Park on the Queens Walk side, and we walked to the club.

The British power elite work and socialize in an area not more than one square mile in size. Here the Prime Minister and his ministers have their offices, and the Parliament meets. Westminster Abbey, Buckingham Palace, Trafalgar Square, Piccadily Circus and other historic places lie within walking distance of London's clubs.

Sir Geoffrey introduced me to the secretary of the Athenaeum Club and ordered drinks—gin and orange for him and a dry sherry for me. We sat at a table and were joined by two men whom Sir Geoffrey rose to greet.

"Mr. Desta, I would like to present my friends: Mr. Jonathan Boyd, from the foreign office, and Mr. Herbert Clark from the home office. Gentlemen, this is Mr. Desta Kidane Wold."

"How do you do?" was said all around.

In British middle class and upper class etiquette, a simple "how do you do" is all one has to say when introduced. This has always puzzled me, for there invariably follows an awkward moment of silence, as it did that evening at the Athenaeum.

Sir Geoffrey told his friends about my recent odyssey, and he told me that Mr. Boyd handled African affairs at the foreign office while Mr. Clark dealt with alien residents at the home office. They were both very interested to know about political developments in Africa without pinpointing Ethiopia at first. British discretion relies on subtle hints and loaded questions.

By the time dinner was over, we had covered much ground, without any specific commitment on their part to do anything, but with hints that "things might be worked out" or "there may be a way to get round that one." And all the while we exchanged stories and jokes, which lubricated the course of the conversation. Boyd and Clark were both about my age and seemed to be decent types, well-informed about world affairs.

"It went very well, old chap," Sir Geoffrey said when he saw me to the door at the end of the evening. "They were very impressed, and they will both be very helpful. You'll see."

My own feelings were divided between cautious optimism and a sense of guilt that I was submitting myself to the care of an imperial power that still influenced Africa's destiny. I shrugged off these feelings as best I could. But my mind was clouded with worries about Mimi.

One day in November Sir Geoffrey rang me up at the Institute for Commonwealth Studies to say that he had heard from the embassy in Addis Ababa, and there was a cable which he wanted to show me.

I could not wait to see it. Sir Geoffrey brought the cable to the Institute to show me. It said: "Gloria Sullivan expelled from Ethiopia. We are trying to find the person in question by other means. Letter follows. Regards."

"That explains her silence," I said.

"Perhaps the promised letter will bring good news," Sir Geoffrey said.

"I hope so. Meanwhile I must travel to France and Italy."

"Well, let me know of your whereabouts."

"I will. And thank you Sir Geoffrey."

"Not at all, my dear chap. I wish it were better news. But we will get to your Mimi, old boy," he said giving a guffaw to cheer me up. But his face reflected the pain that he must have picked up from mine.

TWENTY-EIGHT

I t was a cold afternoon in late November when I arrived at Le Bourget airport, visiting France to observe an Ethiopian student conference. Paris in the fall is grim and gray, in stark contrast to its bright summer days—especially to the visitor who did not live through the slow and subtle autumnal changes, who did not experience the wonders of the changing colors of the falling leaves and the gradual paling of the sky. Life in the autumn withdraws behind shuttered windows and cafe curtains like the closing petals of a sunflower.

Having made all the necessary arrangements to meet the leadership of the Ethiopian Students Union in Europe, I took a taxi to *Rue des Batignolles* on the periphery of the *Quartier Latin*. The address was under the name of Haile Dada, who was president of the movement when Melaku had given me the names and addresses before his death. According to the accounts in our file, Haile would be the brains behind the movement even if he were not still president, and therefore the best contact for me to start with.

I did not know what reception to expect. When I arrived at number two *bis Rue des Batignolles,* Haile was not there, but he had left word about my coming.

I was surprised to be greeted by a tall blonde woman who helped me with my suitcase and led me down the stairs to a basement apartment. The apartment was small and sparsely furnished but quite comfortable, even luxurious, by student standards in Paris.

The woman, Haile's fiancé, turned out to be a Swedish student of

French literature. She made me feel at home, offering me wine with cheese and bread. She said that Haile would be back soon with a couple of friends. We spent an hour or so talking about French literature and student politics since the fall of Charles de Gaulle.

She did not have what you might call a typical Nordic temperament. She spoke and gestured like a Latin.

Haile and two friends arrived carrying a chunk of meat, bread and wine. We introduced ourselves. The names of the other two were Nega Gobena and Fikade Mersha, both Ethiopian students of law.

Haile was tall and gaunt with a long and pleasant face. He was soft-spoken and a good listener. Nega was of medium height with a dark complexion. He was talkative and a shade opinionated. Fikade was stocky, also of medium height, with a fair-skinned round face. He was soft-spoken and courteous, but politely tenacious in argument.

The three were the nucleus of the student movement, and although it was not written anywhere as far as I could gather, Haile was the obvious leader. They were, all three of them, deeply interested in knowing about the inner workings of the government. They had heard about my work with the Prime Minister, and were intrigued to find that I had been, all the while, an underground revolutionary dedicated to overthrowing the government for which I worked.

On this subject it was Nega who showed open incredulity and (I thought) even lingering suspicion. "Are you telling us that Akalu is a progressive man?" Nega fumed, after I had explained my views. He had listened, taking notes and never once smiling or nodding.

"Yes. In his own way, he is progressive in the context of our country," I said.

"That's nonsense," Nega said. His two comrades looked embarrassed.

"How so?" I asked, controlling my anger.

"He is a comprador bourgeois in the service of a feudal autocracy. No such person can be progressive." he said.

"I have noticed that labeling is a common practice in student politics," I said to all three of them. "But labeling a person, a movement or a government is a poor substitute for analysis. It is a way of avoiding a more difficult task."

"And what is that?" Nega asked.

"Every situation, every social force must be examined on its own terms," I said. "We cannot just dismiss everyone as reactionary and heap abuse on people who may help advance the course of the revolution."

"Marxist dialectics teach us that the only meaningful social analysis is one based on class analysis," Nega replied. "On the strength of such an analysis I find that your Akalu and his ilk are members of a comprador bourgeoisie allied to the feudal class executing the plans of imperialism."

"The discussion has shifted to a different topic," I said. "My words were on the current situation in our country, and on the various forces and individuals that might contribute to the revolution and those that constitute a hindrance. From that assessment of the objective situation, we are now being deflected to a lecture on Marxist dialectics."

"It was not a lecture, comrade Desta," Nega interjected.

His use of the word "comrade," usually reserved for members of an inner group, came as a surprise. Was he relenting, or was he being sarcastic? I wanted to find out.

"If you see me as one with a comprador bourgeois, how can I be your comrade?" I asked.

At that point Haile intervened gracefully to save the situation from deteriorating to a shouting match.

"I think comrade Desta's analysis of the situation back home has been very useful to us. It is not everyday that you run into a man who has seen it from the inside, who has been an insider and yet kept the faith. In fact, it is rare if not unique. We are indebted to you, comrade Desta, for helping us to gain such a rare insight into the inner workings of the feudo-bourgeois system. And we look forward to working with you in the future."

He looked at the other two for further questions or comments. Nega bent his head to look at his feet. Fikade spoke briefly in approbation of Haile's little speech and smiled amiably.

"Some wine?" Fikade rose to fill our glasses with beaujolais.

"I still think that we have certain differences in our world view," Nega said toward the end, and I agreed.

"*Vive la difference,*" I said raising my glass. Nobody followed suit.

Haile Dada had a kind of coiled urbanity and quiet authority that seemed at once to intimidate and soothe the people around him. They obviously respected his intellect and dedication. Few, if any, disputed points he raised. Only an occasional tremor in his low baritone voice suggested any uncertainty.

The meeting which he chaired a few days after our first discussion was attended by some fifty students from the Paris branch of the movement. I sat at the back and few noticed my presence. Under an agreement between me and the three leaders, I was to remain incognito; if questions were asked, I was a member of a clandestine labor union passing through Paris on my way home from a private visit.

The meeting was convened to discuss differences arising between the leaderships of the Ethiopian Student Union in North America and in Europe. These differences concerned the question of national self-determination in general, and in particular the Eritrean struggle for independence from the Ethiopian empire.

After Haile dealt with preliminary questions of procedure, he summarized the differences between the two organizations.

Behind the platform there were slogans posted on boards. One of the them which stuck in my mind read: "REVOLUTIONARY INTELLECTUAL—INTEGRATE WITH THE MASSES, LEARN FROM THEM, AND TEACH THEM IN TURN."

The issues that occasioned differences between the movements in Europe and the United States were important in themselves; yet they masked an intense struggle for power that had been going on for some time. That power struggle was to result in the division of the student community into two camps, which eventually emerged as two political parties. The one which Haile led, with its power base in Europe, was to be known as the All-Ethiopian Socialist Movement, often called the Inner Group for convenience. The other faction, which was based in the student movement in Addis Ababa and in North America, was to call itself the Ethiopian People's Revolutionary Party. We will call it the Outer Group.

Haile, to his credit, made an attempt to establish unity between the two factions by paying a visit to the rival Outer Group, led by Berhanu. It did not work. The split was formalized and hardened with the publication of pamphlets which indulged labeling, *ad hominem* attacks and distortions. And always the pamphlet warfare hinged on the issue of nationalities and the Eritrean question.

The Paris meeting did not last long. The student congress approved a pre-arranged resolution condemning the "narrow nationalism" and "adventurism" of the Outer Group. It was disgusting. I could see that, even at that time, the student leadership had been transformed into the typical one-party dictatorship with which much of the Third World is plagued. But I still hoped I could play a part in helping instill a spirit of democratic dialogue.

Four of us went to a cafe after the meeting. Haile led us to a free table amid the hustle and bustle, the din and chaos. The Paris cafe is more than a place where customers meet to eat and drink. It is a social institution where citizens meet to escape from the regimented discipline of jobs, families and schools to a state of glorious anarchy. In this it is unique. The chaos of the Paris cafe has its own inner order; it is anarchy leavened by a cult of reason, that precious product of the Age of Enlightenment to which the French claim intellectual proprietorship. The cult of reason replaced the church.

In the Paris cafe everyone talks, but few listen. I decided long ago, in my Parisian student days, that most of the cafe's denizens were ardent believers in the primacy of the immediate: life is there to be lived from moment to moment; those who think too much about tomorrow are insufferable bores, who take themselves too seriously . . .

Not far from our table, an elderly man with a black beret and a goatee was holding forth on the corruption of modern civilization. He was quoting Herbert Marcuse on the evils of American capitalist society, which, he said, had become a universal model.

"And a corrupt model," he said, as the record machine nearly drowned his words with Edith Piaf's song about Paris poets whose verses live on long after they are gone.

We sat and listened to Piaf's stirring song, a voice that had enthralled a generation of Parisians—"*longtemps, longtemps, apres les poetes
sont disparus, leur chansons . . .*"

"*Messieurs!*" the waiter said, waiting for our order and joking with
Haile, whom he seemed to know.

"*Disdonc!*" he said, patting Haile on the back; "*Tants de guallistes ont
mordus de la poussiere, quoi!*" He took the orders of coffee, beer, and red
wine (for me).

"He hates the Gaullists," Haile explained. "He was referring to their
recent defeat in local elections."

The professor at the next table was speaking louder, still competing
with Piaf. When the music stopped I could hear him say, "American
capitalism has become so alluring in its provision of consumer goods,
seducing the masses. It is ironic, mass-produced goods have defeated
the masses, draining away their revolutionary impulse. In fact consumer
goods have become the unarmed guards replacing the police as the
instruments of repression!"

"How so, professor?" a young woman asked.

"Because the best method of repression is control of the mind, of
daily habits and behavior. The masses sweat day in day out to earn
money to buy consumer goods which are advertized all the time. There
is no let up. Buy this, buy that. You need this and that. The media, the
most subtle instruments of capitalism, define peoples' needs."

"What is the solution, then? Is it a lost cause?" the young woman
asked, getting agitated.

"The solution, my dear, is refusal," the professor answered.

"Easier said than done," an African among the group said. He was
the only African among about a dozen disciples.

"It isn't easy. It is a struggle," the professor said. "We must develop
a culture of refusal to counter their consumer culture. There is, on the
one hand, a capitalist hegemony of consumerism. We must oppose that
by a counter hegemony."

"He is a philosopher in the tradition of Jean Paul Sartre," Haile said.

"Just a cafe philosopher who would not dirty his hands in the real
world of struggle," Nega said contemptuously.

"At least he has the right ideas," Fikade said, seeming irritated with Nega's dismissal of the professor.

"Who is he?" I asked.

"Professor Jean Jacques Duclos. He teaches sociology at the Sorbonne," Haile said.

Listening to the professor and the endless chatter of the customers in every corner of the cafe, I was transported back to my student days. In fact I had ordered red wine in commemoration of the first time I had ventured into the cafe life years back. Haile brought me back from my reverie, however, with a question about my personal (family) life.

"Do you have children?" he asked me.

"Yes. One daughter who will be five soon."

"It must be hard, being separated from your family," Fikade said.

"Yes, it is hard. But it is part of the struggle."

"Yes, indeed; an important part," Haile said. "Let's hope the rewards of our success will compensate you."

"Well, I have learned to believe in hope. A reactionary sentiment," I said, smiling at Nega who smiled back.

"I thought you didn't believe in labeling," Nega said, and we all laughed.

"Labels are an essential part of a struggle," I said. "But the question is where and when and about whom they are used."

"The powerful use them to stigmatize the weak," Haile said, displaying a discerning mind. "And the oppressed must also learn how to use them, because labels have a powerful mobilizing function. The first thing that an oppressed class or nation must do is to reject imposed labels that demean and enfeeble it."

"Then you agree with me about the importance of choosing the right target, time and place," I said.

"I agree completely," he said. "I also think that when an oppressed group makes an inverted use of labels, such as American blacks calling each other 'nigger,' it is a sign of a profound sense of humor born out of struggle."

"Or the notion of the self-hating Jew?" I added.

"Exactly. Now, there is an interesting phenomenon. A self-hating

Jew. Mind you, there are truly self-hating Jews and self-hating blacks. That is a function of the success of the powerful class instilling a sense of inadequacy in the mind of the oppressed. Fascinating, isn't it?"

"And depressing," Fikade said. "I had a problem trying to get my mother to stop calling the majority nation in our country by the name imposed by the ruling nation. She still uses the old name, and will die defending her right to call anything and anybody by the name she chooses."

"That is Humpty Dumpty philosophy," Haile said.

"Ah! Humpty Dumpty. That's right," Fikade said, and looking lyrical continued: "When I use a word, it means exactly what I choose it to mean, neither more nor less."

"'The question is,' said Alice," (I put in) "'Whether you can make words mean so many different things.'"

"'The question is,' said Humpty Dumpty," (retorted Fikade) "'which is to be master—that's all!'"

We all laughed, though Nega looked rather lost and there was a hollow ring to his laughter. It was clear to me that he did not know what the hell we were talking about and resented it.

Oh yes, that was it: Resentment. The word came to my mind then, as it did many times before and after. It was the word that came to mind when Nega spoke to me disparagingly the first day we met and talked about Akalu. It defined the gap between him and the others (and me).

The spirit of resentment was written on Nega's face as we three exchanged quips and jokes that went over his head. I knew then, as I know now, that Nega and his ilk are the source of our trouble. Beware of resentful men, they are dangerous. Their look is not only lean and hungry; it burns with envy and suppressed hatred. The history of our unhappy land has been determined by such men and the mischief that has befallen us must be laid at their door. And they flock together.

When we were about to depart from the cafe, we were joined by the African who had been at the professor's table. Haile whispered, "Here comes a man who may be of interest to you."

"*Salut, Maitre Mekonnen!*" Fikade said to the man who walked toward us with an air of confidence, as though he owned the place. He was dressed differently than Haile and company, who wore army field jackets and jeans; he wore a brown corduroy jacket and trousers to match, an open shirt and a silk scarf tied around his neck. He was of medium height with receding hair and rimless glasses, from behind which large brown eyes presided over what seemed to be a perpetually amused smile.

"*Salut, compatriots,*" the man said, fixing his eyes on me and stretching his hand to shake mine. He did not bother to shake hands with the others, but he patted Fikade on the back.

"This is Mekonnen, a law student working on his doctorate," Fikade said by way of introduction.

"And how is the revolution, comrades?" Mekonnen asked with an impish chuckle. There was a sarcastic edge to the use of the word "comrades."

"Which one, the armchair revolution or the real one?" Nega shot back, glowering.

"All revolutions begin in the armchair. Or are you going to tell me that Marx was a coal miner?" Mekonnen retorted.

"And to you, coal miners or peasants cannot lead a revolution, I suppose," Nega said.

It became obvious to me that Mekonnen and Nega were conducting an ongoing verbal war. I learned later that they used to be classmates.

"That has never been my conclusion," said Mekonnen. "What I do contest, as you well know, is intellectuals in field jackets and jeans pretending to be leaders of miners or peasants, pretending to embody the revolution of the popular masses, pretending . . ."

Haile intervened in an attempt to steer the conversation to other topics. "Tell me, Mekonnen," he said. "What was the good professor going on about? He was full of quotations."

But Nega would not let go. Some old wounds must have been opened. "To hell with the cafe professor," he said. "I want to answer Mekonnen's absurd remarks about intellectuals pretending to lead revolutions." He turned to face Mekonnen, who sat opposite to him.

"Tell me, Mekonnen. Are you saying that Marx, Engels and Lenin were not intellectuals; or that they did not live and work for the revolution of the working man?"

The original plan to leave the cafe was postponed. We all settled for a battle of wits.

"Well, Nega. You began by saying 'to hell with the cafe philosopher.' And I begin by saying categorically 'to hell with your Marx and Lenin.' The masses for whom you have been shedding crocodile tears for more years that I care to remember, the masses for whom Marx and Lenin labored mightily and spoke and wrote voluminously, are now the anchor of the capitalist system. That was what the professor was saying, the one you call a cafe philosopher. And he is backed up by facts and figures, not just abstract theories. That is the first point. The second point is that modern psychology teaches us that the Marxes and Lenins and Stalins of this world are not the saints that you try to make them."

"I have never said they were saints. The notion is ridiculous," Nega interjected.

"Not as ridiculous as you think. You don't understand my point. But my third point was going to be precisely this—to reject any pretense that man can be devoid of selfish motives. In fact I would argue that, at bottom, martyrs are the most selfish people. I don't trust saints and martyrs, any more than I trust so-called revolutionaries substituting themselves for the oppressed masses, and acting in their behalf."

"But you would trust the landlord, or the bourgeois owner of the means of production, I suppose?" Nega said with a rare display of irony, accompanied by an equally rare smile.

"*Maitre Mekonnen,*" Fikade said interceding between the two old protagonists. "Tell us more about your views on what should be done to improve the lot of the working people, say in our own country. Let's forget the West, for now."

"As a matter of fact, it happens to be one aspect of my doctoral thesis," Mekonnen said, throwing a contemptuous glance at Nega—who, I later learned, had failed his examination for doctoral candidature three years earlier.

"First of all, let's agree on a couple of points. Let me ask you: can man, any man, act without an incentive, primarily of a material interest?"

"Let us grant you the point for the sake of argument," Fikade said, "without forgetting that men have been known to sacrifice material interest for the good of others."

"I am talking about the common man, the average," Mekonnen said.

"Granted. Go on," Fikade said.

All the while Haile kept quiet, watching and listening with the calm, disinterested regard of a magistrate—of one who is not involved in the dispute of the moment, but rather ponders its future implications. A remoteness from the immediate, an intellectual disinterestedness, might be an asset for a judge or an intellectual, but for a political leader it could be a fatal flaw, I thought.

Haile occasionally glanced at me, perhaps wondering why I did not intervene. But I was fascinated by the course of the dialogue and wanted to find out where it was leading. It was clear to me that Mekonnen was a skeptic whose critical mind had been honed in the schools of France. His personality would not fit into the mold of revolutionary action. He seemed to be most comfortable in the world of academic pursuit. In that sense, he was a natural antagonist of Nega and what he represented.

Mekonnen was evidently a Parisian, a man given to the joy of the moment. I kept wondering how he would adapt back home. Mekonnen took a cigarette from his breast pocket and lit it before he concluded his argument.

"The common man is interested first and foremost in the satisfaction of his daily needs: bread for his family, shelter, clothing, what have you. If a revolution can give him more of these, or something better in their place, he will support it. But he is also by nature cautious, and therefore conservative. He will not be gung-ho for a revolution simply because a better life is preached by intellectuals."

"Is not the lot of the Russian and Chinese peasants better today than it was before the revolutions of those two countries?" Fikade asked.

"Perhaps. But now the peasant will want more and better things. Have you not heard of another revolution: the revolution of rising expectations?"

"You are shifting ground. First, grant me my point: that the Russian and Chinese revolutions have ushered in a better era for the peasants," Fikade persisted.

"Suppose I grant you that. Now grant me my point. The American worker is better off today than in the time of Teddy Roosevelt. The English worker is better off than in the time of Lloyd George. But is he satisfied? Of course not."

"I thought your cafe philosopher said the American worker, as the consumer of mass-produced goods, had become the pillar of American capitalism?" Haile jabbed.

"Yes, but that does not contradict the basic thesis that the American worker is not the agent of revolutionary change that you Marxists contend. His lack of satisfaction is in the realm of goods and services. Working within the system, he wants more of the same, or better; he does not want to destroy the system."

"In other words, the worker is not and cannot be a revolutionary?" Nega concluded for him.

"Not against what he considers to be his interest as he sees it at any particular moment. *C'est la primauté de l'instant. C'est tous,*" Mekonnen said with a flourish, crushing his cigarette in the ashtray.

He looked at his watch and rose to leave.

"The subject cannot be exhausted in one afternoon. But the bottom line is: nobody acts selflessly, even when he pretends to do so. At heart we are all selfish. Let's face it, *comrades.* The revolution is a lie. You are all living a lie!"

It was a cruel parting shot which stunned us. "What would we gain by becoming revolutionaries, do you think?" Haile asked calmly. Nothing ruffled Haile.

"Power, of course. It is obvious. You are interested in power, but you are not honest enough to say so. You wrap yourselves in the ideology about the right of the masses. *C'est la vérité.* I know you hate me for saying so, but it is the truth. If you can bring some good for everybody with the least harm, you have my blessing, for what it is worth. But history teaches us that revolutions invariably do needless harm. I am not prepared to give my support to needless harm."

We all rose to leave. If eyes could kill, Nega's glare at Mekonnen would have been instantly lethal.

Mekonnen was curious to know who I was and why I did not speak. "What is your view of this sir?" he asked me, before he left.

"Oh, I am for the revolution. But I am of the opinion that with the right leadership a revolution can be a humane event, with minimal harm done even to the oppressors, as human beings. I don't believe in a cop-out."

"You are obviously an optimist and have not read revolutionary history," Mekonnen said. The three looked at me and laughed, all at once. Mekonnen left, perhaps wondering what provoked their laughter.

"*Le salopard!*" Nega said with disgust.

TWENTY-NINE

That evening, Haile's Swedish fiancé handed me a sealed envelope when we got back to the apartment. Heart pounding, I opened it as soon as I was alone. But it was not from Mimi. The note was cryptic; it read: "I must see you today. I am on my way back home after six months training in the United States. You may wish to send a message to our mutual friend. You will recognize me when we meet."

It was signed only, "Room Twelve, Empire Hotel." I did not recognize the handwriting. The episode brought back some of the adrenaline and curiosity of the old days, and I decided to go immediately.

I had a dinner engagement with a dear old professor of mine and his family in the suburbs. When I phoned to cancel, the professor was bitterly disappointed. His wife was more philosophical. "Is this important business an assignation with a new romance?" she teased.

"No. Absolutely not. I swear on my honor. It is very serious business and the person I must see leaves tomorrow."

"Never mind. You can come another time. *C'est la même cuisine*," she cackled, and I could hear the old professor protesting.

"I will make it up to you," I said and left it there.

I took a taxi to the Empire Hotel. The taxi driver was a pot-bellied, red-cheeked man in his mid-fifties, and he wore that ubiquitous symbol of the Resistance, a beret. He talked all the way, telling me about his life and his heroic role against Nazi occupation. What a contrast to the British who make a virtue of modesty and circumspection, I thought. The French and their other Latin cousins feel a sense of inadequacy unless they can lay bare their life to a complete stranger.

My taxi driver bemoaned the plight of the poor French who were squeezed, he said, between the Jews and the Arabs.

"It is a cruel dilemma," he concluded. "On the one hand there are the Jews who make us work, not to say exploit us; and then there are the Arabs who work for us, not to say take away our jobs."

He saw me smiling in the rear-view mirror. "Can you think of a more cruel dilemma?" he asked, then answered his own question: "Of course not." He asked me where I came from just before we reached the hotel. I told him Ethiopia. He saw the hefty tip and said "*Vive l'Empereur!*" assuming no doubt that the money came from the imperial treasury.

The lounge of the Empire Hotel was small with two sets of armchairs, six in all. The name of the hotel was the only thing majestic about it. The receptionist was a middle-aged woman with platinum blonde dyed hair and an eerie smile. I asked for the occupant of room twelve.

"He just left, monsieur, and he left this message. Are you Doctor Desta?"

"Yes, madame," I said and read the note. "If you come before I return, please wait in the lobby. I will be only a few minutes," it said.

I sat reading old magazines. Barely ten minutes later, a smartly-dressed short man in a leather cap came in, smiling when he saw me. "Dr. Desta. So good to see you," he said, taking off his cap.

It was our mysterious officer whom I had last seen at Melaku's funeral in Dessie, before he disappeared into the night, leaving us all to wonder where he had come from and where he was going.

The suit that he was wearing had transformed him, and he had put on weight. He was dressed immaculately in a grey birds-eye suit, hardly the garb of a revolutionary. But then the military men who begrudged the conspicuous consumption of the civilian elite, all too often bought the most expensive clothes for themselves. I noticed that he wore a silk tie and expensive shoes.

"Let's go to a cafe," he said. It sounded more like a command than a suggestion. As always, he exuded confidence.

"Our leader knew your address through his British contacts," he explained. "He cabled me to pass through Paris to meet you."

"I don't even know your name," I said after we had ordered beer and sandwiches.

"Mengesha Haile Mehaiman," he said, smiling. It was the same smile that had greeted me at our first meeting. It was an unsettling smile, mysterious and mocking, even when accompanied by genial words. The eyes were not a part of the smile, but remained cold and aloof, as if they did not belong to the rest of his face.

I wanted to know about his experiences in the United States before we broached the subject of the revolution. I waited for him to start the conversation, but he was not forthcoming. "How was America?" I began, finally.

"Overwhelming," he said throwing his arms into the air, as if he did not know where to begin.

"What part of America did you see?"

"I did not see much outside the area where I was training. The camp is in Maryland, not far from Washington, D.C. I got out for visits on a few occasions. Otherwise, it was hard work all the way."

"What kind of training?"

"Ordinance, which is a branch of logistics," he said.

He did not wish to pursue that topic. He explained his anonymity, probably because he sensed that I wondered why Iman had not properly introduced him in our first meeting at Mama Zen's.

"Our leader advised that we should remain anonymous even to each other. The situation demanded this precaution. But now our movement is quite secure; even if individuals are caught the extent of the damage they can do will be minimal."

"I am glad to hear that," I said.

I briefed him about the situation in Europe and asked him if he had made any contacts in America.

"I attended a couple of meetings of our students in the U.S.," he said. "They spend their time fighting over ideology and are split from top to bottom. They are hopeless. From what I hear, those in Europe are better organized and united. We can do better business with them.

I have heard of Haile Dada and his group. But we will rely on you for guidance on this subject," he concluded.

There was no telling on what he meant by his concluding remark. I wanted to play it safe.

"Well, I will communicate my views to Brigadier Iman in detail," I said.

He gazed at me for a moment. "Good," he said finally; then asked me if I wanted to send a letter to Iman.

We returned to the hotel, where I scribbled a short note. It simply said, "I met your man. All is well at this end, but I am itching to return. I need a word regarding you know who—care of our London contact."

Just to be on the safe side, I signed it "Monty's friend," knowing that Iman was an admirer of Field Marshall Montgomery; I sealed the envelope, and gave it to Mengesha.

"I will deliver it first thing after my arrival. We will meet in victory," Mengesha said, extending his hand which I shook vigorously.

It began in a zoo. Mengesha and I were leaning on a guard rail facing the monkey cage. Mengesha made faces and one monkey rose off its florid bottom and began pacing back and forth in great agitation. It looked at me, as if asking for help, but avoided Mengesha's eyes. Suddenly, without warning, it flew at the fence in front of Mengesha and almost caught his fingers. It gripped the wire mesh, baring its teeth and screaming like hell. We left immediately.

Then we were in a nearby restaurant where a mother was taking her baby from her pram. The mother asked us if we would mind holding the baby while she took out fresh diapers. Without waiting for an answer, she handed the baby to Mengesha, who happened to sit nearer to her.

Mengesha did what we all do with babies: baby language, goggling eyes, and giggling. The baby began to scream.

"Is that man giving you the eye?" the mother laughed, taking back the soggy child. The child was not amused. Like the monkey, it gazed at me, but avoided Mengesha's eyes.

Then we were in the woods. Mengesha wanted to meet Haile Dada.

"Just Haile, no one else," he insisted. The meeting took place in the woods of Bois de Boulogne. Haile seemed changed. He lost his remote, disinterested gaze and became transfixed by Mengesha's eyes. I noticed that Mengesha wore an open shirt, and hanging from his neck was a pair of crescent shaped ivory pieces that seemed to draw Haile's attention.

"Now, repeat after me," Mengesha commanded. "The only way to the revolution is to trust the armed forces." Haile obediently repeated the words. Mengesha then turned toward me, and I saw shafts of blinding light emitted from his eyes. The pain was intolerable. I bolted up from my bed.

"Thank God. It was only a dream!" I said.

In the post-nightmare gloom, my mind focused on Mengesha's eyes. It has been said that eyes are windows of the soul, and I did not see benevolence in those eyes.

But in the morning, after a cup of coffee and a croissant, amid the fresh air and the sound of the traffic, I put such thoughts aside as unworthy of a revolutionary whose tools are—or should be—rational scientific analysis. Who was I to judge a fellow revolutionary on the basis of physical traits which are biological accidents? It was superstitious nonsense to indulge in speculations about the ancient Evil Eye just because a bloody monkey and a six-month old baby had screamed at someone in a dream.

My rational education and scientific vocation had banished such superstitions to the remotest recesses of my mind. The spirit-inhabited woods that were part of my African heritage had been cut down by science and Christianity.

They were all still there, waiting to be rediscovered in my dreams. But daylight and the sights and sounds of "The City of Light"—home of modern, rational man—banished them again.

Thus ended my Paris sojourn.

THIRTY

I traveled from France to Italy, Germany, and Sweden. My purpose was to create and deepen contacts with non-student exiles. I discovered that most of these were members of Haile's student organization, which did not make membership conditional on being a student. A few exiles stayed aloof from the organization on ideological grounds, stating that it was too radical and out of tune with the conditions of our people. But Haile's organization had outmaneuvered them and was accepted by many governments and parties in Europe. The Left parties of Europe in particular, notably the communist parties of France and Italy, saw in it the nucleus of a future Ethiopian government. Some of the exiles were convinced that the Soviet Union provided financial and political support through the West European Left parties, and that the student movement had sold its national soul to the "devil."

Back in England just before Christmas, I found three letters waiting for me.

One was from Gloria Sullivan, mailed from Philadelphia. Gloria expressed her sadness that she could not fulfill her promise to look after Mimi because of her expulsion. She begged me not to believe the wild stories being spread about her.

The second, signed "Monty," was from Brigadier Iman. He said that the situation was evolving rapidly and that I should be ready for recall.

The third letter was from Mimi. I did not know until I opened the envelope that it was from her. It began:

"My dearest love: May this find you in good health and spirit. How I long to be with you, to be held by you and to look at your face and listen to your voice, which I miss more than words can express.

"Not long after you left, I had a miscarriage. Yes, my dearest, I lost our baby."

I stopped reading. The word "miscarriage" stuck in my throat. I read it and re-read it. It dissolved the meaning of every other word in the letter. I felt an acute pain; the pain of separation, which had been buried in my daily routine, tearing through the prosaic, protective cover.

Poor Mimi! Not only did she lose a priceless life that united our lives, I knew that she would suffer guilt and fear that I would blame her. But I did not blame her; far from it. My heart went out to her; I wanted to pack and go and hug her. But alas! That could not be.

Yet, there must be a way, I pondered. There must be a way.

The Christmas party began at the Athenaeum Club, where I met more of Sir Geoffrey's friends. I did not even register their names in my mind, which was still filled with thoughts of Mimi. The party ended at Manor House, the home of Sir Geoffrey's sister, Lady Priscilla Hornblower. Lady Hornblower was the wife of Sir Anthony Hornblower, a Knight of the Garter and a former Chief Justice of a crown colony.

The residence of Sir Anthony and Lady Hornblower was in Middlesex, an hour's train ride from London. The party was made up of about twenty members of the immediate family and close friends, as well as about a dozen neighbors. Most of the latter were country squire types, local lawyers and rich farmers. Among the former were a couple of members of Parliament and a junior minister. In short, the party comprised a microcosm of England's elite.

I was introduced as an Ethiopian scholar; and no politics were mentioned at first, save for a few remarks by the local farmers about the danger to Britain from the European Common market. But toward the end of the party a slightly built, bespectacled young man of about thirty approached me with a provocative question: "The future of monarchy in Africa does not inspire much hope, wouldn't you say?"

"There are only a few monarchies left," I equivocated.

"Is it only a matter of arithmetic?" he probed.

"Yes. When you spoke of the future of monarchy, the question presumed there were many monarchies left," I said.

"Good point. Nevertheless, if the few that are left could inspire confidence in comparison with the one-party republics and the military dictatorships, then the question would go beyond arithmetic, wouldn't it?"

"Would it?"

"Wouldn't it?"

Ah, the subtle British! Their understatement. The lean economy of their discourse. The Socratic method of their probing.

"Well, would it?" I held my ground. After all, he had brought up the subject. Let him prove his point, I thought.

The bespectacled young man smiled and changed tactics, to a frontal attack.

"Tell me. Why would a Brigadier be better than an Emperor in Ethiopia?"

"I wouldn't know. Why would he?"

"Come, come. I know you are a friend of Brigadier Iman."

"I had no idea that Brigadier Iman had presidential ambitions," I said in mock surprise.

"Perhaps not. But if the Emperor's government were to fall, he would be a good candidate, wouldn't you say?"

"Perhaps he would. Then again he may not. After all, the Emperor does have a successor in the Crown Prince."

"Precisely my point, " the man exulted. "These upstart colonels and presidents are no match for hereditary successors. Public expectations of a smooth transfer of power underlies the value of a monarchial system of government."

"That assumes many things," I said. "It assumes that the successor monarch would be an enlightened one. In a constitutional monarchy like yours, it does not matter whether the monarch is a genius or an idiot, because the real government lies elsewhere. I don't have to tell you that this system has evolved through centuries of struggle between kings and nobles and then between noblemen and commoners. That is your history. You can't impose that history on us."

"But the Bolsheviks can impose their history on you, eh?" He arched his brow.

"Did I say that?"

"You don't have to say it. Your movement does."

By that time a member of Parliament and another man had joined us and were listening with great interest. "His movement?" the member of Parliament inquired.

"Yes. Would you like to tell the honorable gentleman from Harrow about your underground movement?" the young man challenged me.

"Why don't you? You seem to know all about it," I said.

"All right, I will. And please correct me if I am wrong," he said.

His account of my activities, my comrades, and my banishment was concise, complete, and accurate.

"May I ask how you came to know all this?" I inquired.

"Tony is a member of the special branch," the member of Parliament informed me.

Tony, or Anthony Hornblower, Junior, son of Sir Anthony and Lady Hornblower, had been born abroad and knew several languages including Arabic, I was told later.

The next day on our way back to London, Sir Geoffrey and Tony Junior engaged me in a serious dialogue on the prospect of a republican government after the demise of the Emperor's regime. Above all, Tony wanted to know what guarantees could be devised to ensure that his sworn enemies, the "Bolsheviks," did not take over. He wanted to know whether I and my group could be trusted to be good patriots and avoid entanglement with his enemies.

"I trust that you are a good British patriot. And I would expect you to do me the courtesy of trusting that I am a good Ethiopian patriot. Indeed, it can't be otherwise," I said.

The discussion ended there and we began to talk about the beauty of the English countryside, punctuated by long silences. We took a taxi from the train station.

"I enjoyed the parties, Sir Geoffrey. Tony, I hope I will see you again," I said when we parted outside my apartment.

"We were all delighted to meet you," Tony said. "And I am sure we will meet again."

"Cheerio, old boy. So glad you could come to meet my crowd," Sir Geoffrey said.

In the end, my life in exile came down to housekeeping, making daily calls to keep abreast of developments, comparing notes with like-minded people, and preparing for the future. Endless calls, endless talk, and ceaseless travel back and forth across the English Channel. Routine had gained supremacy. The vision was getting blurred.

Most people talked about the present, while a few farsighted ones prepared for the future. In the crucible of the revolutionary movement the past was recalled and reintepreted. There were factional splits and national splits; and the scriptures of Twentieth Century Revolution were quoted by every faction and every national movement in support of its case.

There were times when the future seemed to me to be thick with the fog of these acrimonious debates. And then there were the likes of Tony Junior and Nega Gobena, who added insult to injury. Anyway, I had had enough of it all; and had probably outlived my usefulness abroad and even my welcome, though Sir Geoffrey's generosity of spirit and untiring efforts to help stood as a monument to decency.

THIRTY-ONE

Three years after I set foot on English soil as an exile, I went back to the field of action. I went back through a tortuous and hazardous route across the wilds and mountains of Eritrea and northern Ethiopia.

There was no easier way to get back, and Eritrea had become the single most important region of rebellion which threatened the Emperor's regime. One of my old school friends, a former leader in the student movement, joined the Eritrean Student Union in Europe and eventually became a top leader in the Eritrean Liberation Front. His name was Habte Bahru.

Habte arranged my travel through Eritrea and he himself accompanied me from Port Sudan up to the Eritrean border, where I was taken in escort by an armed company of liberation fighters.

There are few borders as dramatic as the border between life under normal law and order and life under a rebellion. To cross into Eritrea at that time was to go from the certainties of imperial law to the hazards of unknown men with guns. It was also to go from a life of relative ease to one of tension and austerity.

The first part of the journey across the rugged mountains of Eritrea was hard. I had blisters on the soles of my feet the first two days, which slowed us down. My escorts bore with me. They helped me with my load and attended to my needs as best they could. After the fifth day the blisters hardened into calluses. My speed increased, to the surprise of my escorts.

We depended on the local population for food and water, because at that stage of the Eritrean liberation struggle there was no logistical support system. Moreover, a civil war was raging between two factions of the movement, which dissipated whatever resources the front might have been able to deploy for purposes such as my journey. The conversation among my escorts was dominated by the civil war. They belonged to the more numerous but more loosely-organized ELF. The smaller but better-organized EPLF was concentrated at that time in other areas. My escorts referred to the rival front as counter-revolutionary and its leadership as a criminal gang.

I pretended to know nothing about the rival movement, even though I knew through Berhane (of our Central Committee) that many of the EPLF's new recruits were friends of our student groups. The leader of my escort asked me questions designed to find out my affiliation. I simply told him that my group was a segment of the revolutionary movement which was dedicated to the overthrow of the imperial regime.

It took us sixteen days to reach the southern border of Eritrea. The rains had failed for two years, and in some areas for three years. We could see evidence of this disaster in the withered flora and the carcasses of livestock scattered everywhere. The bleached bones of the carcasses indicated that they had been dead for two years or more. Whole villages had been abandoned by the people, who were forced to trek to the cities for relief. It was a woeful sight.

We were forced to make several detours in search of food and water. This meant waiting for night to fall, then sending a scout to the home of a trusted supporter. At one village in Seraye we were almost caught by the police. That was the only time we had to use our firearms.

The name of the village escapes me, but it was near a town dominated by the government's loyal supporters—led by a feudal family. We spent the night at the home of an ELF supporter. Early the next morning, one member of our group was sent to buy supplies from a shop. The shopkeeper must have suspected him to be a liberation fighter and alerted the police. But the man, a veteran fighter, sensed the trap and deliberately walked in the opposite direction from where we had spent the night. He then made a detour and came to join us, unobserved by anyone.

We were ready to leave. The team leader divided us into two units as a precaution. His group took up position on high ground. I was sent with the other group, which went past them to take up another position, covering the first group. The first group then withdrew further away and took up another position to cover us.

Suddenly we saw a squad of policemen running toward us. The team leader opened fire with his AK–47. Two policemen dropped, dead or wounded; most of the rest ran away while a few fell flat on the ground. Our leader gave the order to flee, and we all ran and disappeared into a hilly area covered by thorn brush. We heard more firing behind us, but we saw no one in pursuit. We had escaped unscathed.

"That was close!" I said.

They all smiled and looked at one another. "That was nothing!" one of them said.

"What if they pursue us?" I asked.

"They won't. They will spend the whole morning writing reports and boasting about how they chased us away," the leader said. "Your fear would be justified if these were the special commando forces. They are Israeli-trained and are fearless fighters. Fortunately, there are no commandos in this part of the country."

As we got to know one another we became friends. The shared experience of an arduous journey and a common danger forged a bond between us. I understood at last what my teachers in France had meant when they referred to the bond of the *anciens combatants* with mystical wistfulness.

When we began the journey, I had perceived three enemies. The first was the terrain and the harsh environment of the desert. The second was the security forces and their civilian auxiliaries. The third was the tension that I sensed in the company. As I got used to the hardships, the first of the three assumed less and less significance. As for the second, the security forces were not visible and the only actual contact was the one described above.

The tension in the group thus became my principal source of worry. I felt the tension from the outset. I did not think my escorts liked making this arduous journey just to provide a safe passage for one Ethiopian. I represented a people (and had been a member of a government) that in their eyes was the real enemy oppressing them.

Within the group itself, there seemed to be an undercurrent of conflict between the team leader and another member. I heard them raising their voices on a couple of occasions. The other member was a sullen type who did not exchange one word with me throughout the journey. In moments of wild imagining I feared that if a quarrel broke out in which he eliminated the team leader, I could be in for it. The uncertainty oppressed me. Who knows, I wondered, what goes on in the mind of a quiet rebel (with a gun) escorting a member of the "enemy" people?

The incident in the village put my worries to rest. It seemed to have a cathartic effect on the group. Even the sullen one smiled as the team leader joked about the police. To them it was all in a day's work; it was what they were trained for and lived to expect. To me it was the closest I had come to actual combat, and I don't mind confessing that I was scared to death. I even thought of the absurdity of dying there, having escaped the imperial security. How would my epithet read? I wondered.

Fortunately, it all ended well. When we were at a safe distance from the village, all my putative enemies had been left behind and were receding into the distance. A new and final phase of my journey back home had begun.

My Eritrean friends had done a good job. Risk, hardship and privation was their way of life, which they adopted voluntarily for a cause which they considered to be higher than themselves. That was why the Eritreans, though usually outnumbered, outmaneuvered the Ethiopian army in countless battles. Their successful challenge to that army in the north was to prove a critical factor in the eventual demise of the imperial regime.

My ELF escorts saw me safely into my own region, where I had friends who could take me safely on to Addis Ababa. I was sorry to part from these hardy fighters. The unassuming, diligent and business-like character of the Eritreans had always impressed me. Now that they were properly organized and armed, they would be a force to reckon with in the future politics of the region.

I told the leader of my escort that if my own group succeeded in toppling the imperial regime, the first item on the agenda of the new government would be peace in Eritrea.

"What kind of peace? Under what terms and conditions?" he probed.

"I would like to believe that we can form a government dedicated to democracy, and that means the right to self-determination," I said.

"Up to and including independence?" he pursued.

"I don't see why not. Mind you, I personally would wish that Eritrea could remain a part of the whole, with a guarantee of maximum autonomy."

"Like a federation?"

"Yes. As was provided for, before greed and imperial aggrandizement destroyed it," I said.

"And what did you Ethiopians do when the federation was destroyed? How many people protested?" he asked, and I cringed. None of us had raised a voice of protest.

"I grant you the point," I said. "We were remiss in failing to protest. But that is done; what matters now is the future. More people are now aware of the fact that the Eritrean quest for freedom cannot be stopped."

"What would you do if you became a member of a new government?" he pursued.

"I would demand that your quest for freedom be supported."

"Would you be agreeable to an internationally-supervised referendum?"

"Yes, I would."

"Would you accept the verdict of the Eritrean people, should they vote for independence in such a referendum?"

"Yes. If the people chose independence, then despite my own wishes, I would accept their choice," I said.

"In that case, we wish you and your group every success," he said, looking around to see the reaction of his comrades. They nodded in agreement.

"And I wish your people's struggle success," I replied, "because we all have a stake in it. The Eritrean struggle has shaken the empire to its foundations."

"Thank you," he said.

"No, it is I who should thank you, and I do so from the bottom of my heart. I will always remember this help."

They were all moved. We embraced one another as they prepared to leave. Even the sullen one tapped me on the shoulder in the manner of the lowland greeting. They left me outside the Ethiopian town of Makale. As I stood watching them disappear behind a cloud of dust which merged with the darkening sky of the approaching night, part of me went with them. The moment and the scene had a poetic quality.

THIRTY-TWO

I was now moving closer to a fateful rendezvous with history, ending a journey which had meandered through twists and turns. Events that had flowed from diverse and different sources were approaching a point of convergence.

The aging Emperor had celebrated his eightieth birthday with pomp and ceremony, seemingly unconcerned with the deafening clamor for his exit from the stage of history. He seemed to have withdrawn from reality, judging by the obscene spectacle in which he was seen feeding animals on the roadside every week while his people starved.

The cacophony of protests had reached a high pitch and was turning into a tragic symphony orchestrated by invisible hands. The students became more daring in their challenge and were rewarded by open public support, including that of labor unions and small traders. After the worldwide rise of oil prices, inflation had struck at every sector of urban society, and all were now geared for change.

Meanwhile, the war in Eritrea and the famine in Wollo and elsewhere in the north was attracting world attention. A fickle international press, which had yawned with disinterest, was now galvanized by the sight of emaciated bodies. The BBC played a catalytic role by showing a film of these scenes which led to public outcry the world over.

All the while, the military waited in the wings, keeping an opportunistic watch on developments. At first, only those units directly affected by the war in Eritrea would dare to protest. They were followed by other units from every corner of the empire, protesting the deteriorating conditions of military service.

It was the beginning of the end.

In the spring of 1974 the revolution exploded. The world has been fascinated by what became known as the "creeping coup," which slowly unfolded from February to September of that year. Coup watchers and revolutionary enthusiasts, who do not experience the pain that goes into the making of such events, have made endless comments. Most of their comments have missed the point, and none of them has seen the ugly side, as some of us did.

By the time I reached Addis Ababa and linked up with Brigadier Iman in late 1973, the city's nervous system was showing signs of breakdown. It was fretful with paranoia. People hoarded essential supplies. Absenteeism from school and work, disobedience of authority, bold exchanges of obscenities, the flight of capital, and the purchase of private arms at astronomical prices became the order of the day. Other cities soon followed suit.

Brigadier Iman arranged for me to stay in the home of his sister, a devout Christian who cared little about worldly affairs. He told her that I was sick and was not to be disturbed by anyone. No one was to see me or know about my presence, except people he himself might bring at night to meet me.

From the time of my arrival in late December, I had asked to see Mimi, but Iman had just smiled and counseled patience. One evening after I had been in his sister's house for a few days, I asked why I couldn't see her.

"I understand your impatience, my friend," he said. He had just come in, looking tired and preoccupied. He turned on the radio to listen to news; he brought beers and roasted ground nuts and sat opposite me.

"Dinner should be ready soon. You have lost weight, and must be fed properly. These nuts and the beer will help in the meantime," he said, skirting the subject of Mimi.

Iman had been meticulous in working out the plan that brought me from Wollo to Addis Ababa. The communication from London had kept him abreast of my progress in the wilds of Eritrea. Then his own people brought me from Makale through the Wollo region in relays. The plan involved fake military training and transport of supplies. I was impressed and flattered to be the object of such attention, and I said so to Brigadier Iman.

"First of all you are my friend—my very good friend," he said. "Then you are a man who has risked much for our common cause, and you are worth all the efforts. So, stop thanking me."

"All the same . . ."

"All the same, it was done for the cause," he interrupted. He raised his glass: "Chin chin."

"Chin chin," I said and drank my beer quietly.

We sat listening to the music from the radio. He must have guessed what I was thinking.

"Before we talk about Mimi, let me finish what I started telling you the other day," he said. He briefed me in detail on the events of the previous year, with particular emphasis on the last three months—October through December 1973.

"The old man talks to his dogs and shuns his ministers. Did you know that?"

"It is pathetic," I said.

But my mind was on Mimi. Finally, he must have guessed that I was not concentrating and that I suspected he was hiding something from me. He pulled a sealed envelope from his pocket and gave it to me.

"This has been with me for over a month," he said apologetically. "There has been a change in her life."

The handwriting was Mimi's. I was puzzled and sensed disaster. Iman left me and went to the kitchen to talk with his sister.

Very slowly I read the letter, word by word. It was a letter of farewell. Mimi said she had left the city for good and moved back to Wollo. She wished me well, but expresseed no desire to see me again. I read the last page over and over, searching fruitlessly for any expression of love or hope.

Then I asked Iman: "Did you see her before she left?"

"Yes. Lula arranged a meeting outside the Villa Bianca. I saw her briefly and she gave me this letter."

"Is there anything else you can tell me about her sudden departure?"

"All I know is that she had some problems. That she was sad, and that when the Wollo famine became the talk of the town, she decided to go. I learned all this from Lula."

"The letter says she joined a foreign relief organization."

"So it will be easy enough to trace her, if that is your desire."

"It is," I said. "And I would like to ask one more favor. I would like to see my daughter, from a distance. I can do it from a parked car outside her school."

"Okay. We'll arrange that," Iman said.

The New Year came and the slow motion revolution began. The first serious outbreak was a series of mutinies in units of the armed forces in Eritrea and to the south.

At first the incidents seemed isolated; the complaints were narrowly focused on conditions of military service. Then the teachers went on strike to protest a new education policy. The teachers' strike was followed by taxi drivers protesting increases in petrol prices. Bus drivers followed suit, the students egging them on.

Iman took me on several drives at night to see the streets for myself. I wore a military uniform as camouflage. We were often stopped by military police. Invariably, he would be instantly recognized and saluted, and we would pass on.

On February 20 we drove around in many areas of the city. The streets were deserted by ten o'clock at night. I saw several smashed cars. On the car radio we heard a nervous government official explaining the new education policy as a World Bank project. He kept repeating the name of the World Bank, as if it had some final, papal authority over the affairs of a nation like ours.

"Listen to the fool," Iman said.

"I know. I was just thinking of that. The regime is losing its nerve."

"Our moment has arrived, I think. It is just a matter of establishing a command center to coordinate the various movements."

"Beginning with your colleagues in the military?"

"Of course. But it won't be easy. We have begun meeting at the headquarters of the First Division. We must find a safe meeting place outside headquarters until we feel certain that we can openly challenge the regime without fear of a counter-attack."

"Or until you can move swiftly and organize a coup?" I inquired.

"The old man has cleverly divided the military; people don't trust each other. The moment will arrive when most of the officers will feel that it is all over for the regime. Then they will rally around us."

"What about the imperial bodyguard? After all, they tried to overthrow him once," I said.

"They are the most dangerous. Their commander is intensely loyal. If I know him, he will die defending the Emperor."

"That is interesting," I said. "I always thought he was an opportunist."

"Not when it comes to the Emperor."

"So who are your present supporters? I mean in which unit?"

"Mostly in the Third Division. But there are some good officers in the staff of the First Division. I have been cultivating them indirectly."

We reached a wooded area past the Balcha hospital. It was pitch dark; only the car's headlights illuminated the dirt road behind the hospital, which we navigated slowly. We arrived at an isolated house and stopped.

Iman turned the engine off, then turned the lights on and off three times.

After about five minutes we heard footsteps approaching. I could hear the faint sound of a song being whistled.

"That's the counter signal," Iman said, and we got out and followed the whistling stranger who had walked past our car. My eyes had grown accustomed to the dark in my Eritrean adventure.

"You have not told me where we are going," I whispered.

"It is a surprise. A welcoming party for you," he whispered back.

It was indeed a surprise. A wonderful gift of a surprise. The whistling stranger led us through a gate into the house. A door was opened and we entered a large salon. And there were Yohannes and Berhane, both smiling! I hugged them, one after the other.

"You have not changed a bit," Yohannes said, looking me over.

"You haven't changed either. Berhane has grown thinner," I said.

"How was it?" Berhane asked, and I did not know where to begin.

"Well, I must go," Iman said. "I have to attend a meeting. You three have all night to talk about old times. Then we will talk about the future."

"Will you come tomorrow?" I asked.

"Yes. Nobody else must know about this place until we can find a more secure headquarters. Then we can all go there."

"What! and become prisoners of the military?" I cried in mock horror.

"You are a prisoner at large now, and fair game," he pointed out. "It will be better in the barracks when we have enough forces rallying behind us."

After Brigadier Iman left, the three of us exchanged bits and pieces of personal information. The first thing I asked was where they had been during the three years of my absence. Berhane had spent his time commuting between Addis Ababa and Asmara, the Eritrean capital. He had joined the EPLF as their man in Addis Ababa. Only Yohannes (and now I) knew of this.

Yohannes had spent nearly three years in jail before being released under an imperial pardon. He had been tried by a security court and sentenced to ten years.

"What about Bekele?" I asked.

Both of them bowed their heads.

"Has something happened to him? Come on. Tell me."

Yohannes looked at Berhane, who shook his head as if to say, "It is your duty to tell him." Yohannes then spoke.

"Bekele is no more," he said.

"What happened?"

"He was tortured to death. We believe he died under torture. The police said he jumped from his apartment window while he was showing them where he had hidden incriminating papers."

"Was there an autopsy?"

"No. I was in prison and no one else could follow up the case. His brother tried, but drew a blank—blank faces at the police station, blank faces and shrugged shoulders in the ministry. And that was the end of it."

"Were you tortured, Yohannes?" I asked with a shiver.

"Of course," he said. "Don't you know that torture is part of the judicial system?"

I could sense a change in Yohannes. It was not the sort of normal change brought on by the lapse of time. Something was missing— something vital. The openness and trustfulness that had infused his voice and his gestures was gone. He was now circumspect in speech and gesture, and his eyes had lost their gleam.

"How was it?" I asked mechanically.

"Oh. It was not so bad. At first it is intolerable, but after a while the pain gets numbed and you develop a resistance. Also the relationship of the torturer and tortured is something difficult to explain."

"Don't tell me. I have heard and read about it. They call it the Helsinki something-or-other."

"Not Helsinki. The Stockholm syndrome," he said matter-of-factly. "You become like a child dependent on the torturer, who assumes the position of the provider."

"You mean the torturer knows his role? But these torturers must be ignorant second-rate policemen?" I said with anger.

"It has nothing to do with ignorance or knowledge. It is instinctive. Anyway, my torturer knew me and was considerate. He would interrupt when he realized I was passing out or was reaching a breaking point."

"Did you know him?"

"No. They are masked. They know you, but you don't know them. Some of them are sadistic and enjoy prolonging your ordeal. I was lucky. Mine was not one of those. Bekele's must have been, though," he said with a heavy sigh.

His voice was dull. It seemed to me that he had become cynical, a natural defense mechanism against a painful experience.

"How was life in prison?" I asked.

"Not bad for the inmate. It was hell for Saba and all the other wives and mothers. Anyway, let's forget the past. Did you hear about Aberra's whereabouts, by the way?"

"I tried to find out. But no one knew where he was."

"It seems that we got better information in prison than you got out of it," Yohannes said, laughing for the first time.

"Why? Have you traced him?"

"Prison is a university. In fact, it is a small universe. You find all kinds of characters. There was one character who knew Aberra from the United States. Aberra had been a plant from his student days through a secret agreement between the FBI and the imperial security's counter-espionage service."

"Do you think he may be in America?" I asked.

"This character swore that he must be there, probably under a different name," he said. His eyes did not show any sign of anger, but a cloud of gloom invaded his expression.

"The bastard!" Berhane said. "Our people will help eventually in tracing Aberra. For now, let us just celebrate our reunion."

We raised our glasses and drank quietly.

That night I had a dream. In the dream I saw Hanna chained to a rock in a desolate place. It was a damp, drizzly, foggy night. She was surrounded by rhinos stamping their hooves on the steaming ground and brandishing their horns. Hanna was dressed in a pristine white robe that looked like a bridal gown.

I made an attempt to chase the rhinos away. They would scamper a few feet, then pull back, and Hanna scolded me for chasing them. The rhinos surrounded her again and Hanna sang for them, a sort of lullaby which put them to sleep.

Then, above the rock, I saw Mimi flying with wings of fire. She was carrying a child who looked like my daughter. I called after her, but my voice was inaudible and I could not move. She circled the rock, calling Hanna's name, but Hanna behaved as though she did not hear. My attempts to get Mimi's attention were useless. My immobility was excruciating. I did not want to leave Hanna to the beasts, but I did not want to lose sight of Mimi.

Suddenly, I bolted upward like a rocket and flew over the rock and followed Mimi. I could see her wings of fire diving like a lighted arrow toward unknown terrain. I was afraid she might be falling, so I flew faster and faster until I nearly caught up with her. I saw a sharp rock ahead, and both of us were on the point of crashing when I was awakened . . .

I must have been crying out her name. Yohannes was at my bedside. "You had a nightmare," he said. "You were calling Mimi! Mimi!"

"At first I thought it was Mommy!" Berhane said, with a chuckle.

I told them about my dream and Berhane said he liked interpreting dreams. "The desolate place is the empire," he said.

"There he goes again," Yohannes said. But Berhane ignored him.

"The rock is the government and the rhinos are the *kerkedions.* Hanna's captivity and her apparent acceptance of her fate reflect her coming to terms with the reality of the situation. Mimi and the wings of fire represent the revolution, and the child she was carrying represents the future generation, the beneficiaries of the struggle."

"This was certainly the night of the *kerkedions,*" I said.

"We have all lived the nights of the *kerkedions,*" Berhane said. "It's the dark side of the thrill."

"What thrill?" I inquired.

"The thrill of riding the whirlwind, which is what we have been doing," he said.

We fell silent, as I ruminated on Berhane's remark.

THIRTY-THREE

The pace of the revolution was accelerating. A brief chronology of events in early 1974 will give a picture of the slide of the imperial regime toward its eventual demise.

Thursday, 21 February

The tension was mounting. Some civil servants failed to report to work, the ostensible reason being lack of transportation. That was the day after Iman brought me to meet my friends. There were reports of random shootings. At least two students were killed by soldiers guarding buses and installations. The streets were patrolled by soldiers toting machine guns on open army trucks.

There was a radio and TV announcement that the new education policy was suspended. Teachers had carried the day arguing that the new policy was wrong because it would put nine and ten year old children (of the poor) to work after only four years of education.

Friday, 22 February

More soldiers visible everywhere. The Prime Minister's car was stoned, along with those of other dignitaries. Buses were back in service, escorted by armed guards. Shops were closed.

Fear crippled the city—the fear of the unknown future.

Saturday, 23 February

The Emperor appeared on TV and radio, announcing the suspension of the new education policy and a reduction in petrol prices.

Sunday, 24 February

The streets were deserted. The government had arrested one thousand taxi drivers.

The soldiers, now everywhere, were coordinating, not opposing, the stone-throwing students. More cars were smashed. We heard later that evening from Iman that the soldiers were demanding a salary raise. On the evening news it was announced that the salary of soldiers would be raised to $100 a month, effective March.

Monday, 25 February

Mass promotion of officers (including my brother-in-law, Ashenafi, to the rank of major). Some of the promoted officers were taken to the palace to say *thank you* to His Majesty! (With murder in their hearts, no doubt.)

Tuesday, 26 February

Early in the morning it was reported that the ground forces had mutinied in Asmara, the Eritrean capital. Now that the soldiers had seen the Emperor to be without clothes, they demanded a monthly salary of $150. Some also wanted political changes and dismissal of ministers and generals. The Asmara soldiers arrested all officers above the rank of captain.

Wednesday, 27 February

The Air Force and the Navy in Eritrea joined in the mutiny, and a delegation was dispatched from Addis Ababa to negotiate terms of release of the officers. Only one member of the delegation came back; the rest were detained.

On TV it was announced that the government of Prime Minister Akalu had asked to resign and that the Emperor was considering it. The Emperor opened a ministerial meeting of the OAU.

Thursday, 28 February

Troops took up position to guard important installations including the ministry of information, the banks and the airport.

At two p.m., the Emperor read a short speech announcing the appointment of a new Prime Minister, Indeniye Sowyelem. This was followed by an announcement that the minimum salary for soldiers was to be $112, with a ceiling of $150. Pensions were raised to $50 from $30. The pension for soldiers disabled in the line of duty (a bone of contention of the Asmara mutiny) was raised to $85.

What a day! How thrilling for the soldiers. It was so easy, so why stop there?

Soldiers were now everywhere, stopping cars and checking identity papers. I was no longer a prisoner at large. The soldiers had released me without knowing it. I could walk freely and go anywhere I wanted, talk with anyone I wanted. What a day!

The OAU meeting of African foreign ministers had to be adjourned because the government could not guarantee their safety. The African foreign ministers were told to go home, which they did reluctantly. (They loved Addis Ababa's hospitality, day and night.)

The new Prime Minister, an Oxford-educated aristocrat, made an unsuccessful attempt to bring the situation under control. When he addressed the nation on TV he looked like a marionette manipulated by too many strings tugging in different directions.

Students shouted demanding his removal. The soldiers transported the students, urging them to keep up their demand.

Friday, 1 March

More students demonstrated, and shots were fired, with two students reported killed (probably more). Confusion followed. The armed forces were divided between those who supported the new Prime Minister and those who wanted him out.

But with the imperial bodyguard loyal to the Emperor, and the countryside outside Addis Ababa generally quiet, the forces of revolution in the armed forces could not overthrow the government. The new Prime Minister survived his first crisis, and set about forming his cabinet.

The Emperor attended a memorial service at St. George's. Things looked almost normal, but the ritual barely masked the tension simmering below the surface. The forces of change were unleashed. The students and the soldiers had tasted blood.

The new Prime Minister's cabinet appointments seemed to bridge the gap between old and new, between the emerging middle class and the retreating nobility. In this he seemed to continue the policy of the Emperor, with this difference—that young technocrats predominated in the cabinet. If this had happened a year before, it is conceivable that the country might have welcomed it as a great leap forward.

But now the unleashed forces would not be satisfied with what they considered cosmetic changes. Above all, the military were now out to grasp power in their own name.

THIRTY-FOUR

The Emperor addressed the nation on March 1, promising constitutional reform. But his promises were drowned in the clamor for radical change. That same day the labor unions threatened a general strike; the strike took place two days later, and lasted for four days, inspiring more strikes. University teachers struck in favor of political change. Even clergymen struck for a pay raise. There were strikes everywhere.

Anarchy ruled, with employees of government departments demanding the dismissal of their department heads. Government administration came to a standstill, paralyzed by strikes, absenteeism, and lack of direction.

The new cabinet met, but did not produce any new policies that could capture the public imagination. Prime Minister Indeniye Sowyelem could not give a sense of direction because he was consumed with the business of survival. The bureaucracy was thus headless: the senior bureaucrats ran scared, while the army of minor bureaucrats enjoyed the chaos and joined the general public in endless revolts. No one knew from one day to the next what might happen.

Then people started talking about a shadowy coordinating committee of the military that was seizing the initiative and making drastic decisions. Random shootings continued, resulting from confrontations between students (and employees) and the police. And rumors of clashes within the military persisted.

In late March and early April, the new Prime Minister took a bold step that would prove to be his undoing. He appointed a well-known army colonel who was related to him on his mother's side (from Gojam) to be chairman of a security committee. The other members of the committee were junior officers, presumably appointed on the recommendation of the colonel. The security committee began making arrests of "trouble makers" in the military. It declared its loyalty to the new government and said it would not tolerate any further subversion by members of the military. In its brief but spectacular life, the security committee convinced the divided officers of the various units that unless they united, the old government would return—and with a vengeance.

Brigadier Iman knew the colonel and did not trust him; neither did the other officers of the First Division. The colonel was commander of a special airborne brigade of paratroopers headquartered at Bishoftu. On March 16, the colonel's paratroopers called on a tank battalion in Adama to help them arrest "extremists" in the air force. The colonel and his group then persuaded the rest of the air force officers to give a vote of confidence to the new Prime Minister. The slogan was, "Let's give him a chance."

But that was precisely what Iman and his group did not want. They had no intention of giving the new Prime Minister a chance. It is imperative, Iman said soon afterward, that we broaden the membership of our coordinating committee and defeat the friends of Indeniye Soweylem, the new Prime Minister.

They came from all the units of the army, the police, and even the militia, traditionally looked down upon by the military (but politics does make strange bedfellows). They came from the length and breadth of the empire. They came representing their various units to the Coordinating Committee of the Armed Forces, the Police and the Militia. The name of their committee was so long that they began to refer to themselves simply as "the committee," which in the local vernacular sounds like "the dragon." And that was how people came to call the committee "the dragons."

They came to take control of the revolution in the name of the armed forces, and in the name of the whole nation. The shadowy coordinating committee, numbering 120, had expanded to embrace the rank and file, the NCOs and the junior officers (up to the rank of captain) of the entire military.

The original, smaller committee had been chaired by Captain (later Major) Samba Libbu, who was a senior officer from the First Division. Brigadier Iman acted as the "gray eminence" from a distance, guiding and counseling. But when the committee was expanded, rivalries based on personal and ethnic animosities emerged. The rivalry and jealousy was so severe that some feared a shootout between the rival groups.

Then a quiet and respected captain, known for his fairness, proposed a solution that would prove to be fatal eventually. He nominated Captain Mengesha Haile Mehaiman for the chairmanship and Captain Samba Libbu for the deputy chairmanship of the new, enlarged committee.

Captain Mengesha Haile Mehaiman did not represent any major ethnic group, and was thus seen as an acceptable compromise. It was agreed in the corridors during the recess (where I took note of the conversations) that since the real leader was Brigadier Iman, it did not matter who chaired the committee.

And that was how Mengesha Haile Mehaiman came to be the head of the coordinating committee; or, as the people called them, "the dragons."

That was in June 1974. By then the situation had gotten out of control for the new Prime Minister. He had formed a constitutional commission and announced it with pomp and ceremony. A commission of inquiry to investigate the ministers was promised. But these announcements only had the effect of whetting the public appetite for more drastic changes. The public wanted blood and the military was more than obliging; the country was in no mood for constitutional or legal niceties.

When I saw Captain Mengesha the night after his election to the chairmanship, I saw "knife" written on his face. It was an opaque, expressionless face which I could never penetrate, now or the other times I met him. That disturbed me. That his coarse, expressionless face should suggest to me a knife was irrational, and I chided myself that I was being uncharitable to a fellow human being and a fellow revolutionary.

Yet the picture of the knife persisted in my subconscious. We met again at the dinner table at the home of Iman's sister. There were four other officers, including Major Samba Libbu, besides myself and Brigadier Iman. The conversation was about the next steps to be taken in pushing the revolution forward, including cooperation with the university students and other civilian groups.

Brigadier Iman, whom they had promoted to the rank of general, took up the last subject and turned toward me.

"You will understand why I insisted that our brother Desta join us as an honorary officer. Not only because of his record as a revolutionary, but also his contacts with the civilian segment of the revolutionary movement. He will be an invaluable asset."

"We all agree. We know brother Desta," Mengesha said, and the others nodded in agreement. But I had a premonition of danger.

I attended the committee meeting the next day, as an observer. It was a buoyant day, energized by the optimism that captures the spirit when you feel an intimation of a bright future. It was a day to feel good, because the enemies of the revolution were (we thought) on the run.

Looking down from my perch in the assembly hall, I watched the rows of seats filling up with uniformed men coming in groups of twos and threes. As I scanned the assembled committee, I felt a charitable spirit swelling up in me, and I silently chastised myself (and the public) for calling them "dragons."

"An honorary officer," Amare had called me. It was a dubious title, but one of which I was proud, at first. The soldiers cheerfully jousted and waved to one another like schoolboys as they found their seats. They had good reason to be cheerful. They had scaled the dizzying heights; they were exercising the combined power of Emperor, ministers, parliament and judges. They had power over purse and power over life and death, with no one so much as to raise a question.

But even as I witnessed their triumph, I was assailed with doubts. What was to stop these men from unleashing the forces of tyranny on a helpless population? What guarantee did we have against abuse and corruption? Lord Acton's dictum that power corrupts and absolute power corrupts absolutely was a universal truth—and why should there be an exception in our case?

My cheerfulness and optimism gave way to anxiety, as the chairman called the meeting to order and "the dragons" began their violent speeches. Iman was in his office at the ministry of defense, receiving diplomats and giving interviews to the foreign press. Mengesha presided over the meeting, sitting motionless, directing the proceedings with surprising competence.

As dragon after dragon called for blood in speech after violent speech, his inscrutable face absorbed every word. By contrast, Samba Libbu, who sat on his left, registered every emotion in his expressive face, reflecting back to the gathering the sense of the meeting as the dragons gushed out their language of violence. I confess to being enthralled by the display of humble men in uniform, gathered from distant corners of the empire to leave their mark on history. I was fascinated and alarmed at the same time.

It was as if a monster in whose creation I had taken part was growing bigger and more frightful. I felt a sense of loss of control, and centered my hope of redemption on one man—General Iman. Only he, I thought, could maintain control over this new monster.

The imperial ministers had become the object of the accumulated hostility of the military, which was finding violent expression in speech after speech.

"Let's finish off the job. Let's kill the ministers!" shouted one sergeant.

"Yes. I say let's give them a taste of what they have done to the country," said another soldier, a corporal.

"What is the point of the slogan 'Forward Without Bloodshed' coined by General Iman," asked another. "How can there be a revolution without bloodshed?"

"Let us not forget that the object of the revolution is not to shed blood for its own sake," said Captain Gabriel, a police officer from the north. He was booed and shouted down.

Mengesha Haile Mehaiman called for order. And he smiled wickedly.

"Our general has told us that we will do what we have to do if there is resistance, but that our aim is not to shed blood," he said, baring his teeth and throwing up his arms as if to add: "You know what generals are like!" His gesture was greeted with prolonged laughter.

That man knew the mood of the dragons, and he knew when and how to manipulate it. I had a sinking feeling that all was lost, and I wished Iman were there. I had no right to speak, and any words from me would have been dismissed as the sermon of a pious member of the civilian elite who does not know the meaning of hunger and privation. So I kept quiet.

At the end of the meeting I walked up to the platform and observed Mengesha at close quarters. His eyes were like crevices allowing me to peer into his dark soul. He was aware that I was studying him. The shiny sheath covered the knife as he smiled his inscrutable smile.

"Brother Desta, what do you think of our council?" he asked me as we climbed down the steps of the platform together.

"It is extraordinary," I said.

He turned to examine my face and gave a cynical laugh. His eyes did not smile and his thick lips expanded to reveal cigarette-stained teeth like a row of fangs.

"Extraordinary, yes. We are living through extraordinary times. Anyone can see that. I expected a more *learned* reply from you," he said, making two syllables of learn-ed.

"Well, let me try, then," I said. "The slogan 'Forward Without Bloodshed' is a good slogan. Your remark regarding that slogan was intriguing. Are you for it or against it?"

"I bow to the wisdom of our general," he said and left me abruptly.

But I had noticed something about him for the first time. His eyes quivered, moving fast to the left and right like the eyes of a hunted beast when he was angry. And my question had angered him.

By late July of that year the cabinet of former Prime Minister Akalu, some junior ministers and managers known for their corruption, and the prominent members of the feudal establishment had been arrested and thrown into prison camp. Then Indeniye Sowyelem, the new Prime

Minister, was arrested.

It was a measure of the old Emperor's vainglory as well as his loss of touch with reality that he sat silently, turning the other way, while people who had served him well (some for decades) were hunted down, ferreted out one by one, handcuffed and thrown into prison. The pillars of his regime were now removed, and he stood alone at the center of an edifice about to collapse. I felt that the Emperor's benign descent into insanity was complete.

Iman had permitted Mengesha to form an executive committee which acted in the name of the larger council. They kept Iman busy attending to details and ceremonial matters, while they made the important decisions and informed him after the event.

I thought this was a serious mistake, and told him so. "I think you are too trusting," I said. "I don't trust Mengesha and his group."

"Desta, you are exaggerating. You worry too much," he said.

"No, I am not exaggerating. They are doing things behind your back, and when you allow that to happen anything is possible."

"Like what?"

"Like one day you will be stripped of power," I said.

"Come on! These are officers whom I have nurtured and helped over the years. They are like my own sons. After all, didn't they make me minister of defense and virtually head of state?"

This last remark surprised and annoyed me. I detected a naiveté in Iman which I had never thought possible.

"That could be a case of the crow being defined as a pheasant by hungry hunters," I said, referring to a local saying.

"That is uncalled for!" he said angrily. "You are surely aware of what I am trying to accomplish for our country."

"I am well aware of that," I said. "I am also aware of the fact that your vision for equality and justice as the guiding principles of a new, humane society is not shared by all your followers."

"What do you mean?"

"Mengesha made a laughing stock of your slogan in your absence. You are bogged down in details while they are making decisions over life and death. Is that your wish?"

"I am kept informed."

"Yes, after the fact. After they make all the decisions."

"That's enough! I will not tolerate a slander of my comrades-in-arms, who are honest and courageous men."

"Have it your way. But I hope you will at least take some precautionary measures. I tell you, I don't trust these men, and I am speaking to you as an old friend. Your vision and Mengesha's are not the same. Keep a close eye on him, for God's sake!"

As I left him, his face bore the furrowed pain of unpleasant discovery. In his heart he must have suspected mischief at work. But pride and an illusion of a sense of control kept him immobilized. His Achilles' heel was pride and a stubborn self-confidence.

THIRTY-FIVE

I was eager to leave the hothouse of the revolutionary council and the constant calls for "death to the ministers." I decided to shed the military uniform and the protective custody it provided me.

It was refreshing to walk freely on the streets of Addis Ababa. The day after my talk with General Iman, I went to visit Yohannes, whom I found at home by himself, looking morose. We exchanged news and some gossip, and then I asked if there was something he wanted to tell me.

"Yes. I meant to tell you at our last meeting," he said.

"What is wrong, Johnny?"

Before Yohannes could answer, the bell rang and he went to the door. He came back with a young man and a young woman whom I had never seen before.

"Desta, I would like you to meet Mulu and Almaz, my brother and sister in Christ," Yohannes said.

I must have seemed like someone who had seen a ghost, judging from the expressions on their faces.

"What!" I exclaimed.

"That was what I was trying to tell you, among other things," Yohannes said.

We all sat down. Yohannes turned to me and began to explain. "I met the Lord while in prison. These two good people helped me find him. Mulu was in prison with me, and Almaz used to smuggle in literature on the glad tidings of the Lord. In my hour of despair they helped me find him. Prison became my road to Damascus."

"Damascus?" I was confused.

"That was where Saint Paul met the Lord, having been a persecutor of Christians," Yohannes explained.

It was hard not to laugh. The different language that Yohannes was now using struck me as almost comical. I had always respected people's faith, whatever its nature or denomination. But it was strange to hear a man whose bibles had been *The Origin of Species* and *The Communist Manifesto* now speak like a simple, country evangelist.

"Yohannes—" I began. But I didn't know what to say.

"Yohannes always talked about you. He prayed for you in all our meetings," said Almaz.

"Perhaps you can come to our next prayer meeting. Pastor Elias will be there," said her friend, Mulu.

"No, thanks," I said rudely and got up to leave.

Yohannes begged me to stay. But I had had enough. I wanted to go away and sulk somewhere over a glass of whiskey. How I wished I was with Mimi! In fact, one reason I had come to Yohannes was to see if he could go to Wollo and bring her back. But now I was devastated. One of my best friends, a fellow revolutionary with whom I had shared so much, had become a born-again!

"Desta, you should not go away angry. If you only knew how much happier I am today than before, you would not be upset," Yohannes said.

"What happened to your scientific socialism? To Marx and Darwin?" I was outraged.

"That was part of the trouble. Marx and Darwin could not come to my rescue in my darkest hours, in my life of despair in the torture chamber and in prison. The God whom they had banished from the universe came to me instead."

"Does that mean that you are against the revolution now?"

"I am not against anything or anybody. Christ, the Lord, admonishes us not to be against, but to forgive and to be positive. Oh brother Desta, if you could only—"

"Don't *brother* me, please. I have been called *brother* too many times lately, by people who thought daggers even as they said it." I thought of Mengesha.

"—only find the Lord," Yohannes finished, taking no notice of what I was saying.

The mark of a fanatic, be it religious or political, was written on his face; it was in his eyes. He only listened to the inner voice (which he called the Lord), the divine intimation that he placed above anything else. I had noticed the changed expression in his eyes, but I'd had no idea of its source.

"Yohannes, I am glad you found something to give you happiness," I said. "To each one his own salvation. Mine does not lie in that direction. In fact I came here to seek your help to find Mimi for me and bring her from Wollo. I can't live without her."

Yohannes bowed his head and avoided my gaze. We went outside the veranda, and he sat on a deck chair, pointing to another and asking me to sit.

"No, I must go. But tell me, please, if you can do me this favor and go to Wollo for me."

"Mimi is not in Wollo," he said. "Please sit down, I have something else to tell you."

"Is she . . . is something the matter with her?"

"No. She is alright." He hesitated.

"Come on, man!" I cried. "Out with it, where is she, if not in Wollo?"

"She is here in Addis Ababa."

"Where? Why didn't she contact me? What the hell is going on here?" I shouted.

"Desta, please don't swear."

"I will God damn swear if I want to! Now, I asked you a question. Where is she and why didn't I hear from her?"

"She is at work now. But later she will come to a small prayer meeting. You see, Mimi, too, who has had her share of distress, has found the Lord. She is a member of our fold. She has found Christ, the Lord."

The ground beneath my feet began to sink. I felt sick and slumped backward into the deck chair.

"Would you like to lie down inside, Desta?" Yohannes said, coming to my side. "You look awful. Shall I get you something to drink?"

"No. Just leave me alone. Go back to your friends. I will be all right."

Yohannes hesitated and then left me to go inside. He must have told his friends, for they came out and offered to pray for me. I told them I didn't need anybody's pity or prayers.

"If it is any consolation," Yohannes said after they left, "Mimi talks about you and prays all the time for your safety and salvation."

"How long has she been back in Addis Ababa?" I asked him, mustering calm.

"About a month, I think. According to a member of the voluntary group she worked with, she suffered a lot. The death and degradation in the camps got to her. And she saw the care and compassion of these people. She found the Lord with their help."

"What is the name of the group?"

"World Vision," he said.

"My poor Mimi. Her own world, the world in which she was brought up, collapsed. And there they were. They probably saw how vulnerable she was and trapped her," I said bitterly.

"It is not a trap, Desta. You got it all wrong. It is, on the contrary, true freedom. I wish I could make you see. He has the power; only He can show you. All I can do is pray."

"And convert me too? No way! If I get converted at all, and that is not bloody likely, it will be to Islam. That much I can promise you. I am not going to be a bloody born-again Christian!"

"Do you want to see her?" he interrupted.

"Of course I want to see her. Take me to her!"

In the southwest section of the city, there is an area called Little Akaki. It is a lovely place, covered with trees and dotted with modern villas amidst smoky mud huts. Asphalt roads merge into dusty dirt tracks. Well-dressed youngsters rub shoulders with bare-footed peasant folk. Cars stop to let goats and donkeys pass.

We reached the headquarters of Agro-Industry Company, Ltd., a fledgling metal working enterprise. The whine of metal cutters, mixed with the clang of stamping machines, echoed from the workshop. A Mercedes truck loaded with scrap iron and timber weaved its way past, and we followed the truck into a large compound. In a corner, workmen were busy with a saw, sending the smell of sawdust to fill the air.

Agro-Industry was jointly owned by an Italian and a native businessman. The Italian was none other than our friend Enrico, of Villa Bianca. He had prospered and expanded in the past four years.

Mimi was the secretary of the company. When I hurried into her office unannounced and stood facing her, she froze in her chair. Her eyes popped and her hands snapped to her mouth, as if she saw a ghost.

"Desta!" she said.

She looked thin and pale. Her hair was cut short in an Afro style. Her wood-panelled office was covered with pictures of Billy Graham and other Bible-thumping evangelists.

It was an anomalous scene, even eerie, with the faint whining sounds outside. Mimi made an effort to stand.

"No. Don't get up," I said going around the desk and embracing her. She got up nonetheless and yielded to my embrace and kiss. Then she pulled back.

"Desta," she said, and the tears streamed down her cheek.

Yohannes left us, closing the door behind him.

"Desta!"

"Mimi!"

"Are you okay?"

"Yes. I am fine. How about you?" I said, holding her face in my hands and gazing into her misty eyes.

"How did you manage to escape?" she asked.

"I was not a prisoner. And you? Are you going to escape from them and come back to me?" I went straight to the point, looking defiantly up at Billy Graham.

"I am not a prisoner. Yohannes must have told you about his own experience. Mine is similar. They are good people," she said.

"That is debatable," I said.

"It is not something that can be resolved by debate."

"If you are certain of your faith, surely you should not be afraid to defend it in a debate."

"I am not afraid. No one who has the Lord on his side knows fear or despair, believe me," Mimi said without hesitation. She turned her face to avoid my gaze. It was the first time that what I said seemed to be disagreeable to her. Was it the loss of her "innocence" or her reliance on a force beyond my reach? Whatever it was, my reaction was one of bitterness. I was consumed with jealousy and wanted to smash the pictures on the wall. I resented the evangelists. They had robbed me of my Mimi, damn them!

"Tell me, Mimi," I said. "Do these people of God object to people being in love?"

Her face broke into a smile—the sweet smile that I treasured and which had sustained me in banishment and in distant exile. "Of course not," she said. "But the love of Jesus is the greater love."

She sounded like all the rest of them. What kind of faith was this that robbed people of their earthly, human love and turned them into parrots, spouting the words drummed into them by some evangelist claiming to be the messenger of God? What kind of people were these who had turned sweet Mimi from a natural and trusting lover into an automaton?

Who was my adversary? Whom could I fight?

That was precisely the point. There was nobody except Jesus Christ. How could I compete with a supra-natural being, invisible, impalpable?

"Mimi. I prefer you the way you were," I said with a quavering voice, burying my head in my arms. I could not control my tears.

"It pains me to see you cry," she said, her eyes misting.

"I can't help it. I feel that I have lost you."

"Why should you feel that? I am the same Mimi, except that my life is richer because I found Him in my moments of despair." She hesitated, then said: "We lost our child, you know." She too was in tears.

"I know," I said. "You wrote me after it happened. I wish I had been with you, to share your pain and sorrow."

"I found the Lord," she said.

"I fear your new-found Lord. I feel squeezed out from your heart by him."

"There is no reason for fear," she said, and pulled my head to her bosom.

The first faint light of hope began to shine and warmed my heart. But I did not dare to be too optimistic. I asked her to take me to her home so that I could spend the night with her.

"Would you come with me to a prayer meeting?" she begged.

"I'd rather not," I said. "But I can wait outside for you, if you wish."

"Okay, but I will pray for you," she said.

"And I will make a wish, perhaps even pray to Allah to bring us back together as we were before uncontrollable events forced our painful separation. I would give up everything for you. You must know that."

"Dessie!" she said and kissed me softly. "Until tonight!"

I left her and Yohannes drove me back to the center of the city. It was after four o'clock in the afternoon, and I still had unfinished business.

Hanna had become a sales manager at Alitalia, a promotion she deserved. I entered her office unannounced. The secretary outside knew me by sight and did not object.

The last time I had seen Hanna at close quarters was during my banishment at Assela four years earlier. I had often thought about that brief and bitter encounter. I wondered whether my life would have taken a different course if Hanna had taken a more mature view of the situation instead of running amok and leaving town without notice. I had even written her a couple of times, asking her to come to see me and bring our daughter whom I longed to see.

Since my return from abroad I had seen her four or five times picking up Lemlem from school. On at least one occasion I was tempted to walk up to her and greet her, and pick up Lemlem and embrace her. But it had been still too dangerous for me to come out from the shadow of the underground. And then, after the acceleration of the pace of the revolution, I got caught up in the maelstrom.

Hanna looked prosperous. Her fashionable blue dress, her smart hairdo with a gold pin at the back, and her diamond ring—all were testimony to her material well-being.

Her surprise was visible on her expressive face, as she looked up from reading a file and saw me.

"Hello, Hanna," I said.

"Hello, Desta," she said, rising to greet me with an outstretched hand.

"I hope you don't mind the intrusion."

"No. It is all right. How are you?" she said, pointing to a chair.

"No kisses on the cheeks for old times sake?" I teased.

"I am sorry. This has been a stunning surprise," she said, coming around the desk to kiss me.

"How is Lemlem?"

"Lemlem is well. She has found a new father who is devoted to her. And she is fond of him."

"Are you married to him?"

"Yes. We got married last year. He is a good man. Whatever you may have heard about him, he is a decent man who spends time taking care of his family."

"Don't rub it in, Hanna. I know what I could and should have done. That is spilt milk, and I am not crying over it. But Lemlem is my daughter and I have a right to visit her."

"Not now. It will only confuse her."

"What do you mean?"

"If you come into our lives now, and she knows that she has two fathers, it will be very confusing to her. She is too young to under-stand."

"Do you mean to tell me you told her that this man is her father?"

"No. I did not say that. But I did not tell her about you."

"That is cruel and stupid."

"Thank you very much," she said with a sarcastic laugh.

"It is true! Lemlem was old enough to remember her daddy. And you can't take it from her. She will blame you when she grows up if you do that. And I can't take this lying down!" I fumed.

It had been a day of shocking discoveries. Maybe I should not have come to Hanna, on that day of all days, when I'd already had my share of shocks. Yet I came to Hanna, perhaps unconsciously in search of family support to help me absorb the shock. How wrong I was! As I listened to her, in my mind I changed Hanna from an ordinary human to a female *kerkedion*.

"If you think about the welfare of Lemlem you will not take any steps to exercise your rights as a father at the moment," Hanna said. "Give me only two years, until she is old enough to understand things."

"If your husband is a decent man, as you say he is, he would not deny me my right and Lemlem her right to meet her father."

"Give me time, please, Desta. Give me time to think about it and to consult my husband. Don't drag her through an ugly legal fight."

"Don't worry. I won't. If you behave reasonably. I am sure we can work out something. All I need is a weekly visit."

"Give me a week to think about it," she said.

We parted as we had met, with traditional kisses on the cheeks. She did not show any curiosity or interest in where I had been for the past four years. But then Hanna was never distinguished for her imagination or intellectual curiosity.

Mimi had left her residence at the Villa Bianca for good. She was staying at the YMCA, where a young women's section of apartments had been built. The only way to describe her apartment was: no frills. Nothing that could be considered a luxury. There was a Murphy bed, a bathroom, and a small storeroom adjoining a wardrobe. A small table served both as a dining table and a desk.

"You have moved down in the scale of what they call 'the good life,'" I teased her, after we sat down and she put the teakettle on (there was, of course, no scotch).

"All luxury is useless," she said. "It is corrupting, and the source of many problems. What is the use of luxury when people have nothing to eat?"

"There, I am with you, a hundred percent. And that is what the revolution is all about."

"What is the real aim of the revolution?" she asked, pouring our tea into two plastic cups.

"Well, there are different points of view," I said putting two spoonfuls of sugar in my cup. "In my view, a revolution, in the final analysis, is about people. It is about changing their lives for the better. In our situation this means introducing ideas and institutions of democracy and justice for all. This is my vision and the vision of my friends."

"Which friends?"

"Well, some have been killed and others have been forced to commit suicide in the face of intolerable torture."

"I know. I heard. But how can you bring about change without the help of the army?"

"The army contains good people and bad people like everything else. Our problem is how to keep the bad people from taking over. I am really worried that we may fail in that."

"How can your group help?"

"If the students, teachers and other civilians could form a united front and strike a blow in favor of democratic change, the good people would succeed. If we are divided, then the bad people in the military will install a military dictatorship."

"Who are these bad people in the army?"

"You would not know them. They are unknown to the public. There is a Captain Mengesha Haile Mehaiman who is the present chairman, and I fear him the worst. But General Iman does not share my fear."

"General Iman is a trusting type. I could see that the first time he came to tell me about your meeting in Assela."

"Your Wollo intuition again!" I laughed.

"My feminine intuition," she corrected.

"Let's forget politics and talk about you," I said, stroking her cheeks and running my fingers through her hair. She clasped my hands and bent to kiss them.

Mimi told me about her sorrows when she lost our baby. She was depressed for several days, she said, and only the thought of our future reunion kept her going. And also the daily work at the restaurant and

Lula's friendship was of immeasurable help.

We were naked on the Murphy bed with the sheet covering the lower parts of our bodies. The act of love-making and the tender feelings that accompanied it seemed to help her transcend her religious qualms. She told me about the countless deaths in the famine relief camp in Wollo where she had worked for several months, and her growing need for religious faith.

I did not wish to argue or debate the merits of such faith. I preferred to wait and see her grow out of it, for I believed that her Wollo heritage would eventually rebel against the total spiritual submission that the Pentecostals demand.

I did not want to push her into their arms completely by making an open frontal attack on them. On the other hand, I could not let go of her. She had such a hold on my life, with her simple and total love. But even after our act of love that evening, I felt that I had to leave her with some space so that she could reflect and decide for herself. That meant that I should not spend the night.

"Mimi, I must go now," I said.

"Oh, must you?"

"Yes. I think you need time to sort things out in your mind by yourself. If you wish I can give you a number where you can find me or leave a message."

She looked surprised.

"But if you go back to the barracks, it may be days before I see you," she said.

That warmed my heart beyond measure. It was what I wanted to hear, and the ray of hope that I saw when she pulled me to her breast, now became a shaft of light showing a brighter future.

"I'm not going to the barracks yet," I said.

"Where are you going then?"

"I am going to talk to some of the student groups, and I'll stay with one of them."

"I'll pray for you," she said.

THIRTY-SIX

T he Lantern Bookshop was teeming with curious youngsters. Haile and his Inner Group had left France to come to Addis Ababa to coordinate their faction of the student underground movement, establishing the bookshop in the center of the city. At first they sold textbooks on a variety of subjects and gradually introduced revolutionary literature.

Haile showed me around. The shelves in the back room were filled with works by Marx, Lenin and Mao. Haile said that the Chinese had donated thousands of copies of *The Little Red Book* containing Mao's speeches.

I could see that Haile and his group had not graduated from the student stage of their activities.

"Haile," I told him. "Books are fine. Ideas are essential for altering or raising consciousness. But I think you should realize that the revolution has gone beyond that stage."

"What do you mean?" he asked.

"I mean that a revolution is about ideas and also about the means of putting these ideas into action. To be blunt, it is about guns, and the military has the monopoly on the guns. Moreover, they are organized and they control a command structure that can set things in motion as they have done already."

"I know. But they will depend on us for ideas and for the crucial stage of politicization of the masses. There is no way that they can consummate the revolution without us."

"But we are divided," I reminded him.

"We have tried to coordinate our efforts with the Ethiopian Peoples Revolutionary Party. We have made overtures to them to join hands with us and approach the military as a united group. But we have been spurned and ridiculed."

"Why is that?"

"The EPRP wants to have nothing to do with the military. Their slogan is that a people's government must be organized. We told them that it is unrealistic to expect the military to pack up and go, and that we need to create a tactical alliance with the military until the revolution is on a more secure ground."

"And they refused?"

"Yes. And now we are in secret negotiations with the military to go it alone."

"Do you think you can use the military and then discard them?"

"Those of them who wish to consummate the revolution with us will be welcome to join in," he said.

"You speak of consummation, as though this were a wedding night with a happy bride ready and willing to open her thighs to you," I said, with mounting irritation at his naiveté.

"Well it is, in a manner of speaking," he said.

"No, it is not! It is a perilous adventure. Unless you confront the military as a united force, they will use you to eliminate the others and then chew you up," I said.

Haile looked at me, wondering at my passion. I told him about my experience with the dragons, and about the crescendo of demands for blood among their members. I told him about Mengesha and of my worries about his blind ambition.

"Oh, him!" he said. "I heard about him. He is an ignoramus. We can control him better than the generals or the other, better-educated officers."

I gave up trying to point out the dangers and left him with his books.

I went to the university teachers' club, which was frequented by members and supporters of the Outer Group, Haile's rivals. Toward eight o'clock in the evening, Ishete, a young lecturer in economics, came in. I knew he was one of the supporters of the EPRP and a mentor of their university student members. He was well-informed about the intricacies of student politics, so I came straight to the point.

"What is the prospect of forming a united front among the various factions?" I asked him.

"If you mean between the two important factions, the Outer Group and the Inner Group, the answer is—very remote. I just came from a meeting of the teachers segment of the EPRP, and they are out to smash the rival party."

"Why?"

"It is a long story. It goes back to personal rivalries and animosities."

"But surely in the face of a common danger they should bury their differences. Don't the members have a say in this?"

"Not bloody likely. The members follow the orders of the leaders. Democratic centralism and all that kind of jazz."

"Well, the military are now getting ready to overthrow the Emperor. If they do this while the civilian groups are divided, they will feel so bold that their next victims will be precisely the civilian opposition groups which they see as their rivals."

"I know. It is funny, I made the same point at the meeting, and all I got was a slogan: 'Power to the people. A People's Provisional Government.'"

"You know of course that the Inner Group has decided to cooperate with the military," I said.

"I didn't know that. But I assumed that the military would want to use them to work out their programs and to provide them with a kind of legitimacy."

"This will mean civil war, with the military and one civilian faction against another civilian faction," I warned.

"I hope that it won't come to that."

"But if it does?"

"If it comes to that, then the military will tyrannize all of us," he said glumly.

We were joined by a few other members of the club. One of them was Taddele, an old colleague from when I taught history. He was a conservative but opposed to the military, which he regarded with contempt as ignorant and brutal.

Taddele launched into a tale about the secret meetings between a certain Captain Mengesha Haile Mehaiman and an old man who was employed as a servant by the minister of the palace. Taddele had a cousin who worked as the Emperor's valet, and he used his contacts to keep up with palace gossip and politics.

"And do you know what I have discovered?" he asked with jubilation. "You will never guess."

"Tell us," one of the group said.

"Mengesha Haile Mehaiman is the illegitimate son of Ras Kebere, the minister of the palace," he said. "Why do you think Kebere is the only minister still free, and still minister of the palace?"

Taddele took a big gulp from his beer and paused to see the effect of his earth-shaking announcement. His eyes shone. We were all ears, and he knew it. His smile expressed the pride and satisfaction of a professional doing his job well—an investigative journalist with an interest in history.

"How is that possible?" I asked finally.

"It is a fact," he said. "Mengesha's mother was a maid in Ras Kebere's household. Her pregnancy by Kebere was kept a secret and she was wedded off to a servant, who has acted as Mengesha's father ever since. But the real father is Kebere, who has looked after his son and the mother from a discreet distance."

"Where did Mengesha grow up?" Ishete asked.

"That is easy. He grew up in Addis Ababa, as an outcast on the periphery of the privileged class, eating the crumbs from his real father's bountiful table. According to accounts of people who grew up in and around that household, Mengesha's mother whispered the secret of his true parentage and nurtured the boy's ideas of grandeur."

"Was the mother a former slave?" I asked.

"Yes. How did you know?"

"Because I heard one of his colleagues call Mengesha 'that slave' behind his back after one of their meetings."

"How did he go to military school?" Ishete asked.

"Ras Kebere pulled strings to get him admitted. And he failed in every subject except sports. But he was known for his pugnacity and boldness," Taddele said, and concluded his lecture.

There were no more questions. An air of gloom descended upon the entire group, which by the end had grown to be eight or nine people. The idea of the son of a former slave, and an ignorant one at that, being the country's ruler was too depressing for these educated Ethiopians to contemplate. I could not resist a taunting remark.

"Well, perhaps this is divine justice," I said. I was met with cold, censorious faces.

It was midday on September 12, a bright day with a cloudless sky. The air was filled with excitement. The city was stark, raving mad with joyous celebration. People left their work and shops and streamed to the Jubilee Palace.

Taxicabs offered free rides. Bus loads and truck loads of people arrived to fill the open space outside the palace. They had heard the news first on the morning radio broadcast, then from loudspeakers mounted on jeeps and army trucks.

The tyrant had fallen.

Yes. The Emperor had been overthrown by the Coordinating Committee of the Armed Forces, the Police and the Militia—the dragons, for short. I had missed the morning radio broadcast, because I had stayed at my cousins' place after an all-night meeting with a joint conciliation committee of the rival underground groups. And it had been all in vain.

Now it was all over. The military had attained their most crucial objective. They aimed at the head, as every revolutionary worth his salt should, and hit a bulls eye. Not a word of protest was heard from any quarter. The dragons had done an effective job of using the media. Throughout the summer months they had slowly de-mystified the majesty of the Emperor, or to vary the metaphor, stripped him of his clothes and left him stark naked.

Over the past week I had stopped going to military headquarters, or even to see Iman at his sister's house, shying away from my semi-membership of the committee as an "honorary officer." Instead I had been spending my time vainly trying to get the feuding civilian revolutionaries to reconcile their differences.

I was driving my cousin's Fiat when I heard the news. The radio announced the news every fifteen minutes, in between martial music and a jubilant traditional ululation which they no doubt inserted from a previously taped show. It was all done quite cleverly.

I found myself driving toward the palace. The streets were filled with people. I parked and mingled with the crowd, walking then running toward the palace; it seemed that the entire city was converging there.

Around the various gates of the palace a well-coordinated crowd chanted slogans. Some carried placards:

The Tyrant is Overthrown!

We are Free of Tyranny!

Down with Oppressors!

We waited, a crowd of thousands, for hours. Then a squadron of air force jets flew low over the palace, making a spectacular show. A few minutes later an armed contingent opened the northern gate, and pushed through the crowd, clearing a passageway.

Presently, a Volkswagen Beetle emerged from the palace driven by a soldier. The Emperor was in the car, barely visible. He was flanked by two armed guards.

The crowd thundered: "Robber! Tyrant!"

It was later reported that the Emperor asked his captors what the people were saying. When he was told they were yelling "robber," he said, "They are under the impression that our palace is being robbed. We are proud of our loyal subjects."

Clearly he had taken leave of reality. I felt sorry for him when I heard this story from a lieutenant who was one of his guards.

I joined the crowd that followed the Volkswagen on foot as far as the entrance to the detention camp. It was a day I will remember all my life. What impressed me most was the breathless excitement of the multitude. The cruel expressions on their faces seemed to me like the brandishing of weapons that had been concealed deep in the collective subconscious. Their language was harsh and unforgiving. I felt sure that if the Emperor had fallen into their hands, they would have trampled him to death. The unleashed fury of the masses (become the mob) knows no bounds of decency or decorum. It is the pack instinct; the Romans knew this and institutionalized it as a death ritual in the arena of the colosseum.

I was told later that when the time had come to select the officers who would arrest the Emperor, Mengesha did not volunteer. An unknown police officer volunteered to lead the group; he went to the palace and respectfully told the Emperor that henceforth he would live in another place.

In fact, Mengesha had opposed the decision to arrest the Emperor, but was overruled (for once) by General Iman. Mengesha's hesitation, it was later revealed, was due to the advice given to him by his father. It is not known whether the old minister of the palace wanted to save his imperial master, or to spare his son the ignominy of what he doubtless considered the ultimate crime.

THIRTY-SEVEN

And so ended an era of imperial rule under a monarch—and a new one began under the military. General Iman was made the first head of state. His role in planning the strategy was crucial; his popularity was undisputed. At that historical moment there was no better leader.

General Iman was a man with a vision, who wanted a revolution with a human face. He had often talked about his political ideal as a combination of Indian diversity and tolerance, with Swedish social justice. He was aware of the need for controlled violence in a revolutionary situation. He wondered whether it would be possible to reconcile Jefferson, Lenin and Ghandi. He was above all else a decent man, a humane officer and a gentleman. He hated violence for its own sake, and showed a distinct distaste for it even when the situation dictated its use. That was why he coined the slogan "Forward Without Bloodshed."

It was not to be. Mengesha Haile Mehaiman was no visionary. His philosophy, such as it was, pertained strictly to the mechanics of attaining and maintaining power; which in the Ethiopian context and given his own predilection, meant violence.

In fact, Mengesha was a study in contrast to Iman. Where Iman believed in unity and harmony, Mengesha chose chaos and division. Where the general preferred gentleness and creativity, the captain was for violence and destruction, and was devoid of human sympathy. Iman celebrated genius and promoted gifted people; Mengesha resented genius and kept a dossier on all the gifted officers that he knew.

With the overthrow of the Emperor, the revolution now turned inward. Internal rivalries and power struggles intensified. Mengesha was well prepared for that. His most important quality, which was not sufficiently appreciated at the beginning, was his single-minded desire to get to the top and his willingness to use violence to achieve that goal. The rest was a matter of tactics.   Mengesha prepared his ground with meticulous care and ruthless method. His supporters held key positions. His opponents relied on Iman to control him, but Iman remained above the fray and acted as an avuncular arbiter. He did not imagine that the sword was hanging over his neck. Such aloofness might have worked in normal circumstances, but it ignored Mengesha's character and inordinate ambition.

Of all the crises that confronted the military once they had removed the Emperor, the most important was the war in Eritrea. Mengesha, who knew that General Iman favored a peaceful resolution of the war, openly confronted him on that issue and whipped up the chauvinistic passions of the military. When Iman persisted in arguing for a peaceful solution, Mengesha had him charged with treachery. That led to Iman's walk-out in defiance of the majority resolution to wage war in Eritrea.

"Everything is falling apart" I said.

"Not necessarily," General Iman said absent-mindedly.

"Do you remember my warning about Mengesha?"

"Yes."

"Do you still trust him?"

Iman did not answer. And that was an answer. We were sitting in the salon of his sister's house, the day after he walked out of the military council meeting. I wanted to know whether he was taking any precautions, and he had replied vaguely about the loyalty of the troops in the division outside the city. I was not satisfied with his replies and wanted to know more.

"A general must be with his troops to be able to say that the troops are with him, right?" I queried.

"In a way, yes."

"Well, then, let's go to your most loyal division."

"No. I have sworn an oath to lead the revolution. And the center of the revolution is right here."

I tried a blunt approach. "Suppose there is a rebellion in the military council and they appoint Mengesha to replace you," I said.

"If they don't trust me, that is their affair," he said meekly, to my utter disgust.

"For heaven's sake, man, how can you say that? That's being a defeatist, and I have never known you to be a defeatist. Your entire career speaks against it."

"What do you want me to do, run away?" he flared.

"Yes, if necessary! You military people have a word for it. It is called retreat. I mean, I am no Napoleon, but I know enough to see when the game is up. I say it is time for you to join your loyal troops and use that base to lead the revolution from a position of strength. Failing that, we can fly you to Eritrea; we have a bush pilot with a Cessna."

"No way. I am not going to turn my back and flee," he said vehemently. "And that is the end of the matter. No more arguments on this. *Finito.*"

He was standing and his face was wild with anger, such as I have never thought possible in him. I knew then that the game was up indeed.

The phone rang. He picked it up and said, "Yes?" He listened for while and said, "Thank you," and hung up.

"What is it?" I asked.

"It was an air force officer, a loyal friend."

"And?"

"He said that they want me to come to the air base."

"Who wants you?"

"The air force command. There is to be a graduation show."

"Are you going?"

"No."

"Why not?"

"Mengesha is going to make the main speech. They just want me to be in the supporting cast."

"You see. I told you, Iman. Please think about what I said, and be quick before they make a move against you."

"Thanks, Desta. I will think about it, and I am grateful for your concern and friendship."

"I am not doing anything more than what you have done for me, or what you would do for me. But I beg you to decide today and let me know."

His forlorn gaze revealed a soul in doubt and pain. He had put too much trust in young officers whom he did not think capable of ambition beyond promotion up through military ranks. But he was too proud to retreat. He reminded me of Socrates and his refusal to accept the offer of his pupils to help him escape. He drank the hemlock.

"Iman, I can easily arrange an escape to Eritrea. Then you can come back at the head of loyal troops, and in unison with a united civilian revolutionary group we can do a better job."

"No, Desta. I will not run. If they betray me and grab power in their own name, then so be it. History will judge me and them."

"History? Iman, we are makers of history. History is in our hands. By refusing to give yourself a chance you are denying history and letting bad people take over. How can history be kind to you in her judgment?"

"My mind is made up. Don't confuse me with your sophistry."

I left him with those words ringing in my ears.

THIRTY-EIGHT

As he told the story, pastor Elias, the most dynamic and controversial young leader of the Pentecostal group in Addis Ababa, met the Lord on board an Alitalia flight from Rome.

"The pilot had just told us to relax and enjoy ourselves. I was sipping Italian wine and listening to rock music when the pilot interrupted the program to say that he had an announcement to make. 'Ladies and gentlemen,' he said, 'please stay calm, we are changing course. We are being hijacked. There is a man who has a gun pointed at me and a grenade in his other hand. I have to do as he asks. He has companions on your side of the aircraft. Please do as they ask you. Don't try to be brave.'

"As you can imagine, there was pandemonium in the plane; women shrieking, children crying, and I was terror-stricken. It was in that moment of truth that the Lord Jesus appeared to me and said, 'Elias, do you know me? I am the Way, the Light and the Truth. He who believes in me should not fear death, for he shall have everlasting Life.'

"All of a sudden my terror left me. My heavy heart became lighter. And I got up to comfort the other passengers. My life changed in that instant. The shadow of death was removed by the invisible hand of the Lord."

"Amen! Hallelujah!" cried a young woman inside.

I was sitting on the verandah outside, listening to Elias's sermon through the open window. I was captivated by the story line and the drama of the narrative. I was also gaining deeper insight into the workings of the mind in moments of stress, and understanding how people like Mimi and Yohannes could change.

Earlier that day, after leaving Iman, I had gone to the YMCA to be with Mimi. I found the whole place turned into an army camp. The assembly hall had become a karate training gym, and the apartments were all occupied by members of the armed forces, who had thrown the residents out and moved in.

In the gym I noticed a man I had seen at the university a few years back. He was a biochemist trained at a university in California. And there he was, in a karate outfit with a black belt, training a group of about fifty youngsters. I asked an attendant who the trainees were.

"These were common criminals in prison a few weeks ago," he said. "They were released and inducted into a special force commanded by a member of the military council."

"And their instructor?"

"He is Dr. Sennu, a personal friend of Captain Mengesha of the military council."

I left before Sennu could recognize me. I went to the Villa Bianca looking for Mimi. She was not there. "Try the home of pastor Elias," I was told by one of the guards who knew her.

I knew the place; that was where I had waited for her last time. When I arrived, pastor Elias was preaching, telling his hijacking story. It was followed by prayers and songs.

I sat outside on a chair on the verandah, where I could hear everything. The story and the way Elias told it made a strong impression on me. He was a powerful preacher with a resonant voice.

It was a starry night and the air was bracing. The service ended at about nine o'clock, and the members of the small congregation filed out in groups of twos and threes.

Mimi walked out alone and was surprised to find me standing near the gate. As we walked toward my car she told me how she had been kicked out of the YMCA. "I was given three days notice, and that was generous. All the others were simply told to leave."

"Where are you staying?" I asked.

"I am staying with Lula for now. I have applied for a room at a new apartment building near the university."

"At least you have somewhere to stay," I said.

"You sound depressed, Dessie."

"These are depressing times, don't you think?"

We agreed to have dinner together. She followed me in her car to a Szechuan restaurant, a quiet place in the center of the city. A smart waitress in a black chinese robe brought us two menus and a pot of tea.

Mimi sat primly. The restaurant was half-filled, mostly by Americans and Europeans, none of them known to me. That suited me.

"Is there hope for us?" I asked abruptly.

"Of course there is hope for us. What a question! Why should you doubt?"

"It is a hopeless situation. The revolution is being hijacked. It's funny, but when your pastor told the story of the hijacking of the Alitalia flight, I was thinking about us, about you and me and the revolution. About love and revolution."

"If you can think about love, and peace, maybe . . ."

"Mimi. Spare me. I am not in a mood for any preaching."

"I was not preaching. I want you to have peace, peace of mind. The revolution seems to have robbed you of that peace. I am not saying that I am opposed to the revolution. But you have suffered banishment, exile, separation and God-knows-what. And for what?"

"I chose the hard road."

"Yes, and it is getting harder and harder. I can feel it. I can feel your suffering and I am suffering with you, and praying . . ."

She turned her face and fumbled in her purse, but could not find a handkerchief. I did not even have a clean one to offer her, so she used the napkin.

"Don't cry, Mimi. Please don't cry."

"I'll be all right."

"I wanted this to be a memorable evening," I said.

"Why? You are not thinking of running away, are you?"

"Anything is possible. The way things are going, the country will go down the drain. I am not sure about anything anymore," I said. I must have looked lost.

Mimi leaned forward, putting her warm hands over mine, and gazed into my eyes with a diffident smile.

"Don't lose faith, my dearest. Don't lose faith in yourself. And if you can possibly bring yourself to do it, have faith in God."

"I am not . . ."

"I know, I know!" she cut in. "You are an agnostic. I remember what you told me five years ago."

"Five years! Has it been that long? My God!"

"You see, you do at least say, My God!" she said trying to cheer me up.

The mood changed. I begged her to have one glass of wine.

"Just one," she said.

"Here's to love and revolution," I said, raising my glass.

"You crazy man," she said, raising her glass, her face breaking into a broad smile.

"I am crazy about you," I said, holding her hand and kissing her fingers.

"And the revolution?"

"The revolution is taking a dangerous course, and it will take its toll."

"How can you speak about love and revolution in one breath?"

"You have to love before you can be a revolutionary," I said. "But now I am wondering whether I would be a good lover if I became a disappointed revolutionary."

Mimi squeezed my hands tightly. "I want all of you for myself," she said, "but I know I can't have you if I demand that you give up what you have dreamed about for years. So I try to accommodate your revolution, even if I cannot be a revolutionary."

She was back to her earthy, homespun wisdom again, and I was glad.

"I think you have expressed, better than I ever could, my own dilemma concerning your new-found religion," I said. "I want you completely for myself. But you are not the same Mimi of five years ago."

"We all change. But the house of my religion has rooms in it for you."

"And for others?"

"No. Not in a romantic sense. But yes, in a larger sense. When I was doing famine relief in Wollo, I saw death stalking and ravaging lives; I saw healthy, productive human beings become skeletons, day after day. My despair gave place to compassion. I was referring to that when I said there is room for others."

"The house that I imagined in my revolutionary dream is one in which there would be plenty, so that people would not go hungry; and one in which people would care about one another. So, it seems that there is a similarity in our dreams."

"Except that God is part of mine," she said.

That, more or less, took us back to square one, with the difference that her earthy Wollo wisdom was intact. I pinned my hopes on that wisdom and on Mimi's innate goodness and capacity for love. Even her new-found God could not change that, I wagered silently, settling to enjoy the beef Szechuan and the wine. Mimi, too, ate and drank heartily.

"More wine?" I asked.

"No, thanks. You don't have to get me drunk. The spirit and the flesh are both willing. I am yours tonight," she said seductively.

THIRTY-NINE

I t was an event that produced a fixed memory; people remember where they were at that time. It was six o'clock in the morning of November 18, 1974. I had not slept for much of the night—which I spent at the home of an old friend. I had been advised to sleep at different places for security reasons. The nomadic life had become part of me.

The previous evening we had heard gunfire crackling around the area of the central prison. And the day before, the residence of my old friend, General Iman, had been surrounded by armed guards. The military council explained this as a protective measure, but I knew better. They had put him under house arrest and cut his telephone line. I had last talked to him in the morning, just before the line was cut.

The morning radio opened with martial music. Then followed the ominous song that was to become the signature tune presaging terrible announcements.

Then came the announcement itself.

Oh horrible, horrible day! Oh damnation of a revolution gone awry! Oh cursed land, has there ever been another place on earth where so much hope nurtured for so long, by so many, was dashed by so dastardly an act?

Actually, the end could have been seen from the start like a Greek tragedy. The thing you fear most will happen, and the person you hate the most will inherit the earth. It is the local vernacular's version of Murphy's law.

When the signature tune ended, the announcer, known for his

intimidating voice, began to tell the grisly story. It was Mergemu Wonaf, who had also served the Emperor well. His preparatory remarks about the "sword of revolutionary justice" were enervating.

"I wish he would come to the point," said my friend. We were huddled around the radio, breathlessly waiting.

He then began to read the names of the "counter-revolutionaries and traitors" to whom revolutionary justice had been meted out. Heading the list, of course, was the architect of the revolution and its military hero, my friend, General Iman. The names of fifty-nine others followed, including former Prime Minister Akalu, his successor, and most members of the old cabinet, generals of the army and the police, including that bear of a man, General Dima. There were also other unknown men.

It did not make any sense. But then murder, any murder, makes little sense. No revolutionary end, no lofty principle, could explain, much less justify, the deliberate, cold-blooded murders that were perpetrated on the night of November 18, 1974. The entire country, and the whole world, was outraged.

The music which punctuated the repeated announcement of the execution became like poison to my ears. I was never fond of military bands, but after that morning all martial music became anathema to me.

Murder, most foul! Murder! I kept repeating it to myself as if the repetition of the word that expressed the deed could ease my pain. Would people forget this dastardly act of midnight massacre one day? I wondered. Would people ignore or come to terms with the stain of the crime? Would it be forgotten as just one of those mad moments in history, an aberration of the revolutionary process, an unfortunate incident born of necessity?

People would come up with all manner of explanations to extenuate the act, once the perpetrators had consolidated power and put on a mask of legitimacy. How many tyrants in history have waded in blood and then lived to absolve their sins with the act of accession to the throne and the anointment at the hands of bishops!

This is, after all, a revolution, they might argue, not a *minuet* at the court of His Majesty. Didn't Robespierre and company brutally wipe out heirs of the *ancien regime* in order to consummate the revolution? Would the French Revolution have been secure if they had not erased the aristocracy?

I could imagine the arguments multiplying with the help of different proverbs and metaphors. You have to be cruel to be kind. You can't make an omelette without breaking an egg. But what if the omelette turns out to be unsavory, or even poison? I held my ground as though I were engaged in a live debate. And before answering my own silent questions, I vowed vengeance on the dragons. The blood of my friends must be avenged, I decided. Life would not be worth living with their blood on my conscience. First, there was Melaku and now there was Iman. To hell with the revolution! Revenge, sweet revenge, was all!

In my feverish state of mind I did not even think of Mimi or Lemlem. Mengesha and his gang had displaced them from my consciousness. Revenge had displaced love and even fear. I wanted revenge and I knew how to get it.

People came in and out of the house of my friend all day, bearing news about the events of the bloody weekend and its consequences. I sat and listened, concealing my identity, with my friend acting as host and interlocutor.

After hearing, for months on end, the soothing slogan, "Revolution Without Bloodshed," people were obviously confused by the Saturday night massacre. Their stories reflected despair as well as a defiant hope, involving a straining of the imagination, to make sense out of the shocking announcement, to find a rational explanation for that supreme act of irrationality—murder.

Already, before the blood had dried on the edge of the mass grave where the dragons had dumped the bodies of their victims, a legend was emerging. I was not surprised. In Africa, legends are expressions of a creative imagination which magnifies or distorts reality in order to fortify people in celebrating virtue or fending off evil.

General Iman, who embodied popular aspirations for freedom and democracy, could not possibly die. How could he, when there was unfinished work? Didn't he have an unwritten compact with the people, to take them to the promised land? No, he was not dead. He was in hiding somewhere, awaiting the arrival of his loyal troops; then he will march on the treacherous dragons.

Another version had him hiding in the American embassy. In yet another, he had been flown to Eritrea in a small plane (oh, irony!), and he would come marching back at the head of a triumphant regiment to deliver the country from the dragons.

Here was a subject that had always fascinated me—the revolutionary leader as the incarnation of a popular cause, often with divine qualities and powers. If I survived, I promised myself that I would write about the subject someday.

My friend interrupted my thoughts. Since it was Sunday, he suggested that we go for a drive around the city to observe the scene firsthand. He had one minor errand to run, which was to bring his mother-in-law home from the Church of the Savior of the World.

His mother-in-law was waiting outside the church. She was a plump, middle-aged woman, who was very wealthy and well-connected in society. I knew that she had several small shops, plus other business concerns that were less visible. She believed in placing her eggs in many baskets and also in being discreet. She often entertained influential members of society, knowing full well that such expenditure was a worthwhile investment as well as tax deductible.

I learned the latter fact when I was a member of the tax appeal commission. In fact, the first time I met her was when she appeared before the commission—unaccompanied by a lawyer—to argue for a reduction of the tax assessed on her business. She impressed us all with her incisive logic and eloquent speech, to say nothing of her feminine charm.

That morning on the way back from church, she told us an interesting story. It seemed that the spouses and daughters of the detained ministers and generals had made several desperate attempts to save their husbands and fathers from the firing squad. As it turned out, most of the attempts failed. But one young woman's efforts succeeded in saving her father's life.

"And who is this enterprising woman?" my friend asked his mother-in-law.

"You know I don't like naming names," she answered with impatience. "Let us just say that she is the daughter of a former high dignitary."

"And what was her approach?" I asked.

"Now that is an interesting question," she said. "'Approach' is an interesting word. It is so neutral and professional."

My friend pressed for details, but she knew she had us on tenter-hooks and she took her time.

The story she told us was very similar to that of a mysterious young woman in the French Revolution, at the height of the Reign of Terror. French historian Georges Lenotre called the young woman Mademoiselle de M. According to Lenotre, Mademoiselle de M. approached and captured the fancy of Fouquier, whose word could send anyone to the guillotine. Suppressing her feminine pride and aristocratic disdain for the "lesser classes," she threw her beauty and her youth—that is, her body—at the feet of Fouquier and saved her father's life.

Our Ethiopian version of Mademoiselle de M. may or may not have been aware of French history. But she seemed to have done no less. Anticipating the worst, long before the Saturday night massacre, she sought out the most influential individuals on the military council and placed herself at the disposition of more than one of them.

Thus she saved her father. Who could blame her? Addis Ababa society was divided on the answer to that question. Whichever side was right, everyone admired the audacity and resourcefulness of the young woman. No diplomatic mission can call for more finesse than was displayed by our Ethiopian Mademoiselle de M.

"first things first" said Berhane, his Eritrean decisiveness showing, as always, in moments of tension. "We must get you out of here, before they get you."

We were sitting in the office of a lawyer friend of his, another Eritrean. It was seven o'clock Monday evening, the day after the massacre was announced on the radio. The whole city was downcast, as if in mourning. Such is the irony of life! Only three months before, the citizens had exulted in the downfall of "the tyrant," and throughout the summer they had called for the blood of the ministers.

In fact, the word "minister" had become synonymous with evil. The whole nation had become giddy with a false sense of accomplishment, seeing the powerful dismissed and thrown into prison. And the dragons mistook the public mood, interpreting it as a *carte blanche* for murder and mayhem. Many innocent victims suffered death and torture as a result. But the citizens turned out dressed in black to mourn the dead. That shocked and jolted the dragons.

I wanted to settle scores. I had obtained two hand grenades. I planned to conceal them under my clothes, enter the council of the dragons, and take them to Hell with me.

"That will not serve any purpose, Desta," Berhane said gently; he did all he could to persuade me to abandon my mad plan. "A better avenue would be for you to survive and carry on the struggle."

"But how? Where?"

"We will take you to Eritrea, where you can join the group which has been training to wage a protracted armed struggle. This is the only way."

"I am not sure anymore," I said bitterly.

"Believe me, Desta. It is the only way. You can't conduct a revolution from the city. You have to start from the countryside and gradually engulf and take over the cities. If you haven't learned that lesson from what happened here yesterday, then there is no hope for you."

"There is no hope for me anyway. I want revenge now, not revolution," I said, getting up.

"Desta, please! Think of the future. Think of all those who have sacrificed themselves for the cause—Melaku, Bekele, Iman and many others. They would want you to carry on. You must survive to carry on. And another thing, what about Mimi? Have you thought of her, of how long she waited for you and sacrificed for you?"

"Mimi can take care of herself. She has her God and her crowd."

"Don't you believe it. I talked to her this morning; I went to her aunt's place looking for her. And she is worried to death about you; you haven't even thought of her. Shame on you, Desta Kidane Wold!"

That last remark hit me hard; it relieved me of my momentary madness and put things into perspective.

"Where is Mimi now; do you know?" I asked meekly. "Can you take me to her?"

It was time to go; time to slip out of town once more, and escape. Survival, the primordial instinct, now ordered and dominated all my thoughts and actions. Much as I mourned Iman's death and the tragic turn of the revolution, there was room for gratitude; I was grateful to be alive.

I was also grateful for the reaction of the good citizens of Addis Ababa, which had so frightened the dragons that they, too, were temporarily preoccupied with survival. They had crawled into the old palace and surrounded it with tanks and armored personnel carriers. An inside informant told us that it would be at least a week before the dragons crept out of their holes again, to face the public and plan more arrests and executions. It was my time to slip out.

This would not be a dramatic exit, with forged passports and Mercedes limos with phony plates, like my escape to Djibouti with Gloria Sullivan. It would be quieter, and perhaps riskier.

"Are you sure you want to go with me, Mimi?" I asked her the evening before our flight.

"Yes, of course, I am sure."

"Absolutely sure?"

"Absolutely, positively, decidedly," she said spitting out the words emphatically.

"But the risk, and the . . ."

"Don't even think of it. I want to be with you. You'd better get used to the idea. I am not going to let you out of my sight again."

Berhane and his Eritrean underground comrades had everything ready. A Land Rover belonging to the ministry of land reform (where one of them was a surveyor) was to take us to the border, across Wollo and Tigray provinces. The surveyor would go as our driver.

There would also be an expert on land reform (suitably armed with forged papers) and I would be a consultant advising him; Mimi was the secretary of our "survey team." Our "land reform expert" was also armed with an AK–47 concealed in the vehicle. He was a veteran fighter who had been studying the revolutionary situation in Addis Ababa.

Lula was the only outsider informed of our plan. Mimi had to tell her. She was not only a trusted person, but she made money and other provisions available to see us to safety in Eritrea. From there, if need be, we would seek the assistance of international organizations like the Red Cross or the U.N. High Commission for Refugees. Or we could join the struggle. That was not an issue to discuss right away. We concentrated our attention on what Berhane called "first things first."

Survival. Escape.

And so, at two o'clock in the afternoon of Saturday, November 24, we started our journey out of Addis Ababa. It was a trip away from certain death toward an uncertain future. Fear dominated my thoughts until we crossed the city limits and hit open country.

I had my two grenades wrapped in a towel hidden under the seat of the Land Rover. Just in case, I thought. But no one else knew.

Mimi sat by my side in the back seat. She wore sunglasses and tennis shoes, jeans and a khaki shirt, and covered her hair with a green kerchief. I wore khaki trousers and a khaki shirt, as did the other two members of our group.

"You look like a tourist on safari," I said to Mimi, once we were out of the city limits. "But remember, there may be hardships ahead."

"I am aware of that, and I am prepared for the worst," she said, holding my hand and leaning her head on my shoulder.

"I can face anything with you at my side," I whispered to her.

"And I will be at your side always, come what may," she said before dropping into slumber. I held her head on my lap as we journeyed toward the north.

While our Eritrean friends chatted and Mimi slept peacefully, I looked at the countryside, remembering our journey to Melaku's funeral, remembering the past, and thinking about the future with hope. I remembered, with a smile, Dr. Johnson's remark about the second marriage being the triumph of hope over experience.

But what are we without hope? I thought. Mimi's words rang in my ears like sweet music: "I will be at your side always, come what may." Even before we crossed into Eritrea, I felt reassured about the future. I had found my final refuge, even as I headed north on yet another hazardous journey.

About the author

Bereket Habte Selassie is a professor of Law and politics at the University of North Carolina at Chapel Hill. He is a practitioner and a scholar of law and politics. This fact is reflected in his writings. He is the author of *The Executive in African Government, Conflict and Intervention in the Horn of Africa, Behind the War in Eritrea* (editor and contributor) and *Eritrea and the United Nations* (RSP 1989), among other works. Dr. Bereket has served as the Commissioner of the Constitutional Commission of Eritrea (1974-1997). This is his first novel.

Praise for *Riding the Whirlwind:*

"Mr. Bereket has shown both candor and courage. The novel goes beyond being a mere object of aesthetic contemplation, and asserts itself as a political testament as well as a lesson in history."
—Yanas Admassu, *UFAHAMU*

"Even those unfamiliar with the momentous events of Ethiopian history in 1974 will find Bereket Habte Selassie's novel fascinating. For those whose lives were in any way touched by those events, the book offers a dramatic and evocative reenactment of that historic episode."
—Donald N. Levine,
Professor,
The University of Chicago

"This suspenseful and deeply-felt novel provides a fascinating picture of Ethiopia's social earthquake of the early 1970s. With his affecting drama about a decent, conscience-stricken young official's personal and political odyssey, Bereket Habte Selassie has given us a wise insider's insights into the 'revolution with a human face' that disintegrated into one of the horrors of the century."
—Richard Lipez